Once upon a
Chapter o

The clearing was cool, the sun slanted down i
Rustling grasses hid unknown plants that poked tl
fragrant greenery. Birds passed lazily below clouds of brilliant white. And hornets flew with military precision around jewel-coloured bluebells.

As she sat, her back against the rough bark of the tree, Ellie looked about her with new and hungry eyes. Every detail devoured and savoured; seared into her memory. The beauty of the scene a balm to her soul. Each scent and sound swirled about her senses as if for the first time. Vibrant, alive. The verdant green of the canopy shimmered with an ethereal energy that reflected starkly in the single cold tear that slipped from her eye. Her hand lay gently against the blades of grass that struggled for life at the base of the tree, blood snaking down from the wound on her wrist to replenish the soil. An empty bottle of vodka lay discarded and forgotten beside the four bottles of over-the-counter pain relief that she had diligently been saving to fill. Two of the bottles were already empty, and with great care and deliberation, Ellie reached for the unopened bottle of tequila in the Tesco bag to her side. Slowly, with exaggerated effort, she twisted off the cap and raised the bottle to her lips. As the sun warmed glass touched her slack and senseless mouth, she slid to the ground, the bottle rolling from her grasp. The clear and potent liquid soaked thirstily into the earth as she sank into oblivion.

Unseen hands pulled Ellie to her feet, then to her toes. A feeling of immense pain and nausea swept from her numb extremities to her slack and gaping mouth, and then poured forth from her lips to splash at her feet. Again and again her stomach was pulled through to empty on the ground. A bitter and pervading odour surrounded her causing Ellie's stomach to painfully eject what was left of her stomach lining. Then, as if a doll dropped by a giant, she crumpled to the floor. She landed in the puddle she had made and felt the gelatinous ooze enter her nose and gasping mouth. She felt the slime mix with her tears and tried to close her eyes. With more effort than she could believe possible, she rolled over and out of the mess. On her back, panting with purulence and effort, Ellie felt her eyes pulled roughly open. A light that was too, too bright filled her vision and bought fresh tears to bear. Unceremoniously, she was lifted and thrown over a shoulder, then thankfully lost consciousness again as her assaulter began to walk.

Gingerly Ellie dared to open an eye. Fear and pain froze into an icy knot in her throat. She did not know where she was. She remembered being in the woods and taking the vodka and pills but nothing else. So, was this it? Was she dead? Dead sure felt comfortable. Dead felt like a feather bed. Heaven had a clean white duvet with tiny blue rosebuds sewn on it. Heaven had a cool breeze lifting the organza curtain at the wooden sash window to her left. Heaven also had a fat brown tabby cat sitting next to her, staring intently.
The cat looked away, through the open door.
  "She's awake." He called.
  "Oh god, now I know I'm dead." Ellie mumbled to herself, and with a wry smile she fell back to sleep.

Next time Ellie opened her eyes, a woman of such beauty sat beside her, that Ellie was now sure she was dead.

"Are you an angel?" She asked, hushed; reverent.

A light tinkling laugh, like sleigh bells on a winters' morning, issued forth from a mouth shaped in a perfect bow, deep pink lips surrounded the straightest, whitest teeth Ellie had ever seen.

"No my dear, I am certainly no angel," came the reply. The woman's voice was fresh and light, like a cool clear stream tumbling down-hill. The sound of it filled Ellie with a peace that she had never known before.

"My name is Fae. I found you in the woods. I bought you here to recover as I did not know where you live. You have no I.D on you."

"I thought I died." Ellie whispered. "How long have I been here?"

"Oh, only a couple of days. I think we have all the poison from your system now. What on earth made you do that to yourself? How could you not want to be?" Fae's face was filled with such concern and pity that Ellie turned her own to the pillow and sobbed quietly.

"I just... I thank you for your help, but you should have just left me. I can't..." Ellie found that the words were stuck in her mouth. She wanted to tell this beautiful woman everything. She felt a compelling need to make Fae happy, to tell her anything she wanted to know, but shame and despair kept her words behind her teeth. Ellie pressed her face further into the pillow and shook with despair. Fae gently brushed Ellie's hair from her face. The places her hand had touched felt cool and soothed. With this beautiful creature beside her, Ellie fell into a deep and dreamless sleep.

As Fae stroked the troubled girls hair away from a soaked and sweating brow, she closed her eyes and took a breath. Very gently, she placed a hand either side of Ellie's face and furrowed her brow in concentration. Carefully she entered into Ellie's thoughts. All appeared black and red and vivid. Pain, loss and loneliness battled each other in a quest for dominance and Fae felt herself grow heavy with grief. With a mental shrug, she pulled her feelings back into herself and waded further in. There was Ellie as a small child, hiding under the stairs in fear. There again, Ellie as a child of six being kicked and beaten by a tall blonde woman in pointed shoes. Ellie limping away holding in her tears so as to not further antagonise. Yet doing so anyway. Ellie as a child of seven being abused by a slim, dark youth whilst a slightly older girl goaded and tormented her. As a teen, in hospital, on a drip being coaxed back to life as her wasted body struggled for energy to breathe. On the phone, calling her mother and being dismissed. Visiting the blonde woman and not being allowed in because she had no make up on? Seriously? On the phone again, the blonde woman yelling at her that...

"I have no daughter, you are nothing to me". Ellie crying. Ellie with a knife and bloody wrists. Ellie in the woods with Vodka and pills. Ellie in the dark. Alone. Fae could take no more and pulled out quickly. With tears on her own cheek, she left the broken girl to sleep.

The smell of fresh, hot toast and coffee teased Ellie out of her slumber. The pull of the bed kept her supine. As her eyes slowly lifted, Ellie watched the beautiful woman carry a tray toward her and place it on a small table by her side. The fat cat jumped up onto the covers and plopped down beside her.

"You're awake then". Said the cat, looking at Ellie.

"Oh my god! Oh my god!" Ellie mumbled, unable to take her eyes off the cat. "What the... where am I? What the...? Did that cat speak? Did you hear him? He spoke!"

"I know, try not to worry daughter. That is only Peter, my cat."

"What do you mean only your cat?" asked the cat, seemingly put out. "Only a cat indeed!" Peter sniffed, "How rude!"

Ellie couldn't help it, she smiled at the absurdity of it all. This sure was a great dream, she could stay here forever, no rush to wake up at all. No siree! She decided that as it was only a dream, she may as well enjoy it.

"And who do I thank for taking such good care of me?" She politely asked.

"Ah, I thought you might forget. My name is Fae. I found you a couple of days ago in the woods. You appeared to be... ahem, in a little trouble, so I bought you to my home and tried to... well, I tried to help you." Fae placed a hand lightly over Ellie's.

"Thank you very much." Said Ellie courteously with a smile. Strange, but she felt like a little girl in the presence of a wise and grown up princess. But hey, this was a dream, so why not? This lady, Fae, she could be a princess in her dream couldn't she? After all, it was *her* dream.

"I imagine you must be hungry, so I made a little toast. If that hurts your throat, I could make something else perhaps? I have coffee here and there's juice too if you would like some. I'm afraid I have no idea what you like eat."

"Toast is great thank you." Ellie replied as she sat up and took a piece. The toast was thick and rough cut, laden with melting butter and tasted like nothing on earth. Her throat hurt a little as she swallowed, but nothing was going to stop her from finishing. The coffee was rich and smooth, made with the creamiest milk that felt very satisfying as she drank. She felt fuller somehow.

"Oh, that was just fantastic thank you. I feel fabulous, it must have been all that sleep. I can't believe how good that all tasted."

Fae and Peter shared a look and a small smile.

"You're welcome." They said.

Fae had laid out Ellie's clothes having washed and ironed them earlier, so when she was alone, Ellie reluctantly got out of bed and dressed. Walking down the stairs, she came to a large, sun dappled room. Real wood cabinets lined the walls of the kitchen and every surface held a clutter of plants, bottles and books. Clean jam jars were scattered about the worktops with posies of fresh garden flowers inside. At a large round table in the centre of the room Fae sat with Peter on her lap, absently scratching behind his ear.

"Uh... hi, thank you for cleaning my clothes," Ellie mumbled, "I guess I should be going home now though. Thank you so very much for all you have done."

Slowly Fae looked up and there was pity in her eyes.

"Are you sure you want to go? There is no rush, you can stay as long as you like. There is plenty of room and I was about to make lunch."

"Well, if you don't mind, I would quite like some lunch. I feel so reluctant to leave for some reason."

"That's because you aren't ready to go yet." Peter told her.

Ellie sat down with a bump. "I guess not if I am still hearing cats talk," she whispered.

The Fae

Fae laughed her light tinkling laugh, and at once Ellie felt better. She felt as though she had danced through a light summer rain that had left her feeling breathless and refreshed.

"Oh, Peter can talk, you are not going mad. He is a somewhat special cat." Fae paused and looked thoughtful. "Although usually nobody can hear him but me and mine. Strange that you can. Oh, possibly it is because I had to give you some of my blood when you were ill. That must be it. Hmm! That opens up a whole new can of worms as it were..." Fae looked up at Ellie in concern.

"Not sure that's such a good idea." Commented Peter in a voice that could only be described as supercilious. "She's hardly in a position to understand is she?"

"Well," said Fae, "Having given her my blood, she kind of needs to know something, or else she is going to run into some very sticky situations. I can keep it light and relevant."

"I am in the room" Ellie snapped. "Number one, you gave me blood? Why? And number two, what's the biggy? Do I become a vampire or something?" She laughed. Not quite sure why. *Probably nerves*, she thought.

"Vampire indeed!" Hissed Peter. "The very thought!"

"No dear, not a Vampire," smiled Fae. "Fairy."

"Of course. Fairy. I should have known." Ellie didn't seem particularly impressed. Perhaps she really was still asleep.

Fae looked amused. "I'm not really used to having to explain myself," she smiled, "but as you have some of my blood now, you will need to know. Things could change a little for you now. You may feel things stronger, taste things better, see further, just feel...enhanced. Sort of."

"So, I'm like a superhero now?" Ellie didn't seem to be taking this seriously at all. "Do I get super powers? Can I fly? Jump tall buildings? See through walls? Have mega strength?"

"No. Sorry, just a bit... well, enhanced is all. I wish I hadn't told you now. It all seems such a disappointment to you." Fae smiled fondly.

"Oh no... no, I'm grateful. Really I am. You saved me, gave me blood. Eow! Gave me 'enhancements' what's not to be excited about? I'm sure when I wake up I will be very grateful. This is the most fun I've had dreaming since...well, forever." Ellie was giggling now. "Oh say, do I get enhanced body parts? I've been thinking of a boob job for some time now."

Peter had become restless throughout this exchange, and it was obvious that he felt the ungrateful girl should just shut up and be glad she were alive. He looked as though he felt she were mocking his mistress and he couldn't bear it. In a flash, he hissed and lashed out at Ellie, catching her arm with a sharp scratch.

"Oh!" Ellie managed to say before she fell to the table in a dead sleep.

Ellie awoke in her own bed, the duvet wrapped tight about her, feeling thirsty but rested. She had slept long and hard with no dreams but awoke with a sense of purpose and energy. She fairly leapt out of bed and bounded to the bathroom to attend her ablutions. Ellie smiled at herself in the mirror and admired her thick, lustrous hair that seemed to shine with a life of its own. Feeling a slight tingle on her arm, she looked and saw the faintest of scratches. She couldn't remember how it had come about but it was almost healed.

In the kitchen, Ellie drank two cups of coffee and polished off three thick slices of toast, generously spread with her favourite lime marmalade. It tasted so good, she considered making more. The sun shone through the window and made her homely kitchen gleam. The scent of fresh mown grass found its way through the crack in the glass and tickled her nose. Ellie hunted for her hay fever tablets and swallowed one down with the last of her coffee. Grabbing her bag and jacket, she left the house for work.

The walk to work took Ellie past the churchyard, where the vicar was humming a hymn to himself as he tacked up the latest poster on the display board outside. She waved to him as he glanced her way and she was rewarded with a smile that could light the way to heaven. On past the shops selling vegetables and fruit, their earthy smells permeating the air whilst their colours beckoned to her. On an impulse, Ellie stopped and bought a pear. She bit into it and the gritty juiciness filled her mouth with its wet sweetness. Ellie made short work of the pear, stopping only when she had finished every bite and licked the residue from her fingers.

The sounds of the traffic seemed muted in contrast with the sweet trilling of the birds in the trees. Ellie gazed up as she walked, marvelling in the differences in each birds song. A rustling of feathers flashed glossy, emerald and black as a magpie took flight. All too soon, Ellie arrived at the shop in which she worked. The bell jangled harshly as she opened the door and stepped inside. Ellie walked to the back of the shop and hung her coat and bag on the hook by the toilet door and pasted a smile on her face as she re-entered the shop floor. Jack, her boss, was already at the till, counting out the day's float and checking the till rolls were inserted. He nodded a hello then went back to his task. Ellie sighed. She was not happy here. No particular reason other than she thought she could do better. Ellie leant her elbows on the counter and her head on her hands. She sighed again and closed her eyes.

"Goodbye Mrs. George." She heard Jack call as the shop door swung shut with a jangle. "Time to close up then. Glad that's over." Said Jack.
Ellie looked around in a daze.
"What? Did you call me?" She asked.
"Not really, just saying that I'm glad the day is over. I can't wait to get home, my feet are killing me." Jack replied.
Ellie stared at Jack for what seemed an age, waiting for him to explain.
"Are you wanting to get off home or shall I lock you in?" Jack asked with an amused expression on his face.
"But we only just opened. It's still early." Ellie replied, still waiting for Jack to laugh at his joke.
"It certainly seems that way," Jack sighed, "The day has flown by. That's the great thing about being busy, the time flies."
Jack stood by the door, holding it open for her. Ellie looked at her watch and saw that it was indeed five o'clock. Her coat and bag were also in her hands and not on the hook. But surely no! Not possible. What the hell was happening here?
Feeling extremely confused, Ellie left the shop.

Ellie could not account for it. One minute she was walking into the shop to start her day, the next it was closing time. Odd to say the least. And what was Jack talking about, being busy? That shop is lucky to see one customer a day, that hardly qualifies as busy. Maybe she wasn't feeling well? Yes, that had to be it. She would have an early night and try to shake off whatever this was. But she didn't feel unwell. In fact, Ellie couldn't remember ever feeling as well as she did at that moment. And yet...

Back at home, Ellie settled into her soft and cosy couch with a large mug of hot chocolate and a book. She was completely hooked on the Sookie Stackhouse books and was currently getting through one a day. That probably accounted for her 'lost day'. Too much fantasy on her brain. She probably got caught up dreaming about Eric the Viking Vampire and lost track of time. Okay, so she had never lost a whole day before, but it was the only thing that made sense. Right?
Later, as Ellie curled up in her bed, she felt a weightlessness overtake her. It was as though she were cocooned in warm, soft nest that moulded to her body and supported her weight. It took no time at all for Ellie to fall asleep.

The alarm clock hadn't gone off. Oh hell! Now she would be rushed. Quickly, Ellie swung her legs out of bed and her feet automatically found her pink fluffy slippers. Blindly, she stumbled her way to the bathroom and clumsily set about her morning routine. Feeling slightly more awake, Ellie entered the kitchen and fumbled the kettle to 'on'. Whilst waiting for the water to heat, Ellie stared out of the window. The small crack in the pane allowed the familiar aroma of grass to seep through, and Ellie breathed it in deeply. It felt satisfying somehow, almost filling. Out of the corner of her eye, she saw a fat brown cat skit out of the garden and up, over the fence and away. She thought absently that it had looked directly at her, but so what? It was only a cat, who knows what it was looking at? Ellie made her tea, dropped the used tea bag in the bin and went to sit on the couch. Idly, she flicked on the T.V and turned to the news. The reporter was winding up a story of a young woman found dead in the town centre, it appeared to be a hit and run. Ellie was only half listening, not being fully awake. As the reporter recapped the story, a photo of the young woman was flashed on screen.
"Jane Torrenson, twenty nine, found dead at the side of the road in an apparent hit and run. If anyone has any information..." But Ellie wasn't listening. She was staring at the picture of the girl on the screen. It was like looking in a mirror. The girl looked exactly like her, same eyes, same hair, lips, cheekbones, even the nose. The only difference, Jane Torrenson had her nose pierced and her hair parted in the middle. Ellie shivered, as though someone had walked over her grave. *Phew, there but for the grace of God and all that*! She thought to herself. Feeling a little unnerved, she went and finished dressing, then left her house for work.

At work, the shop was unusually busy. Old Mrs MacGyver came in for her usual incense sticks. Polly from the shop next door called in for a chat on her break and bought a new tarot pack as a gift for her sister. Mrs Henson came by to put another instalment on the large amethyst crystal she had set aside and her daughter Jade bought a few small crystals to hang at her bedroom window. Whilst talking to the customers, Ellie felt that they were all looking at her strangely, but could not think of any reason why this would be. She shrugged it off as coincidence and continued with her day.

Just after lunch, the door jangled harshly and made Ellie jump. She had been at the back of the shop, engrossed in the new display of Zodiac Mugs that she was arranging.

"Oh!" She said, "I'm sorry, you made me jump. How can I help you?"
The man that had come in walked slowly toward her, and as he did so, she could see that he had a slight limp. He wore a long raincoat, which struck Ellie as odd given that the sun was shining brightly and it was the middle of a particularly hot summer. *No business of mine*, she thought to herself. The man had coarse black hair that seemed incapable of laying flat. Tufts stuck out at obscure angles around his head, defying the laws of gravity. He had very thin black eyebrows that Ellie tried desperately not to stare at. His face was pitted and his nose appeared to have been re-set at some time. He had unusually large, full pink lips and a pointed chin with a few wispy hairs masquerading as a beard. As he opened his mouth to speak, Ellie could not help but notice that his teeth were brilliant white and mesmerisingly crooked. His voice however, was deep and melodic, sounding like the tail end of a lullaby, and Ellie realised she'd not heard a word that he had said, so soporific was the sound.

"I'm sorry, but could you repeat that? I didn't catch what you said."
"I asked if you knew me." The man repeated.
"I don't quite understand. Are you lost?" Ellie was confused. What did that mean? Did she know him? Know him how? Okay, so she had a few boozy nights out that were a bit blurry in the morning, but she was quite sure she would have remembered this man.
"I was in here yesterday, we chatted about Earth Magic and you said that you knew someone that you could recommend I see. You asked me to come back today to find out if they would let me visit with them."
Oh boy! Okay, so this must have been during her lost time at work yesterday. What on earth had she said? She knew nothing about Earth Magic, knew nobody that did, what could she possibly have told this man?
"Erm, I er... I'm so sorry, but I don't really remember the conversation." *Honesty is the best policy*, she thought to herself. "Could you maybe remind me of what we discussed?"

The man looked at her oddly.
"I came in here about half past two yesterday, you were busy serving a woman with her small children. The children were running about touching things. The woman was getting anxious so you recommended a calming spell for her to use on her children. I think you said that it involved lavender, rain water and myrrh. The woman seemed happy, bought the ingredients and then you spoke to me. I asked if you practiced spell casting, you said yes and we talked about my problem a little. You said that it was beyond your skill and that you knew a woman, Fae I think you said her name was, and that you would ask her if it were okay for me to see her."
"I... erm... I really don't remember, I am sorry. I don't know anyone called Fae and I certainly don't know any Earth Spells, or any kind of spells for that matter. Are you sure it was me you spoke to?" Ellie was completely at a loss. She had no idea whatsoever what the man was talking about. She couldn't even remember what happened throughout the day. It had just sort of disappeared on her.
The man looked at her through narrowed eyes, and Ellie became a bit nervous. What if he yells at me? Attacks me? She thought to herself. I'm here on my own. The man looked at her some more. It felt to Ellie as though he were reading her very thoughts. She shuffled uncomfortably from foot to foot.
"Yes, maybe you are right. My mistake." The man turned abruptly and strode out of the shop.

The Fae

Ellie sat down heavily. She felt shaken, and yet nothing untoward had happened, or even been said. She just felt, well, wobbly. The rest of the afternoon passed in a blur. The shop was uncommonly busy, Ellie sold more that one day than in the previous week altogether. By time she locked the door at five o'clock, she felt exhausted.

Instead of walking straight home, Ellie decided to sit in the park and watch the world for a few minutes. This generally soothed her. As she walked through the large, black wrought iron gates, Ellie felt the stresses of the day slide off and stay outside the barrier. The grass was green. The flowers were pert and fragrant. The birds were pecking at ice cream and crisps dropped by squalling children, and the squirrels were scampering about begging for morsels to eat. She found an empty bench and sat with her ankles crossed, head back and a satisfied sigh escaping her lips. Oh, this was much better. The brilliant blue sky was unbroken except for the dancing of birds. They whirled and dove in a complicated pattern for her delight. They called out to each other singing loud and clear as they navigated impossible paths. She closed her eyes and breathed in deeply, greedily inhaling the scent of flowers growing nearby. If she concentrated, she could pick out the individual flowers. There, near the roses, a bee buzzed busily as it went about its work, collecting and tasting. Ellie followed its path with her ears and identified the changes in tone as the bee alighted and alerted its hive. Funny how she had never noticed before, the bee was so loud, so clear. The flowers were so fragrant, the air so warm and enveloping. Feeling greatly refreshed, Ellie walked out of the park and stood at the traffic lights waiting for them to change so that she could cross.

From the corner of her eye, Ellie saw a grimy white van with tinted windows come too fast down the street, her last thought was, *That will never stop in time.* Then she was flying through the air and her world had gone black. Again.

Waking to the amused face of a nurse peering at her from inches away came as a bit of a shock to Ellie.
"So, you're awake then. That's a good sign." The face slid out of view to be replaced by that of Jack, her boss.
"God Ellie, I was worried sick. The hospital called me because you had a card from the shop in your purse. Do you want me to get hold of anyone for you?" He looked so wretched standing there face pale, hands wringing, that Ellie laughed.
"Oh, Jack, I don't know what you're so worried about. I'm fine. Really. I must have slipped on the kerb and knocked myself out. I'm okay now. Honest."
"Ellie, you were hit by a car. You have been asleep for two whole days. I was really worried about you."
"I promise," Ellie replied, "I feel fine. Look, not a mark on me. They must have made a mistake." She proved her point by languidly stretching her arms and legs for Jack to see that there were in fact, no marks.
"Well, you certainly seem okay. I'm just going to speak to the nurse. I will be right back. Okay? Wait there, I will be back in a sec." Jack scuttled out of the room, his eyes searching for someone to explain this to him.

Ellie took a deep, luxurious breath and snuggled down further into bed. Minutes later, a short, harassed and bespectacled doctor came to see her. His stethoscope swayed at his chest; in perpetual motion like his hands and eyes. He seemed unable to look directly at her. He spoke above her head or to the flowers in a vase next to her bed.

The Fae

"I don't understand how, but you're injuries are all cleared up. It must have been a combination of the medication and the sleep. You also appear to be quite a healthy young lady, so I am sure that also played a part. But I must say, this is amazing. I have never seen a hit and run recover as quickly as you before." The doctor's accent made some of his words thick and hard to follow, but Ellie got the gist of it. She, apparently, was lucky to be alive. Well fab.

"When can I go home?" She asked.

"I would like to keep you in another night, then, if you are still this good tomorrow, I see no reason why you can't go home then." With that, the doctor left the room in a shuffling slide that seemed to propel him smoothly along the floor like a snake.

As the doctor exited the room, the air seemed to be a little clearer, easier to breathe. *Medication, must be*, thought Ellie as she settled down with the remote control and flicked on the T.V.

There was her face.

"Ouch!" Ellie squealed as she pinched herself. "No, definitely awake" she said out loud. Her voice seemed to bounce back at her from the glossy white walls surrounding the bed. But it was surely her face. There, on the telly. What was going on? She depressed the mute and the presenter finished off the story of how lucky Ellie was to be alive after being hit by an unidentified car and how the driver didn't stop. They were appealing for witnesses to come forward. Then another picture flashed up on the screen. The girl that looked like her. What was her name?

"In a related story, the driver of the vehicle that hit and killed Jane Torrenson has still to be identified. Jane, twenty nine, who lived here in Colchester, is being buried at the Mersea Road Cemetery at three pm tomorrow. Family ask that flowers..."

Ellie tuned the sound out. She felt odd. Yes she was definitely lucky to be alive, and yes Jane Torrenson looked just like her, and yes she was also hit by a car, but coincidences happen all the time. Don't they? It didn't mean anything. Surely?

As Ellie lay in bed, slipping into a sleepy funk, a scratchy, scuffling sound reached her ears. As she looked up, Ellie caught what could only be the tail end of a cat, passing the doorway. It appeared, in her very brief glance, to be large and brown. Also, somehow familiar. *Definitely bumped my head. Must have been harder than I thought*, she murmured as she fell back asleep.

During the night, Ellie was awoken for observations by the nurse, awoken for medications by the doctor, awoken by bad dreams from her accident and awoken by an uneasy feeling that she put down to being in a strange bed. As the sun oozed up over the roof of the neighbouring building, a brightly cheerful nurse bounced into the room, asking:

"Did we sleep well my dear?"

Ellie bit back the sarcastic retort that threatened to choke her and spill out of her mouth, and replied that yes, thank you, she had.

"Any news on when I can go home?" She asked hopefully.

The nurse replied that the doctor had to check her out first, but it shouldn't be long.

"Bloody liars!" Ellie complained to Jack, who had come to take her home. "Bloody, bloody liars! I've been waiting since seven this morning, it's now three and still I haven't seen the bloody doctor. This is ridiculous! I'm fine, I just want to go home. All he has to do is hold my wrist, flash his torch thingy in my eyes, say 'hmmm' a few times and let me go! God, I could scream! Oh, who is looking after the shop?" Guiltily Ellie remembered that Jack must have taken time off to collect her.

"Oh… we are so quiet, I decided I may as well close up for the day."

"But I thought… I mean, wasn't the shop picking up? I was rushed off my feet the other day."

"Well yes, that was so odd. We were really busy then all of a sudden it was back to normal, quiet as the grave. Oh, excuse me. It was well… actually, about the same time you had your accident. Luckily, I mean… well, not luckily, what on earth am I saying? I mean it was… I mean we were quiet. Yes quiet, so I could close up. Sorry. Well, I mean, it's odd. Really."

"Yes." Ellie looked at him, really looked at him. He seemed to be nervous. A slight tremble visible in the hands that held his jacket, twisting, ruining the fabric. Jack had a faint sheen of sweat glistening on his brow. His eyes seemed restless, unable to settle, darting back and forth. His hair was a mess. Messier than usual. Jack had pale, mousey brown hair that normally had the strongest hair gel running for cover when introduced to his mop of curls.

"Jack, are you alright? You seem, well… you seem not yourself."

"Me? Oh no. No, no, I'm fine. Worried about you, I suppose that's it. No, I'm fine. Really." If anything, he seemed to become more agitated, so Ellie decided to leave it and tackle him later. She had never seen Jack distressed before. Normally, he was pretty unflappable. So laid back he was horizontal she used to joke to him. Clearly something was bothering him, but if he didn't want to talk about it… well okay. For today anyway.

Finally the doctor made a sweeping visit, took her stats in a desultory manner, huffed and puffed a little, merely for show, thought Ellie, then let her leave. Ellie could not wait to get out of there. She fairly ran out of the door. Jack hoppity shuffled behind, half heartedly trying to catch up.

Chapter two

The next few days were spent in the usual way, walk to work, do the work, walk home, shop for tea, sit in the park a bit if it was nice. The shop was back to being slow. The customers were back to being garrulous. Jack had finally stopped fussing over Ellie and seemed a lot more relaxed than he had been at the hospital. Ellie was so caught up with the mundanity of each day; she forgot to ask Jack about his behaviour at the hospital.

Standing half in the shop and half 'out the back', Ellie was nursing a cup of tea when the door jangled open. The air seemed to have been sucked out of the room, the temperature appeared to have dropped by several degrees and the hairs on Ellie's arms sprung up as though electrified. A small, old woman walked slowly and carefully to the counter. As Ellie watched, the air around the woman seemed to shiver in a dark and ugly way. A faint odour of burning hair seemed to emanate from her, and as she reached the counter, dropping her bag on the floor, Ellie could have sworn that she saw the woman's face shimmer and seem to settle. Like a television that is just tuned in.

Ellie gave herself a shake and chided herself for being fanciful, then looked the old woman square in the eye. Except it wasn't an old woman at all. It was a pretty young girl of about eighteen, wearing a pair of ripped and faded jeans, belly top and with her hair tied back tightly in a pony tail. Her eyes were a greenish brown, and as Ellie looked, they appeared to swim, the colours were actually moving, like paint swirled on water. Ellie hiccupped a quick breath and looked again. The young girl stood there, politely, waiting to be acknowledged.
"I'm sorry," begun Ellie, "I don't know what came over me. How may I help you?" The young girl did not seem in the least put out, and replied in a sweet and melodic voice
"I am looking for a lady called Ellie; I was told she worked here. Would that be you?"
"Yes, how may I help?" Ellie politely enquired.
The young girl reached down for her bag, and as she rose with it in her hand, she had turned again into a gnarled old woman. Her skin was tough and leathery, with hairs sprouting at oblique angles; her hair was cut short, with shears apparently, and was the colour and texture of wire wool. The woman's face was pulled back in a snarl that forced her wild and bushy eyebrows to stand on end, making her green and brown eyes appear even smaller, like two pebbles in the sand. Her lips, stretched over her teeth, revealing broken stubs and the foulest stench Ellie had ever encountered. She wore a shapeless wool cloak that was tied with rope around her waist and a pair of men's boots that had green and yellow electrical tape wound around the tops to keep them up.

With an animal snarl, the old woman threw the bag with all her might then leapt up at the counter and grabbed Ellie by the hair. She pulled Ellie forward and leaned in toward her neck, filthy teeth bared and ready to sink into Ellie's flesh. With a shout of surprise, Ellie grabbed hold of the counter and tried to pull herself backwards, out of the crazy woman's grasp. Hissing and spitting, the crone sank her nails into Ellie's

The Fae

scalp and redoubled her effort to pull Ellie toward her. Fear and shock fought inside Ellie's mind.

"What the?" She yelled between pants. "Who the hell?" She managed to get her feet on the shelves under the counter and throw her body backwards. The cup of tea she had been holding flew into the air and landed on the floor with a crash, the crone lost her hold as Ellie fell backwards against the doorway.

In a flash, the old woman was up and back at Ellie, throwing aside the clump of bloody hair in her hand and pulling at any part of Ellie that she could grab. Spitting and cursing like a wounded cat, her nails, like claws, reaching for her eyes. The stench of her making Ellie gag. Drool flew all around as her teeth and stumps could no longer hold back the flood. Ellie's stomach climbed up into her throat and threatened to erupt. She pushed and pushed at the woman, but she was making no headway at all. Tears of pain and shock were leaking from her eyes, blurring her vision. All her senses were concentrated on the woman. Trying to stop the pain, the stench, the gut turning awfulness of this insane mass of flesh that was even now biting Ellie's cheek. Ellie tried to twist her face away, but the woman clung on. Her teeth were pulling and tearing at Ellie's face, the pain was indescribable, but the shock was worse. What on earth was happening? How could this be happening?

And then, just like that, it was over. Ellie lay curled in a foetal ball behind the counter and the woman was splayed against the wall. The crone's fingers were scratching at her throat, trying to release unseen hands that were squeezing the breath from her body; just as her feet were scrabbling for purchase on the floor. A wild and terrified look in her eyes as she stared straight ahead to the man that was standing, calmly, in the doorway to the shop. The man was very tall and very lean. His golden brown skin glowed as the sun reflected off it. His long and silky hair had dark brown, red and blonde swirling amongst the curls that shimmered around his head. His high forehead swept down to meet two finely arched brows, his golden eyes slanted slightly at the ends, and his long, aquiline nose sat above a full and generous mouth. He wore a long and sweeping coat of an indeterminate colour and fabric, but which seemed to swirl about his feet as he stood, still, tall and proud.

The crone was losing colour, her lips were turning blue and her eyes were rolling back in her head. Her hands appeared to become heavy and dropped to her sides, her feet stopped kicking. She hung, limp, against the wall. As she took her last breath, she seemed to fold in on herself. Like dough being kneaded in a bakers bowl, the sides met in the middle and disappeared. With a flutter she was no longer there. Just a slight dusty residue about the floor where she had hung. The air in the room improved immediately, to be replaced with a fresh, summery breeze, gently rooting at the corners of the shop and chasing any malignancy away. The man turned and made to walk away. He hesitated, then turned and spoke. His voice was at once heavily sibilant, yet strong and mellow.

"Please take better care of yourself. I am not always here to help, you know." And with that he walked away.

In a daze, Ellie struggled to her feet and lurched toward the door, clutching her bleeding face in her hand.

"Wait. Who are you? What is happening? Wait!" As she reached the doorway, she looked in the direction the man had taken, but could no longer see him. She looked up and down the street, waiting for some several minutes before giving up and going back inside. As she closed the door and slumped against it, a large, fat, brown cat shot across the road and out of sight.

Ellie sat heavily on the stool behind the counter and stared at the dust on the floor. What on earth was happening here? What had that woman wanted? Clearly she wanted to harm her, but why? Was she confusing Ellie with someone else? And what about the dust thing? What was that about? And that man?
"Oh god!" She moaned and, putting her head in her hands, she sobbed.

Jack returned from the bank and found Ellie sitting at the counter, head in hands and tears streaking her face. He ran to her side and took her in his arms, brushing her hair from her eyes, he asked
"What is it Ellie, what's happened?"
Where would she start? Would he even believe her? What would be the point? She was too exhausted to explain, so instead; she lied.
"Headache. Bad." She mumbled.
Jack looked long and hard at her injuries and desolate face, but said nothing except acknowledge that she was truly upset.
"I'll call you a cab, on me, don't worry. You are going home. Bed is the best place for you right now." And frankly, she couldn't agree more.

Ellie got home and curled up in her bed. She pulled the duvet tight around her shoulders and snuggled down deep into the soft embrace. In no time at all she was asleep, as the sun poked through the chink in the curtains, warming her face. The birds chased each other merrily with chirps of delight and the flowers seemed to exude an extra perfume to fragrance her dreams.

Sleeping through to the next morning, Ellie awoke feeling fresh and alert. The memory of the previous day still with her, but not as vivid, somehow less real. She could view it objectively, like a third party. Her face was raw and painful, there were scratches and bruises all over her and she had even broken a couple of nails. But she was ok. Whatever that was yesterday, she was ok. She would figure it out, but not right now. Right now she wanted a shower and a cup of tea, maybe even some toast and Marmite.

Running the water as hot as it would go, Ellie jumped into the shower. She pampered herself with the new, pricey, shower gel she had splurged on last pay day. Soaping her skin, washing her hair then roughly towelling herself dry, had Ellie feeling fresh and ready for the day. Just as the toast popped up, there came a knock at the door. Putting down her cup, and belting her robe, Ellie went to answer it. She stepped back in surprise; a large and unattractive 'O' in place of her mouth as the man from yesterday stood there. He looked as aloof and unapproachable as ever. His golden eyes travelled down the length of Ellie's tatty dressing gown and stopped at her odd socked feet which were pushed into the faded and threadbare pink fluffy slippers. Eventually, he raised his eyes to meet hers and he forced a polite smile onto his face.

"Oh, hi." *As greetings to the man who saved your life go, that was pretty poor*, thought Ellie.

"Hello, I thought it might be an idea to see how you are after yesterdays little contretemps" The man said to her. "I was concerned about you."

"That's very considerate of you." *although he doesn't look particularly concerned,* she thought. *Wait, why am I being so mean? He went to all this trouble to find me and...* "Hey, hang on. How did you find me?" She asked him indignantly.

"Oh, it was no bother I can assure you. Are you going to invite me in or not?" He just couldn't seem to shake that condescension thing, she thought.

"Sure, as long as you don't turn into a crazy old lady and try to eat me." Ellie's attempt at humour fell flat.

The man stepped past her and into the kitchen, where he pulled out a chair and sat down. He picked up the teapot and poured himself a mug of hot, strong tea.

"Where do you keep the sugar?" He asked. "Never mind, found it." He got up and stepped to the cupboard. Without looking, he opened the door, reached in and took down the sugar canister then returned to the table. He poured a little milk into the tea then took an appreciative sip.

"Now that we are all cosy, would you answer a few of my questions?" Ellie wanted to know. "Firstly, the little trick with the sugar? I'm assuming it was for show as you haven't even used it."

"A vanity, forgive me."

"Then, please, in words of one syllable. What the hell was yesterday all about?" Ellie fairly shouted the question at him, her composure becoming a little unstuck at the physical reminder sitting at her kitchen table. "Oh, yeah. And who the hell are you?"

"You can call me Felix. A friend of yours has asked me to keep an eye on you for a while, to see that you come to no harm. I apologise for not reaching you in time at the park, but I let my concentration wander for a second, and well, there you are."

"Which friend?"

"Her name is Fae. She knows that you probably don't remember her, but all the same, here I am. I should ask how are you doing, after yesterdays little incident?"

"Not quite so little, have you seen my face? My body? I'm a mess, and I hurt like hell."

"Oh, pish" He said as he waved his arm in an offhand manor, roughly in her direction.

Ellie felt a tingle of anger roll across her face and down to her toes.

"I know that you will be back to your old self in no time at all." He smiled at her.

Ellie jabbed her finger toward his pompous nose.

"You, you.." and noticed that the grazes and bruises were gone. She raised her hand to her cheek and gently stroked the smooth, unblemished flesh. The bite marks were gone too.

"How?" She sat, bewildered, then started to laugh at the absurdity of it all. She laughed so hard that her sides hurt. She laughed so hard that her face felt as though it would split. Felix just sat and stared at her.

Eventually, with a sniffle and a swipe under her nose with her hand, Ellie pulled herself together and sat, staring at the man. This man, Felix, who had saved her life, then cured her injuries, and who was sitting in her kitchen, drinking tea and looking like the Queen of bloody Sheba, like the cat that got the cream. *A bit like that cat that, oh don't be so ridiculous!*

"Please, whenever you are ready, explain it to me." She was quite proud of how calm she sounded. "Please explain to me what is happening."

"When you were in the woods and tried to take your own life..."

"Whoa there cowboy! What the hell are you talking about? I was never in the woods trying to take my own life, are you crazy?"

"If you will let me finish?" Felix calmly countered. "When you were in the woods and tried to take your own life, my friend Fae found you and took you back to her house. She nursed you back to health and, in an effort to help and protect you; she wiped your memory of the incident." Felix took another sip of tea, "When you were able, she took you home and has asked me to keep an eye on you, to make sure that you don't try to do it again. Unfortunately, something else has happened that now we really need to have you understand. We had hoped to keep our existence secret from you. We didn't believe that you needed to know, but, after yesterday, and I believe, the incident with the car, you have to be aware."

"Of what?" Ellie was now convinced that even though the guy had saved her life, and yes, healed her injuries, and was damned cute. *Where did that come from? Concentrate Ellie, stay focussed.* Anyway, just because of all that, it didn't stop the guy being a complete whack job. Cute and sexy, *stop it*! But crazy as a loon.

She could feel herself blush, and sensed Felix look at her quizzically.

"I'm a fairy." He kept such a straight face.

"Oh!" She seemed surprised, then Ellie realised "Oooh! You mean you're gay? Typical!" *Just when I find a fit bloke, he's bloomin gay.* She thought to herself. *Again, stop it*!

"What is gay? Happy? Yes, we used to be gay, not so much now. Dark things are rising. No, not so gay now." Felix seemed lost in some memory.

Ellie sniggered, she couldn't help it. Here was this gorgeous man, in her kitchen, talking about being gay and having dark things rising. It was like being in high school. Felix gave her a very dark look.

"I don't think you understand how serious this is. If they sent one, they will send another. We have to find a way to protect you. You must take this seriously. Your life depends upon it."

Oh, this was too much. Ellie burst into a fit of the howling giggles and nearly fell off her chair in her mirth.

Felix stood up and paced about the room. Every time he opened his mouth to speak, Ellie laughed harder and louder. Felix was becoming very annoyed. Clearly he was not used to being the subject of such merriment.

With tears rolling down her cheeks, Ellie tried to suppress her laughter. But Felix looked so serious, she just couldn't.

"Oh, this is just too much." Felix waved his arm and Ellie felt herself squeezed very tightly. She struggled vainly against the invisible bonds. As she fought, the bonds grew tighter, she started to panic, her breath coming short and fast. Just when she thought she would pass out, Felix waved his arm again and she fell, released, to the floor, panting.

"Hey, that was, so, unfair" Ellie panted "Why did you do that?"

"You have to listen to me. This is serious."

"And so what, if I don't you will kill me?"

"For goodness sake, Ellie, pay attention. We need you to understand what is happening here. It is not a joke. It is not a game. It is not some idle fancy. You are in danger. You need to trust me."

"Oh, I need to do I? Mr. complete stranger tells me that I need to do as he says. Why the hell should I? Who are you?" Ellie was scared and Felix was just staring at her, insisting in his calm and soft voice that he was there to save her. Eventually, she gave up arguing, he was no fun anyway, he wouldn't argue back.

"Start at the beginning." She said.

So he did. He wove a tale of Fairy Folk who lived alongside mortals, working, playing, and loving alongside mortals. Their existence a secret and their numbers few. He told of the Great Fairy Wars and how their race was nearly wiped out. He told of the Fairy Queen and her sadness at having no heir to pass the throne to. He told of how the Fairy moved from town to town so as not to arouse suspicion at their very long lives. He told of the Fairy children, losing their powers as they assimilated into human society, and the worries of the Fairy Folk at the possible extinction of their race.

Ellie listened to all he said. She watched his eyes take on a wistful look as he spoke of his kind, saw his eyes light up as he spoke of the children, then darken as he told of the dwindling population. He was so beautiful. She saw in him, a tall and proud Fairy Prince, with flowing hair astride a stallion, swooping down to gather her in his arms.

"Ahem!" She coughed, breaking her dangerous train of thought. *What in hell is wrong with me?* She thought. *I may not have had a date in a couple of years but I am not usually so ready to throw myself at any passing Fairy who happens my way. Behave yourself,* she told herself.

"So, er, where do I come in?" Ellie asked.

"Well, we are not completely sure."

"That's promising."

"As I said, we are not completely sure, but, we think that when Fae gave you her blood, you may have inadvertently, well, you may have…"

"Oh, come on, spit it out. How bad can it be?"

"Well, you may now be part Fairy. We don't really know. It has never happened before. Usually we just let humans go about their own business, we never involve ourselves. When Fae helped you, she broke a lot of our laws, and, well, like I said, we think you may be a bit Fairy."

Ellie sniggered.

"Oh for heaven's sake, do not start all that again. Please."

"But how can you be a bit Fairy?" Ellie wanted to know. "Surely you either are or you are not. Fairy that is." She tried to hide the laugh that was bubbling up inside.

"We think it is the blood. No human has ever had Fairy blood before. We have no information to work with. And, well, you saw what it does to the Gnomes."

"Look, I hope you appreciate how hard I am trying to take this seriously. But Gnomes? Really? Come on!"

"Ellie, the woman that attacked you was a Gnome. She must have smelt you out. Did you not notice the odour?"

"Oh, yes. I certainly got a bellyful of her odour. The minute she walked through the door, I smelt her. I have never smelt anything like it before."

"That is one of the ways you can tell that they are not human. Each Magical Creature has its own scent. The Gnomes, as you found, are quite disgusting."

"But why was she trying to hurt me? I never met her before."

"She was trying to kill you Ellie that is what I have been trying to make you understand. The Gnome was trying to kill you."

"I'm not sure I can take this. I probably believe you, after all, I was there and I saw it myself, but well, you have to accept that this is all extremely way out of my frame of reference. It's just not something I ever thought I would be sat calmly discussing at my kitchen table."

"Yes, quite. I agree, it is a lot to take on board. But I am afraid, Ellie, that you are going to have to get up to speed quickly. We have received word that there is a Gnome in the town and he is looking for you."

"But didn't we, I mean, you kill him yesterday?"

"No, that was only a scout. They are a lot smaller and weaker than the soldiers. Usually they are sent ahead to reconnoitre the area and report back. Allowing the soldiers to plan and use their time more effectively."

"Ok, if they get bigger and badder than that thing yesterday, I'm scared. What do we do?"

"Well, there is a Fairy Council called for this evening, and I think it would be a good idea for you to come along. You need to know how serious this is, and to be frank, several of us would like to meet you and talk. This is such a strange and I suppose exciting thing to have happened. I am sure that the Folk will have lots of questions."

Being ever the human and the female human at that, Ellie asked the most pertinent question of the day.

"And what do I wear for this council meeting? Is it formal or more casual?"

"I think that you and I are going to have some communication problems. Do you not grasp the significance of this? Do you not speak the same language as I? Do you not understand what is happening?"

"Sure I do, but seriously, what do I wear? I have never met Fairies before and I guess I want to make a good impression." Ellie pouted just a little. After all, she really was nervous and when nervous, she tended to concentrate on the frivolities. It was a kind of defence mechanism she supposed. And anyway...

"Don't you use contractions at all?" She asked.

Felix harrumphed and turned toward the door, telling her that he would collect her at seven that evening.

"I suppose it would not hurt to dress smartly, after all, the Queen may just show up." And with that he left.

Ellie stepped to the window to watch him leave but he was nowhere to be seen.

Ellie spent the rest of the day in a complete daze. She wandered aimlessly about her home, touching things, picking them up, putting them down. She sat in front of the television for an hour without turning it on; she ran a bath and then watched it go cold. She could not wrap her mind around the things that Felix had told her. She was completely at a loss to know what to do next. She didn't really have any close friends, just people who popped into the shop to chat. Ellie had always valued her privacy; her home was a quiet and restful place for her to unwind with a book. So, she had nobody to phone with "You will never guess the day I have had." Today was the first day that she wished she did have someone. But who would believe her? She didn't even have the wounds as proof.

Oh well, time was marching on. After a day of procrastination, the afternoon sped into the evening and now Ellie had to rush to get ready. She jumped into the shower and lathered her hair. It felt so thick and smooth, full of silky soapy bubbles, and when she rinsed it off, she could have sworn it felt longer than usual. As Ellie

The Fae

towelled herself dry, she luxuriated in her soft skin and natural, fragrant odour. Whilst she rubbed the towel over her flesh, it seemed that the skin itself exuded a soft scent of flowers; there even seemed to be a dewy glow about her that she had never noticed before. Whilst sitting at her mirror, combing out her hair, the setting sun highlighted the rich tones of her lustrous mane and Ellie decided against make up as she was feeling pretty good about herself. Her reflection in the mirror was definitely looking wholesome, winsome even, she thought.

Ellie dressed in black slacks and a jewel coloured T shirt that looked quite smart. Being quite tall, she wore flat black sandals and tied her hair back from her face with a matching scarf, letting the ends dance with each movement. She poured herself a glass of water and leant against the sink whilst she drank it. She realised that she was nervous. She was about to step into a room full of Fairy Folk. For crying out loud! What the hell was happening to her? She was not, however, afraid. Ellie found that she was quite excited about meeting the Fairies. She was full of anticipation and her mind bubbled with possible scenarios that may arise. Would they be dangerous? Would they like her? What on earth would they talk about? Why did they really want to meet her?

The doorbell rang just as the clock struck seven. Ellie opened the door to find Felix, resplendent in a long, deeply purple jacket that buttoned to his throat with buttons covered in the same fabric. The jacket reached down past his knees and stopped just shy of his boots, into which were tucked his rich black silken trousers. His hair was swept from his brow and held in place by a simple silver circlet. He was breathtaking. He looked like a prince from a fairy tale. Of course he did! He stood tall and erect, hands clasped lightly in front and incongruously holding a bunch of keys.
"Ah, you ready?" He asked
Ellie took a deep breath.
"Whenever you are." She replied.
They got into his car and started off.

Felix drove for about half an hour, there wasn't much conversation, but it did not feel uncomfortable. Ellie just sat back and enjoyed the ride. She reasoned that she would know soon enough what was happening. Felix, in turn, did not seem to be the talkative type. He was polite enough, but the word taciturn went through Ellie's mind more than once. She snuck glances at him and noted the tilt of his head, the strength of his jaw, the dark lashes that flicked at his cheek as he blinked. Oddly, Ellie felt that her interest was not sexual, merely curiosity. Oh yes, he was stunning. He was tall, handsome, proud and a fairy for goodness sake. But no, she wasn't interested in him as a potential mate.

In no time at all, they arrived at their destination. The car had pulled up at a high gate set into a forbidding wall. Passing through the gate, Felix and Ellie drove up the long curving driveway. Each side was rich with tree, flower and bush. The air was thick with the heady scent of the flowers. Butterflies lazily bounced out of the way as the car crunched gravel in its wake. As they rounded a large bend, a picturesque cottage came into view. It had a thick thatch overhanging rounded whitewashed walls. The windows were large and sparkling, hung with baskets below, filled to bursting with flowers of every hue. The door to the cottage was of heavy oak and studded with giant black rivets. It stood ajar.

The Fae

Felix cut the engine and both he and Ellie made their way through the door and into the cottage. A clean white hallway with faded runners on the floor and jam jars full of fresh flowers was Ellie's first glimpse of a fairies home. There were no pictures on the walls but petals and leaves seemed to have been captured in the plaster and spread about in no discernable pattern. The overall effect was one of comfort and rest. A small table sat against the wall and upon it was a wooden plate filled with bunches of keys with wallets and purses. Felix placed his car keys and wallet on the plate and motioned for Ellie to do the same.

Gradually, a murmur of voices reached them and Felix turned toward the sound. Beckoning Ellie, he walked through a doorway. As Ellie stepped over the threshold, she nearly fell on top of Felix in surprise. Firstly she felt a cool mist of rain scented water tickle her face, then she opened her eyes to see not the room she was expecting but a sun dappled clearing in a forest. Trees stood tall and erect whilst lush, fragrant grass carpeted the ground. Small daisies poked their heads through the blades and tiny tuneful birds darted about the sky. In the centre of the clearing were several fallen branches and tree trunks, roughly arranged in a circle. In the middle of the circle Ellie could see a tall, willowy woman with her back turned, talking to two small girls. On the tree stumps sat several other people chatting quietly.

Felix took Ellie's hand and led her toward the woman, and with a slight bow of his head, said "Your majesty, may I present Ellie, of whom you have heard tell."
The woman turned with a smile in her eyes and accepted Ellie's hand from Felix. Ellie felt an overwhelming desire to curtsey, she did so, somewhat clumsily saying
"Your majesty, it is an honour to meet you."
"Stand child, we bow to no one here." Spoke the queen as she pulled Ellie to her feet and toward her in one fluid movement. Before she knew what to do or say, the queen had leant in and kissed Ellie on each cheek and then the lips. The queen turned to Felix.
"Brother, kind of you to escort our guest. Perhaps you will both be seated so that we may begin."
With another short bow, Felix motioned Ellie to follow him as he went and sat on one of the fallen tree trunks.

Ellie gently sat then jumped up again and looked behind her at the tree. She reached out and felt the bark. Instead of the harsh and jagged bark surface she expected, the wood gave beneath her hand and felt, well, like her sofa at home. It was soft and inviting. She sat again.

At a movement from the queen, each person took a seat and quietened to listen. The queen acknowledged each guest with a nod or a smile then began to speak.
"Family, brothers, sisters, I ask you here today because it has been too long since our last meeting and we have news to share." The queen smiled out at the people seated but noted the stolen glances toward Ellie.
"I see that our guest has caused some curiosity. Let me introduce her to you. Ellie, if you please?" The queen motioned for Ellie to join her and with a great deal of trepidation, Ellie did so.

The Fae

"I know that all here present have heard of Ellie. She was found and rescued by our sister Fae. This in itself is unusual, but Fae took the forbidden step of giving Ellie, a human, some of her blood." The queen continued.

Although the queen's words felt ominous, she stood serene and beautiful. Her blonde hair lifting slightly in the breeze, as the hem of her cobweb light skirts kissed the grass. "We shall decide upon Fae at another time, for today's meet is to discuss far greater concerns."

At this a murmur, no louder than a butterfly's heartbeat, went around the circle. The queen heard this but acknowledged it only with a slight movement in her hand. Almost a soothing gesture one might make subconsciously.

"As Ellie now has fairy blood, we must accept her as our family. Every drop of our blood is precious and must be protected. However, as Ellie is human, we must keep her safe and teach her about our ways. This is an interesting and exciting development that, though unprecedented, could provide us with insights and directions previously unthought-of to us."

The queen indicated for Ellie to re-take her seat, which she did so, gladly. Felix winked as she glanced his way and Ellie was so surprised that she felt herself smile widely and begin to relax.

"Now." The queen resumed. "Onto matters dark and dangerous. Mertensia, perhaps you would like to send Begonia and Bluebell home? This is no tale for young ears."

A woman of indeterminate age, dressed in a green and brown, floor length dress, stood and held her hands out to the two small girls. Without complaint, the girls stood and went to their mother.

"Straight home now girls, I will return shortly."

"Yes mama." They chorused. Then, kissing their mothers cheek, they stepped outside the circle. Holding each others hand, they smiled at the group and vanished. One moment they were there and the next, only a slight shimmer in the air and a few glinting dust motes remained. Mertensia retook her seat.

"Thank you." Said the queen. "Now, what I have to share with you is indeed grave and not for general knowledge until we have reached a decision. This itself is also unheard of, but this news is potentially of such magnitude that I feel we must discuss fully how we are to proceed before we frighten the family. A united and unified response and plan of action is the only way, I believe, to try and avert panic."

At these words, the gathered fairies looked about and at each other nervously. None seemed to know why they had been called and none appeared to know why the queen appeared so distressed.

"I wish to call forward Yarrow and Milfoil." The queen clapped her hands and two fairies appeared inside the circle. Each was dressed in the earth tones that the fairies seemed to favour and each was as beautiful as the other. Although they stood calm and serene, there seemed to be a slight hint of panic in their eyes. Ellie thought she had never seen anyone so pale and shocked. She was curious to know why. The male of the pair stepped forward and spoke. His voice was fresh and lilting, full of quiet strength and resolve.

"My wife Milfoil and I are, as you know, healers. In the human world, we work as doctors, where we can use our gifts to aid, but never to cure. As is our law regarding interfering in the course of humanity." With this, Yarrow sent a clear and pointed look at Ellie.

The queen cleared her throat and invited Yarrow to continue.

"Two nights ago," continued Yarrow. "A man came into the hospital with severe burns on his hands. Now this in itself is nothing unusual, but when I undressed his wounds, I smelt the Undead upon them. The man was human. I tried to hide my surprise and called Milfoil in on the pretence of a second opinion. She also smelt the Undead. I cleaned and re-dressed his hands and questioned him as to how they came to be burned. The man was not forthcoming, instead he became verbally aggressive and left before I could glean any information from him. I sent Milfoil to follow him. I have never used our powers in the Mundane world before, but I believed that this was an exception to our rules." Here he stepped back and glanced at his wife. Milfoil stepped forward and took up the tale.

"The man was not very difficult to follow; the scent of the Undead was very strong upon him. The man also harboured a lot of aggression and fear. As we know, these have their own odours. I followed him to a school. It was late and the school was locked, but the man had a key and let himself in. He hurried to the back of the school and down a set of stairs, where he unlocked another door and entered into a laboratory. The room was clean and set out along the workbenches were the usual paraphernalia that you would expect to find. However, the man walked straight to the back of the room to a bookshelf. He pulled on a book and the shelves slid aside to reveal another door. This door, he also unlocked and entered through."

Milfoil stopped for a moment and wiped at her brow. She was becoming visibly anxious, yet she continued.

"The man could not see or even sense me so I followed him through the door. At the far end of the room were two cages, one filled with the Undead, in such a state of agitation, the like of which I have not seen for a millennia. In the other, smaller cage, were Gnomes and Pixies. They each sat as far away from each other as possible, and their feud seemed forgotten in their shared doom. Their fear was palpable."

"The man went to a glass cabinet and removed a box. He placed it on the counter and lifted the lid. He reached in and took out a fist sized, spherical object. The Undead were watching him and you could plainly see their agitation. The man took a long handle with a silver noose at the end and passed it through the bars of the cage and managed to snag it over one of the Undeads' head. He then pulled and pushed until the Vampire was against the bars, where he secured him against them with a silver cuff about his waist. The man returned to the object and broke a piece off. It crumbled into a gritty powder which he scooped up with his uninjured hand. Cautiously approaching the Undead, the man threw the powder at him and jumped back. He returned to the counter and started to type into his computer."

"For several seconds, nothing happened, then the vampire began to shake, his eyes rolled back up into his head and he moaned. Such a pitiful sound, the like of which I never wish to hear again. There was so much pain and torment in that cry. The Vampire stopped shaking but began to foam at the mouth, he snarled and bit at the air around him, trying to attack anyone in his path like a rabid dog. The power of speech seemed to have left him, he could only yelp, snarl and growl. He was a terrifying sight and the other Vampires in the cage pressed themselves as far out of his reach as possible. They were calling to the man to stop, to release them, to let them go, but to no avail." Milfoil stopped to take a shuddering breath and wipe at her eyes.

Yarrow stepped up to his wife and took her hand.
"You must tell it all my love." He gently pressed.
Milfoil visibly drew herself together and with a shaky breath, continued.
"I have never seen anything so cruel." She continued. "The Vampires were terrified. The Undead that was locked against the bars was tearing at his own throat in an effort to get free of the silver binding him, so that he could attack his kin. Great handfuls of flesh and blood were ripped from his throat by his own hand and yet still he did not tire or stop. The pain he must have felt! I cannot imagine it. Mercifully, the man took a steak and drove it through the heart of the wounded Vampire. Then, quick as a flash, he pulled on the silver loop so tightly that the Vampires head came off and he turned to dust. The remaining Vampires were in frenzy, screaming to be released, but one had stopped and was sniffing the air. He had spotted me. Although he could not see me, he knew I was there. "Help us." He begged me."

"At first the man must have thought the Vampire was talking to him and told him to shut up. He was busy making notes at his computer. Again the Vampire begged me, "Help us. I know that you are there. How can you watch? Are you not Fairy?" What could I do? The man looked at the Vampire and followed his line of sight, right to me. I know he could not see me but he was now aware of my presence. What could I do?" Milfoil wiped at the tears on her cheek and Yarrow squeezed her hand to continue.
"Nearly there my love." He told her. "Nearly over."
Milfoil drew herself in, squared her shoulders, took a deep breath and continued.
"I lifted a tray of glass vials and dropped it on the floor. The man jumped in surprise and took a step back. I lifted a book from the counter and slid it across the work bench to land near him. He was visibly afraid now, as he did not know what was happening, he still could not see me. He must have thought me a ghost I suppose. He took several steps back now, darting looks about him, searching for the source of this development. He stumbled backward again, toward the cage, as his foot caught on the broken glass. He could have no idea what was happening, only seeing the effects of my actions, and he was afraid. I heaved his computer monitor to the floor and he jumped back enough for a Vampire to reach through the bars of the cage and snap his neck. Just like that, he fell to the floor dead. I became visible and the captives all started yelling and pleading at once for me to release them."

"I searched through the dead mans pockets and found his keys. I tried several in the locks before the right ones turned. I was shaking. I was terrified. My hands shook so much that turning the keys took an eternity. I had killed a man. I was responsible for his death as surly as if I had snapped his neck myself. I am a healer, I swore to help and protect, not take life." Milfoil sat heavily on the ground and began to rock gently as she cried.

The fairy folk seated just stared, open mouthed in shock. They looked at Milfoil, being comforted by Yarrow, as she sobbed into his shirt. The Queen stood and went to the pair.
"It is indeed an horrific thing that has happened, and though you played a part, the death was not yours to claim. You did not kill that man. Be content with that and

The Fae

take what comfort you can from it. I do not think though that your tale is finished. Perhaps if you will continue? When you are done you may return home to rest and we will speak more tomorrow."

Milfoil wearily stood and took up her tale. Her voice flat and emotionless.
"I healed as many of the wounded as I could and gathered up the black balls so that the Undead need not touch them. They burned my hands, but we heal fast and well, there appeared to be no lasting damage or effect. When the prisoners had left, I set about collecting as much information as possible. I took the balls and all of the research I could find then flew home to Yarrow."
Yarrow stroked his wife's hair then spoke to the group.
"I managed to reverse engineer the balls and have discovered how they were made. Why they were made can only be guessed at. Indeed, how the man knew of Others is a mystery. I have discovered that the balls are designed only for Vampires and that, according to the research material, if a Vampire is newly turned, he reverts to being human, however if the Vampire is an ancient, i.e. over two hundred years turned, he becomes feral, vicious and unaware of his actions; needing only to rend and feed. So, we bring this information to our Queen and she to you."
The Queen stood and looked at Milfoil kindly.
"Go to your home now, rest. We will speak tomorrow." She turned to the seated Fairies gathered and spoke again. "Now you know what has befallen our sister Milfoil and our brother Yarrow, we must decide how to proceed."

"We can wipe out the Undead." Shouted a voice from the back. "Finally, we have the means to protect the Mundanes and even the rest of the Others. We can be free of them forever."
"Lupin! How could you say such a thing?" Came a shocked voice.
"Lupin may be right." Joined another. "How long have we dreamt of ridding the world of the Undead? Now we have the perfect tool, I say we should use it."
And so the Fairies argued back and forth until the sun started to set and dusk crept up to the circle.

Ellie sat, her mind kaleidascoping with images from Milfoils tale. Vampires from movies and books fought for attention in her mind. Memories of characters that she had invited into her imagination now took on a terrifying reality. Thoughts of barbaric demons stalking the earth drinking the blood of innocents struggled against the glamorisation of the High School Student Vampire Buddies that filled her TV screen. TV Vampires that were good and only drank synthetic blood, or Day Walkers that curbed their atavistic desires with miracle drugs, circled her mind like psychotic Town Criers. Were Vampires Evil?

Everyone stopped talking and looked at Ellie. She blinked in surprise and confusion.
"No." The Queen told her. "Not all Vampires are evil. They have good and bad like any other race. We even have some that we consider friends of our family. They fought alongside us in the Great Fairy War. But we have long memories and some amongst us prefer to remember darker days." The Queen beckoned Ellie to stand by her side. "What would you have us do were it your decision?" She asked Ellie.
A chorus of gasps and incredulous mutterings swept the gathering. The Queen silenced them with a look.

"I would never presume to have an opinion on something I know nothing about." Ellie managed to say. Her heart was pounding and she could hear the blood rushing in her ears, making her dizzy.

"And yet I wish to know what your instinct would be." The Queen quietly demanded. "What would you do, with the information we hold that could potentially annihilate a whole race of beings?"

Ellie was sure she would pass out now. Her legs were weak and her head was spinning, the pounding in her ears was becoming deafening.

"Speak." The Queen bade.

"I would ask the Vampires to join the discussion. It affects them the most, they surely must be involved in any decision."

Again, gasps and mutterings. This time louder, more aggressive, more incredulous.

"You cannot possibly consider the opinion of an outsider in this?" Came a voice.

The Queen drew herself up.

"An outsider? Did I not introduce this girl as family? Did I not wish you to take her to your hearts and show her our ways? Is she not now one of us?"

"Well, yes, but surely you cannot mean to involve her in this? It is a decision for us, the High Council, not a Sub with no knowledge of our ways? Our history?"

"It is precisely that which compels me to do so." Spoke the Queen. "We have become too embedded in our own ways. We no longer consider the value of others, or as you call them, Subs. We for far too long have become insular. We have kept our walls high, have internalised our problems. I believe that the time has come for fresh perspective."

"But…"

"I have spoken." The Queen gently but firmly said, loud enough to be heard by all.

The Queen paced the clearing, deep in thought and the fairies sat in silence, watching her. Each of them desperate to be heard but compelled to silence. Their Queen had spoken.

After a few agonising minutes, the Queen stopped pacing and returned to the centre of the clearing. She looked about at those gathered. With a long look at Ellie she spoke.

"I have made my decision. Before we bring this to the family, we will invite the Vampires to attend. As Ellie has said, this affects them the most and they must be involved in any decisions made."

The gathering clearly wanted to protest but, kept silent as the Queen continued.

"Milfoil, Felix, myself and Ellie will meet with Marcellus, the Hive leader tomorrow at midnight. We shall hold the meet on neutral ground. I believe that the Castle Park, in the Band Stand will suit. I shall contact Marcellus to ask him to join us. I will decide whom of the Council will join us and let you know in the morning."

The fairies mumbled and muttered. Ellie looked as if she had been hit by a brick wall and Felix sat, imperial and aloof.

"Please return to your homes and await my decision."

With that, the Queen stepped out of the circle and vanished.

Ellie returned to her seat and sat heavily on the log. Her mind was numb. Mere days ago she had been going about her life, simply and uneventfully, unaware of the existence of Supernaturals excepting as fiction in books and on TV. Now here she was, smack bang in the middle of a surreal nightmare which, to all intents and purposes, was about to get worse.

The Fae

She did not notice that Felix was guiding her out of the clearing, through the house and back to the car. They had travelled several miles before she realised she was being spoken to.

Chapter 3

Ellie awoke in her own bed, fully clothed except for her shoes. The sun was streaming through the open curtains and bouncing off the mirror above the fireplace. Her head felt thick and her teeth seemed to be covered in foul tasting goo. She glanced over at the clock on the table by her bed. It was eleven in the morning.

"Hell!" She thought out loud, "I'm late for work." She grabbed her phone and clumsily punched in the number for the shop. Jack answered on the third ring.

"Oh Jack, its Ellie. I am so sorry, I just woke up. I am so late. I'm going to brush my teeth and be right there. God. I am so sorry."

"Ellie, its fine. We're not busy. Grab a cuppa and take your time. You can make it up to me by closing up. I need to getaway early. Is that ok?"

"Oh man, thanks. I will be in really soon. Thanks. You are the best. See you in a couple of minutes."

She called and booked a taxi to take her the ten minute walk to work and jumped in the shower whilst she waited.

Ellie arrived at work to find a hot cup of coffee waiting for her.

"Oh, Jack, you rock. Thank you."

"I knew you wouldn't take time to get one, so, well, here."

Ellie lifted the cup and sipped appreciatively.

"Oh that's good." She sighed.

"New blend, well, for me. Its one of the flavoured ones from that new shop across the road."

"Well thanks. I like it." She sipped some more. "So, how come you are leaving early? Do you have a date?"

Jack turned red as a beet and looked sheepishly at the door. Classic escape body language.

"Oh my god! You do don't you?" Ellie grinned so hard her face hurt. "Who is it? Do I know them? Who? Where did you meet? Tell me all. I want details."

Jack blushed a deeper shade of crimson but his eyes were delighted.

"Her name is Scarlett. I met her yesterday. She came into the shop and well, we got chatting. She asked me out! Can you believe that?"

"Of course I can silly. You are a great catch."

A shadow passed briefly across Jack's eyes, but he blinked and was back to his happy self.

"So, how come you slept late? Hot date last night?" He teased.

"No, no, just up late watching TV. I got caught up in a movie. You know how that is." For some reason, Ellie felt reluctant to go into details. Jack would be supportive and understanding, but really! Could she really tell her friend and boss that she had been cavorting with Fairies? Probably best to not even go there.

The day was a little busier than usual, but not so much that Ellie didn't find her mind going over the events of the night before. Not to mention her being distracted by the sheer panic at the thought of meeting Vampires later that night. Real live Vampires! Well, kind of. What on earth do you wear to meet Vampires? The meeting would be at night and in the park, so probably best to dress warmly she thought.

The door jangled and in walked Ciara. She stopped by the shop once or twice a week on her way to work, to buy incense or gifts for herself and friends. Ellie believed, or rather hoped, that it was really just so that she could have a chat and a friendly gossip. In the few seconds it took Ciara to reach the counter, Ellie considered telling her about her encounters with the Fairies, but decided against it. She really wanted to be friends with Ciara and reasoned that this would not be conducive.

"Hi Ellie." Breathed Ciara.
"Oh, honey, do you have a cold coming?"
"I think so. I was in the woods yesterday, taking the rabbit for a walk. It was quite misty and I think it got to my chest."
"How is Flopsy coming along with the whole harness and walkies thing?" Ellie asked.
Ciara spent the next five minutes regaling Ellie with anecdotes of her attempts to take her rabbit for walks. Ciara lived in an upstairs flat whilst the rabbit lived in a hutch on her small balcony. In an effort to get them both exercised, Ciara had decided to buy a harness and take it for walks in the woods.

Ellie's mind lightened as she listened to Flopsies latest adventures. By the time Ciara left, Ellie was feeling quite cheerful and the impending meeting with the Vampires was firmly at the back of her mind. The rest of the day passed uneventfully. A steady trickle of customers caused the days takings to be up on her previous day at works. Jack had left at four o'clock to get ready for his date. Ellie knew that this was his first date in almost a year, and it was making him quite nervous. Jack was distracted and fluttery, easily loosing his train of thought. Ellie teased him mercilessly then eventually wished him good luck as he went out of the door.

Just as Ellie was locking up, Ciara came running over, bending over to catch her breath. "Oh, I'm glad I caught you." She managed to say. "The reason I called in this lunch time. Phew, hang on a minute." Ciara sucked in a great lungful of air. "Wooh! Okay, the reason I called in was that..." breath, "okay, what it is. When I was in Friday Woods last night with Flopsy, a really weird thing... This peculiar old woman asked if I knew you. She tried asking me all kinds of questions. Wanted to know if you go to the woods, how well I know you, if you keep animals. Seriously odd. I tried to get away from her, but she followed me, asking all these questions, right up to the edge of the woods, where she... Well, this is a bit embarrassing, she... well... she disappeared. One minute I'm scooping up the rabbit, next she is nowhere to be seen. You probably think I'm crazy, but... well, I thought I should tell you."

"Wow, how weird is that!" Ellie's smile was forced and unnatural as her mind jumped to the Gnome that had tried to kill her. A shiver ran down her spine. "Uh, well, thanks for letting me know. How weird is that right? Well, I really need to get going. Thanks again for telling me."
With that, Ellie rushed off home. Upon reaching it, she slammed the door behind her and ran to her bedroom, where she threw herself on the bed and began to shake. What the hell was happening to her?

Just like the previous night, Ellie found that she was listless and could not sit still. She tried reading a book, but somehow Andrew Marr's 'The Making of Modern Britain' couldn't hold her attention. She tried watching TV, but the soaps were just grating on her nerves. She turned the radio on and off a couple of times before just giving in and sitting in her armchair, staring into space and trying to quiet her mind. As she sat, in total silence, she became aware of her heartbeat. At first it was just a gentle thrum in her chest, but as she concentrated, it became a deep resounding boom, vibrating her ribs. By and by, she believed that she could actually feel the blood moving, hotly, through her veins. She traced its journey up her arm and down her chest. A small smile at her lips as she felt the power inside the veins, replenishing her. A light tickling along her arms as the downy hair stirred with her breath. Ellie revelled in the aliveness of her body and realised that she was now much more relaxed than she could remember being in quite some time.

Eleven o'clock came around before she knew it and Ellie went to her bedroom to dress. She chose a thick turtle neck jumper, jeans and low heeled boots. It was a midnight meeting and so probably it would not be as warm as it had throughout the day. She refreshed her make up and ran a brush over her hair. She decided to tie her hair back as, for some reason, she was feeling very alive and attractive. Her eyes sparkled in the mirror with anticipation and a hint of amusement. A few hours ago, she had been very nervous about meeting with the Vampires but now, well, she was almost looking forward to it.

Felix knocked on her door just as Ellie was clearing away the remains of the sandwich she had made for herself.
"Ready?" He asked.
"As I ever will be."
"Come on then. Nervous?"
"Actually no. I was pretty much all day, but now, no I'm not. I'm quite looking forward to meeting a real live Vampire."
"Humph!" Was Felix' eloquent reply. "When we arrive, I believe that it would be best if you just stay quiet, do not speak unless spoken to. Certainly do not, I repeat, do not address Marcellus unless he speaks to you first. Vampires are very hierarchical. They observe tradition and have little patience for ill manners. You do not want to annoy a Vampire. For obvious reasons."
"No problem mummy. Do I get a sweetie if I'm a good girl?"
Felix just turned and looked at her with his eyebrow arched and lips pursed.
Sarcasm was completely wasted on Fairies Ellie thought to herself. She made her way to the car and climbed into the passenger side, buckled her seat belt and settled back to see what the night would bring.

Felix parked in Priory Street and they both walked up the road to the Castle. The large war memorial that stood in front of the high iron gates, seemed brighter than usual, as if the stone had been cleaned and polished just for them. The guardian angel stared down imperiously as they approached. There was a slight shimmery haze about it that appeared to reflect the street light back into the night. Up above, the stars glinted and winked, whilst the moon smiled down on the quiet town, illuminating the red eyes of the bats that hovered nearby.
"Are they the Vampires?" Asked Ellie in an excited whisper.
"For goodness sake!" Exclaimed Felix. "Where on earth do you get these ideas? Just follow me, stay close, and remember, manners!"
The pair walked over to the gates. They were high, ornate, impressive and shut. Behind them, Ellie could see the castle, spot-lit. Shadows of the sculpted bushes threw shapes across the pathways and snaked away, into the park. Night birds sang in

The Fae

the depths of the gardens and the roses, so beautiful in daylight, swayed darkly, perfuming the air.
"How do we get in?" Whispered Ellie. "Do you have a key?"
"Why do we need a key?"
"The gates are locked."
"What gates?" Asked Felix as he walked straight through, as though they weren't there.
"Show off!" Said Ellie as she hurried to catch up.
Felix and Ellie walked past the play area and around the Roman wall to the Band Stand. The air was still and fragrant, it tingled as if in anticipation and Ellie drew it deep into her lungs, feeling it fill and cleanse.

Up ahead, the Band Stand stood, proud and ancient. It's ironwork black against the deep night sky. At its steps stood the Queen, Milfoil and one other person that Ellie did not recognise. She and Felix walked over. The group turned at their approach and Ellie bowed deeply toward the Queen.
"Your majesty." She said.
"Ellie, Felix." Said the Queen. "Ellie, I have told you that we bow to no one. Please stand. You have not been introduced to Foxglove."
The introduction was made and Ellie shook his outstretched hand.
"Glad to meet you." She said.
"Likewise." Said he.
Foxglove was tall; straight blonde hair brushed his shoulders. His aquiline nose sat above a full and sensuous mouth. His coat was long and fitted, deep green velvet with covered buttons, a gilly shirt open underneath. His trousers were dark and tight, ending in a pair of highly polished boots, with long pointed toes. He appeared quite the dandy, like a character from a Bronte novel. He smiled impishly at Ellie as he noticed her looking him up and down. She in turn blushed and looked away.

The queen took the steps up into the Band Stand and disappeared from sight, Milfoil closely behind her. Felix and Foxglove turned and ushered Ellie ahead at the same time, causing them both to look at each other and glare. Ellie took the steps and entered into a large tented room. It reminded her of a Sheik's tent, all swags and silks. Low tables were dotted amongst the floor cushions, holding jugs and crystal glasses alongside platters of fruit. At the far end of the tent was a raised platform, about a foot off the floor. Here there was a table much the same as the others, but this one held a large thermos jug. Ellie had an image of it being full of warm blood for the Vampires and quickly shook that idea out of her mind. She filed it in the 'don't need to know' draw of her mind. The Queen was seated on the platform whilst Milfoil, Felix, Foxglove and herself arranged themselves on the cushions below.

At the stroke of midnight, the entrance to the tent was swept aside and in strode a short, swarthy man with black curly hair, behind him came two others. These men wore expensive looking single breasted suits in a soft and supple fabric that seemed to skim just above their skin. Their shoes were equally expensive looking and appeared to be just like the ones in the men's section of Vogue Magazine that Ellie had seen in the newsagents. The three men swept up to the dais and inclined their heads respectfully toward the Queen. The Queen, in turn, rose and offered her hand to the shorter man in the lead.
"Marcellus, thank you for agreeing to meet with us. I trust you are well?"

"Madam Queen, well enough thank you. Shall we do away with the pleasantries and get on with it?"

The Queen's lips narrowed briefly and she indicated that Marcellus be seated, at her table.

The other two vampires sat at a table away from the fairies. They looked about, stared imperiously at the fairies and then turned their attention to their leader.

Ellie stole glances at the Vampires. This was her first ever sight of a being that she had always believed to be fantasy. She was strangely disappointed. They looked like normal men, the kind you might find in any pub on a Friday night. Really ordinary. One was dark like Marcellus, considerably taller perhaps, but still dark, compact, kind of tight looking. His movements were small and strained, as though he were in pain. The other was also tall but very thin, with bright ginger hair. He had freckles and snaggled teeth. When he moved, he made large open movements; almost clumsy in his gangliness.

"They look so normal." Ellie sighed.

"What were you expecting?" Asked Foxglove.

"I don't know, just something more." Mumbled Ellie. "I don't really… its just that I thought they would be… well, more impressive."

The ginger Vampire glanced over at Ellie and gave her a filthy look.

"Well," Foxglove continued smoothly. "Their hearing is impressive certainly."

"Perhaps she expected shape shifting bats?" Mocked Felix.

Ellie gave him an old fashioned look. "Perhaps I did. So far my only experience of mythical creatures has been Fairies, and they, I mean you guys are all so… I mean, well… Never mind. But I just expected the Vampires to look more, well… menacing. That's all."

"Fairies are more what?" Asked Felix.

"Oh, nothing really. Forget I said anything."

"Uh huh! No way, I want to know. Fairies are more what?"

"Beautiful. There, you happy? Fairies are more beautiful."

"Well of course we are. Were we not beautiful, we would be goblins." Said Foxglove in a perfectly reasonable voice.

"Oh man!" Sighed Ellie.

The Queen, who had been quietly conversing with Marcellus, cleared her throat and everyone talking stopped.

"Ellie, if you would please stand."

Ellie stood.

"Marcellus, this is the human of whom I spoke last night."

Ellie bowed toward the Vampire. "My lord."

"How strange that you should bow." Marcellus intoned imperiously.

"Sir, I am not Fairy." Ellie replied.

"Sit. Sit." Marcellus waved a dismissive hand toward her.

"I thought you said that they valued manners above all else?" Ellie whispered to Felix as she sat.

The Vampires all turned toward her. The ginger one smiled. At least, Ellie chose to think it was a smile.

"Did I not also tell you not to speak unless addressed directly?" Asked Felix.

The Queen shot her a look then leant in and whispered something to Marcellus. He in turn directed his attention back to the Queen.

The Fae

"Milfoil, please share with Marcellus the information you bought to the High Council last night." The Queen asked.

Milfoil stood and recounted her tale. She appeared to still be distressed and when describing her part in the death of the man and she had to take several steadying breaths to continue. The Vampires listened intently but did not interrupt. Only the gradual darkening of their faces and the clenching of their fists betrayed any emotion. When she had finished her tale, Milfoil sat again.

"We have here all the information that Milfoil gathered, all the reverse engineering data that Yarrow completed and the balls that were retrieved for you to do with as you will. But I am sure you will agree that there is a larger problem here that we need to discuss." The Queen spoke to Marcellus.

"How can we know that this is all of it?" Questioned the other, ginger Vampire.

"Silence Dougal!" Marcellus growled. "My apologies Queen Alcea."

The Queen inclined her head in response.

"Dougal does raise a valid point Alcea." Marcellus continued.

At the insulting use of the Queens name, both Felix and Foxglove jumped up from their seats. Both of them had a sharp looking stick in their hands.

"Apologies again, *Queen* Alcea." Smirked the Vampire.

"Be seated, I am sure the slight was unintentional," spoke the Queen, waving her hand to encompass her would-be defenders. "This information is enough to distract anyone. We do however have matters to discuss. Firstly, did you not know of these experiments? Also, how did this human come to know of Others? How did he come to make these balls? And why? Have your Hive been active lately?"

"By active, I assume you are asking if any of my Hive have been feeding in the open? The answer to that is no. I would know. Nothing passes me."

Except this threat, thought Ellie. Very quietly... to herself... in her head.

Marcellus lifted the flask from the table and poured it into a crystal goblet. Yeuk! It *was* blood! Marcellus lifted it to his lips and drank the glass dry. A small trickle escaped and rolled down his chin. He slowly replaced the glass on the table, looked Ellie straight in the eye and wiped the drip with his index finger. Still looking her in the eyes, he sucked his finger noisily.

A disgusted shudder ran down Ellie's spine. Foxglove shifted in his seat and the slight noise made Marcellus break his gaze. He turned to the Queen but was not fast enough to see the revolt on her face.

Marcellus jumped up. "I will send my deputy to discuss this with you tomorrow night. I have an appointment that I am running late for. If you will excuse me." And with that he swept out of the tent, closely followed by the two other Vampires.

"Oh my god! I cannot believe how rude that man is!" Ellie sputtered. "How can he speak to you like that? We are here for his benefit, not ours. I mean yours! I mean, oh hell! I don't know what I mean. This is certainly not what I was expecting."

The Queen looked at Ellie with a half smile on her lips.

"And what were you expecting Ellie dear?"

" I don't know. More, I suppose."

The Queen laughed, "Too many story books I think. This is the real world Ellie, people do not conform to the traits written about them."

"But you do." Ellie replied. "You the Fairies, are beautiful, gentle and kind."

The Queen tilted her head to one side and studied Ellie for a moment. "You think us kind?"

"Well, yes. Of course. Felix says that Fae saved my life, I saw Felix save my life, you have shown me nothing but kindness since I met you. Of course you are kind."

"Does that not depend upon which side you sit?" Asked the Queen. "Had the Vampires found you, or even the Pixies, would they not be your saviours? Would you not think them kind? Instead of rude and insolent?"

Ellie stopped talking and sat down. She had no words to say. No smart alec reply. Well, what could she say to that?

The group stayed chatting for a few more minutes then broke up. Foxglove offered to take Ellie home but Felix assured him that it was not necessary. In the car Ellie was full of questions but not sure if she should ask them.

"I don't mind. You may ask me anything." Said Felix.

"Are Vampires always that rude?"

"Some are. I guess that you have to bear in mind that Marcellus was turned in ancient Rome. He came over when the Romans invaded Britain. He actually stayed in the castle when it was new. He supervised the building of it. He has been alive for a very, very long time. Many times the lifespan of a human. With that comes ennui, tiredness. Can you imagine nothing ever being new? Nothing ever lasting. No uniqueness, nothing is special. He has seen civilisations rise and fall. He has been over every inch of this planet. He has loved and lost countless times. He has killed in every way imaginable, loved in every way imaginable. Nothing ever touches him because he is inured to it." Felix seemed to be almost sorry for the Vampire.

"But you, the Fairy live as long. Don't you too feel like that? Don't you also tire of life and existence?"

"Oh no." Felix visibly brightened. "We are so much different. Vampires are born of death and destruction. That is a bleak and miserable place. Fairies are born of life and regeneration. We create, never destroy. Our lives are enhanced with every breath we take, every flower we pass, every rainbow. We are so much more... so alive. We burst with life. We bring and give life. Our lives could never be tiresome."

Ellie smiled at him. "I wonder what will happen now? Is our part done?"

"With the Vampires?" Asked Felix. "Probably, we will know more tomorrow. The Queen will meet with Marcellus' deputy and they will reach a decision. Despite the insult, we still wish to reach a conclusion. This weapon could be devastating if it fell into the wrong hands."

Ellie giggled.

"What on earth is funny?" Asked Felix.

"In the movies, whenever anyone says that, or they say something like 'What could possibly go wrong?' Something always happens. Something bad."

"Well, this is not the movies. As I keep trying to make you understand, this is real life."

Suddenly, Felix jammed his foot down hard on the brakes, throwing himself and Ellie forward with a jolt. Their seatbelts prevented them from hurtling through the window and the airbags exploded in their faces. Dazed and in shock, Ellie felt hands roughly pulling at her from outside the car. Her seat belt held her fast but the pulling continued.

"Ellie, Ellie, can you hear me? Felix, are you alright?" She heard from a long way off.

Ellie fumbled the seatbelt catch open and felt the fabric of the belt whip past her face as it retracted.

"Felix." She croaked. "Felix. Are you okay? Can you hear me? Felix!" There was no reply but for a low moan. Ellie felt along his seatbelt to the catch and struggled to open it backwards. Felix slumped against the airbag, a large gash on his head where he had hit it against the door.

As she reached to feel for a pulse, she felt herself pulled backwards out of the door. Strong hands lifted and carried her to the grass verge. As she sat there, trying to keep her head from exploding she saw that the car was on its back. Felix was squashed between the roof and the airbag. Foxglove was desperately trying to open the door to release him.

"Felix!" He was shouting. "Felix! Can you move? Help me you great lump! Wake up!"

Felix groaned and stirred, he opened his eyes slowly and looked at Foxglove with incomprehension.

"Felix, for crying out loud, help me. Open the door. Come on!"

Felix gradually turned his head, wincing as blood ran down his face. He gingerly reached out to the door and got his fingers wrapped around the handle. In apparent exhaustion, Felix leant his wounded head against the glass and closed his eyes.

"Wake up! Felix! Wake up. You cannot stay in there. Help me open the door. Felix!" Foxglove was pulling at the handle but it did not budge.

Felix gingerly pulled on the handle and as it popped open, he fell sideways through the door. Foxglove caught him and carried him to Ellie's side.

"What the hell happened?" He demanded.

"What? How are you here? Where were you?" Ellie asked, still in shock.

"I felt it and came." Foxglove told her. "Can you tell me what happened?"

"I don't know, we were driving and talking, then we were crashing. I don't know why. I was looking at Felix when he slammed on the breaks. Oh Foxglove, thank god you came."

"Fox, call me Fox. Foxglove seems so formal don't you think?"

"Sure, whatever, Fox. Thank you. Oh god, is he okay?"

Felix was laying on his side, his knees drawn up to his chest and was making a low keening sound as he gently rocked from side to side.

"Oh, yes, he will be fine. Do not worry. It's not as bad as it looks."

"Are you sure? He looks kinda messed up."

"He will be back to his own self in moments." Fox assured her.

As he spoke, the moaning ceased and Felix slowly straightened out. As he rubbed his hand over the injury on his head, his hand came away bloody but the wound had disappeared.

"What happened?" Felix asked. "How come you are here?" He asked Fox.

"He felt it and he came!" Ellie intoned in a hammed-up mysterious voice.

"Do not mock it. It saved you from the Gnomes did it not?"

"So, what happened here?" Asked Fox.

"I saw someone in the road, one minute I was talking with Ellie, the next, there was a person slumped in the road. I slammed on the brakes but I think I still hit them. Can you please check for me? I am still a little dizzy."

Fox slid upright and strode to the back of the car. "Where exactly was this?" He asked. "I cannot see anyone here. The road is clear for at least a hundred yards. How

The Fae

far back do you think it was?" Without waiting for an answer, Fox walked back along the road. He returned in a few minutes, shaking his head. "Are you sure? Because I can see nothing that would cause you to crash."

"I don't mean to be rude, but have you farted?" Asked Ellie.

"Fairies do not fart." Came Felix shocked reply.

"Well, what is that awful smell?" She wanted to know.

Both Felix and Fox stopped and raised their faces. Both sniffed the air and scowled.

"Gnomes!" The chorused.

"Well that explains why you crashed." Fox said. "They do seem to be very active lately. I wonder what they are up to?"

"It certainly needs looking into." Felix agreed. "Okay, now we need to get the car back on the road and get this lady home."

Felix and Fox walked over to the car, Felix at the front, Fox at the back. They each bent and took hold then, as if it weighed nothing, they turned it the right way up. The car bounced slightly as it settled back on its wheels.

Felix leant in through the door and flattened the air bag. He then climbed in and started the engine. After a couple of dry coughs, the engine caught and turned over. In no time the car was purring and Felix called Ellie to get in.

As Ellie buckled her belt, Fox opened the back door and arranged himself artfully on the back seat.

"I am just making sure she gets home in one piece." He told a slightly annoyed looking Felix.

The drive back to Ellie's was mercifully short, as both Fairies seemed intent on trying to out sullen each other.

As they pulled up at her home, both of them jumped out and escorted her to the door.

"Um, thanks guys. It's been, well, eventful." Then without her mouth consulting her brain, she asked them "I don't suppose you two would like a coffee? Or a hot chocolate?"

"I thought you would never ask."

"I suppose I could." They spoke over each other.

As soon as Ellie had opened the door, they were both in and at the kitchen table in a blink. Ellie wondered what on earth she had done. But in her heart she knew that she felt too wierded out to be alone for a while.

As the three of them sat nursing their hot drinks, Ellie was fidgeting in her seat, bursting to get some answers.

"Spit it out." Felix said. "Ask your questions."

"How many species are there? Why do you call them Others? What about the black balls? Why are Gnomes trying to kill me? Are all Fairies beautiful? What did you mean when you said that…"

"Whoa!" Interrupted Fox. "Slow down, one at a time. Ok, Humans are mostly called Mundanes. Supernaturals, us, Vamps, Pixies etcetera are Others because its less camp than calling ourselves Supes. As to how many species, well, there are dozens. Yes all fairies are beautiful, as I said earlier, if we were not beautiful, we would be Goblins."

"What does that mean?" Interrupted Ellie. "Why Goblins?"

"I think that is enough for one night, do you not?" Felix shot Fox a look that prevented him from arguing.

The Fae

"Oh I suppose so. Well… One of us should stay with you tonight to be on the safe side and the other will accompany you tomorrow. I think that until we have this unravelled and resolved, it would be wise to not leave you alone."

Ellie opened her mouth to protest but closed it when she realised that she really would like the company. Ellie was mostly a solitary person, with very few friends. Absolutely no friends that she could call on to borrow a fiver let alone save her from rampaging Gnomes.

"Ok, I'm happy with that on one condition." The two fairies looked surprised, as though they were expecting an argument.

"What is the condition?" Fox asked.

"Simply that we just have a drink and go straight to bed, no talking. I am exhausted, and not afraid to admit a little scared, but I would appreciate one of you staying with me."

Fox and Felix argued quietly in a language that Ellie had never heard before. She found it restful and soothing just listening to them and was a tad disappointed when they stopped.

Felix stood, clearly unhappy. "Fox will stay with you but I will be back at dawn. I have programmed my number into Fox' phone, so call me at anytime." at this, a look at Fox, "If you need me I will be here in seconds."

With that he literally swept out of the room and left.

Fox opened his mouth to speak.

"No talking. The couch pulls out into a bed, everything you need is there. See you in the morning."

Ellie turned and left the kitchen. As she entered the bathroom, she closed the door quietly behind her then sat on the lowered toilet seat and dropped her head in her hands. There were no tears, just numb exhaustion. The weight of her head seemed to sink and melt into her fingers, her hair oozed through the cracks and her skin melted away for the bones to be supported. Her curved back was taught and aching with the effort of sitting upright. She felt the faint stirring of air and Fox was stood before her with a pensive look on his face,

He lifted her effortlessly and carried her to her room. Fox carefully lay her down and pulled the duvet up to her chin. He bent and wiped her hair from her eyes then turned and left the room.

The downy hairs on her brow tingled where he had touched her and she felt the tension seep away as she fell asleep.

When night was at its deepest, the stars hidden behind distant clouds and with creatures scuttling for shelter; the heavens crashed and poured forth a torrent of earth scented rain. The coin sized drops pounded at the window and caused Ellie to wake with a start.

In the corner of the room, strobe lit by lightening, sat Fox. His eyes were closed and his breathing was heavy. His chest rose and fell with each breath and his gilly shirt slid open to reveal a smooth, golden chest. Her skin began to pucker slightly with the cold and Ellie rose, gathering her throw. Gently she placed the fabric around Fox. She felt his breath, sweet and fresh on her cheek as she bent to tuck the throw behind his knees. A shiver ran down her spine. Unconsciously, she reached her hand inside his shirt and ran her fingers across his skin. Her nipples hardened immediately, so she drew her hand back quickly and scurried back to her bed, pulling the duvet over her head and squeezing her eyes closed. As she curled into her bed, she missed the small smile at the side of Fox' mouth.

Chapter Four.

Ellie awoke feeling rested and alert. She glanced at the corner but Fox was no longer there. She smelt the wonderful fresh coffee aroma coming from the vicinity of her kitchen, so threw on a robe and made her way to the kitchen with a sense of trepidation. As she entered she took a deep breath and gabbled…

"Thank you for spending the, Oh, its you. Where is Fox?"

"Good morning to you too. You are very welcome. Oh, its not me is it, it's Fox you want to thank. For what though I wonder?" Felix had a cross between a sneer and a smirk on his face. Ellie decided to ignore his sarcasm.

"You made coffee? Fab, do you want a top up?" Avoiding eye contact, Ellie went to the coffee maker and poured herself a large cup. She added the milk then sat at the table, wrapping both her hands around the cup. Keeping her head down, she took short sharp sips of the scalding liquid.

"I trust you slept well and that the night was uneventful." Felix said.

"Oh, yes thanks, slept straight through, very good, not a peep, dead to the world. Yep, I slept like a log." Ellie fumbled. Feeling her cheeks redden, she busied herself by staring into the steaming depths of her coffee.

Felix stared long and hard at the top of her tousled head, a faraway look in his eyes.

"Well then. If you are sure." He finally spoke. "What are your plans for today? Do you have to go to work?"

"Uhm, yes. Yes I do. What time is it? Oh my god, I slept in again, I can't believe that I'm going to be late. Again!" With that, Ellie jumped up, slopping her coffee on her hand. "Ow! Bloody hell!" She cursed as she made her way to the bathroom, sucking her hand as she went. Ellie brushed her teeth, washed her face and got dressed in record time, and then she was back in the kitchen, slurping down the cooling remains of her coffee as she struggled to get her jacket on.

"Are you coming with me? If so, we gotta go. Now. Sorry to rush you but I keep sleeping late. It's the dreams; I can't seem to wake up from them some days. They are so vivid, it's like I'm really there. Anyway, here we go, late again. You ready?"

"Slow down, we have plenty of time. Finish your coffee, have some toast or something. You have to eat. Come, sit down."

"But we are late, its," Ellie looked at her watch. It was only eight thirty, she had plenty of time.

"Oh! Fancy that! Well, I…" Ellie sat with a flump and finished her coffee.

As they walked the short distance to the shop, Ellie and Felix settled into a comfortable silence. The air was heavy with the scent of the previous night's rain. The earth appeared aromatic, rich and brown, proudly supporting the myriad of flowers that had awoken just for them. The small birds that swooped and darted in the clear blue sky had held back their most beautiful songs to serenade the pair on their brief walk. Ellie breathed deeply, inhaling the invigorating scents that accompanied them.

"Is this you?" She asked.

"What do you mean?"

"This, the beauty, the air, the flowers. It all seems to be enhanced somehow. Sort of like it's always been there, but now it's more. Stronger, brighter, deeper, fresher. I know that doesn't make any sense. It's hard to explain."

The Fae

"I think that about covers it." Felix smiled, not unkindly. "As Fairies, we are connected to nature. All that we are stems from all that is around you. I suppose that when we walk through, we sort of enhance each other. We are all, magical and Other, made of energy. We interact by giving, receiving and sharing that energy. When you understand that, you are able to affect the energies of everything around you, which then 'enhances' all about you. Yourself included." Felix smiled brightly and Ellie was sure that she saw the flowers open just a little more as he did so.

In no time they were at the shop. As they entered, Jack looked up with a smile which disappeared as swoon as he saw that Ellie was not alone.

"Hi." Ellie beamed at him. "Come on, tell me all. How did it go? What was she like? Where did you go?"

"What?" Jack appeared flustered. He shot a look at Felix then said "We have a full day ahead, I expect us to be very busy, no time for dilly dallying."

Ellie was so surprised by his off-hand behaviour that she didn't know what to say except, "Oh."

"Yes well." Jack seemed completely out of sorts. "Who is this? The new boyfriend?"

"Oh no. God no. This is Felix, he's a... well... he's. What it is, is he is..."

"Good morning. My name is Felix. I am a student at the college. I am studying the after effects of accidents. How the victims get back to normal as it were. Ellie has very kindly said that I can shadow her for a few days. I sincerely hope that you do not mind. I promise not to get in your way."

"Well, I erm. Well.." Jack seemed to have the wind taken from his sails and was not sure how to proceed.

"You could look at it that you now have a free staff member for a few days, if that helps?" Felix offered.

"Oh well, in that case." Jack tried to smile, but it didn't go any further than his mouth. "Welcome on board. Ellie will show you around. Make yourself at home." With that he disappeared into the back room and stayed there most of the day.

Surprisingly, the day was great fun. The customers were very impressed with Felix' knowledge of all things magical and mystic. The women customers were more than happy with his breathtaking beauty and old world charm. He had the knack of making everyone feel that they were the only person in the world. That they were the most fascinating person ever to grace his presence. There was never a single trace of irony or amusement. Ellie believed that he genuinely enjoyed the experience. The takings were up considerably and five o'clock came round in a flash. Ellie was a little disappointed when the time came to close up.

"Oh, that was so much fun!" Felix practically bounced out of the shop. "I cannot believe that you do this every day! And you get paid to do it too! What a fantastic way to pass your time."

"I'm glad you had fun." Ellie couldn't help but smile back at him. "I have never seen you so happy. Have you never worked before?"

"Of course not. We don't work! Well, not as you would know it. We do not exchange labour for money."

"So, pardon me for asking, but, how do you support yourselves then?"

"It is no great secret. We usually... Ellie, back in the shop. Now!" Felix whole body had tensed, he practically pushed Ellie back through the doorway they had just exited.

The Fae

She stumbled backwards but managed to stop from falling by grabbing onto a shelf. As she righted herself, her nose wrinkled in distaste.

"Oh my god. It's them again isn't it? It's Gnomes."

"Stay back. Do not come out unless I call you. It may be an idea to hide in the back room for a while. I will take care of this. Try not to worry."

With that Felix shut the door and was lost from view.

Ellie ran to the back of the shop and wrenched open the door to Jacks tiny office.

"What the? Ellie? What's going on? I thought you had left. What's the matter?"

"Oh, Jack. I just need to, well, I just need to wait, yes that's it. I just need to wait in here for a minute or two. Felix has just gone to check on something for me. You don't mind do you?" She tried very hard to look winsome and appealing.

"You scared the pants off me." Jack answered.

"Now there's a picture to haunt me for a few days." Ellie tried to joke, forcing a thin smile.

"Take your bloody hand off me, you stinking great Fairy. Just who do you think you are? Where is Jack? What have you done with him?" Came an extremely upset female voice from the other side of the door.

"That sounds like Scarlett." Jack said as he opened the door. He stood with his mouth open in surprise as Felix stood, holding Scarlett by the elbow; clearly against her will. Felix was calm although he did have a fresh scratch running down the side of his face. Scarlett was flustered, red in the face, spittle at her mouth and invectives on her lips. She was thrashing and spitting, cursing and trying desperately to get free of Felix.

"Let go of her at once!" Demanded Jack. "What the hell do you think you are doing?"

"Do you know this creature?" Felix asked calmly.

"This is no creature. How dare you. This is my girlfriend, Scarlett. Answer me damn you. What exactly do you think you are doing?"

"Your girlfriend?" Asked both Ellie and Felix at the same time. "Really?" Continued Ellie in disgust. For she had caught the scent of her, filling the air with its putrescence.

"Yes, my girlfriend. Now let her go immediately or I shall call the police."

Felix let go of Scarlett's arm and she stumbled over to stand under Jacks armpit. She wrapped her arms around him whilst shaking and simpering pitifully. Staring up into Jacks eyes like a terrified fawn.

"You still haven't explained what you were doing?" Jack continued. His free arm reached around Scarlett and stroked her soothingly. "There, there my darling, all better now." He cooed.

"Can't you smell her?" Asked Ellie. "It's disgusting. I don't know how you can stand it."

Jack turned to Ellie with disappointment and disbelief in his eyes.

"What did you say?" He asked very quietly.

Ellie turned red and realised that nothing would explain this. Jack clearly could not smell the Gnome and nothing she said would make this ok.

"Look, Jack. I am so sorry that this has happened. I don't know what to say to you. I think it's best if I go now. I will see you in the morning."

"No, I don't think so." Jack said slowly.

As he spoke, Scarlett raised her tear stained face slightly toward Ellie and, staring her straight in the eyes, licked her lips very slowly. A shiver ran down Ellie's spine.

"No, I think that you should take a few days off. The accident has affected you more that we realised. Take a few days off and we will see where we stand say, in say a week?"

Ellie and Felix walked to the park. They didn't speak as they walked past the castle and around to the band stand. They settled themselves on one of the benches facing the stand and watched the squirrels scurry about scavenging for food a few minutes. Eventually, Felix spoke.

"This is potentially very serious. I believe that the Queen was right to have us guard you."

Ellie felt a stab of disappointment. "Oh, it was the Queen's idea? I thought maybe it was yours?"

"No. Queen Alcea is concerned about so many aspects of your existence right now, that she assigned your safety to Foxglove and myself."

"Oh, well then. So long as someone baby-sits me. I don't suppose it matters at all who gets lumbered with the job. I don't know why I imagined anything else." Ellie was suddenly very afraid and very pissed off.

"What on earth is the matter now?" Asked Felix.

"Absolutely nothing!" Sulked Ellie.

The continued to sit, in silence, for many more minutes.

"How the hell is my boss dating a Gnome?" Asked Ellie. "I know he hasn't had a date in a while, but seriously? A Gnome?" With that, she burst out laughing. "He will have to move out of his flat and into a house with a garden, else where will all the little baby Gnomes sit with their fishing rods?" She laughed so hard that tears were running down her face.

"Do I have to choke you again?" Asked Felix in a very stern voice.

Ellie looked at him, her eyes bright with laughter, "Probably." She roared.

Felix turned away as a smile spread across his face. His shoulders shuddered slightly and when Ellie spun him back to face her, he was laughing quietly. One look at her face and he erupted into full scale trumpeting laughter that caused passers-by to glance their way. In no time at all, the pair of them were sniffing and wiping at their eyes, trying to pull themselves together.

"Well." Said Ellie. "My life is certainly no longer boring."

As they drew near to Ellie's house, they saw a large fat brown cat curled up in front of her door. The cat seemed to be familiar, but Ellie could not think where she had seen it before.

"Hello gorgeous boy." Ellie said as she leant down to stroke the cat.

"Hello yourself, beautiful." The cat replied.

Ellie was so shocked that she toppled backward and landed on her butt with a bump.

"Peter!" Came a musical voice that sang of fresh fields and sunny days. "Are you teasing Ellie again?"

From the garden came a beautiful woman that Ellie felt was also vaguely familiar. The woman stepped to Ellie with her hand out.

"My child, I am so very happy to see you again. Perhaps you do not remember me? That is as it should be. You will forgive the intrusion, but Peter felt I should come. Do you mind if we go inside?"

The Fae

"Oh, of course." Ellie unlocked then opened the door.

Peter sashayed ahead of the trio and entered her home first, followed by the woman, Felix and then Ellie.

"Please, sit down. May I get you a drink? Tea? Coffee? Water? Felix, what would you like?"

"Water for both of us." Answered the woman.

Ellie handed round the glasses then sat at the table herself.

"I know!" She exclaimed. "You must be Fae."

"Yes," smiled Fae, "Do you remember me?"

"I'm sorry, no."

"Perhaps my son has spoken of me?" Fae asked.

"Your son?"

"Yes, Felix here. Has he not told you who he is?"

Ellie looked at Felix who sat, back straight, eyes on his mother.

"No, I guess we didn't get to that bit yet. I have pretty much been on a rollercoaster lately. It seems every time I open my eyes, something new and incredible happens."

"So I hear." Smiled Fae. "In part, that is why I am here. I feel responsible for all that has befallen you. Had I not given you my blood, you would be unaware of, well, any of this." Fae spread her hands to encompass the world. "Also, I believe that I have placed you in great danger."

"Well, thank you but I don't really mind." Ellie smiled at them.

Felix and Fae stared at her in surprise.

"Oh, don't get me wrong. I am terrified most of the time and all that but, jeez! The things I have seen and now know. Well, it's incredible. I truly would have it no other way. When I look back to before all this, my life felt so... so one dimensional. Now I feel fuller somehow. More awake, more alive."

Felix smiled and Fae looked discomfited.

"Well. Be that as it may." Fae continued, "We do have a problem in that the Gnomes seem to be very interested in you. It must be more than the mixing of blood, after all there are still several Fairy in the area. So, I wonder what it could be. Tell me Ellie, has anything untoward happened lately?"

Ellie and Felix looked at each other and giggled.

"Where would you like me to start?" Ellie smiled.

"Yes, I suppose that would be a silly question." Smiled Fae in return. "I mean, has anyone been asking questions? Or approaching you unexpectedly?"

"Oh. Yes, actually. Well, not me so much but I heard of something strange."

"Carry on."

"Well, okay. My friend Ciara. Well, she's not my friend. Not yet anyway, we are kinda working toward that. She pops into the shop to say hello occasionally. We have a little gossip and a catch up and... Ah! That's not what you... okay, well. Ciara stopped me at the shop as I was closing up and told me about an old woman in the woods, Friday Woods. You know them right? Up on the way to Mersea Island?"

"Yes dear."

"Oh, okay. Well, she told me that this woman appeared out of nowhere asking if she, Ciara that is, if she knew me. Asked by name. Asked if I went to the woods, had animals, that sort of thing. That's weird right?"

"Yes, did your friend to be get a description of this woman?"

"Not really. Ciara did say that the woman disappeared into thin air, so I'm guessing she was Other."

"How soon it all becomes normal." Smiled Felix.
"Indeed." Said Fae. "Any other instances?"
"No. Well, I don't think so... hang on a minute. There was this episode in the shop. About a week ago. I had a sort of lost day. Do you ever get them? You have no idea where the time went, how you got to your destination, what you did? That sort of thing? Well, anyway, I had this lost day. One minute I am arriving at work the next it's time to close up. Absolutely no recollection of the time in between."

"You say this was a week ago?" Asked Fae.
"Yes. I am pretty sure it was a week. Why, is that important?"
"Well, it was just over a week ago that I found you and gave you my blood. I imagine that your lost day was the after effects of that. We have never done it before, so we do not know how it will affect a human. I must say though that you seem to have adapted very quickly."
"I'm not too sure about that." Ellie countered pleasantly. "But that was not the odd thing. The lost day I mean. The odd thing happened the next day. I was in the shop and a man came in. He was quite insistent that I had served him the previous day. He told me that I had said I knew how to perform magic. Oh! He also said that I told him I would arrange a meeting with you. But how could I? I hadn't met you then. Oh, you know what I mean. Anyway, I told him he must be mistaken and he left. Now that I remember it, it was quite disturbing. I remember feeling quite shaken after he left."

"Do you remember anything about the man?" Fae asked her.
"Not really, it seems such a long time ago. I do remember him being dark. Not just dark haired, but dark all over. His coat... well, it seemed that he was just like... shrouded in dark. He had a thin nose and brilliantly white teeth. I'm sorry, but that's all I can remember of him. And I suppose you have seen the news? That girl that got hit by a car? I thought that she looked remarkably like me. Then of course, I got hit by a car too. Oh, the attack in the shop when I met Felix? The car accident? Ha! When you put it in a list like that, I've had quite an exciting time of it this last week. Oh, not to forget, my boss is dating a Gnome!"
"Yes, you certainly have had a time of it." Fae looked very serious. "It's the man in the shop that concerns me the most. Think hard my child. Did anything else occur to you about him? Or at the time? I know it's difficult, but please try."
"How about smells Ellie?" Asked Felix. "Do you remember any smells about the man?"

"Do you have the nose Ellie?" Asked Fae in delight. "How wonderful! Even some full Fairies do not have the nose. I see you got some good from the blood too."
"Oh, much more, my life is much more. I feel enhanced. Everything is better."
"Smells?" Felix interrupted.
"Actually." Ellie said. "Actually, if I remember correctly, he smelt like cookies. I was surprised, because he was so ugly. Not the nasty ones in a packet that smell like chemicals, but the gorgeous ones hot out of the oven of a grandma who has flour on her apron and apples in her cheeks." Ellie blushed at her words and looked away.

The Fae

"Elf" Said Fae and Felix together. They turned and looked at each other and smiled in relief.

"I'm guessing that Elf's are our friends?" Ellie asked.

"Elves." Felix and Fae echoed again.

"Elf's, Elves. Are they good guys or bad guys? Was he out to kill me too?"

"I doubt that. Elves are pretty much solitary. They appear as ugly because they do not really like to interact with Mundanes. Oh, excuse me, humans. But they are quite harmless and actually quite beautiful. Well, unless roused. But they tend to spend their time out of the way in the woods and forests. I have heard of a group that have set up home by the sea, but I believe it is too exposed for that here in Essex."

"So...." Ellie prompted.

"So what dear?" Asked Fae.

"So, why was he in the shop asking questions? Who is he?"

"I am not completely sure." Said Fae. "I must look into this first." Fae seemed to close in on herself as she sat and thought. Her face closed down and she looked like a marble statue as she sat, eyes closed and directed toward the fading sun.

Felix and Ellie decided to leave Fae alone with her thoughts for a while, and they went and sat in the garden.

"You keep the garden well." Commented Felix.

"Thank you. It brings me peace."

"From what?"

"Do you know? I am not so sure anymore. It's like a great big door has closed on a room full of pain and anxiety. I cannot nor want to open the door, but I know that whatever is behind it is mine. I feel no desire to go into the room, but it's always there, just behind that door." Ellie shook herself and asked. "So, correct me if I am wrong, but..."

"Oh, oh! But what?" Teased Felix.

"But. But I have noticed that so far, all the fairies have flower names. But you and Fae don't. how come?"

"I do. My correct name is Flax. It means symbol of domesticity. You can imagine why I use Felix."

Ellie tried to hide the smirk that arrived unbidden.

"Sorry, and Fae?"

"Well Fae, her name is actually quite sad. She was named Ophrys Fly, which means mistake. Her parents were particularly literal unfortunately. Now, we would never say that one family is better or more beautiful than another, but Fae did suffer as a child for her unfortunate name. She therefore renamed herself Fae. Which I am sure you know is a way of referring to Fairy Folk."

"And yet she gave you such an odd name too."

"No, she did not. Myself and my sibling were taken at birth. Even though there were many, many years between us. I think our abductors must have tried to give us fairy names. I think we were placed into other families and we were only made aware of our true mother when we came of age. At least, I believe that is... Anyway, I took it upon myself to find my mother. And well, here we are."

"So, have you found your sibling?"

"Unfortunately, not yet. Although I continue to search, and will continue until I find her or the earth takes me home."

"So, how come you were taken as babies? Who took you? Why?"

"Oh, my sweet Ellie. So full of questions. That is a story for another time."

The Fae

And that was all he would say on the matter.

Whilst Ellie and Felix sat in the garden soaking up the last of the sun, Fox arrived. As the gate banged shut behind him, Felix looked up and scowled. From the kitchen, they heard Fae bustling about apparently, making a meal.

"Here he is. He who shall not be mentioned." Felix said nastily.

Ellie shot him a look, then glanced at Fox and blushed.

Fox appeared not to notice this unfriendly welcome and sat in one of the chairs near the garden table.

"So, how has today been? Uneventful I hope?" Fox enquired.

"Not hardly." Said Ellie.

"Really? Tell me more sweet Ellie."

Felix scowled even darker and indicated Fox to follow him inside.

"Come inside and I shall explain. Let Fae have a moment with Ellie alone."

"Oh, is she here? I must say hello." Fox bounced up from his chair and disappeared into the kitchen, followed more sedately by Felix.

Fae took the seat that Felix had vacated. The plates she had carried from the kitchen were placed on the table. Each plate heaped with delicious smelling finger food that teased and tantalised Ellie's nose.

"Where on earth did all this come from?" Ellie asked in delight, scooping up a handful and nibbling with pleasure.

"Oh, I hope you do not mind but I had a look through your kitchen cupboards."

"You never found this in there? I don't even recognise half of it." Ellie was amazed.

Fae laughed her clear water laugh that caused Ellie to look at her. She felt the smoke of a memory evaporate as Fae took up her glass to drink.

Ellie followed her example and took a long drought of a honey flavoured cordial that left her feeling refreshed and tingly. Her hair crackled with electricity and stood momentarily at angles from her head. Her toes and fingertips felt warm and she felt an overriding urge to jump up and dance. She laughed out loud at the sensations coursing helter-skelter through her system. She felt as though everywhere the liquid passed was left feeling vibrant and alive in a way she had never known before.

Fae smiled at her and settled back into her chair. She turned her face toward the sun again and closed her eyes.

"I love this time of day." Fae sighed. "Everything is awake. Just listen to those birds."

Ellie put down her half full glass and leant back. She tried to adopt the same relaxed position as Fae, but the events running through her mind prevented her from relaxing.

"Have you remembered?" Asked Fae in a faraway voice.

"Remembered?" Asked Ellie. "Remembered what?"

"It will come." Said Fae sleepily.

"Why was an Elf asking me about you?" Ellie wanted to know.

"I believe that his name is James. He and I used to know each other many, many summers ago." Fae's voice had become very soft and when Ellie looked over, she looked to have fallen asleep.

Ellie tried very hard to settle back and relax. She closed her eyes and tried to pick out the individual scents in the garden. This was always one of her favourite relaxation

The Fae

games. The sweet heady aroma of the honeysuckle reached her first, followed by the deep and evocative tea rose. The geraniums from next door added a fresh layer but she could not determine the finer nuances. She was too distracted. Unable to settle, Ellie quietly left Fae to sleep and went to join the others in the kitchen. She walked in to find both Felix and Fox seated at the table, glaring at each other, with arms crossed and backs straight. When they became aware of Ellie's presence, they relaxed their postures and each forced a smile.

"We will continue this another time." Felix told Fox.

Fox nodded solemnly then turned to Ellie. Immediately he became bright and effervescent again.

"So, my child, tell me of your day." Fox invited.

"Where would I possibly start?" Ellie laughed, glancing at Felix. "Have I interrupted anything?" She asked.

"Oh, no, we were just talking. Nothing to concern you." Felix supplied.

"Actually," interrupted Fox, "it very much concerns you."

Felix gave him a sharp look but Fox carried on unperturbed.

"My brother Felix here was enquiring as to the arrangements for tonight. He does not believe that it would be suitable for me to guard you again. It would seem that he is concerned with your honour."

"That is not what I said, and well you know it!" Felix jumped to his feet, glaring at Fox. "I merely suggested that one of the women might be better suited."

"Ah!" Fox snarled. "What exactly do you think will be the problem with my being on guard tonight? Do you not trust me to protect our sister? Have I not proven my worth on many a campaign? What is it that you object to Felix my dear?"

"It was merely a suggestion, I do not know why you have taken it this far. I honestly thought that Ellie would be better... more comfortable, with a woman."

"And not a lecherous old Fairy like me do you mean?" Fox was becoming incensed. "How dare you suggest that I would violate our oldest law? I would never..! I have never..! Never crossed species before. What makes you think that I would now? Now whilst there is such danger? I cannot believe that you think so little of me!"

"Nor me!" Interrupted Ellie angrily. "Do I have no say in this? Am I such a weak willed and wanton woman that I could not say no to a big bad fairy? Even were I so inclined, I should think I would like to get to know him a bit first for crying out loud!" Fox turned to the window his shoulders tense and face a mask of indignation.

"My apologies." Felix muttered. "I did not mean any offence and certainly had no desire to offend you. I should go now. I truly am sorry that you had to hear that. I will call in the morning. Again, my apologies."

With that, Felix took up his jacket and left.

Fox turned from the sink and sat across from Ellie.

"I too apologise. I had no right to lose my temper and insult you."

"Yes, well. Okay then. No more said." Ellie sat fuming but not sure why. Actually, she was damned sure why. How bloody dare he not want to cross species with her? What was she? A cat? A horse? And surely there was no need to be so bloody, bloody adamant about it! Ok, she knew that there were laws, but he could have been a bit less disgusted at the idea.

"I think I would like to go to my room for a bit now." She said quietly. Ellie stood and walked out of the kitchen. She went to her room and quietly closed the door

The Fae

behind her. She sat on her bed and fiddled with the pillow whilst she waited for her emotions to settle down.

There was a gentle knock at her door.

"Please Fox, I will be out in a bit. I have a bit of a headache and just want to lie down for a minute."

"It is me." Said Fae. "I just wanted to check that you were alright. May I come in? I will not disturb you for long."

"Oh, of course." Ellie opened the door and Fae entered the room.
They both sat on the bed and Fae took Ellie's face in her hands.

"Do not be angry my child. I know that you are hurt and that my son Felix has caused this. But please, you have suffered so much in your short life, do not let this minor squabble rouse painful feelings."

"I'm not angry so much as hurt I suppose." Ellie tried to explain. "I know that you, the Fairies, can't be with people of other races, which I get. Well, kind of. But, well, he didn't need to be so bloody disgusted by the idea did he? I mean, I'm not so terrible that, well. I mean, if I were a... I mean, oh, I don't know. I don't even know why I'm so upset. It's not like I even thought of Fox that way, but to be so horrified by the prospect! It's, well, it's insulting. It's not like it was even something that I had considered."

"Are you sure?" Asked Fae kindly. "Generally all fairies are extremely attractive to humans. Regardless of sex. We tend to be like a magnet to them, even if they are not sure why. We have found it to be a bit of a problem at times, so perhaps, you may have mistaken this for something else?"

"Oh no. I don't find you all attractive at all."

"Really? How strange." Fae said with a raised eyebrow.

"Oh, there I go again! I mean, of course you are all beautiful, and I love being around you guys. Well, a lot. But, well, I am not attracted to you like that. I just feel sort of more whole when you are around. Especially you and Felix. Even though I only truly met you today, I feel as though I have known both of you forever. Its different with Fox. I don't feel that way about him."

"How do you feel about him?" Asked Fae.

"Well, of course, I find him deeply attractive, he is Fairy after all, but I don't have the same feeling of, well, of 'belonging' that I do with you and Felix. I can't explain it. Ok, when we were at the Fairy council, I felt at home. Even though a few were a bit unhappy with my being there, I still felt that peaceful, at home feeling that I always get around Fairies. I think, or well, I assumed that it was pretty much how humans are around you guys. But I didn't feel the 'at hominess' that I feel with Felix and you."

"That is indeed strange. We have never had that before. Perhaps it is another effect of you having my blood. I do forget sometimes that you are human, you seem to be becoming more Fairy every day. Have you noticed that your speech patterns are changing? Also, although you were always beautiful, you seem to glow now. Your hair has grown in length and lustre. What else have you found? We know that you have the nose. That you can smell the different species, which not all Fairies have."

"Don't Fairies all have the same powers then?" Asked Ellie.

"We do not think of them as powers, as such. We simply can or cannot do things the others of us can. For instance, Fox and Felix can communicate without speaking

The Fae

aloud. I can enter minds and heal. Alcea, our Queen can live in the here and the then. Yarrow, whom you have met, can fly without being seen. Iris, whom you have not yet met, escorts our departed souls to the Great Garden. We each have a gift that we believe is bestowed upon us for the good of the family."

"So, you guys must have some powerful blood running through your veins, if the bit that you gave me is having such an effect on me. I imagine it could become very sought after if others knew about it."

"Well, yes. I do not think that is something we need to concern ourselves with though. It is strictly against our laws for the sharing of blood."

"Yes, have you heard any more about what will happen to you for giving me yours?" Ellis asked.

"Not yet no. I believe that the queen wishes to resolve the issue with the Undead first."

"Any news on that? The last I heard, the queen was to meet with the Vampires second in command." Ellie asked.

"The meeting will take place tonight, but we are not required to be there. I believe that the queen will call a council later to discuss the outcome. These are very strange times."

Ellie looked at Fae for a long moment. She saw how the Fairy had a strange look in her eyes, one almost of hunger, like a burning need. When Fae saw that Ellie was staring, she blinked and the look was replaced with one of compassion and love.

"Well, you seem to have recovered from your earlier ill temper, I believe that I shall have a brief word with Fox, then take my leave of you."

Fae stood and crossed to the door, she then paused and looked back.

"I will also leave Peter here with you, if you will agree to it. He can be pleasant company and he never seems to sleep. It would be good to have another guard I think."

"Oh, thank you that would be nice." Ellie replied. *Nice? A talking cat for company strays more into the realms of utterly bizarre, and all I could think to say was nice!* Ellie smiled to herself.

The valance that fringed the bed rustled slightly, making Ellie freeze. Then a black nose peeped its way from the fabric, closely followed by a large, furry, brown cat.

"Did I startle you?" Asked Peter.

"Uh, well, maybe for a second. How long have you been under the bed?" Asked Ellie.

"Pretty much since we got here." Peter replied as he sprang up to sit beside Ellie.

Peter reached his paws in front and arched his back into a long stretch, his tail straight and stiff behind him.

"Ah, so much better. Nothing beats a good stretch."

"Peter, may I ask you a question?" Ellie tentatively enquired.

"Sure, go ahead."

"Well, what I was wondering was, how come you can talk?"

"How come *you* can talk?" Peter asked in response. "All animals can talk. Well, all creatures really. Actually, if you want to be pedantic, even plants can talk if you are prepared to listen."

"But I have never heard an animal talk before I met you."

"Were you listening?" Peter licked his paw then swiped it over his ear.

"Oh, well, I suppose not. Are you serious? Can they really?"

The Fae

"Er, are we not talking now?"

"Good point. Okay, so if you are all so smart and can talk, how come you don't run the world? How come you are happy to be pets?"

"Who said we are the pets?" Peter asked. "Humans wait on us hand and foot, we don't have to lift a paw for anything. Who is in charge in that relationship do you think? They don't call our females queens for nothing!"

Ellie was not too sure if he was joking or not, and the weirdness of having a sensible conversation with a cat was beginning to really make her question everything now.

"Peter."

"Yes Ellie."

"Is that you that has been following me?"

"Following you?"

"Yes. Quite a few times, I catch sight of a brown cat. At the corner of my eye. I've seen it here, at work, in the park, all sorts of places. I know that cats cover a lot of territory, but, well it seems that almost every time I look around, there he is."

"It is not me." Peter replied. "Are you quite sure? When did it start?"

"About a week ago. The only reason I ask is that the other cat looks a lot like you."

"How does he smell?"

"I don't know, I haven't been close enough to smell him. Also, I wasn't really sure if he was following me. It wasn't until today that I realised that cats can talk, so I never really thought one might be tailing me. Pardon the pun."

"I must say that I think you are taking this change in your life very well." Peter commented.

"Well, I don't really have too much choice. Plus, my life was not that great before, this is quite exciting. I never know what will happen next. I kind of like that."

"Please make sure that you are careful, exciting isn't always a good thing."

"Ah, spoil sport!" Laughed Ellie as she got up from the bed and went to the living room.

Peter oozed down from the bed and swung his rear into the lounge after her, purring Tom Jones' 'What's new pussycat' quietly to himself.

Chapter Five

Fox lay sprawled out on the sofa, watching Emerdale. He had a glass full of cola in one hand, and the other behind his head, scratching his ear. He looked very at home. When Ellie walked in, he jumped to sit upright and in doing so, spilt his drink on his trousers. It made a huge wet patch that had him jumping up and holding the fabric away from himself with his free hand whilst he looked about uncomfortably for something to wipe the spill.

"Oh, I am so sorry; it's all over your couch. Do you have a cloth for me to clear it with?"

Ellie looked at him and battled between annoyed and amused. Amused won. She went to the kitchen and got him a cloth.

"Here. Take your trousers off and I will run them through the wash, I need to put a load on anyway."

"Oh, I erm, I can not do that." Fox blushed.

"Oh don't be so daft. Get them off."

"No, really, I can not."

"Why on earth not. You've nothing there I've never seen before!"

"I seriously doubt that." Blushed Fox. "You see, I ah, well I do not have any under garments on."

Ellie smiled. Widely.

"Go in the bathroom, there is a robe in there you can put on."

Fox wasted no time in complying.

When Fox returned to the living room, he was wrapped tightly in Ellie's purple silk robe. It was stretched so tightly that she could see his abs clearly defined through the fabric. The curve of his hip was a little distracting too. Luckily the robe hung down to mid thigh on him, stopping just at the point where the well developed muscles in his leg... *Stop it Ellie!*

Fox clutched his sodden trousers and shirt in his hand. He was quite clearly uncomfortable.

"If you show me how the machine works, I will see to this." He said.

"It's okay, I will do it, pass them over."

Ellie took his clothes and added them to the load in the machine and set the dial. Switching the machine on, she stood to find Fox standing a little too close. Her breath caught in her throat and she felt a flutter erupt in her stomach. Swiftly stepping around him, she kept her head down so that he could not see her blush.

"What would you like us to do tonight?" Fox asked.

Oh boy, oh boy, oh boy, Ellie thought. *Stop, stop, stop with this crazy stuff. Get a hold of yourself. It's only Fox for crying out loud.*

"Uh, well, I don't have plans. What did you have in mind?"

"What would you normally be doing?" Fox wanted to know.

"I suppose I would be curled up with a book and a glass of wine."

"Ok, that is what we shall do then. Peter! Peter, where are... oh, there you are. What are you going to be doing?"

Peter stretched lazily and looked at Ellie.

"I believe that I will spend the night outside. Ellie told me of a cat that has been following her and I would like to investigate a little. You two will be alright without me won't you?"

The Fae

"I am pretty sure that we can manage." Fox smiled. "If we need you, we will call out the door. How far can you hear?"

"I'm usually good up to about a mile on a clear night, but I wont be going that far tonight. I plan to stay close to the house."

"There is a cat flap when you want to come in. It was here when I moved in. I always meant to get a cat. I think I feel a bit odd about that now."

"No reason to. My friend is having kittens soon; it would be nice if you had one of those." Peter said. Then added, "Another slave to do our bidding is always welcome!"

"You know?" Ellie said, "I'm not altogether sure when you are joking."

"You know?" Peter replied, "Neither am I!"

When Peter had devoured a tin of tuna that Ellie found in the back of her cupboard, and drank a bowl of milk, he belched a loud burp and said,

"That was great. Fae never gives me milk. She says 'my poor wittle tummy wummy can't handle it and I will get sick!' Pah!"

"Oh, great, now I've poisoned the bloody cat." Ellie was aghast. "Why didn't you tell me?"

"Well, because then you wouldn't have let me have it, would you?"

"Clear off and investigate you old reprobate!" Ellie laughed, opening the door.

"See you later." Peter called as he sprung up to the top of the wall and disappeared over it.

Fox and Ellie settled down with a book each. They had a glass of wine within reach and a comfortable silence enfolded them as they turned the pages. Ellie stole glances at Fox whilst he stared intently at the text in front of him. Ever since he had so vehemently voiced his lack of desire to mix the species, Ellie had been consumed with self pity. She had been honest with Fae when she said that she had not considered anything happening with Fox, but his adamant denial of any possibility of it happening, saddened her. She could not understand why she felt that way. All of a sudden, he was the sexiest man, or fairy, alive. His very presence made her shiver. If his breath touched her bare arm, she all but imploded on the spot. It made no sense.

"Are you aware that I can read your mind?" Fox asked quite casually.

"What?" Ellie screeched.

"What?" Asked Fox. "What is it? What happened? Is it the Gnomes?"

"What?" Ellie asked. "What did you say?"

"I asked if it…"

"No, before that. You said that you could read my mind!"

"I most certainly did not!" Fox sputtered. "Nor, in fact could I if I wanted to!"

"I could have sworn that you…"

"Believe me, I did not." Fox looked thoughtful. "But I did think it."

"Oh my god! Why would you think that?" Why would you want to freak me out like that?"

"Ellie, I am not responsible for any random thoughts I may have. I cannot possibly be held accountable for thoughts."

"But why that? Why would you think that? 'Are you aware that I can read your mind?' That is what you said… thought. Why those words?"

"I do not know." Fox blushed a deep crimson. "I think it would be best if we forgot this and just read our books."

"But why that?" Ellie insisted. "Why would you be thinking that?"

"Look, what do you want me to say?" Fox was becoming very frustrated. "Ellie, I must insist that you drop this."

"I can read your mind. That is what you said. Don't you realise how disturbing that is? I don't want you reading my mind Fox. You just can't, it's not right."

"Ellie, I promise you, I can not read your mind."

"But you and Felix can read each others mind. Fae told me you can."

"No, we can not. We can talk to each other with our minds, but we can not read what the other is thinking, or access their memories and thoughts."

"Look, Fox. I swear to you. I heard you loud and clear."

"I believe you. I do not know what to say. I did think that, I do not know why," he blushed deeper, "I am sorry. Please, can we end this now? Can we just go back to our books?"

"What were you thinking about?" Ellie persisted.

"Oh no. No. My thoughts are my own. I do not wish to share them."

"Look, Fox. My whole life has just been pulled inside out. I have a talking cat in my garden, a fairy on my sofa and a Gnome trying to kill me. With all due respect, I haven't known you very long. I am trusting you with my life here. How do I know that you too aren't here to hurt me?"

Fox looked absolutely crestfallen.

"Oh, I swear to you. I would never hurt you. I could never hurt you."

"Well, in that case, I need to trust you, and what I heard leads me to question the sense of that. If I don't know why you 'thought' what you did, I am going to keep wondering if I should ever trust you. Don't you see? It was such a frightening thing to think. Please, help me here."

Fox sat up and put his head in his hands.

"Ellie, please do not ask me to do this."

"You have to."

"Ellie?" Fox looked devastated. "Ellie? Please?"

"Tell me." Ellie quietly commanded.

"Oh. May the gods help me. Alright. But please, remember that this was just random thoughts. I have no control over them. Alright then. Okay. Well, you see. What it was…"

"Oh for heavens sake, spit it out!"

"Yes, well. I was thinking that, obviously, if we did not have such strict rules, well, that it would be nice to get to know you better. Then I was thinking that maybe it could not hurt if we just… well. Anyway, I was thinking that I did not know how to approach the subject with you and that it would be so much easier if I could read your mind. So that I could judge how you would respond." Fox was visibly shrinking with shame.

"Go on."

"Well, and then I thought back to last night. When you covered me with the blanket thing. I remembered that when you touched me I thought that… Well, I thought the 'I can read your mind bit'. There. That is it. I am utterly mortified. Are you happy now?"

"No." Ellie stood and walked toward the kitchen. "No, I am not."

Ellie continued into the kitchen and leant back against the counter, deep in thought.

After a few seconds, Fox stepped through the door and asked if she were alright.

The Fae

"Yes." Ellie replied distractedly. "Give me another couple of seconds."

"You have been standing there for ten minutes already. I was worried. I did not mean to upset you. I am sorry Ellie."

"Oh, okay. Give me a minute please, will you?"

"Of course."

Fox returned to the living room and Ellie returned to her musings. After a few more minutes, she took a deep breath and returned to the couch where Fox was sitting. She knelt down in front of him, between his open legs.

"Ellie, what are you…?"

"Ssh!"

Ellie leant in and took Fox' face in her hands. She brushed her lips very gently against his.

"Ellie! What are you doing?"

"Ssh!"

She pressed her mouth harder against his and her tongue slipped past his lips. Fox responded tentatively. The warm wetness enveloped her tongue as she slipped past his teeth. She felt his hands move up to bury themselves in her hair and pull her deeper into him. Ellie Snaked her arms around him and ran her fingers across his back. Fox groaned deep in his throat and Ellie felt all the air leave her. The smooth warmness of his chin rubbed against her own and his hair tickled her face, she felt parts of her body come alive that had lain dormant for a long while.

Fox reluctantly pulled away and held Ellie at arms length. Evidence of his reluctance strained against the filmy fabric of her robe.

"Ellie, we can not do this."

"I know." Ellie almost whined in response. "But who would know?" She nuzzled closer, her mouth seeking his again.

Fox set Ellie away from him.

"Ellie, no! We can not do this. It is forbidden. Please."

Ellie shifted further away from him, looked at his face and saw the resolve there; battling the desire.

"Who but us would know?" She whispered.

"We would. I can not love a woman in secret. I have to be able to tell the world, and I could not do that with you. There are rules."

"Rules are made to be broken" said Ellie in a sulky voice.

"Ellie, we can not break these rules. Do you not know what happened to Fae?"

"Fae? What has she to do with this?"

"The reason her babies were taken? Do you not know?"

"Why were they taken? Felix didn't tell me."

"Because she broke the rules. She loved an Elf. We can never mix our blood, the outcome could be catastrophic."

"I think you may be being a little dramatic there."

"I am serious. Fae loved an Elf and her children were taken as punishment."

"I simply don't believe that Fairies are that cruel." Ellie responded, with a pout.

"Oh my child you have no idea how cruel Fairies can be. But it was not the Fairies that took her babies. It was the Gnomes."

"Gnomes? Oh my god! Why? What did they want with the babies?"

The Fae

"Well, imagine what could happen if the power of Fairy and Elf were mixed? There is no knowing what could ensue, what power may be created. That is why we must never mix."

"But I am human, I have no power. If we 'mixed' as you so delightfully call it, there would be no super being created, I have no powers."

"No, but you have had our blood. We do not know what would happen."

"Okay, so if I now have some Fairy blood, is that not enough to, well, enough that the rules are not broken.?"

"Ah, a good question. The truth is that I do not know. I know not who to approach to find out, and I am afraid to ask."

Fox looked so dejected. He sat with his shoulders slumped and his eyes downcast. Misery rolled off him in waves.

"But." Ellie took his face in her hands and forced him to look at her. "But. If we could be together, is it what you would want?"

"Since the moment I saw you." He mumbled in reply. "Yes." He said louder.

"Okay then. Fine. We shall just have to figure it out. I know that we will be alright. It can't be possible for something this good to be bad. Right? There has to be a solution. We just have to figure out what it is."

The rest of the night was spent talking of trivialities, sipping wine and listening to Ellies latest find on C.D. A delightful, contemporary Jazz artist called Victoria Hart that Ellie had found in a charity shop and was playing daily. It set a lovely light backdrop to their musings and even provoked the odd wry smile from the pair. They sat with Fox' hand gently covering Ellies, but did not attempt to kiss again.

Ellie yawned and looked up at Fox.

"I believe that the wine is getting to me. I am so tired. I think I should get to bed. Would you like me to get you a blanket or are you going to spend the night in that uncomfortable chair again?"

Fox smiled softly and replied, " A blanket would be fine thank you."

Ellie got the blanket and set it on the couch. She then bade Fox goodnight and went to her room and bed.

For a long time, Ellie lay staring at the ceiling, re-living the kiss and feeling again the sensations that it created. She had not realised that she was attracted to Fox, but having kissed him, held him, she now felt that it had somehow deepened. It was more than sexual. She wanted to know everything about him, every little detail of his being, every thought in his head. They just had to find a way to be together. The power of her need surprised her. She had never fallen for anybody this quickly before. Or this deeply.

Maybe he cast a spell on me, she thought sleepily, *or sprinkled me with love dust or something.*

Whilst Ellie lay fast asleep, she felt a weight upon the bed and someone curl up behind her. She breathed a deep sigh of satisfaction as Fox' arm slid around her waist and he nestled his face into her hair. Moments later, she heard his breathing deepen with sleep. Within seconds, hers matched his.

When Ellie awoke, the bed was empty but the room was not. Peter sat in the window, staring through the glass at the road on the other side.

The Fae

"Good morning Peter. How was your night?" Ellie asked brightly.

"Good morning. Very eventful. I only got back a few minutes ago. Fox has prepared you a breakfast and asked me to wake you. We have much to do today."

"But I have to go to work. Oh, I forgot." Ellie felt a stab of disappointment as she remembered that she had a week off and why. "Okay, if you wouldn't mind telling him, I will be there in a minute."

Peter jumped down from the window and padded out of the room, humming the Macarena as he went.

Ellie grabbed the robe from the back of her door and held it to her face. She took in a deep breath and tasted Fox in its folds. She smiled as she put it on and tied it around her waist.

Walking into the kitchen, she saw Fox, ladling porridge into bowls. He had a pile of fresh chopped fruit on a plate in the centre of the table, a jug of golden looking cream and a pitcher of iced water. He had lain the table with cutlery and dishes. Her glasses sparkled in the morning sun and Ellie noticed a jam jar with wild flowers set beside the fruit, their aroma sweetened the air and caused her to smile again.

Ellie's biggest smile was for Fox when he sheepishly looked up at her.

"Good morning Fox. Wow! This looks wonderful. Thank you. I may have you move in permanently."

Fox reddened slightly and held out a chair for Ellie to sit in.

"Uh, you are welcome. I hope you do not mind that I made breakfast? I saw that Fae had dropped some provisions and a note to say that you particularly enjoyed the cream when you met before."

"Oh, she is so kind. It looks perfect, and of course I don't mind. I may get used to it though, so be careful!" She joked.

As they ate breakfast, Peter sat at the table also with a large saucer of the cream.

"Shall we keep this a secret too?" Ellie asked him.

"I am allowed this, it is of Fairy hand, so for some reason, I can eat, or rather drink it and it does not upset my stomach. It just makes me feel full, whole and kind of wonderful." Peter replied.

"I know just what you mean." Ellie told him. "I have only had a little, yet I feel incredible. Usually I eat like a pig, but I am content with just a small amount of this. It makes you feel fabulous inside. Nothing I have ever eaten before comes anywhere near it."

"It has wonderful properties." Supplied Fox. "A small amount keeps you satisfied all day."

"What do you call it?" Ellie enquired.

"Cream." Said Fox, straight faced. Then he laughed.

Peter looked from Ellie to Fox then back again. He narrowed his eyes and lifted an eyebrow. But he said nothing.

As they sat eating, Felix arrived and joined them. He looked at Ellies smiling face and then at Fox' sparkling eyes.

"Oh, by the gods! Please do not tell me! I warned you, did I not? Please say that you have not crossed the line? I knew this would happen!"

Ellie's face fell instantly and she looked from Felix to Fox. Fox also looked stunned. He sat staring at Felix, mouth open and a cross between defiance and fear in his eye. Ellie leapt up from the table, causing her chair to scrape back. With a hand over her mouth and her eyes bright with tears, she ran to the bedroom and threw herself on the bed. She lay and sobbed. Was this what Fox meant? Would everybody be so disgusted with them? How could this thing, whatever it was, be wrong? How could something so wonderful be so disgusting?

There was a light scraping at the door, and Peter asked to be let in. He joined Ellie on the bed. Ellie sat up near the headboard, her knees tucked under her chin and her arms wrapped around herself. She had large fat tears on her cheeks and her eyes were red and puffy. Peter sat dead centre on the bed and looked at her for what seemed an age.

"I don't understand this." He told her. "What is Felix so upset about?"

"He thinks that Fox and I have broken the law."

"But you haven't been anywhere."

"No, the law about crossing the species. He thinks we have had sex or something."

"Well, haven't you?"

"No!" Ellie asserted. "We most certainly have not!"

"But you want to?"

"Wanting to and doing are not the same!"

"Only to humans. Oh, and ex-mates. Well. That can be problematic. What will you do now?"

"I don't know. I need them here, and you. I just don't think I can face Felix today. He was so shocked. How can it be so wrong? He was so very disgusted. What can I do? I know that we can't be together, but I cant help how I feel."

"Do you think that Felix wanted you himself?"

"Oh god no! Felix has never looked at me like that. Now he will never look at me the same again. I am a sub-species to him and all the Others. Its not my fault that I am human!" Ellie dissolved into self-pity and Peter left her to it, returning to the relative peace of the kitchen.

A short while later, Ellie realised that she would have to return to the kitchen and face them. She was still hurt but increasingly, she was embarrassed at having to face Felix and Fox. Knowing that she would have to do it sooner or later, she stood, took a deep fortifying breath and went in.
Both Felix and Fox were seated at the table, deep in 'silent' conversation.

"If this concerns me, I would prefer that you spoke out loud." Ellie told them.

"Yes. You are quite correct." Felix said formally. "We were discussing Fox' breach of the law and how we would handle it."

"We have not broken the law!" Ellie almost shouted. "How am I supposed to stop my feelings? We did nothing! Nothing!"
Ellie threw herself onto a kitchen chair and put her head in her hands.

"Perhaps you did not act upon those feelings. That is a matter for another time. But you both do have those feelings. It is then only a matter of time before you do break the law. Supposing of course, that you have not already done so."

"You pompous arsehole! How bloody dare you! I cannot believe that you can sit in my house and be so bloody judgmental on a subject that you know nothing about. I thought that we were at least friends."

"As do I." Felix interrupted.

"Well, any friend of mine would know that I do not jump into bed with the first bloody man, fairy or hobbitybeast that comes along. You, you…"

"Arsehole?" Enquired Felix with a raised eyebrow.

The Fae

"Oh go to hell!" Ellie slumped. "Are you just going to sit there?" She sneered at Fox. "Do you have nothing to say here?"

"There is nothing to say. I have feelings for you. It is against the law. I will have to atone for that."

"Oh for Christ' sake! Did we or did we not discuss whether or not my fairy blood would exempt me from this?"

"What do you mean?" Asked Felix.

"Well, me having fairy blood, would that not mean, for the sake of argument, that I was part fairy and therefore, our being together would not be against the law?"

"It is certainly something to consider." Felix mused. "I must seek clarification on this. Meanwhile, what to do about today? Clearly, Fox will no longer be able to guard you. We must seek advice and request another guardian."

"Is that really necessary?" Ellie asked in a resigned voice.

"Yes." Replied Felix. "I believe so."

"For crying out loud!" Ellie huffed.

Some time later, there was a knock at the door. Ellie opened it to find a short-ish, older woman. Although she were beautiful, she had fine lines around her mouth and at the corners of her eyes. Her long black hair was tied back in a pony tail, but silver threads could be seen running through it. She wore a knee length cotton skirt in a swirl of pastel pinks, greens and blues, her blouse was white with every button a different colour and her cardigan was a loosely knit aqua green. Her bare feet and orange painted toes were encased in clear plastic shoes that appeared almost invisible. In her hand, she held a brown paper bag, crumpled with use and torn around the top. Over her shoulder, a bag of violet and emerald cotton patchwork squares that sprouted large red silk flowers in a haphazard pattern. The long fabric strap was plaited with threads of every colour and an occasional loose ribbon tied in a knot. A wide and toothy smile was spread across her face as she looked up at Ellie.

"Oh my dear, I am so glad to meet you. Peter has told me all about you. I am really looking forward to getting to know you. You are so very pretty. Where is that naughty cat? Ah, Felix, Fox, come here at once. Ah, Ellie dear, take this please." And she handed the brown paper bag to Ellie as she held open her arms to be hugged by the boys.

Ellie placed the bag onto the counter and out fell a couple of revolting looking seed pods. Ellie had never seen anything like them before; they were long, shrivelled and brown, looking for all the world like discarded pupae. Meanwhile, Felix was trying to extricate himself from the woman's fierce embrace. Fox had already been squeezed and had his cheek pinched before suffering a large sloppy kiss on his cheek. Felix seemed intent on escaping the same fate.

"May I introduce Mertensia, she was at the meeting you attended and has agreed to join us today." Peter bowed to Mertensia with a flourish as he introduced her.

"Pleased to meet you." Ellie replied. "Oh I remember now, you have those two adorable little girls. How are they? Will they be joining us?"

"Oh yes. My angels. They are so very precious to our whole family. No, no not today, they have lessons to attend. Maybe some other time." Mertensia took a seat and reached for the brown bag with the pods. She offered the bag around but each declined. Mertensia took a pod and squeezed it from the bottom. A thick golden, gritty looking paste oozed from a crack in the top and Mertensia sucked noisily until the pod had collapsed in on itself.

"Ah, how lovely. Are you sure that I can not offer you one? They are particularly sweet. And oh so good."

"Thank you but no." Ellie said.

"Oh, have you heard the news?" Mertensia lowered her voice conspiratorially. "The queen had her meeting with that Vampire. Aurellio his name is. By all accounts he is almost as unpleasant as Marcellus. But then, what would one expect from an Un-dead? Well, anyway. He and the queen met last night as you know and they discussed those dreadful ball things that Milfoil found. It seems that the Vampires did not know of them until we told them. Rather careless if you ask me. Well, I mean, how could you not notice that members of your hive are missing? I am quite sure that if even one of our family were missing, we would be sure to notice. I am thinking that Vampires have no sense of family at all."

"They simply have different ways of doing things than us." Felix interjected. "They have quite a strict code of behaviour, with many checks and balances. It would be impossible to run a hive were it not so. I find it surprising in the extreme that Marcello knew nothing of the disappearances."

"Well, all I know is that the queen had a long talk with Aurellio and they agreed to hand over the balls in exchange for information and aid."

"What would we need the Vampires for?" Asked Fox, surprised.

"Well," Mertensia looked at Ellie, "It seems that the queen is very worried about Ellie and the attacks on her. She has therefore asked that in exchange for information on the Gnomes and help in resolving the problem, we will hand over all the information on the balls."

"We need no aid from un-dead." Protested Fox hotly. "We can take care of our own business."

"But not if we need to 'final sanction' the Vampires." Felix supplied quietly.

"Oh, no. The queen would never agree to that." Mertensia gasped.

"What is final sanction?" Asked Ellie.

"As it sounds. It is the ultimate sanction. Death." Said Felix.

"But I can not believe that the queen would countenance such an idea!" Fox insisted.

"Nor I." Felix said. "But if she did, would you or I be able to take a life? Even in defence of our family."

The next hour was spent discussing the situation with the Gnomes, and many ideas were put forward as to why they were interested in Ellie. Each suggestion became more and more outlandish and eventually they changed the subject. The topic of Jacks new girlfriend was raised and Ellie wondered aloud whether his new girlfriend were really interested in him, or merely trying to get at Ellie.

"All I know is that she is pretty gorgeous, very vociferous and even a little trampy looking. Not at all what I would have imagined Jack finding attractive. And how did they get to have a date? I know that he has been single for months and months, but, oh I don't know! Jack blushes when he has to speak to old Mrs McCafferty. How on earth did he manage to ask Scarlett out? Oh, I sound like such a bitch. I am happy that he has someone, but I can't help but wonder if it is genuine or not. And now that I am off work for a week, I wont even be able to find out."

"It is certainly something that needs looking into." Mertensia agreed. "Oh, boggy bark! I meant to tell you when I got here. I am so sorry Ellie. The queen asked that

The Fae

you and Felix meet with her this afternoon. She has invited you for tea and to discuss what is to be done about you."

"I sometimes feel like everything would be normal if I hadn't had Faes blood. I seem to have caused such a ruckus!"

"Nonsense dear. We have been quite sleepy lately, it will do us good to be shaken up for a bit. Besides, I would rather this than you be dead. Which, you may recall, was the alternative."

"Actually I don't. Recall that is, but I take your point. Ok, wow! Tea with the queen of the fairies."

"A dress. Before you ask." Felix smiled.

"Ah such a wealth of knowledge in such a short time." Ellie smiled at Felix for the first time that day, and they both felt the better for it.

After Fox had left to get some sleep, and Felix was sitting talking with Mertensia in the garden, Peter and Ellie sat chatting at the kitchen table.

"Have you met the queen?" Ellie asked him.

"Oh, once or twice" Smiled Peter. "I used to live with her before I was with Fae."

"Oh, really?"

"Yes, when Fae's second child was stolen, the queen asked if I would stay and keep Fae company whilst the matter was looked into. I pretty much haven't left. Its been many years now. I am quite happy there. It's a simpler life certainly, but it has its advantages. The peace and quiet for one."

"If you don't mind me asking, how old are you?" Ellie enquired.

"Oh, hmm! I haven't thought about that for some time. Do you know? I am not completely sure. Well over a hundred, I know that."

"Oh! Well, you don't look a day over ten." Ellie laughed at him.

Peter harrumphed but looked quite pleased.

"Peter?"

"Ye-es?"

"Why did Faes babies get stolen?"

"Well. We believe that the Gnomes took them."

"Yes, but why?"

"We are not completely sure. However," Peter continued after seeing the impatience in Ellies face. "However, what we think is that... Right look at it this way. Fairies have powers right?"

"Yes."

"Elves have powers, so if you put those together, you could get double powers. At least that is the belief. As you know, it is against fairy law to mix for that very reason. We can only imagine that the Gnomes thought they could use that in some way."

"Doesn't Felix know?"

"No. He suffered such trauma that it has been wiped from his mind for safety. The Fairies would rather not know than risk him again."

"Oh, that is so sweet. And so sad." Ellie said as she got up from the table.

"I have to choose what to wear for the queen, are you coming to help me?"

"Oh heaven! I can think of nothing I would rather do!"

"You know, for a cat, you can be bloody catty!" Ellie laughed.

Peter sat on the bed, one leg up behind his ear as he washed himself.

"Tell me," Ellie wondered. "Why do you guys lick that in front of people?"

"Wash dear, not lick."

"Ok, why do you guys wash there, in front of people?"

"Well, why do you think? Because we can!"

"I'm serious."

"Me too. We do it because it drives humans nuts and we think it's hilarious." Peter chuckled.

Ellie was fairly certain she even saw him smile.

"Yeah, I thought so. Showing off really aren't you?"

Ellie opened her wardrobe and leafed through her meagre collection of smart clothes. She only had two dresses as they were not her first choice for comfortable clothing.

"I don't really think that either of these are suitable for tea with the queen." Ellie sighed to herself. "Are you sure I have to wear a dress?" She asked Peter.

"Yes." Peter slinked off the bed and stretched his front legs out on the floor. He jumped into Ellies wardrobe and started pulling clothes aside, with his mouth, from their bottoms.

"What about this one?" He asked, with a piece of fabric between his teeth.

Ellie took the fabric and felt up to the hanger, she then pulled it out and looked at it with a strange look on her face.

"Well? What about it?" Asked Peter. "Why the funny face?"

Ellie held the dress against herself and twirled in front of the mirror.

"I have never seen this dress before, but somehow... I don't know... but it is beautiful." Ellie quickly slipped the dress on and stood in front of the mirror.

"I have never seen anything so beautiful in all my life. It is a perfect fit. But where did it come from?"

"Probably best not to ask, but Mertensia did have a bag with her when she arrived."

"That had those pods in it, and she hasn't left my sight. Oh! It was you! I never saw you come in. But how? How did you? Oh thank you, it's beautiful." Ellie leant down and hugged Peter to her. She mussed the top of his head and put him back down on the bed. "Thank you so much. I love it."

"As much as I would love to have made you so happy, it was not me. The queen chose this for you herself. She thought that it would please you."

"But Peter, how on earth did you get it into the wardrobe and onto a hanger?"

"You ask so many questions!" Peter said as he jumped off the bed. He twitched his tail jauntily as he left the room.

Ellie, Felix, Peter and Mertensia sat in the garden with tall glasses of iced water on the table between them. Peter had a straw sticking out of his.

"You look stunning. The queen has a good eye." Mertensia told Ellie.

"And a good memory, she only met me briefly. This dress is incredible. The colours are perfect for me. I have never seen the like."

"Nor shall you again probably. The queen only allows one of each creation to be made. She has only one vanity and that is it. She does not want someone else to show up in the same dress as her." Felix supplied.

"Well, she is the queen. I imagine it would be mortifying. I'm only a human and I know I would hate it."

So the conversation went. Idle chatter about nothing of importance. The sun smiling down and warming their skin, melting their ice. The flowers turning their faces to the warmth and excreting their heady perfume in thanks. The birds singing distractedly as they pecked at the nuts hanging from a stocking on the tree. The background sounds fading away as the tensions eased and friendship reasserted itself.

Chapter Six.

Felix and Ellie drove through the town and up Mersea Road. They passed the bakers and the mini roundabout, continuing straight on toward Mersea. As the passed over the low bridge, they took the left turn and made their way to the beach. This was not the beach that tourists came to, it was wilder and not an ideal place for children. Occasional dog walkers wandered here but mostly it was deserted.

As they parked up, they could see a marquee set up on the sand. It was very large with what appeared to be fairy tale turrets around the edges. The entrance flaps were tied back with huge white ribbons and there was a table set just inside, out of the sun. Upon the table were silver and golden platters heaped with fruits and cakes. There were large crystal jugs, clear iced water sat beneath great chunks of orange and lemon. Beautiful goblets marked the place where people would sit and gleaming knives and forks twinkled as the sun found them. Fresh combs of honey dripped seductively next to a loaf of crusty bread and delicate curls of butter softened in the sunshine.

The queen was at the water's edge, her skirts held up with one hand as she walked through the shallow surf. In her other hand, she held a child's bucket and spade, dirty with use. The queen was laughing and calling to a man further along the beach. She looked so carefree and young. Her hair was down about her waist and lifting gently in the slight breeze. Her cheeks were red from the sun and her nose seemed to have sprouted a few freckles. She was a poster child for good health.

Upon spotting Ellie and Felix, the queen lightly ran over to them.
"Oh Ellie, I am so glad that you came. Come, take off your shoes and join me. The water is delicious." She threw back her hair and smiled widely.
Ellie smiled in return as she pulled off her sandals and ran with the queen back to the waters edge. Like two small girls, they laughed and kicked up the water, splashing and squealing as they were gradually soaked. All inhibitions fled with the receding waves.

Breathless and giggling, the queen and Ellie made their way to the marquee, where Felix handed them both towels to dry off with. They collapsed into upholstered chairs spreading sand and water everywhere. The queen sipped at a glass of water whilst dusting the sand from her long, smooth legs. Her hair lay in damp draggles and curled slightly at the ends. Her lips, puckered around the glass, were full and pink. Her hands were smooth and ageless.
Ellie wondered at the queen's age.
"Oh, well over three thousand years." The queen smiled. "We do seem to carry it well. For that, and my vanity's sake, I am glad."
"I did not mean to be rude," Ellie replied. "You look so young, like a girl really."
"We choose at which age to stop ageing." The queen told her. "When I reached twenty two, I thought it a pleasant age to stop. It has some drawbacks, but on the whole I am pleased." She smiled and sat back in the chair. Looking at Ellie, she continued.
"Thank you for agreeing to meet me. There are some things that we must discuss, but I believe that you have a question that you would like to ask? Regarding Fox?"
Ellie was suddenly annoyed. Who had been telling tales?

The Fae

"Do not look alarmed," the queen soothed, "I did not read your mind. You were projecting your thoughts so strongly that I could not help but know. You wish to have a relationship with him? Yes… I see, that would be problematic."

"But I was wondering if…"

"Yes my dear?"

"Well, seeing as how I have Fae's blood, and her being Fairy, would that not override my being human? After all, it has been mentioned that I am to be considered Fairy now."

"Delicately put." The queen mused. "In truth, this is not a problem we have encountered before. I will have to think on it. You do raise a good point."

Ellie sat back in her chair. She had done all she could think to do. If not the queen, then who else could help her? She would have to be patient and wait.

"Unfortunately, it does mean that Fox will be unable to guard you."

"But…"

"At least until I have made a decision." The queen interrupted. "Mertensia will suit in the short term. Which brings me to the reason I asked you to join me."

As the two sat in the marquee, sipping water and nibbling at fruit, the queen gathered her thoughts; then, taking a deep breath, she spoke.

"Ellie. My dear child. We find ourselves in a quandary. I have asked the Vampires to try to find out why the Gnomes want you. They have agreed to look into it, but as you can appreciate, they can only work at night. We can think of no reason ourselves, so have made a bargain with the Vampires. In exchange for the balls and technology, they will aid us in this matter."

"I heard that Marcellus did not know of this. How is that possible?" Asked Ellie.

"A very good question. How indeed?"

"Are the Vampires so spread out that they didn't notice some missing? What happened to the ones that Milfoil freed?"

"You are thinking well my child. According to Aurellio, Marcellus knew nothing, which is quite extraordinary. They are not spread so far that they would not be missed. There is no other hive for some miles, so the only explanation so far is that the captured Vampires came from another town. That itself is odd. I want to know how this human knew of their existence, but this was not a question raised by Aurellio. Perhaps they knew, perhaps they did not. I wonder if it is a matter that we need to concern ourselves with."

"But what of the freed ones? Where would they have gone, if not back to the hive? You would think that after an ordeal like that, you would want to return to the people that you know and trust." Ellie said.

"It is certainly something that we need to consider." The queen replied. "Come, we only have a short while before the sun fades. Let us play."

With that the queen jumped up, grabbed Ellies hand and ran with her to the water.

"Oh, I never thanked the queen for my lovely dress." Ellie turned and said to Felix as they drove home. "She must think me so rude."

"If she wanted your thanks, she would have presented the dress to you herself. I believe that this way she tried to be discreet. She is aware that you have few dresses."

"Oh!" Ellie turned to look out of the front window. "And how would she know that?" She asked sulkily.

The Fae

"The queen knows everything she needs to know." Felix replied mysteriously. "Besides, Peter probably told her. He is a dreadful gossip sometimes. No harm would have been meant. The queen enjoys giving gifts."

"Well then. That's okay, I suppose." Ellie huffed, with less enthusiasm than before. "As long as it wasn't out of pity or anything."

"Why ever not?" Felix sounded genuinely curious. "Surely pity is good. Without pity, there is no love. No caring. If not for pity, thousands would die from starvation each year. If not for pity, animals would die cruelly."

"But to be the object of pity?" Ellie turned to him. "To be the object of pity is, well, it's demeaning. It implies that you cannot provide for yourself."

"But you can not."

"Yes I can!" Ellie blustered. "I have a job, I pay my own way. I neither need nor rely on anyone."

"What a sad way to live."

"What's so sad about it? I take care of myself. I don't need anybody's charity!"

"I will never understand humans." Felix was bemused. "You love to help but refuse to be helped? You are very contrary."

"Oh, forget it! I thank the queen for her gift, truly, but I hate the thought that she pities me, or thinks I can't take care of myself."

"But you can not take care of yourself." Felix was perplexed. "Why else are we guarding you?"

"Oh, that is not the same and you know it!"

"I do not."

"I am not arguing with you, Felix. I refuse to talk about this any more!"

"Ellie, you are no fun today."

"Harrumph!" Ellie harrumphed.

As they pulled up outside Ellie's home, the gate was opened by a small, mixed race girl with long curly hair tied in two bunches, one either side of her smiling face.

"Mama, she is here." The girl called Turning and looking back at Felix she said "Mama wants you two in the kitchen."

"Hello, what's your name?" Ellie asked.

"I am Bluebell." The girl replied with a small curtsey, then she ran giggling into the house.

"Hello Bluebell, I'm Ellie. Hi Mertensia." Ellie called laughingly as she stepped through the door to her kitchen. "Oh wow! What are you cooking?"

Mertensia stood at the oven with a tea towel over her arm and a large dish steaming in her gloved hand. Her hair was tied back in a loose bun and she had flour on her cheek. The door to the oven was open and inside, Ellie could see a tray of golden vegetables roasting merrily.

"I made a pie for supper." Mertensia replied as she managed to set the dish down onto a trivet on the counter. "Mushrooms, sweet potatoes and some quorn stuff that I found in your freezer. I do not know what it is but as it said it was vegetarian, I supposed that it would be suitable. Is it alright?"

"More than alright." Ellie beamed. "One problem though, having met you guys, I am really worried about my waistline!"

"That is not something that you need…Begonia, be careful! Bluebell, can you help your sister to set the table please?"

Mertensia swerved her hip as a carbon copy of Bluebell raced past her with the agility only a small child can display.

"Say hello to Ellie." Mertensia prompted. "And Felix."

"Hello Ellie, hello Uncle Felix." Begonia curtsied sweetly.

Ellie smiled widely and curtsied in reply.

"Hello, Begonia. Pleased to meet you."

"Mama says that you are sleeping at our house tonight." Begonia informed Ellie.

"Well." Mertensia interjected. "We must ask Ellie if she minds first. It would certainly help, their father is away for the next few days and although I could set them down here, it would help me greatly if you could stay with us instead." Mertensia seemed a bit embarrassed.

"Oh ple-ase!" Echoed the twins. "Ple-ase say you will. It will be so much fun." Begonia continued.

"Mama said that if we were good we could stay up another hour, we promise to be good. Honest." Bluebell lifted her great big brown eyes and melted Ellie's heart.

"Now, how could I say no to that face?" Asked Ellie. "I would love to come. On one condition."

"Oh, anything." The girls chorused.

"You have to read me a story before you go to bed." Ellie told them.

"Easy!" They chimed.

"Well then, after we eat, we go!" Ellie laughed.

"Speaking of going…" Felix went to the door. "I must be on my way. Mertensia, see you tomorrow." He bowed low to the twins. "Ladies." Then he turned and smiled at Ellie. "Sleep well. I will see you in the morning."

After a most delicious meal, Ellie, Mertensia and the girls, climbed into an old style Renault. The kind that look like an old upside down pram and usually have peace stickers on the bumper. This one was clean with flowers painted on its sides. There were silk flowers across the dashboard and hanging from the rear view mirror. The car had a pleasant floral fragrance that danced along the nostrils and the seats were covered in a fur fabric that seemed to envelop and caress. The journey was short, just to the other side of town.

Ellie was very surprised when they pulled into the parking lot of a new housing development. She remembered watching the flats go up only a few years previously, and knew them to be small and pokey inside. This was not what she had expected and already Ellie began to worry that there would not be enough room. They walked to the entrance, Ellie closely behind Bluebell with Mertensia and Begonia following. Surprisingly, Bluebell did not go directly to the door but stood in front of the wall slightly to the left of it. She turned and smiled at Ellie whilst waiting for her mother to catch up. Mertensia reached the wall and waved her hand in front of her face. She mumbled a few words that could hardly be heard and the silver outline of a door appeared on the wall in front of them. Begonia clicked her fingers together and the door opened. They all hustled through and the door swung shut behind them. As Ellie turned to look, the door appeared as a thousand other doors. Painted wood, a bit scuffed and in need of a clean.

They walked forward a few paces to another door, this one much cleaner, new looking and painted in a fresh mint green. Mertensia took the handle and turned it. Like a thousand other doors, it opened. On the other side of the door was a flight of stairs leading up. They swiftly climbed them and found themselves on a landing painted in a crisp, clean white. There were a great many framed pictures of the twins on the

The Fae

walls and upon a small table was a jam jar of fresh wild flowers and a photograph of Mertensia with a tall, handsome black man. The picture showed the pair gazing lovingly at each other in front of a beautiful oak tree. Mertensia appeared the same age as she was now, so there was no guessing when the photograph was taken. Looking closer, Ellie saw that the man held his hand protectively over Mertensias' slightly swollen belly. A small sigh escaped Ellies lips and she could have sworn that at the same time, the man in the photograph winked at her.

The hallway led into a large airy room where the walls were now in a soft sage colour. There were wooden bookcases along the far wall, crammed haphazardly with books of all shapes, sizes and styles. The floor was wooden boards painted a deeper shade than the walls and strewn with mats in varying hues of brown. The couch was long, low and deep, begging to be sprawled in and there was a low table in front of it with more jam jars and flowers. An empty mug sat forgotten on the table and the remnants of a sandwich curled dryly on a dainty pink tea plate.

The twins ran and jumped onto the couch, fidgeting until they had found a comfortable spot, where they curled their legs underneath them and sat looking at their mother. They reminded Ellie of two satisfied kittens. Mertensia led Ellie toward the door to their right and they stepped into her kitchen. The counters were long and appeared to be made from whole trunks of trees. They were planed and sanded to a glossy finish, their knots and whirls beautifully preserved to delight the eye. The cabinets were wooden also, but a pale lemon wash had been applied. The floor was wooden boards too and painted a fresh green. The window held a row of jars with yellow flowers bursting from the tops. The overall feel was of being in a sun dappled glade. It felt refreshing and homely all in one and Ellie felt as though she had spent many an hour there already. Mertensia indicated that Ellie sit at the table which was a great slab of tree, polished like the counters but scarred with the memories of countless family meal times.

Mertensia went to the fridge and took out a large jug full of a golden, shimmering liquid and poured out four glasses. She replaced the jug in the fridge and carried two glasses to the girls on the couch. Coming back into the kitchen, she sat lightly on the chair facing Ellie and let out a satisfied sigh.

"Ah, home! I love coming home." She said. "There is nothing quite like it."

"You certainly have a beautiful home." Ellie agreed. "Funny though, I feel as though I have been here before. I feel so comfortable already."

"Good. That is good." Mertensia smiled. "I invite few people here, so it is gratifying to know that you feel as I do about it." She picked up her glass and took a long sip. "Oh, heaven. I simply love this. I should not really drink so much of it, but I cannot help myself. It is like an addiction." She smiled conspiratorially.

Ellie took a small mouthful and felt her taste buds come alive. The fresh citrus flavour was mixed with a sweet honey undertone. There was also a hint of papaya and coconut along with a sweetness that Ellie had never tasted before. She took another, longer sip and reluctantly placed the glass back on the table.

"Well, I understand why!" She agreed. "I could develop quite a habit myself. It's glorious. What is that flavour? I can't place it."

Mertensia sat back and smiled.

"That, my dear, is ambrosia."

The Fae

"Really? Wow! I thought that was made up. Or a rice pudding company. My god, it's gorgeous." Ellie took up her glass and had some more.

After a while, the girls came in and asked their mother if it would be alright to go to bed. Ellie was flabbergasted. She admittedly had little knowledge of children but was quite sure that this was unusual.

"Yes my dears, you may. Clean your faces and brush your teeth." Mertensia reminded them.

The girls each gave their mother a hug and a quick kiss on the cheek then turned and skipped out of the kitchen. Begonia turned, looked at Ellie then skipped back and gave her a chaste hug before joining her sister. Ellie couldn't help but smile and be pleased. They were such lovely children.

"We love you too!" Ellie heard the girls reply in her head.

"Oh my!" She jumped., startled.

"What is it?" Mertensia looked at her enquiringly.

"Please do not tell mama. She does not know." Bluebell begged silently inside Ellies mind.

"Oh, nothing! Nothing, I think I just realised that I think I am now addicted to this drink too." Ellie took up her glass and drank deeply to try and hide her surprise.

"Can you hear me too?" She asked of the girls with her mind.

"Oh yes." They chorused.

"Oh my god! I can't believe this, it is incredible!" Ellie was amazed and excited. This was truly fantastic. She could hold a conversation telepathically.

"But why don't you want your mother to know?" She silently asked the girls.

"We think it might scare her." Begonia replied. "She has such limited powers herself, she thinks that the old ways are dying out."

"But surely she would be thrilled to know this?" Asked Ellie. "But I will respect your choice. However I feel really strange talking to you in front of her, so to speak."

"Ellie, are you alright?" Mertensia asked, concern written all over her. "You appear to be in pain. Can I get you anything? The cordial may have been too cold for you? Perhaps I should have warmed it first."

"No, no, I'm okay. Just a twinge. All the excitement of the last few weeks I suppose." Ellie sort of lied.

After reading the promised book, the girls fell asleep so Mertensia and Ellie settled on the couch with glasses of warm milk and cookies. They talked of sunshine and flowers, sparkling brooks and rainbows. For Ellie, it was a magical evening with no cares or worries. Mertensia was delightful company, providing Ellie with a maternal affection that was completely alien but not unwelcome. She was warm, giving and enveloping, her open and supportive nature had Ellie instinctively trusting her; to the extent that she found herself telling her host about the situation with Fox.

"I don't understand, one minute I'm ambivalent, then, when I think that he isn't interested, I think he's the greatest thing since sliced bread. And there is no way we can be together anyway. I am really confused."

"Yes, I imagine you are," Mertensia comforted. "Fox appears to be a bit of a cad, but I can not remember the last time he got involved with a woman. It has been at least twenty years. I do not think he will be taking this lightly."

"My point exactly! What if I only want him because I can't have him? Oh, what am I going to do?"

The Fae

"Wait and see. It is all you can do. If your blood is not enough to allow the union, then you have nothing to worry about. I suggest that you wait and see. Try to be strong."

"I understand the reasons for the law about mixing, but I am human, I have no powers, surely I'm no threat?"

"That is the thing, we have never had this before, and so we do not know what it would mean." Mertensia mused.

"But what of Felix? He is half Elf. Doesn't he know? I mean, what extra powers does he have? And why is it okay for him? God, please don't think that I'm being unkind to him, I would never dream of that. It's just that, well, how come? That's all."

"Felix was nursed for a very long time after we found him. For a long while we thought that we would lose him, so great was the damage done by the Gnomes. They tortured him horribly. The only way that we could help him, was to erase his memories. We have no idea what he went through, we just saw the physical damage to his body. There are people in the family dedicated to trying to find a way to help him know and come to terms with his lost years, but we must go carefully. He is too important a person to damage further."

"Oh, I had no idea. I suppose I thought that he was just raised as a Gnome, it didn't occur to me that his life would have been so bad. Poor Felix. I wish I could help him."

"We never know when or how we help. Sometimes just listening, or making time is helping. Felix has made peace with his life as it is now, and we allow him courtesies that we would not another Fairy, which he knows. He is not comfortable with this, but has come to accept it."

"But surely you know which of his powers are Elf?"

"No. Because we all have different abilities, it is next to impossible to know what is different enough to come from Elves."

"So what of his sister? Is there any way to find her? Would the council allow her back if you did? Find her I mean."

"I believe so, yes. It was not the fault of the sister that she was of mixed heritage. I do believe that the council would welcome her. I know that Fae would be complete if she were found. Of course, we do not know how Felix would be, he never met her."

"Oh, of course! I never thought of that. Poor Fae, I can't imagine what she went through. How long ago? How old would the sister be now?"

"Let me see, she would be about twenty four in your years now. Just a child in ours. The poor girl. I tremble to think how her life has been. Let us talk of lighter things?"

"Yes. Forgive me."

The sun was long set when Ellie yawned loudly then covered her mouth with an embarrassed laugh.

"Oh, I am so sorry. I am tired. Would it be okay to go to bed now?"

"Oh my dear, how awful, I have kept you up for hours, tattling and trilling. You must be exhausted. Come, let me show you where you can sleep."

Mertensia led Ellie down a bright corridor, lined with a mixture of ultra modern and ancient looking doors. There were about nine in total. She stopped outside a door that was carved from rough hewn oak, with metal bands at the hinges and an old fashioned latch of worn and blackened iron.

The Fae

"Mm! Yes, I believe that you will sleep well here." Mertensia said as she opened the door and gestured Ellie to precede her into the room.

The door opened onto a small, low ceiling room that was dominated by a high, four poster bed. The bed was piled high with what appeared to be thick feather filled comforters and pillows, all in a dark and dusky rose. At the side of the bed stood a small battered table, inlaid with mother of pearl. Upon the table was a candle holder with a tall, cream coloured candle sitting ready to be lit. There was the expected jam jar filled with pink roses and carnations, and the air was lightly scented with the fresh floral fragrance that had perfumed the car. The overhead light fitting regally presented a fine crystal chandelier that threw teardrop splashes across the antique rose printed wallpaper. The floorboards were pained white with thick, mismatched rugs strewn randomly upon it. The small window was set low in the wall and the muslin curtains sat peeping out behind heavy, shot silk drapes in the palest clotted cream and rose. Ellie lay down on the bed and was asleep before the covers were fully pulled up.

Ellie dreamt of beaches and queens, of sandcastles and lemonade. She dreamt of talking cats and new dresses, of kisses and chandeliers. Ellie knew that she was sleeping, and she knew that she was dreaming. Into her dream walked a cat. At first she thought the cat was Peter, so she called to him. The cat kept walking, he did not turn or acknowledge her. She called again and started to walk toward it. The cat kept walking, but increased its pace. Ellie called out to stop, wait, talk to her, but the cat started to run. Ellie ran after the cat, begging it please stop, wait, don't you know me? It's Ellie. But the cat kept running. Through fields and woods, past a river and toward an old crumbling building, the cat ran never looking back. Ellie stumbling after, tears in her eyes, feeling abandoned and forgotten. Calling out, oh please stop, its me. You know me! Please stop and wait. Running faster but never catching up. Her feet leaden and weighted in honey. Each step an age but run she did. The cat always out of reach, too fast, too far, but Ellie persevered. Breathless and crying, alone and cold, legs cramping from effort, she reached the building and slumped in the door-less entry, lungs burning. In the centre of the empty, dusty, cobwebbed room, the cat sat staring, straight at her.

"Why are you here?" The cat asked.
"I don't know." Ellie cried
"Why are you here?" The cat repeated.
"I just don't know. You bought me here. I followed you, here. Why didn't you stop? I called and called. Didn't you hear me? See me?"
"Why are you here?" The cat asked.
"I don't know what you mean." Ellie was becoming frantic. Why didn't he answer? Why did he keep asking the same question? "What do you mean? I don't understand!"
"Why are you here?" The cat repeated.
"I don't know what you want!" Ellie screamed. "What do you want?"
"You need to go. Now!" The cat shouted and leapt at her.
As the cat hurtled through the air toward her, Ellie threw up her arms to protect her face and let out a long scream.

Mertensia was shaking Ellie gently be the shoulders.

The Fae

"Wake up, Ellie, it is a dream. Wake up."
"Oh my god! Oh my god! There was a cat, he ran and I followed, and he kept asking me, and I didn't understand,, then he shouted and I was scared and I..."

At that moment, there was a loud crash from outside. It sounded as though the door were being kicked in. There was a loud commotion in the front corridor, and the twins came running, crying and tripping to their mother. Mertensia swept up the girls and pulled at Ellie to get out of the bed. They stumbled over to the window and threw the curtains aside. In the living room, heavy footsteps could be heard coming toward them. Mertensia pulled up the sash window and pushed the girls through.

"You next." She whispered to Ellie.
As Ellie lifted her foot to climb through, she slipped and twisted her ankle. Yelping in pain, she told Mertensia, "You go, I will be right behind you. Go!"
Mertensia disappeared through the window and Ellie manoeuvred her injured leg to the sill.

Strong hands grabbed her hair and pulled her backwards to be held roughly against a large, unknown person. Ellie was terrified and screamed as loud as she could. A foul smelling hand was clasped over her mouth and a sibilant voice hissed

"Shut yer stinkin mouf!" into her hair. She was dragged backwards against her assailant and toward the living room. Her newly injured ankle protested and gave way. As she stumbled, the assailant backhanded her violently and she crashed to the floor, cupping her cheek where it was struck.

"No stopping. Get up." He spat, dragging her by the arm and across the wooden floor until she managed to lurch to her feet. She was pulled through the door and down the stairs, out of the building to a car waiting, engine running, at the kerb. Ellie was flung through the open back door and landed heavily on the seat. Her attacker climbed in behind and pushed her along so that he could sit beside her. He held her down with one hand, her face pressed into the leather. Ellies hands were pulled behind her back and tied together. Almost immediately, the tingling from loss of circulation shot hot spikes into her fingertips and Ellie yelped in pain.

"Yer fink that 'urts? You know nuffin." The voice mocked. "Just wait till ee gets is ands on ya."
The man pulled her head up by the hair and wrapped a course cloth over her eyes then tightened it behind her. He dropped her head back with an extra shove causing it to bounce. All Ellie could see was a gauzy, indistinct outline, nothing substantial. Straining to make out shapes hurt her eyes so she kept them closed. Ellie felt the car jolt and swerve as it sped toward its destination. Her abductors did not speak, so the swoosh of passing traffic was the soundtrack to her fear.

It crossed Ellies mind to memorise the twists and turns, so that she could inform the police. But what was the point? If she survived to tell, it would make no difference and it wasn't like she could alert anyone to her direction so that they could charge in on a white horse and rescue her. Then she thought that it would be so romantic if Fox found and saved her, but he didn't know she was missing. She worried what had become of Mertensia and the girls, she hoped they had gotten away. Then she remembered that the girls could speak telepathically and tried to call them. They didn't answer. Surprisingly, she fell asleep for a few moments, only realising it, with a jolt, when she felt the car judder to a halt and the doors open.

The Fae

The man next to her dragged her across the seat to the opening, then pulled her upright and out. He slung her over his shoulder, where she hung like a sack of laundry, and bounced her over the gravel for quite a way. He stopped only to hitch her up where she had started to slip, then he knocked on a door.

"I see you managed not to screw up this time." Came a pleasant female voice. "Bring her in and put her in the back. He will be down soon. When you are done, go to the kitchen and eat, Cook has left some food out for you."

Ellie was carried through an echoing space, she was tipped onto a small, soft and squeaking surface, then the footsteps receded. She struggled to sit up and realised that she was on some sort of a couch. As she manoeuvred upright she heard a lock being turned and assumed she had been locked in. Ellie sat very still and tried to steady her racing heart. She took deep breaths and held them for a count of ten before releasing slowly. She felt her pulse creep back to normal. She sat very still, her arms bound uncomfortably behind her, and listened. She tried to make out any sounds that might identify where she was. At first, all she heard was the pounding of her own heart and the tinnitus buzz of fear. Gradually a faint rhythmic ticking made itself heard, a clock. Old fashioned sounding, deep and resonant, somewhere in the building. Ellie used it to measure her pulse and calm herself further. A slight sighing of wind reached her ears. It sounded like it was rustling through plants and whistling down a chimney. As she thought this, she noticed a faint odour of ashes, of fires long dead. She smelt also the dusty decay of an unused space and the slight mildew of an old piece of forgotten furniture. Faint traces of ammonia tickled her nose and she imagined rats scurrying and defecating in this unlovely place. Images of shadowy figures with violent intent swam across her mind and taunted her with implied violence.

Ellie was almost paralyzed with fear, she was so far out of any frame of reference that her mind refused to accept the brevity of her situation and she started to laugh. It began as a pitiful, mewling giggle and grew into a side splitting, nose running, eye watering belly laugh that had her breathless and snotty with no free hand to wipe the mess. Which made her laugh the more.

"I am happy to see that you are enjoying your stay." Came a voice very close by.
Ellie stopped laughing and pushed herself as far away from the presence as possible.
"Who are you?" She asked. Terrified.
"Oh my dear, I ask the questions here." Came the reply, rough notes over silky a tone.
"Why am I here? Who are you?" Ellie begged.
"I see you don't listen. We will have to teach you how." The voice sounded so reasonable, but at the same time a pain shot through Ellies injured foot, the like of which she could never have imagined before. It felt as though her ankle had been grabbed and turned with force, causing the already painful appendage to protest vehemently, in agony.
"Stop, stop. Oh please stop." Ellie sniffed and begged.
Her ankle was twisted the other way, causing great waves of pain to darken the edges of her mind.
"When I am ready! You will tell me what I want to know. Now. First things first. Your name?"
"Ellie. My name is Ellie."

The Fae

Great, wracking, poker hot waves of pain swept up from her ankle as it was crushed and turned anew.

"No lies. Your name?"

"It's Ellie. I swear. It's Ellie."

"No lies." More pain.

"Ellie. My name is Ellie. What do you want from me?"

A crashing blow smashed against the side of her face and she fell back stunned and throbbing. She could feel the flesh swell as she lay panting for breath.

"I told you no questions." Another smack to the face, this one stinging as what felt to be a ring, tore at her skin.

"What is your name."

"I swear to you, my name is Ellie. It has always been Ellie. I don't understand this."

She was pulled upright by the hair and what had to be a fist crumpled her nose against her cheek. She felt hot, viscous blood burst and flow as she thankfully passed out.

Ellie was in a black, airless room. There were no dimensions, no obstacles, no other presences. She was utterly alone and she knew she was dreaming.

"This way." A voice whispered just ahead of her. "Come, quickly. You will be safe here."

"Who is this?" Ellie asked, fearfully.

"You need not be afraid. This is a good place. You can hide here."

"Who are you?"

"Come, come, quickly."

Ellie tentatively followed the whisper. She had her hands out in front, feeling for unseen obstacles, she slid her feet on the smooth floor in case she tripped. She moved very slowly, not sure what was ahead and afraid to trust.

"Come, come, hurry up."

"I'm coming, but who are you?" She asked in a half whisper herself, not really sure why. It did not seem appropriate to shout here. Wherever here was.

"All will be well, come girl."

Ellie found herself against a solid obstruction that felt like a wall. She moved her hands across the surface until she found a door, then the handle.

"Hurry, hurry."

She took hold of the handle and turned. The door swung open to reveal another room that had a long banqueting table in the centre. It was highly polished and bare except for the ornate candelabra slightly off centre on the top. The candles were lit, of differing heights as if in varying stages of use. The room had a natural woodland scent and a bare polished floor. There were tall arched windows that were opened allowing the sun to throw itself against the far wall in kaleidoscopic exuberance. The air sparkled with swirling dust motes caught in the suns dazzling rays and by the far wall, in the doorway, stood a small boy, beckoning to her.

"Hurry, hurry." He urged. "Come girl, you will be safe here, come, let us reclaim your place."

"What?" Ellie said. Rudely. "What are you saying? I know this is a dream, but usually I am in charge in my dreams. What is happening?"

"Come girl, come. We will explain. Do not be afraid. This is your safe house. Come. Everyone of us has one. Come. Quickly, she is waiting."

The Fae

Ellie followed the small boy through the room and into a bright courtyard. There were two semi circular stone walls set at knee height and encompassing tall Grecian urns, filled with trailing flowers. In the centre was a large stone pond festooned with floating lilies and numerous well fed Koi nibbling at the fingers of a goddess straight from a Greek Myth, who was seated sideways on the wall. She had on a long white robe, tied at breast and waist with a golden rope, her black hair was piled in the fashion of the ancient gods and held in place with matching, smaller ropes. Gold glimmered and hung in whorls from her ears. Her feet were clad in gladiatorial sandals of the same golden colour and her ankles glinted with hair fine golden chains. The woman stood and held out a slender arm toward Ellie. Her bangles jangled melodically as they bumped together and the band wrapped around the top of her arm, fashioned in the form of a snake, lifted its head, yawned, then settled back down.

"Welcome daughter. We have waited long for you to find us again." The woman had the most mesmeric voice, and Ellie found herself drifting toward her, taking her hand, kissing it then curtsying.
"Rise, daughter, we bow to no one."
"Are you Fairy?" Asked Ellie in breathless wonder, for though the Fairies were certainly beautiful, this woman stole your breath.
"No. Though we share many traits, we are not of the Fairy. We are Elves."
"I met an Elf, he did not look like you."
"We chose not to show our true face in the world. We have found that it can be...distracting." The woman smiled gently. "Please, daughter, sit. Let me refresh you."
There by the wall, appeared a tray laden with grapes and a fine silver jug with two matching goblets. The jug was filled with a rich purple red liquid that smelt strongly of pomegranate and raspberry. The goblets were suddenly filled where moments before they were empty. The level of the jug remained unchanged.
Ellie dreamily sat on the wall and the woman arranged herself fluidly next to her.
"I am sure that you have many questions," the woman continued, "please, drink, eat and ask. I will endeavour to answer all that I can."
Ellie took up the goblet and placed it to her lips. The fresh fruity smell seemed to refresh and invigorate her. Where she had felt leaden and tired, she now felt alert and awake. She took a deep sip and felt summertime slide down her throat and sooth the redness from screaming.

"Where am I?" Ellie asked at length, her voice intact.
"This is your safe house." The woman explained. "We all have one. It is where we can escape to when we are frightened or alone, in pain or lost. This place is where you can refresh and relax, build your strength and gather your wits. Weeks here are but moments in the world, so you can take as long as you need."
"But how did I get here?" Ellie wanted to know.
"You needed it, so here it is." Came the answer. "The first few times, it is here when you are most in need, after time, you are able to enter at will. Many stay here for lifetimes at a time, then return to the world."
"Do they all look like this? Are they all the same? I mean, actually, I don't know what I mean. I am a little overwhelmed."
"In answer to your question, I think. No. Not all houses are the same. The owner designs each in their mind. The house provides what they need as it is needed. It can be added to or changed however the owner wishes. Rooms are added, activities

The Fae

introduced; people even, if it is wished. More about that another time I think. Let me see. Hmm! Yes, I have it. In your world, you have computer games yes?"

"Yes."

"Well, this is like a virtual world, and you are like an avatar. No, well, not quite. Oh dear, I do seem to be confusing this more than is necessary. I assure you that it is a good and safe place. You will be happy here."

"But what of my life in the world? What happens to that?"

"Oh, nothing. You are still there. You are here in your mind. You're body is still laying unconscious on the floor. Broken and bleeding in that dank room. But in here you are whole and unhurt. You can stay here whilst the Gnome tortures you if you wish. You will be aware of what he is doing, be able to answer him but that will feel like the dream and this the reality. Or you can go back and return here another time. It is entirely up to you. My role is to help you whatever you decide."

"Why on earth would that be? Why do I not know of this place? Why would you help me?"

"Oh my child, do you not know yet?"

"Know what?"

"It is for you to discover, not I to tell. I am sorry my daughter. As to why I would help, well, my role as it were is to guide and protect you on this your newest journey."

"You make it sound like I have done this before."

"You truly do not remember, do you?"

"Apparently not!" Ellie was a little annoyed at everyone knowing more about her than she herself did.

"Why did the Gnomes take me? What do they want?" Ellie demanded.

"We are not wholly sure yet."

"The one who... The one who... hurt... is hurting me. That one, he doesn't believe me. He asked my name and I told him, but he doesn't believe me. If he doesn't believe my name, he will never believe anything else will he?"

"I am afraid not. They do seem intent on punishing you."

"Oh, I just don't know what the hell is going on! My life was fine a few weeks ago, now its just crazy! I have Elves, Fairies, Gnomes, talking cats, torture, a stalker cat and god only knows what else. Oh lets not forget the bloody Vampires! What the hell I have to do with them is completely beyond me too!"

"Vampires?" The woman asked her quickly, taking her gently by the shoulders and staring into her eyes. Willing the answer from them. "You are involved with the Vampires? Please, you must tell me. What has happened?" The woman was suddenly very agitated.

Ellie explained about Yarrow and Milfoil, about the balls and the threat. She explained about the agreement that queen Alcea had struck and her role in it. The woman paled and trembled slightly.

"This is indeed grave news. We had not thought the Vampires were involved. I must go immediately and report this turn of events. I will be but a moment. Meanwhile, Joachim will keep you company." And with that, she literally vanished in a twinkling shimmer of dust and sunlight.

Chapter Seven.

Joachim came and sat next to Ellie on the wall. He appeared to be a boy of about seven years old. He had smooth black hair cut in an old fashioned page boy style, with fine black eyebrows barely glimpsed beneath his heavy fringe. His large brown eyes were bright with merriment and his rounded cheeks were flushed with mischievousness. His rosebud mouth was squirming to stay closed and his fingers opened and closed on his lap. His left foot tapped irritatingly against the wall and his whole body hummed with unspent energy. Joachim also wore a toga style robe, stopping just above the knees and incongruously white. His was tied with a fine silver rope at his waist but his garment was bunched and untidy.

Just like any other small boy, Ellie thought to herself. *A bundle of energy.*

"Would you like to explore?" The boy asked shyly.

"Why not!" Ellie replied ungraciously.

They got up, he jumping, she slowly. Joachim reached for Ellies hand and, surprised, she took it. Hand in hand they walked back into the house and climbed a large, curved marble staircase.

Joachim chattered away like a baby starling and appeared only to require the occasional grunt or nod to mark an interest. His incessant babbling provided a soothing background to Ellies musings.

"Oh you must look in here, this is my favourite. I love the toys." Joachim pulled Ellie through door after door. Every room holding a treasure or memory that the boy was bursting to share.

"Look, here, the wall has painting of fairies on it! Look, you can see their wings! Everyone knows they do not have wings, but the picture is so pretty do you not think? Ellie? Do you think so? Pretty?"

Joachim seemed to notice Ellies lack of interest and slowed to a stop.

"I am sorry. I get so carried away. I thought you would enjoy seeing all your old rooms. I thought perhaps if you saw them, you would remember me." He said, bright tears shining in his eyes.

"I am so sorry Joachim. I don't know this place. I have never been here before, and I am afraid that I don't know you." Ellie was sad to hurt the boy's feelings.

"It is okay, I know that it's hard, but you will remember, and I will always be here for you to play with. Just like before. I can be older if you prefer."

With that, the hand in Ellies grew in size to that of a man's, the boy himself became taller and more filled out, his hair shortened to a more adult cut and his Adam's apple protruded where before that had been none.

Ellie dropped his hand in surprise and stood staring up into Joachim's face. Well, what used to be Joachim's face. The man before her was stunningly beautiful. The same features as the boy but fleshed out and aged. He appeared to be about thirty.

"Don't do that!" Ellie snapped in shock. "My god, that's incredible. Are you a real person? How could you just change like that?"

"I am real. We were friends a long time ago and I hope we will be again. I know I'm not supposed to tell you, you are to remember on your own, but we swore an oath. No secrets, ever! I cannot bear to see you like this, knowing who you are but not being able to help you remember. It is not fair!" Joachim the adult actually stamped his foot in a fit of childish temper and reverted back into Joachim the boy.

The Fae

Ellie stepped around the man boy and descended the stairs. She went back outside and walked over to a fragrant orange tree that stood on the beautiful lawn. Under the tree was an iron bench, all swirls and curlicues. She sat down.

Joachim came up beside her and knelt on the ground. He hung his head and peered up at her from beneath his fringe.

"I am sorry Ellie Belly, I did not mean to make you mad."

"Its not you Joachim. My life is so crazy at the moment. I just don't even know which way is up anymore. I have no control over any aspect of my life and it seems that everyone knows me more than I know myself. I haven't forgotten anything. I know I haven't, so why does everyone believe I have? How come people think I know things? Why do you believe I know you?"

"I have no idea what is happening in your world Ellie." Joachim looked thoughtfully into her eyes. "But we were best friends when you were here before."

"I have never been here before!" Cried Ellie.

"I know you do not remember and it must be really scary. Trust me though, we spent years and years here, playing in the gardens, climbing trees, swimming in the lake. You will remember, although I do not know why you cannot now. But this is a good place, nothing bad can enter. You will remember when you are ready."

"Okay, let's say that all this is true." Ellie mused, "Why would I forget? If this is such a good place, why would I forget it? God! I can't believe that I'm even contemplating this."

"Okay, let us look at it this way." Joachim smiled and pinched Ellie hard on the back of the hand.

"Ouch! What the hell was that for?"

"So, you felt that?"

"Of course I did, it bloody hurt."

"So if you felt it, it must be real?"

"I don't understand."

"If, in this place, I can pinch you and you feel it, it is a real sensation, a real feeling and a real reaction. Yes?"

"Yes, I see. So what you are saying is that I should just shut up and accept that this is real whether I believe it or not?"

"I would not put it that way, but yes." Joachim seemed pleased that she had finally got it. He continued, "Every one of us has a safe place. It is where we go to be, well, safe. Not everyone needs it and therefore not everyone uses theirs, but the place is there. It is a place that we build with our mind, we furnish it with our mind and people it with our mind."

"So it's imaginary? You are a figment of my imagination?" Ellie tried hard to grasp the concept.

"No. It is not imaginary, it is real, but we create it from our imagination."

"So if I had a crap imagination, my house would be crap too?"

Joachim looked hard at Ellie.

"No. Don't be obtuse! If you were lacking in imagination, which by the way I could not imagine! We all have a guide to help us, how else do you think young children build their first house? Left to their own devices, they would be made of candy canes and liquorice sticks. The children would be sick all the time."

"So, you can get sick here?"

"Certainly. Though it is quite hard to do so, it is possible."

The Fae

"If I get sick or hurt here, does it affect my body back in the real world? And vice versa?"

"Good question. No. Well, if you are hurt here, it will affect you in the other world, but unless you die, the other world does not affect you here. After all, back there you are currently being tortured, yet here you are whole. Take a look."

Ellie lifted her hand to her face and felt her skin, whole and unbroken. There was not the jarring pain that she had expected. She lifted her hands and saw that they were free from injury.

"You say I am being tortured. Do you mean right at this minute?"

"Why yes, can't you tell?"

"Ah, no. Should I be able to?"

"Oh my. I have never known this to happen before. Yes my child, you should be able to tell. Are you positive? Nothing at all?"

"Positive. How do you know? That I am I mean."

"Well, you are supposed to be able to see out of those eyes at the same time as these, just as I can in my real life. I know what is happening in yours because I can see it in the reflection."

"What is that?"

"A reflection is a shiny surface like a mirror or a body of still water; a lake, a glass or anything that you have chosen to see a reflection in. You ask it to show you the life you wish to see, and well, you see it. It is pretty neat really."

"Where is mine? I want to see." Ellie jumped up and grabbed Joachim's hand for him to lead her.

They climbed back up the beautiful marble staircase, followed the gallery round then ascended another, less imposing stair. At the top, they walked along the corridor to the other end and another, more unkempt stairwell. They climbed to the top and stood in a bare and dusty space. Cobwebs hung majestically from forgotten cornices and fly blown windows. Old broken chairs piled in a corner haphazardly whilst a dressing table lay upended in the centre of the room. The mirror mounted on its utilitarian plinth was marbled with cracks.

"Is that it? How can we see in that? I thought it had to be reflective." Ellie was disappointed.

"No, not that one." Joachim reached out and pulled open the stiff and creaking drawer. He reached in and pulled out a dulled silver hand mirror. Its once intricately carved back now worn and scratched. He handed the mirror to Ellie and bade her look.

"This is it." He took a couple of steps back then turned and righted two of the chairs. Joachim sat in one and Ellie the other. She seemed reluctant to look into the mirror.

Ellie turned the mirror over and over in her hands whilst she looked straight ahead, and avoided looking into the glass itself. She was nervous and unsure of what she would see. So much had happened to her already, surely it would be easier to just stay here in this wonderful and safe place? The woman had said that she could live out her life here and not have to return to the world. That would work. She could be safe and free from any more outrageous occurrences. No more Fairies, no more Gnomes, no more Vampires, no more Elves and people trying to run her down in grotty white vans. She could live in this lovely house, walk in the fragrant gardens, swim in the lake Joachim had mentioned. Yes, it would be quite lovely here. Safe.

"You do not have to look." Joachim seemed anxious that Ellie had not moved. "It is not important. Or... or I could look for you. If you wanted. Or... you do not have to look at all. Not if you do not want to."

"I'm okay. I can do it. I will look, just give me a few moments." Ellie closed her eyes and took a deep breath. She held the breath deep in her lungs for a few seconds then opened her eyes and looked directly into the dirty glass of the mirror.

At first there was nothing; just a filthy, smudgy swirl on the glass. The reflection itself murky and indistinct. Ellie was about to look away when the image became clear. She saw in the glass, a reflection of herself, sitting, on the chair in the dusty room, Joachim to her side and cobwebs above her head. Just as she had convinced herself that this was a joke, she saw behind herself a different room. One with tall curtained windows and an old battered couch. The image of the new room became more and more clear until it was the only image in the mirror. On the couch Ellie saw herself, crumpled and broken, blood over her face and her eye swollen, viciously red in the places it could be seen. Her hair was clumped and matted with dried blood, handfuls of her torn out hair lay on the floor, ripped bloodily from the roots. The other Ellie had a piece of dirty grey cloth tied around her eyes but the now Ellie knew she was awake. The Ellie on the couch jerked her head and appeared to be listening for something, then a small smile appeared as she became aware of her other self watching, safe.

The man in the room with Ellie smarted at the sight of the smile and screamed indecipherably as he struck her over and over, almost as if trying to knock the smile away. He was not very tall, with shoulder length greying brown hair tightly tied back in a tail. He had widely spaced eyes under bushy brows, a thick nose and fleshy mouth. His neck was hidden under a heavy looking jumper, his jeans appeared clean and had an ironed crease down the front. His feet were clad in low end trainers that could be bought in any supermarket. The man was so angry that spittle was flying from his mouth as he continued to scream and strike at Ellie. She, in turn, kept her smile in place and tried to curl protectively; seemingly immune to the pain being inflicted.

"Can she... I feel that down there?" Ellie asked in horror.
"Yes. I am sorry, but yes."
"How can we help her?"
"You, not her. And this is helping you. You cannot escape him in the flesh, so your mind has bought you here. Here you are safe. Here you do not feel the pain of there."
"I can't bear to look, take this away please." Ellie held out the mirror and Joachim put it back in the drawer. Ellie's head collapsed onto her hands and she sobbed quietly. She cried for the woman in the mirror and she cried for the woman that she was. Ellie could see no way out for the her being beaten by the man in the mirror. Moments ago she had wanted to live her life in obscurity here in her safe house, now she wanted to free herself and rend her tormentor limb from limb. She had so many emotions battling inside her that she was struck immobile.

"I don't know what to do." She told Joachim. "What can I do?" She looked at him with such fear and futility in her eyes, that Joachim sprang to his feet and threw himself into her arms and cried...

The Fae

"Please do not give up. I know we will find a way, we must. Nothing can last forever, it has to stop at some point." He hugged her tightly and whispered fiercely, "We will think of something. Frances will be back soon, she will help us. She knows how things can be, she will know. Come child, please do not cry!" Joachim lifted his seven year old hand and gently wiped the tears from Ellies cheek.

"We will get through this. We will think of something. I promise. Remember? No lies, no secrets? Do you remember our promise?"
Ellie sniffed and buried her face in the boys' hair. She breathed in the scent of him and gathered herself together. This boy child was right. They would fix this, they would think of something. Nothing went on forever, there would be a solution somewhere, they just had to find it.

Joachim and Ellie returned to the garden and sat in the stone circle at the edge of the pond. Ellie trailed her hand in the water and felt a tickle as a large white Koi came and nibbled at her fingertips. Joachim lay on the stone, on his back with his eyes closed against the sun. He intermittently plucked fat juicy grapes from the platter and dropped them into his mouth.

"Please close your mouth when you are eating." Ellie asked.
"Some things never change!" Grumped the boy, but he complied. "You should try these, they are lovely." He said.
"I don't want any thank you." Ellie answered. "Can we get hungry here? If so how do we get food and stuff?"
"We do not really have to think about it. It is like the place knows what we want and there it is. So in that respect, no, we do not get hungry. If we chose not to eat then yes, I suppose we would then."
"What about toilets? Do we have to go to the toilet here?"
"Ellie! I thought I was the child! What questions you ask! Toilets indeed!" Joachim popped another grape into his mouth then went back to staring at the sky.
"Can we have rain and snow if we want it?"
"Why would you want it?" The boy wondered lazily.
"I dunno. I suppose because I like the rain. We do need it for the flowers."
"Well, if you wanted it, you could have it. I have never heard of anyone actually wanting rain here before, but I do not see why you couldn't." Joachim rolled over and propped himself on one arm.
"Do you really not remember?"
"Do we have to keep going over this? Seriously?"
"I am sorry but it is so unbelievable. To have forgotten all this so completely. I just cannot imagine it." Joachim looked genuinely amazed.
"Believe me. I am more amazed than you, but there you have it! Repeatedly asking about it will not change anything!"
Joachim smiled a crooked, cheeky smile.
"It may. It could jog your memory. I could be doing you a huge favour and you would be so grateful. You would be in my debt."
"I somehow doubt that!" Ellie sniffed, but her mood was lightening.
"In fact." Continued the boy, warming to his tease. "If I keep on and on asking you, you may even remember all the way back to the beginning. You could even remember that you are…"

"Joachim! What are you doing?" Came a stern voice, just out of Ellies eye line.

"I am sorry my lady." Joachim stood and hung his head. "I was only teasing. I did not mean anything. I would never have forced her memory."
Ellie saw that Joachim had his fingers crossed tightly behind his back and she couldn't help but smile.
Ellie stood and turned to face the woman, Frances, who had returned looking pensive.

"I have spoken with the others, told them of your plight. They are looking to speak with the fairies to see how we can rescue you. They are quite concerned about the involvement of the Vampires but will address that at a later date. We are all agreed that your safety is paramount. We need to rescue you but must have more information. We do not know where the house is that you are being held in. We must find a way to gather more information." Frances sat on the wall and absently dropped a grape into her mouth. As she slowly chewed, she looked to Ellie.

"Is there anything you can remember that would help us to find the house?"
Ellie mentally kicked herself. *Oh no, I don't need to remember the twists and turns do I? The police won't need to know will they? Because I will be safe by time I see them! Bloody, bloody idiot!*

"It isn't a lot of help," Ellie started, "but there was quite a long walk over gravel between the car and the house. The walk from the door to the room I am in was quite long too. The rooms seemed high and musty. I got the impression that the house was quite old. It has a fireplace in the room I am in and wooden floorboards. I can't tell you any more as I have a blindfold on in there."

"Well, that is a start. It sounds like a large old house with a longish drive. How long was the drive from…? Where was it you were taken from?"

"I was at Mertensias. She lives in the new development near the college. The ones with the odd circular shaped flats at the front. They have blue lights on them. I don't know the name if the road though, it used to be a rough ground car park a couple of years ago."

"Oh, I know where that is. So, how long do you think the drive took?" Frances asked.

"Well, I would say that all in all, we drove for about ten, fifteen minutes. I was so scared that a minute felt like an hour, so it's only a guess."

"It is a start." Frances encouraged. "When you left the flat, the very first turn the car made, which way did it go?"

"Oh, left. Definitely left. I remember that because as the man lifted my head to tie my eyes, he tilted to the right to keep his balance."

"Good, you are doing well. Okay now, did the car go fast or slow after the turn?"

"Oh. Really quite slow, but there is only one way out of that road. I remember that we turned right; we must have gone up Balkerne Hill because I remember feeling like I was being tipped back a little. Ok, so let me think now. We would have gone up to the roundabout. Where from there? Not the Southway because that would have meant an immediate left turn. I am pretty sure not Butt Road, it felt like we carried further round. It must have been Lexden Road. If we had gone further, we would have been back where we started and that would seem pointless. I had a blindfold, so they probably thought that would be enough of a deterrent."

Frances was pleased.

"You are doing so well Ellie. Okay, so going toward Lexden. That would account for about seven or eight minutes, depending on traffic. What time was it, do you know dear?"

"Time? Wow! No. I was asleep. We had gone to bed about eleven, I was fast asleep so really no idea. I'm sorry, I don't know. Very dark. Very little traffic too. I could hear quite well because they didn't talk to each other. I don't really remember any other cars on the road."

"That sounds like it was early hours of the morning. That is the only time I have known that road to be empty. Okay, good. Do you remember how long you drove next?" Frances encouraged.

"Uh, let me think. Hmm. We seemed to go slowly along the road for about a minute or so, then I felt the car take a left, then another quick left and then…Oh, let me think. After that we…Oh we…Let me see, after the left turn we…"

"Relax Ellie." Frances urged. "Do not try to force the memory. It will come, or not, in its own time. Let us think of something else. Okay, so we know we are in Lexden. We are looking for a large old house with a long gravel drive. That doesn't really narrow it down much." She smiled. "Smells musty. Hmm! So a house that is either unused or belongs to an elderly person. Ok, elderly are in abundance there… unused, that would narrow the field somewhat. If only we could be sure." Frances tapped her teeth whilst she thought. "Ellie, open your eyes and look around, see what you can see."

"How do I do that?" asked Ellie, scrunching up her face, not particularly keen to find out.

"Just open your eyes." Frances told her.

"But my eyes are open."

"No, they are not. Open them, oh and do not forget to come back. Remember, just wish to be back in your safe house. Okay, ready? Now!"

Ellie slowly closed her eyes then squeezed them shut for a second or two. She very, very slowly opened her uninjured eye. All about her was tinged in red and blurred. Waves of pain started at her toes and washed over her. All of her. Ellies stomach clenched in memory of recent fists. Her face, freshly released from some invisible vice, strained at the skin, trying to burst. Every strand of hair hurt. Her hands, which were still tied behind her back, were mercifully numb. Her shoulders, where they were pulled unnaturally, ached with a delicious lightness in comparison to the rest of her body. Her throat was razor raw from screaming and her nose was plugged with blood and mucus. The cover over her eyes had slipped and she could finally see her surroundings. As she had guessed, and as she knew, she was in an old, musty room. The walls were dank and peeling. Racial epithets and miss-spelt vulgarities adorned the mouldering walls with spray can artistry. The fireplace, once used but now long forgotten and filled with detritus. Broken bottles and crushed, rusting cans littered the grate. Cigarette ends lay about the floor, discarded and forgotten. Unimportant.

Ellie took each breath with as much care as she could. She had never had a broken rib, but was sure that this was how it felt and she was afraid that she would injure it further by moving. Oh why hadn't she paid attention when she was in the car? She desperately wanted to turn around and disappear back in her safe house. But she had to try and gather as much information as she could first. She sat perfectly still and strained to hear any possible sounds or noises that would speed her return.

Gradually, the sounds of the house became clearer, she could make out the ticking of a clock, and the sighing of the wind outside. She listened harder and was able to hear people talking in another room. One voice complaining of the paltry food rations

The Fae

available and the other saying not to worry, the job would be over soon and they could get home and eat as much as they liked. That did not fill Ellie with confidence. Nor did it give her any indication of her location. There was a wooden squeaking somewhere outside her room and seemingly to her left. It sounded like stairs being mounted. The step was not very heavy, so it could be a woman, she reasoned. She remembered that she had heard a woman when she arrived, so that would fit. Okay, so definitely a woman and two men so far. But there should be another somewhere. There were the two in the car with her, the man here already and the woman, that she knew of. So, where was the other man? Ellie whipped around to look behind her, expecting to see him lurking there. But the room was empty excepting herself. The movement caused bile to rise in her throat and threaten to erupt. The pain was intolerable. She leant back against the sofa and closed her eye whilst her equilibrium settled back down.

Whilst Ellies eye was closed, her hearing became a little sharper and she picked out faint traces of traffic outside. There seemed to be quite a few cars passing not too far away. *That must help. Keep going Ellie*, she thought to herself. Over the sound of the traffic, Ellie heard an irregular scritching sound. She turned as gently as she could toward the filthy window and made out a tree, scratching against the glass. The tree had no leaves but seemed to be covered in pine needles, only it didn't look like a Christmas tree. She had seen one before, but could not think what it was called. *Don't try, it will come to you,* she thought. *Worst case, you can draw it for Frances. Okay, what else? What else? Come on! I can't stay here, listen*! She urged herself. A church bell struck the quarter hour, very faint in the distance. *That wont help*, she thought, *that could be anywhere from here*. Then Ellie realised that she could hear children, lots of children, laughing and shouting, screaming and yelling. A school playground! Not too far away either. That has to be useful! She tried desperately to think how many schools were in Lexden. She knew there was the Boys school on Lexden Road, where there any others? Oh, she just didn't know. But how many abandoned buildings with monkey trees...Monkey trees! That's what they are called. Monkey puzzle trees! So how many neglected houses near a school with a monkey puzzle tree near the window could there be? Oh! What if she wasn't in the front of the building? Would they even see the monkey puzzle tree from the front? She was so sure that she had been carried down a hall, she couldn't be in the front of the house could she?

"I want to be in my safe house." Ellie said aloud and closed her eye.

Ellie gingerly opened her eyes to find Frances looking at her with deep concern on her face. Joachim stood beside her and was actually wringing his hands.

"Are you okay?" Asked Frances.

"Yes, I'm alright. God but it was horrible. I don't know how much help this will be but there was so little to see or hear."

"Go ahead my daughter, anything will help." Frances sat beside Ellie and took her hands in her own.

"Well..." Ellie told Frances and Joachim of all she had seen and heard. She did not mention how afraid she had been, nor how much pain she had been in. It seemed churlish somehow.

"Oh, my child, that is very good. We should be able to find you in no time. Whilst you were away, I spoke to Alcea and she has agreed to ask the Vampires to join in the hunt for you. Fairies are forbidden to hurt, whether by accident or intent, so they would be pretty useless in any form of rescue attempt." Frances sounded bitter, but shrugged it off and continued in a more pleasant tone.

"There are still a couple of hours until dark, do you think you will be able to hold on that long?" There was such pity in her eyes, that Ellie lied.

"I'm sure I can. How bad can it be?" She tried to laugh.

"Oh my daughter, be strong." Frances squeezed Ellies hand and stood. "Come, let us walk in the garden."

"Uh, actually. I cannot believe that I am saying this, but I think I should go back."

"My child, that is not necessary. You can wait here until you are rescued."

"I understand that, but well, I don't want to leave her on her own to cope with what's happening down there." Ellie shrugged in embarrassment.

"But she is you. You wont feel it here, but there you will be in great pain." Frances was genuinely worried.

"I sort of get it. But, well… when I am rescued, I will have to go back anyway and… please don't think I'm crazy, but I think that it will be a bigger adjustment going back not having gone through it. Does this make any sense to you?" Ellie asked with raised eyebrows and wrinkled brow.

"Yes, it makes sense, but it is not necessary. You can stay here whilst you recover, you don't have to be in pain." Frances was openly begging now.

"But, and please don't think I'm not grateful." Ellie said. "But, if I stay here, everyone will be working on my behalf and I will be, not to put too fine a point on it, I will be absent. I will have no input, no control. It's my life that will be at risk, my life that people will be risking theirs for, the very least I can do is actually be present for them whilst they do it."

Frances had tears in her eyes.

"Daughter, please reconsider. This is unnecessary and madness. Please stay here with me until you are healed."

Ellie stood and took Frances' hands in her own, she bent and kissed her fingers. When she stood, she had tears on her own cheeks.

"I wish I had a mother like you. I wish you were my mother. But I have to do this. If I survive…" Here Ellie took a deep breath and continued. "When I survive, will you be here? I so want to see you again."

Frances pulled Ellie to her and held her tight. She kissed the top of Ellies head and buried her face in her hair for a moment whilst she whispered.

"I am always here for you child. I am honoured that you wish it."

And with that, Ellie closed her eyes and returned.

Chapter Eight

Ellie opened her good eye to see the man with the grey pony tail, leaning over her and whispering. The smell of him making her dizzy.

"There is absolutely no way out of here unless you answer my questions. If you think you are in pain now, you have no idea of the things I am authorised to do to you. Do you have any idea what I would like to do to a pretty young thing like you? I don't mind a bit of blood and bruising. Truth be told, it makes me hot that way."

He stared in her uninjured eye and slid his hand down over her breast. Ellie strained away from him, but was already against the back of the sofa, so couldn't move very far.

"Go on, fight! You'll love it all the more." The man whispered cruelly as he took her breast in his hand and twisted it painfully, taking evident pleasure in her tears of pain.

"Please, please don't" Ellie panted.

The man pulled his fist back and punched her full in the face. Ellie felt heat explode at the impact, and then numbness set in. After a few seconds, the crunching bone blossomed in pain. Like a rose unfurling, layers upon layers of burning pins shot outwards and Ellie felt that one of her teeth was broken inside her mouth.

"Did I tell you to speak?" He asked pleasantly. "No, I didn't fink so. Now, where were we? Ah yes." He stood and reached for the zip of his jeans and pulled it down, He fumbled open the button and eased his jeans down around his ankles.

Ellie tried to climb backwards into the couch, shaking her head and moaning. Eyes wide in terror. Afraid to speak. Unable to scream.

The man kicked off his trainers without untying them, then bent and pulled his jeans off. He threw them behind him and reached his hand to stroke himself through the fabric of his Mickey Mouse boxer shorts.

"Oh god! Oh god! Oh god!" Ellie repeated her mantra over and over and over, quietly like a magic spell. As if it would protect her.

I have to stay. I want to go. I must stay. Why? I can leave. I can't leave, I have to stay. Ellie's mind imploded with indecision. Should she return to her safe place? But if she did and this creature raped her, her body would have the memory of the assault but her mind would not. Surely that way madness lay? How had this happened? How could this possibly be happening to her?

The man had rubbed himself hard and was straining against the fabric of his shorts. Mickey's face and one ear were now protruding and slightly damp. Ellie felt the bile in her throat and she fought to swallow it back. She was becoming faint but refused to pass out. If this bastard meant to rape her, she would damned well be awake to remember because one day she was going to rip his fucking bollocks off! Getting angry was giving her strength. She would survive this and then, when she was able, she would kill him. The knowledge shocked her, that she would so easily consider taking a life after her lifetime of passive conformity. But if this bastard so much as put that thing anywhere near her, she would rip it off and shove it down his throat! Oh yes! This was working. She had never felt angry before in her life, but oh boy! Did it feel good now! Oh yeah!

"You think you're putting that shrivelled piece of crap anywhere near me pal, you have another think coming!" Ellie surprised herself by spitting out at the man.

He looked completely stunned. Here was this pathetic, broken woman. Threatening him? He let go of himself and took a step toward her. Fist raised.

"Oh, that's right!" Sneered Ellie. "Need to smack me around to get it up don't you? You pathetic worm. Why don't you go back to the toilet and beat one off? Make yourself feel like a man for a second." Ooh, she was enjoying this.

The man's erection started to fade.

"Ah. Wassa matta? Poor little fella only work when he's hitting a defenceless woman?" She taunted him. "Can't maintain if she talks back? Did mommy hit you as a kid and play with your winky?"

Smack! Okay, so she had probably gone too far she realised as he struck her so hard that she flew across the sofa and landed on the floor. At least he wasn't thinking of rape now. She had bought herself some time.

The man grabbed his clothes and stamped out of the room, slamming the door behind him.

"Temper, temper." Ellie whispered to herself just before she passed out.

"The owners must be dead." Came a voice from outside the door. "That certainly saves time. Are those Elves in yet?"

"Why are you asking me? I walked in at exactly the same time as…Look out, on the stairs." Came another voice.

There followed a few bangs and crashes, followed by a blood curdling scream that cut off abruptly. The door to Ellies room opened and she tried to pull herself under the sofa, out of sight.

"Ah! Here she is. I must say, she is making me quite hungry, what with that blood all over her." The first voice said.

Ellie peeked out of her good eye and saw a pair of shiny expensive looking men's shoes just in front of her. Then there was a face bent over and peering into hers with a look of detached amusement. There was a slight smear of what appeared to be blood on his lip and a charming smile beneath that.

"Ellie I presume?" He asked.

"Uh, yes." Ellie managed between swollen lips. "How do you do?"

The man held out his hand and indicated that Ellie should get up.

"I think I will stay here if it's all the same to you." She told him.

"What?"

"I believe that I will be a lot more comfortable here on the floor thank you. Are you my rescue party?" She asked, all too aware that she was possibly in shock as this was not generally the way to speak with your rescuers. "I was expecting a big white horse." She giggled.

"You could say that." Laughed the other voice, and its owner, Aurellio stepped into Ellies line of sight.

"I'm afraid you haven't caught me at my best. I didn't know you were coming so haven't had time to make myself pretty." Ellie was now quite sure that shock was responsible for her absurd behaviour.

"Oh, I don't know." The first voice said. "You look pretty tasty to me."

"Don't be so crass!" Aurellio told him.

"Ah, you found her." Came a completely new voice.

"Welcome." Ellie said. "Come, join us, we are having a party on the floor. Pull up a floorboard." She giggled to herself then passed out again.

The Fae

Ellie awoke to find herself in the arms of the most beautiful man she had ever seen in her life. He had long black hair that shone in the moonlight and was repeated in the lustrous lashes adorning his almond shaped black eyes. His straight nose proudly bore two perfect nostrils that were currently quivering with effort. Ellie supposed she was a bit on the heavy side, but he bore her well. She smiled to herself, *guess the crazies haven't completely gone then*, she thought. As he breathed a little heavily, (*but consider the weight!*) his breath brushed against her bloodied skin, the scent of cherries perfuming her face. Ellie turned to look at him fully and noticed that the arms holding her were long, sinewy and imbued with an effortless strength. *Again consider the burden here!* Ellie giggled to herself. His arms were encased in a smooth, soft, dark coloured fabric that felt warm where it touched her skin. And when Ellie looked down, his trousers appeared to be of the same fabric. To the side of her angel stood his twin. Or a man so like him as to be a twin. He was tall and willowy, with the same long black hair and comparable beauty. He walked with an easy grace, eating up the ground with his long strides. His hair fanned out behind him framing his angelic countenance.

Ellie was gently lain on the back seat of what appeared to be a very expensive car. The leather of the seat was soft and yielding, the coolness soothing to her broken face. The inside of the car smelt of leather and cologne. A rich citrus with bergamot undertones. The smell was relaxing and spoke of gentlemen with means. Ellie supposed it belonged to the Vampires.

"But surely you don't need cars!" She mumbled into the darkness. "Don't you fly?"

From the front of the car came a soft chuckle.

"Where do these humans get their ideas from?" Smiled the voice of Aurellio. "Fly indeed."

Ellie felt the seat next to her give slightly as somebody climbed in beside her. She felt her hair being gently swept from her face and a fabulously cool dampness wipe at what she thought must be the bloody mess of her face.

"Ah! Hurts." She managed to sigh.

"I am so sorry; I must clear this blood to assess the damage. I will try not to hurt you further." The fresh voice told her. Then she felt again the cool wetness across her hot, tortured skin.

"Drive faster please Aurellio, this is torture!"

"You think I do not feel the hunger as you do?" Aurellio answered.

"I do not mean to question you, but this is hell on earth. Can I not take a small sip? She is asleep and would not know."

"Awake. Hands off." Ellie managed through her torn lips and swollen tongue. "No snacking."

"There you have it. Five minutes and we will be there." Aurellio answered.

He too had hunger in his voice and Ellie could tell that this was hard for the Vampires, being in the car with this much spilt blood.

"Where? Go where?" Ellie struggled to say.

"We are taking you to Fae's home. The queen will be there, as will Frances of the Elves. Try not to speak, save your energy." The Vampire sitting next to Ellie told her. Given the amount he must be suffering, he was very gentle with his words and his hands as he continued to minister to her wounds.

The Fae

They arrived at a small cottage set back slightly from the road. Ellie managed to catch glimpses of colour and the scent of stocks as she was carried into the house and placed softly on the couch.

"Oh daughter... oh child, look at you! You are so... my child, why did you not return and forgo this?"

"Must remember. Get strong." Ellie managed.

"Let her rest now. We shall attend her. I must speak with our friends." Alcea beckoned to the Vampires to follow her into the kitchen. "Come, we must talk."

Queen Alcea and the Vampires left the room.

"Elves? Where Elves?" Ellie asked Fae.

"They arrived seconds before you, they are in the kitchen. Come let me clean you up. The Vampires did a good enough job I suppose. It must have been hard for them."

"Mmm, yes, hard." Ellie was becoming sleepy.

"I know it is not easy my child, but try to stay awake."

Fae gently took Ellies hand in hers and started to clean her injuries. She chattered about nothing in particular, providing a background noise of familiarity for Ellie, to reinforce the fact of her rescue.

The queen came back in the room, followed by Aurellio and the two angels. Frances stepped in after them and sat beside Ellie on the couch. Frances took Ellies bandaged hand and rested it atop her own. She looked long into Ellies eyes and seemed to find something there that pleased her, as she smiled a tight smile and said, "You were very brave daughter. I am so proud of you. You fought right to the end. These injuries are going to heal and I believe that the other ones you suffered will heal quickly too. The Vampires did not manage to capture your assailants." Here a sharp look at the Vampires. "But the Elves did find some bits of information that we will be able piece together. Hopefully we will be able to find out why you were taken. We would like to ask you some questions, but I see that you need to sleep. With your permission, Fae can look inside your head and that way we need not disturb you unduly. If you wish, she can also soothe your memories to help you recover better."

"Yes, look. No soothe. Need pain."

"Why on earth would you need that pain? How? Oh, we will discuss this when you are well again. Now sleep daughter. Rest and refresh, we will see to your injuries as you sleep."

"Thank..." Ellie fell into the black pit of nothingness, the only sensation being the gentle touch of Fae's hands on her head.

Ellie lay on the couch, covered by a fresh white cotton duvet. The cover had pink peonies embroidered along the top and smelt of flowers after the rain. Her head was supported by cloud soft pillows that encompassed and cooled. The window was open and a soft summer breeze brought the fresh evening air into the room. Ellie gingerly turned her head and found that the pain had gone. She noticed the queen, sitting on a high backed chair beside the couch, holding her hand.

"I don't hurt." She said in surprise. "How?"

"We tried to soothe your injuries and your pain. As you wished, we left the pain in your memory, but we took it from your body. I hope that you do not mind?"

"Mind? Wow! I can't believe it. I can barely feel anything. Is it permanent?"

The Fae

"Yes child." The queen placed Ellie's hand on top of the duvet, stood and walked to the window. "Fae told us what she saw in your mind. I am so sorry that you had that happen to you. Please let her take it away."

"Thank you but no. It is important that I feel and remember this. Something happened to me there."

"We know."

"No, not just that, something in me changed. I became strong, angry, powerful. The more he hurt me, the stronger I felt. I wanted to kill him."

The queen took a sharp, deep breath.

"I know that is completely against any fairy beliefs, but that is how I felt. I wanted to rip him apart."

The queen looked down at the floor to hide the sadness on her face.

"I do understand child. We hurt none because of the power we have. Over the years we have learnt to override our destructive aspects. But I do remember how it feels to wish pain on another. To rip and destroy."

"Oh, I am so sorry. Of course you do. The children!"

The queen stiffened and seemed to shake off the memory.

"Yes. Well. As you wish. But remember that at any time, we can remove this for you."

"Thank you. Is there any news? Do we know why yet? He didn't believe me when I told him my name. That was all he asked me. Who do you suppose he thought I was?"

"That is a very good question. Who indeed!" The queen returned to her seat.

"Oh my god!" Ellie exclaimed. "Mertensia, the girls! Are they okay? Did they get away?"

"Yes, yes, they are quite safe. You have made some good friends there; the twins have been driving me to distraction wishing to see you. I promised that they could visit you soon, if it is agreeable to you?"

"Oh thank god. Yes, I would love to see them. I was so worried about them. If I hadn't twisted my ankle, it would have been Mertensia that they took. I can't bear to think what those two girls would have gone through!"

The queen gave Ellie a strange look but said nothing more.

The next couple of days were spent confined to Fae's house. Ellie was moved to the bedroom at night to sleep but during the day could move no more than a step or two from the couch, else she incurred fuss and frustration from her loving captors.

"I really am better you know!" Ellie called out to nobody in particular. "I should be going home soon don't you think?"

Frances walked into the room with a bowl of broth that she placed on a side table next to Ellie.

"More soup? Please let me go home where I can eat! I swear you two are having way to much fun playing nurse. I am quite well you know!"

"It would appear so." Came a man's voice from behind Ellie.

She tried to turn but the layers of duvet, pillows and throws successfully kept her tied in place.

"Is that you?" She asked hopefully. "Fox?"

Fox stepped around so that she could see him. He bent and placed a kiss on the top of her head.

"I am happy to see that you are back to health." He said somewhat formally.

Oh, he must be playing cool in front of Fae, Ellie thought to herself. Then found that she was ungraciously wishing the others would leave so she could be alone with him. She tried to project thoughts into their heads that would induce them to go. But as with most wishful thinking, it came to nothing.

"Do I not get a hello?" Asked Felix.

"Oh Felix! I am so glad to see you. Where have you been? Why didn't you come sooner? Where were you? Have you any news? Did you come to take me home?"

"So many questions!" Felix laughed as he bent to kiss Ellie.

Ellie was so pleased to see him that she threw her arms around his neck and hugged him tight.

"Well, it certainly seems that you are glad to see me." Felix smiled. "As it so happens, I do have some news." He said. "But I think it best that we wait for the others before I tell it."

"Wait, wait, wait. All I do is wait!" Ellie sulked.

Felix sat on the couch beside her and held her hand very tight. He rubbed the back of her hand over his cheek and his eyes misted for a second.

"We thought we had lost you." He said roughly. "If we had lost you..."

"Yes. Well. We did not lose her and that is the important bit." Fox interrupted rudely. "As you can see she is well and seemingly back to normal."

"Quite." Felix said giving Fox a long, pointed look.

"Ahem!" Came a perturbed voice from the floor. "Down here?"

"Peter! Peter, I missed you so much. Come here." And with that, Ellie swept Peter up in her arms and buried her face in his fur as she hugged him tightly to her.

"Where have you been? Oh Peter, I missed you."

"Put me down please, this is most unseemly!" Peter said with very little conviction as he purred against Ellie's chest and burrowed his nose deeper into her neck.

"Most unseemly indeed." Peter showed no sign of getting down, so Ellie sat back with him cuddled on her lap, purring. Peter stretched out his claws then settled into a ball and went to sleep.

"Well, the gangs all here." Ellie giggled.

Just as Fae walked back into the room, there was a knock at the door.

"What is the world coming to?" Fae mumbled. "Vampires, here in my home! Whatever next?" She went to answer the door then returned moments later with Aurellio and the other Vampire, Vicente, that had helped to rescue her.

"I am happy to see you recovered." Aurellio bowed toward Ellie. "You certainly look a lot better than the last time we saw you."

"Would that be the time your friend wanted a wee snack?" Ellie teased.

"What?" Fae's hand flew to her mouth in shock.

"It was nothing!" Ellie backtracked. "These two showed remarkable restraint and I cannot imagine what would have happened had they not rescued me."

"We were there too you know!" Came a high pitched, nasal voice from the direction of the kitchen.

"I believe you may remember Andrew." Fae supplied by way of introduction.

Andrew was one of Ellie's angels, and she did indeed remember them. But she could not imagine that this sulky, whiney man was one of her rescuers. Sure he looked like one of the guys that had saved her. But that voice! Wow, he sounded like a six year old. In tight underwear. With a cold. And pissed as hell about it to boot.

The Fae

His mirror image walked in behind him and bowed slightly to Ellie then all others present, excepting the Vampires.

"I am delighted to see you looking so well." He said to Ellie.

This was much better. This guy sounded normal. As beautiful as the other but as deep and adult as the other was high and juvenile.

"Thank you so much for rescuing me." Ellie said politely. "You two, are you twins?"

"Yes. My name is Sean, and this is my brother Andrew. We were only too happy to help." Then he turned and spoke to Felix. "Are we all here?"

"I believe we are just waiting on our queen, then we can begin. May I add my thanks also. To you two and also to Aurellio and Vicente. Thank you for bringing our sister home."

"Yes, me too. Thank you." Fox added, almost as an afterthought.

What was going on with him? Ellie wondered. *He never behaved like this before. Why was he acting like such an ass?*

Queen Alcea arrived and they settled down to business. They each took a seat at Fae's large kitchen table. All had a glass of tea in front of them, but the vampires' were only for forms sake. There were chunks of bread, two dishes of butter, a tray of cheese and several jars of different types of jam for those that wanted to eat. In the centre of the table was a large jar with blue and purple wild flowers that Ellie could not name.

For several moments, nobody spoke. They all looked about; at each other, out into the dark sky through the window or even to the floor. Anywhere it seemed, except at Ellie. The reason they were all there.

"I'll start then shall I?" Ellie scolded. "Firstly, again, thank you to Aurellio, Sean, Vicente and Andrew for rescuing me. Thank you." She smiled at each of them, and they each in their fashion, smiled back. "Next, Felix, what have you learnt?"

Felix looked toward the queen who nodded her assent.

"Right." He began. "I also wish to thank you four. I know that it was difficult for you especially." Here he nodded toward the Vampires. "But I wish to tell you that I am now in your debt. To refrain from feeding at such a time deserves my respect, and I wish you to know that it will not be forgotten. Nor taken lightly."

"Agreed." Ellie put in.

"Ellie, do not agree to a pact that you cannot possibly understand." The queen interrupted sternly. "Felix has entered into a blood debt that can be called upon at any time. You are absolved this once, but in future, do not be so rash, and choose your words with care."

Ellie was stunned and turned to see Felix staring at Aurellio, who in turn was nodding his acceptance.

"As it is, so it shall be." Aurellio intoned. He then took hold of Felix' forearm in the manner of the Roman soldier and Felix did the same.

"So it is and shall be." Felix replied solemnly.

"Anyway..." Ellie interrupted. "Now that we are all buddies, what did you find out?"

"Ellie! Take care." Frances whispered. "You do not anger the queen or our guests. Take care with your manners, remember in whose company you sit!"

The Fae

"My apologies." Ellie sulked, chastised. "But I am on pins here, I need to know what Felix has found out. I truly don't mean to be rude, but please can't we get on with things?"

"Indeed." The queen said. "Felix, please tell us what you have discovered."

"Your majesty." Felix acknowledged. "I managed to trace one of the Vampires that had been held in the cage that Milfoil and Yarrow spoke of."

"What..? When..? Who..? Why do we not know of this?" Demanded the second Vampire.

"Vicente! Be still!" Aurellio instructed. "Continue please."

"As I said, I managed to find one of the Vampires, his name was Freidrich. He was in hiding and it took many days and much currency to find him. He told of how Milfoil had rescued them, much the same as she had reported to us. He also told of how he had been captured."

"A Vampire would never allow himself to be captured!" Interrupted Vicente again, indignantly.

"Be still." Commanded Aurellio.

Felix continued. "Freidrich had been lured to an abandoned building at the Hythe. The place that used to be a snooker hall? He had been following a drunk woman who was on her own and very much the worse for wear. He got to the building and as he was walking past it, a lasso of silver came out of nowhere and caught him about the waist, successfully trapping his arms at his side. He said that he tried to fight, snarling and biting, but there was no enemy to be seen. The silver sapped his strength quickly and as he lay, useless and spent on the ground, two men came and picked him up between them. Freidrich said that he tried to struggle but was becoming weaker by the second. He was bundled into a van and driven off. He told me that he was taken to the place where Milfoil found him and thrown into a cage with other Vampires. In the cage next to him were other Others. Freidrich was not sure how long he was held captive, but many days must have passed. All the captives, both Vampire and Other were weakening rapidly as none had any food. They were given water to drink from a bucket on the floor. At first, he told me, they could not bring themselves to take the water but eventually, dehydration won out and they all drank from the filthy pail. Every day the same man would come and work on his computer, attend to his vials and test tubes, scribble in note books and appear to be making something."

"After a few days," Felix continued. "The man started to take one of the prisoners at a time and perform experiments. He alternated between the Vampire and the Others. He had the black balls that we have since found, and handed to the Vampires. With these victims in a separate cage, the man would crumble the balls and throw the powder over the captive. It appeared to have no effect on any of the Others, but on the Vampires, the effect was startling. You must understand that I am paraphrasing here. The language that Freidrich used was unacceptable in mixed company."

"Yes, thank you. Go on." The queen said.

"The powder appeared to affect the Vampires differently, depending on how long they had been turned. You understand that the captives spoke to each other when the man was away. Vampires that had been less than two hundred years turned, changed back to human. Now this was all well and good but the human then aged in seconds to whatever age he would have been. I am sure you can imagine the mess. The Vampires that were older turned feral. They lost all humanity for want of a better word and turned completely atavistic; snarling and tearing at their own flesh to escape. Foaming at the mouth, biting at the air, trying to rip the bars of the cage apart. Sometimes, the man would force another into the cage and make notes of how the feral Vampire annihilated them. Other times, if a Vampire had survived becoming human, he was given to the feral Vampire also. When the feral Vampire had grown weak, or damaged themselves too much, Freidrich told me, the man would dispatch them quickly with a silver lariat and a stake. There were to be no survivors. Had Milfoil not freed them, they would have died in those cages."

"Were there no clues as to who this man was?" Asked Aurellio. "I wonder also why the escapee's did not come to the hive for protection. We have heard of none of ours missing, so I wonder also where they came from?"

"Yes, it certainly bears thinking over." Frances interjected.

"I do know that the Vampires came from other hives. Freidrich told me that he was from Sunderland and was down this way visiting friends. Some that he spoke with were from Scotland, some France, others as far away as New Zealand. He told me that many had been here visiting, travelling, what have you. I suppose that taking from different nationalities, the loss would be less noticeable. As to who the man was, he never knew. One very disturbing fact emerged that I am obliged to tell, though none will thank me for it."

"Continue." Aurellio commanded with a very wary look in his eye.

"I am so very sorry but Freidrich told me that on several occasions, the man had company in the laboratory. He said that this person was very comfortable around the man and even assisted in some of the experimentation. He was quite clear that the man behaved deferentially toward this other person and he got the impression that this other person was the instigator of these crimes."

"Who was it?" Asked Ellie.

"Freidrich did not know him personally but he knew what he was."

Aurellio took a deep breath and narrowed his eyes in anticipation.

"And what was he?" He asked quietly.

"Vampire."

"No! Impossible! How dare you say such a thing?" Vicente was incensed.

"Was he absolutely sure?" Aurellio asked in a resigned and defeated voice.

"Believe me, I was quite thorough and Freidrich was horrified... loath to tell me. But yes... The other person was a vampire."

"How could a Vampire do such a thing to his own kind?" Ellie was shocked beyond words. "To any kind? But to his own kind? That is incredible."

"It is lies!" Vicente shouted. "Where is this Freidrich? I will make him tell the truth. How dare he say that a Vampire could do this thing? Where is he?"

Aurellio sat in complete shock, his head in his hands as the noise of incomprehension and shock pounded against him. He appeared to visibly shrink in front of Ellies eyes. All the majesty and assuredness that filled his expensive silk suit, drained away to leave an aged and weary man. He looked up at Ellie, watching him. Then he stood and his clothes filled out incrementally with every breath he took. When he was solid and whole again, he looked at every person at the table, lingering longest on Ellie.

"This is not such a shock to me."

"What?" came the chorus of surprised, angry and confused voices.

"I am not at liberty to discuss hive business, but I have long suspected that one of our own is working against us. I could never have imagined that this would be the

fruit of his insanity! To create and be a part of such a thing? It is difficult to believe. You may imagine that Vampires are no strangers to pain and violence..."
Here the queen flinched and Frances' mouth turned down with distaste.
"No, no strangers to the worst one man can inflict on another." Continued Aurellio. "But to turn against our own kind? That is not our way."
"But who...?" Vicente started.
"Not now." Aurellio answered. "Not until we have proof. Are you with me brother?"
"Until death!" Vicente stood and with one fist raised, struck at his own chest.
"Come, we must go." Aurellio turned and beckoned to Vicente to follow him. "Felix, you may soon regret your oath."
"I stand by my words. Call me and I will be there." Felix replied.

The rest of the meeting fell apart after the Vampires left. The queen and Frances went to sit and talk together in the garden, Felix and Fox retreated to a corner where they whispered fiercely between themselves. Sean and Andrew were left at the table with Ellie. None quite sure what to say to the other, Andrew becoming restless.
"I see you are healing quickly." Sean attempted weakly.
"Oh, yes. Thank you. I am being well cared for." Ellie replied awkwardly.
"Bloody odd that! The Vamps." Andrew squeaked. "Wonder what its all about? I should like to get my hands on one of those balls, that's for sure."
"Yes, it's lucky for us that the fairies found them then, isn't it?" Sean smiled indulgently at his brother.
"But think of the fun we could have. Are they all gone then? None left at all?" Andrew seemed disappointed.
"Yes brother, all gone." Then turning to Ellie, "my brother was wounded some time ago and it has left him a little bloodthirsty. We are not sure why, but I endeavour to keep him safe." He chuckled lightly. "Have to keep him away from the beer though."
"Oh! I'm sorry to hear that." Ellie felt completely uninterested in the brothers' domestic situation. She was deflated and infuriated at the same time because, yet again, she had no answers. Frankly, she could care less about the traitor Vampires and the crazy Elves. She had just been through the most terrifying ordeal of her life and she wanted to know why. Nobody else appeared to think it was important. So she sat with her arms across her chest and pretty much sulked.

"Ellie Belly, can you hear us?" Came the sweet voice of Bluebell. "Why are you so sad? We were scared for you, but are so happy to see you are safe again."
"Where are you?" Ellie asked them silently.
"We are at home. We are experimenting to see how far we can hear. We have to hold hands and concentrate really, really hard, but we managed to get you. Aren't we clever?"
"Yes, very clever, I am very proud of you."
"What is that dark scary stuff in your head Ellie?"
"Oh precious, you mustn't look in there, its not nice. Try and stay here, at the front with me." Ellie tried very hard to shut that part of her mind off from the girls. They certainly need not have that kind of exposure at their young ages.
"Oh, silly Ellie." They laughed. "We are not young, but we will try to stay at the front."

The three spent the next few minutes chatting with their minds and Ellie felt her spirits lift slightly.

Fox returned to the table as Felix went out into the garden.

"Decided to talk to me now?" Ellie tried hard to sound snotty.

"Ellie, I explained to you before why this cannot be. I am hurting too you know." The Elves both pricked their ears and started to pay an interest in the conversation. Ellie, aware of the listening audience, tried to change the subject.

"Do we know why I was taken, or is tonight just about the Vampires?"

"Ellie! I am shocked at you. This is an important development for the Vampires, they have a traitor in their midst and are faced with an horrific weapon that could wipe out their species! Show some perspective. And some respect!" Fox was incredulous.

"I know that." Ellie spoke slowly with anger. "And I understand that. But I was just captured and almost raped, beaten and almost killed for reasons that I cannot begin to imagine. I would be interested to know if anyone has any idea why this may be. I appreciate that in the scheme of things, it ranks pretty low on your list of priorities, but to me, it is incredibly important. Excuse me if I wallow a little in self pity!" With that, she got up and returned to the living room. She started to pack away the blankets and duvet that she had been sleeping on. She tidied up all her mess, then picked up her belongings and let herself out of the door. Nobody noticed.

That's just about bloody right! Thought Ellie angrily, as she walked down the path to the road. She stood for a moment to get her bearings then walked to the nearest bus stop to get home.

Chapter nine.

Seconds after Ellie had thrown her bag and coat on her own couch, in her own home, and stomped to her own kitchen to put her own kettle on to boil, there came a loud knock at her own front door.
Ellie took a cup from the cupboard.
There came another knock, louder this time.
Ellie took a fresh Earl Grey tea bag and dropped in into her cup.
The door knocked again, and there was a muffled voice calling to her from the other side.
Ellie leant her weight against both hands on the counter and stared at the kettle, willing it to boil faster. She chewed the inside of her cheek as the evenings events played out in her memory.
The kettle boiled. The door banged louder.
Ellie poured the boiling water over the tea bag in the cup.
The door sounded as though it would come away from its hinges, and the voice was becoming more distinct.
Ellie jumped at the noise that until then she had not fully noticed. As she jumped, the boiling water splashed onto her hand and burned her.
Ellie yelled out in pain and surprise.
Within a second, Felix was at her side, holding her with one arm and looking about him frantically, the other hand wielding the tea towel that he had snatched up from the counter.

"Do you intend to waft my protagonists into submission?" Asked Ellie pleasantly as she sucked at her injured hand and twisted out of Felix' grasp.

"I thought you were being attacked!" Felix dropped both his arms and twisted the cloth in embarrassment. "You screamed!" He told her.

"I screamed because the commotion at my door made me spill the kettle." Ellie huffed.

"Can you two keep the noise down please? I am trying to sleep here." Came the voice of Peter from Ellie's bedroom.

"Peter! What are you doing here?" Asked Ellie as she walked toward the bedroom and saw the cat laying stretched out on his back across her bed.

"It didn't take a genius to figure that you would come back here, so I got here before you." Peter said simply.

"Oh. But how did you get in?" Ellie was confused.

"Same way he did." Peter rolled over and curled into a ball. He started humming some kind of tune to himself and said no more.

"Well? How did you get in?" Ellie asked Felix. "And what are you doing here?"

"Never mind that for now, let me look at your hand." Felix took Ellies hand and bent over it, examining the damage.

"Nothing there, I do not know what all the yelling was about." He said as he roughly dropped her hand.

"Nothing? But I..." Ellie looked at her injured hand and indeed, it was undamaged. "Thank you." She said ungraciously.

"Welcome." Felix quipped as he wandered over to the living room and dropped onto the couch, making himself comfortable.

"I'll make you a cuppa then shall I?"

The Fae

Ellie and Felix sat in silence, staring at the television. Which was switched on to a programme about teen sex.

"That reminds me," Felix said switching off the television. "The queen has told Fox to keep away from you until all this has been sorted out, then they will look at the question of whether your blood is enough to counter the rules."

"Oh, okay then. Sure." Ellie replied in a distracted voice.

"I thought that you would be pleased." Felix pressed.

"Oh… yes well… of course I am its just…"

"Just?"

"Well, why couldn't he have told me that earlier instead of acting like such an arse?"

Felix chuckled. "That's one word for it." He turned and gave Ellie his full attention. "Is that what you really want? To be with Fox? Regardless of the consequences?"

"Oh, please god forgive me, but I don't know! When I'm with him, it is so perfect, I know exactly what I want. But when he is away from me, well…I'm just not sure. That makes me awful doesn't it?" Ellie was dejected. She couldn't look Felix in the eye and avoided his gaze.

"Not awful, Ellie." He said gently. "Just young. Fox is, we all are, centuries older than you. We have seen so much and lived so long." He sighed. "I do not know how Fox feels, but I know that were it me, I would wish to know of your doubts before I upended all our rules and customs. You… we, anyone cannot make good decisions without all the information. If it was meant to be, it will be." He took her hand and brushed his lips over it. "You are one of us now, regardless of your relationship with Fox and none of us wish to see you in pain. Nor to be the inflictor of pain." He added.

"Gee! That helped!" Ellie pulled her hand back and jumped up off the couch. She walked back and forth in front of the cold dead television screen. She was so distracted that she didn't see Peter come in and sit on the couch. Nor did she see him talk quietly with Felix. Back and forth she walked, unaware of her surroundings, deep in thought.

"We need to leave now." Peter told her loudly.

"Ok, thank you for visiting." Ellie replied dazedly.

"No, Ellie! Pay attention! We, all three, need to leave now." Peter insisted.

"Really?" She asked. "Why?"

"The cat that has been following you, I saw him from the window. He was sitting in the garden watching your window, come on, we need to get out of here."

"No! I will not!" Ellie stormed over to the window and threw open the sash. She looked about until she saw the cat, dead centre on the lawn.

"What do you want?" She called. "Who are you and what do you want?"

The cat cocked his head and looked her in the eyes.

"Come here please." Ellie called, "we need to talk to you."

The cat padded over to the window and looked up at her.

"Here." Ellie said stepping back and allowing room for the cat to jump in. "Come on in, that's a good boy. In you come."

Ellie stepped over to the couch, where Felix had turned to watch. Peter sat on the back of the couch, staring at the cat intently.

"Do I know you?" Peter asked.

The cat looked at Peter but said nothing.

"Why are you following me?" Asked Ellie.

The cat swung his gaze back to Ellie but still said nothing.

"Speak up." Ellie demanded. "Who are you and why are you here?"

The cat took one more look at Peter, then lifted his leg and started to clean his bits.

"Oh for gods sake!" Ellie was exasperated. "Are you sure this is the one? Is this a trick? I thought all animals talked"

"Uh! Well! I may have been exaggerating a bit there." Peter shifted position uncomfortably. "Not really all animals. Only magical ones. This must be a regular cat. He doesn't appear to be talkative at all."

"So why was he following me? Ask him Peter. You speak cat!"

"I did, he seems to think he lives here. He has a great chunk of memory missing. From what I can tell he was hit by a car and woke up outside your door. He doesn't understand why you keep avoiding him."

"What?"

"Basically." Peter explained. "You now have a cat. He doesn't remember what his name is, so you will have to think of one."

"What?" Ellie stood, mouth open in shock. This is not what she expected at all.

The cat finished cleaning and jumped onto the couch. He padded around in a circle three times, then settled into a small fluffy ball and went to sleep.

Ellie was pretty sure that she saw him wink before he fell asleep but she let it pass.

After a strained night with Felix, Peter and the odd little cat crowding her on her sofa, Ellie announced that she was going to bed. Felix informed her that he was there for the duration, so Ellie threw a blanket at him and went to her own bed at last. Ellie lay flat on her back, with the duvet pulled up to her chin. She felt herself slowly relax as the familiar sounds and smells of her room welcomed her home. Just as she was dozing, she felt a soft thump as Peter jumped onto the bed. Then a second as her new house guest made himself at home too.

The following morning Ellie was presented with breakfast in bed. Beside her as she woke, was a tray bearing a small jar with fresh flowers. Also present were three slices of thick toast, a pot of jam and a glass of apple juice.

Ellie's new guest was eyeing up the toast when Felix walked in, followed closely be a chattering Bluebell and Begonia.

"Good morning Ellie." They chorused in her head.

"Out loud please ladies." Ellie told them silently in a mock stern voice.

"Good morning Ellie." The repeated out loud.

"Good morning girls." Ellie smiled.

Both girls jumped onto the bed and gave Ellie a hug and kiss on the cheek, then swiped a slice of toast each and started to load it with jam.

Felix bent and grabbed the last piece with a smile as Mertensia walked in bearing a new plate full of steaming hot toast and a wide smile.

"Good morning sister. I am glad you are well." She beamed as she placed the new food on the tray. "Girls, mind the crumbs!" She chided.

"Good morning Mertensia. I am so glad to see you. Are you okay?"

"Me? Goodness yes, of course I am. It's you we have all been worried about. The girls here have been fretting constantly to come visit. We wanted to make sure that you were well before we invaded."

"You are always welcome here Mertensia. I cannot imagine my life without you guys in it now." Ellie smiled again.

The Fae

"And who is this?" Mertensia blushed and asked with a crooked smile, indicating the new cat.

"Well, that's a bit of a story, but it looks like he is here to stay. For a while at least."

"Oh, he is sooo gorgeous. What is his name?" Asked Begonia.

"I don't know." Ellie turned to her. "I haven't thought of one yet."

"Can we name him?" The girls asked in unison. "Can we? Oh please?"

Ellie laughed and agreed. "Of course you can. What are you thinking of?"

"Bunbury!" They said together, then looked at each other and laughed.

"Bunbury? Hmm! I like that. From The Importance of Being Earnest?" Ellie asked.

"Huh?" The girls raised their shoulders in a shrug and looked blank.

"Never mind. I think Bunbury is a fine name. Bunbury it is then."

"Woo hoo!" The girls cried, yelling and sweeping the cat up, dancing around the room with him flopping over their shoulders. Each taking it in turns to sing to the cat and chatter to him about his new name.

The morning was spent in and out of the garden. Begonia and Bluebell helped Ellie weed the flower beds then they washed their hands and helped their mother prepare lunch. Felix set the table in the garden whilst Ellie went inside to clean up. When she returned, there were sandwiches and cakes with glasses of lemonade set out prettily on the table. The sun was shining brightly and the flower beds had the fresh, earthy smell from being newly turned. The flowers were trying to outdo each other with their dazzling beauty and soporific scents. The five friends sat and relaxed at the table whilst Peter took Bunbury on a hunting raid in the neighbours garden.

Sporadically Peter and Bunbury would come back with ever amazing bounty they had liberated from other people's gardens. Bunbury tended toward worms, which he dropped clean and wriggling into Ellie's lap. He seemed to be settling in quickly and was inordinately proud of his hunting prowess, if the big grin on his whiskered face was anything to go by. Peter could pass for an ordinary cat. He had thrown off his cloak of aloofness and reverted to playful kitten within minutes of being outside with the latest addition.

"It has been centuries since I saw him behave like that." Mertensia commented. "I think that Bunbury will be good for him."

"Both of us." Completed Ellie, smiling fondly at the pair of cats scampering over the wall.

As the day drew to a close, the happy group were seated around the kitchen table, each clutching a steaming mug of thick and creamy hot chocolate. There were cake crumbs and sandwich crusts happily decorating the table along with sticky smears where lemonade had spilled from laughter and story telling exuberance. The friends were relaxed and at ease, the cares of the last few days seemed to have happened elsewhere, to someone else. The sun reluctantly set and twilight took its brief turn. The shadows started to lengthen and the cooler air bought new, elemental scents to tease their noses.

The girls had been chattering idly inside Ellie's head and she listened with half an ear as she talked with Felix and Mertensia. Peter and Bunbury came back from their bonding session and sat by the door, nose to nose, eyes closed. Ellie smiled at them and thought to herself that if every day were like this day, she would indeed be happy to live forever.

"Oh Ellie Belly." She heard inside her head. "Don't you know?"

"Know what?" Ellie asked them silently.

"You are one of us now."

"I know my angels. And I am very happy that I am, but you should remember that I am human. Even if I forget myself sometimes."

"Oh! We forgot too!" The twins said sadly.

Ellie felt a small pang at that thought and determined to put it away in the back of her mind. The queen may yet count her blood sufficient to let her be with Fox. But what if she didn't want that? How had this all gone so wrong? First she had no feelings, then she's crazy about him, now she's not sure. What on earth was going on in her head? *Maybe it was the attack,* She thought. *Maybe I'm still messed up from that. Yes, that must be it. That would send anybody to crazy town wouldn't it?*

"Ellie, what is that peculiar look for?" Asked Mertensia.

"She's in lurve!" The twins teased. "She's in lurve with Foxy Woxy."

Ellie blushed.

"I was thinking about him. I was thinking about whether my blood would be sufficient to allow us to be together. So much has happened, and so quickly, my head is all over the place. Who would have thought that I would be considering a fairy for a boyfriend?" Ellie burst into giggles.

"What is so funny?" Asked Mertensia.

"Oh, I think I know." Felix replied. "We had a conversation before about the use of the word fairy, and I think our Ellie here is well, let us just say that I may have to choke her if she does not desist." He looked at Ellie and winked.

She tried to calm her mirth but it was not easy. *Stress,* she thought to herself. *It does the weirdest things.*

The rest of the night was blessedly uneventful. Mertensia and the girls left after dinner, leaving Felix and the two cats to keep her company. They all lounged on the sofa swapping stories of ordinariness and trying to get to know Bunbury. He still did not talk, so it was agreed sadly that he was indeed a regular cat; though a very handsome one. Just in case he understood! Bunbury seemed very happy to curl into a ball on Ellie's chest and sleep. She could move him around and he would sleep through undisturbed. He didn't mind what position he slept in as long as it included contact with Ellie. The closer the better it seemed.

When it came time to sleep, Felix took the couch and the cats climbed onto the bed with Ellie.

"Peter, won't Fae be missing you?" Ellie asked sleepily.

"Trying to get rid of me now you have a new cat?" Peter asked a little sharply.

"No. No. Of course not. I just wondered that's all. Fae has had, I mean, you have stayed with Fae so long that it must be odd not having you around."

"Humph!" Peter harrumphed.

"Oh don't be like that. I meant absolutely nothing by it." Ellie scratched Peter under the chin and smoothed out his bristling whiskers. "I would be happy for you to be here forever. I just hate the thought of Fae being alone."

"Oh, she is not alone!" Peter replied haughtily.

"That's good then." Ellie sleepily snuggled down into her duvet and fell asleep.

The Fae

She felt Bunbury curl up by her chin and purr contentedly whilst Peter fidgeted and wriggled until Ellies dreams took her deeper.

Whilst Ellie slept, she went to her safe place. There on the wall sat Joachim, smiling and expectant.

"Oh I am so glad you are okay." He beamed as he jumped up and ran to embrace her.

"Me too. I was pretty scared there I can tell you!" Ellie returned the hug and twirled him in the air. "Are you always here? Are you just for me?" She asked him. Joachim laughed. "Sometimes. We are connected but I am real. I have a life outside but I know when you want me; so I come."

"How do you know? I didn't even know I was coming. I'm asleep down there. Or wherever 'there' is."

"You will remember, I promise."

"Remember what? Why can't you tell me?"

"I am bound to honour Frances. She believes that your memory will come of its own accord. Or not, as the gods will it. But I must be careful not to force you, or I could cause you damage. I don't understand really, but Frances does. What she says goes."

"Who exactly is Frances? Is she the queen of the Elves?"

"Oh no. We don't have queens or kings. Frances is like, sort of like, our spiritual leader if you like."

"Like a priestess?"

"Oh no, not at all. More like a person, or Elf, that sort of takes care of us. She is very wise and we can go to her for help, support, anything really. Like the elder in a tribe. Yes, that's a better analogy, she... we are like a tribe of Elves, and Frances is our elder."

"Okay. That makes sense." Ellie took some berries from the platter that appeared by the pond. "Whilst I am here, what shall we do? Can you show me around a bit?" Joachim jumped up and took her hand, almost dragging her off the wall.

"Come on then. It will be like old times. We can start at the woods. We used to play there lots. Come on."

As Ellie ran, hand in hand with Joachim, she felt her cares and the years roll away until she were a child again. They spent many happy hours exploring cool and shady woods, packed full of wildflowers and birds. The grass was thick and springy underfoot. They played hide and seek behind trees that reached as high as their eyes could see. They chased each other for what seemed like miles and collapsed onto the bank of a small river that snaked its way between the majestic trunks. They sat with their backs against the warm bark as their toes dipped into fresh cold water. They spoke of flowers and birds, of games and cakes, but never of pain and fear. They were happy. They were children. There was no world outside. When Ellie woke, she was refreshed and calm.

Peter jumped down from the bed whilst Bunbury stretched his back and licked Ellie's nose in greeting. She in turn ruffled his fur and gave him a hug before tucking him under her arm and making her way to the kitchen. She filled the kettle and switched it on, she opened the back door wide and lay out food for the cats putting Bunbury down in front of his dish. She dropped tea bags into two cups then went through to the bathroom to take care of business. As she was coming out of the bathroom, she

The Fae

noticed for the first time, that Felix was not on the couch. The bedding was untidy and appeared to have been slept in, but he was nowhere to be seen.

"Felix, cup of tea for you." She called out. "You woke up early! Its on the table when you're ready." Ellie wrinkled her brow wondering where he had got to, but thought little more about it as she prepared her breakfast then sat and ate.

As the morning wore on, Felix' absence became more of a concern.

"Peter, do you know what has happened to Felix? I haven't seen him all morning. He usually tells me if he is going out."

"Nope, pretty sure he will be back soon though." Peter replied whilst laying in a sun spot on the couch. "Did he say anything last night?"

"Not that I remember, anyway you were there too. Oh!" She said as she heard the garden gate close. "That's probably him now." She looked out of the back door. "Fox! Hi. What are you doing here? Have you seen Felix?"

"Hello to you too. Such a loving greeting. No I have not seen Felix, the queen is concerned and sent me to see if I can be of any help."

"Concerned about what?" Ellie asked perplexed. "What is happening now?"

"Felix got word to us that he was going to try and find out more about why you were taken and I have come to see what he knows and whether I can be of use. You say he is not here?"

"Yes, I woke this morning and he was gone. I didn't think anything of it until just now, but it's not like him to just disappear."

"Indeed." Fox stated as he entered the kitchen and sat at the table.

Ellie placed a drink in front of Fox whilst Peter jumped up and sat on the table next to Ellie. Bunbury leapt into Ellie's arms and wriggled down to get comfortable.

"Who is this?" Fox asked sharply.

"He is a stray that has adopted me." Ellie told him as she scratched lightly behind the cat's ear.

"Are you sure?" Fox' voice was laden with suspicion. Eying the cat critically he asked "When did he get here?"

"Oh let me see, yesterday? The day before? I think the day before wasn't it Peter?"

"Yep. He's a normal cat. Has no magic, can't talk at all." Peter replied as he sniffed at the biscuits Ellie had just reached over and grabbed from the counter. Ellie idly handed Peter one of the biscuits as she looked at Fox.

"Why? You look so serious. He is just a cat, we have named him Bunbury, haven't we my precious?" Ellie nuzzled the cat who purred in return, seemingly glaring at Fox. Who himself settled back in his seat with his lips compressed.

"We shall see." He said grudgingly.

"Fox?" Ellie started.

"Now is not the time for this, we have more important matters to consider."

"Of course, you are right. I just wanted to say that I have missed you." Ellie was hurt. She could not account for this complete turn of Fox' attitude. They were alone here apart from Peter, nobody would know. Of course Felix disappearing was important, but a little warmth could not hurt surely? Ellie blinked back a tear and busied herself brushing the crumbs from Peters' biscuit into her hand.

"Do you know where he went? Or who he planned to meet? Fox asked.

"He said nothing at all. We all went to bed after a lovely day and when I woke, he was gone. I had no idea he was even going out. Normally he would tell me."

The Fae

"Yes, all very cosy I am sure, but he must have said something?"
Surely Fox wasn't jealous? Would that account for his ungracious attitude toward her? But he must know that she and Felix were like brother and sister, nothing would ever come from that. Besides, it was forbidden! Oh, so was Fox. Ellie thought to herself. *"Bugger it*!

Fox, Ellie and Peter went over the previous day's conversations and events for what felt like a hundred times but they were no nearer to an answer.
"I will have to request help." Fox said reluctantly. "Can you ask the elves to join us? I will go and speak to the queen." Fox passed Ellie a tiny pink mobile phone.
"This is a phone…"
"Well duh! Really?" Ellie interrupted, examining the phone for herself.
"This is a phone." Fox continued in an overly patient voice. "When you flip it open, we will know that you need to contact us. Just say the name of the person that you wish to speak to and they will be with you. It is not, however, for chit chats and gossip. You cannot call your friends or play games on it. It is a very serious thing. Do you understand me Ellie?"
"For gods sake!" Ellie exploded. "I don't know what has come over you, but sort your damned self out and grow up! Of course I understand. I am may be a human, but I am not a bloody idiot!"
"Yes, well then. If you would be so kind as to contact the elves, I shall return shortly." With a last pained look, Fox left.
"For goodness sake!" Ellie spat. "Who in the hell does he think he is?"
Bunbury wriggled in her arms and opened one eye to stare at her.
"Sorry Bunbury, I didn't mean to wake you, its just that bloody man!"
Bunbury turned over for his belly to be scratched and Ellie was pretty sure that he smirked.
"Another one of those days I think." She mumbled to herself. "Peter. How am I supposed to summon the elves? What am I one eight, eight elf hot line?"
"You only have to call them, or visit your safe place and ask there." Peter said simply as he dropped down from the table and padded out to the garden, where he lay in the shade under the lavender bush.

Ellie closed her eyes and found Joachim chatting with Frances and another man by the lake. Ellie waved to them as she approached and the trio looked up. To her complete amazement, Felix was the third person.
"Oh my god! What are you doing here? We have been so worried, Fox has gone to the queen and I am here to ask for help in finding you, yet here you are!" Ellie gabbled in surprise. "How on earth are you here? Why are you here?"
The man, Felix, stood and held out his hand.
"Be calm sister, I am not whom you seek."
"But…But…You…" Ellie stuttered looking from the man to Frances then to Joachim. "But, you must be, you look so much…who are you then?"
"Phew!" The man blew through his teeth. That would take a whole book to explain! Let us just say that my name is James. There appears to be an emergency, so perhaps the background can wait for another time?"
"Sure, I never get answers anyway." Ellie half laughed, half pouted.
"Tell us what has happened." Said Frances, rising to join James.
James took Ellie's hand and gently led her to a soft couch that had appeared at the base of a tree. They both sat but Ellies hand remained gently clasped in James'.

101

"Well..." Ellie started, then scooted closer to James to make room for Frances to sit. "When I woke this morning, Felix was missing. He never goes anywhere without telling me. First I was not concerned then Fox showed up looking for him and then I got worried. Fox is worried too so he has gone to ask the queen for help, he told me to come and see you for help as well."

"He TOLD you?" James demanded, raising his voice and stiffening his spine. Ellie looked at him with alarm and snatched her hand back.

"Gently James. She does not know." Frances soothed. "Ellie, James is very protective of you. He finds the thought of someone ordering you around very frustrating."

"You should have seen me when I was kidnapped then!" Ellie half joked.

James stood and turned his back, his voice was strained as he said. "Had I known, that would never have happened. I am so sorry that I did not get to you."

"That's okay." Ellie said, not understanding anything at all. "So much weird stuff has been happening these last few weeks, I would not be surprised of horned toads and diamond ponies jumped out of my porridge in the morning!"

James turned back and smiled slightly. "Tell us all you can about Felix, what he said, where he has been."

So Ellie told again of the little she knew. "If I hadn't been so focussed on myself, maybe I would have a better idea of how to help him." She finished self indulgently.

James and Frances shared a look. "Yes well." Frances replied. "Now is hardly the time."

Ellie looked at her in surprise. *Wow! What was that?*

Ellie opened her eyes back in her kitchen to see James and Frances walk through the gate.

"Beat you!" She smiled at them. "I'm not sure how long Fox will be, but generally the fairies are as quick as you two appear to be."

Peter rubbed against Ellie's leg and she absently petted his head.

"Hello Peter. Long time no see." James was oddly formal with the cat. "Hey you, how are you?" His attitude changed completely when Bunbury walked in, sweeping him up and holding him against his chest. James ruffled the top of Bunbury's head and asked. "What did they call you then friend?"

Bunbury purred loudly and snuggled into James' neck where he promptly fell asleep.

"We call him Bunbury." Ellie smiled. "Looks like you have him for the duration, he is a very friendly little thing. He seems to have taken to you."

"Oh we go back a long way." James smiled, then amended, "Cats and I, cats and I go back a long way. They can tell don't you think?"

Frances gave James a look then said. "If you have quite finished, we have plans to make. Peter, what do you know? All of it this time."

Peter looked around the room uncomfortably and cleared his throat.

"I think it best if we wait for the others."

"Peter! Is there stuff you haven't told me? Why would you keep things from me?" Ellie asked in alarm. "Anything could have happened to Felix, why would you keep quiet?"

"I am sorry Ellie. I am not always at liberty to tell all that I know." Peter gave James a dirty look, "sometimes I must consider 'the greater good'!" He mimicked rudely.

"That is enough!" James spoke over him. "I will not continually enter into this every time I see you. Say no more about it."
Peter turned his back and stared out of the window, whilst James absently stroked Bunbury's head.

The atmosphere was plunged lower by the arrival of the queen, Fox and Yarrow.

"James! I did not expect to see you." The queen said frostily. "You remember Fox and Yarrow?"

"Of course," James greeted each politely and bowed before the queen. Who in turn thinned her lips in displeasure.

"You know that we bow to none, therefore we expect none in return. Please stand." The queen stiffly walked to a chair and sat imperiously. "Now, what do we know?"

"We were just getting to that." Frances interjected before James could anger the queen further. "Peter has more to tell but wished to wait for you." Here Frances looked pointedly at Peter, who cleared his throat loudly.

"Yes, well, as some know, I am companion to Fae." Here he looked at James. "And also companion to Ellie. This allows me to have a paw in both worlds as it were. After Ellie told me of the cat that had been following her." Again, a look to James. "I ascertained that the cat was no threat and told her so."

"Yes, yes, we know this. How does it help in the search for Felix?" Frances interrupted, as if to prevent James forming the words on his readily opened lips.

"Well, Felix did not believe that the cat was no threat, so took it upon himself to find out for himself. So to speak. Anyway, he followed the cat and discovered something very interesting." Another, longer, contemptuous look at James.

"And that was?" The queen asked sweetly.

"He found that the cat was a…" With another look at James, Peter seemed to shrink in on himself slightly.

"Yes?" Asked James with one eyebrow raised and an odd tone in his voice.
Ellie looked from one to the other wondering what on earth was the problem. Clearly some old grudge was being played out here, but surely Felix was more important to the both of them?

"Well, he didn't tell me, but he did say that he agreed the cat was no threat. He did also say that whilst looking for the cat, he saw that Ellie was still being watched and followed."

A shiver ran down Ellies back and she saw James and the queen stiffen and look at her. Her breath had caught in her throat and choked back a small cry.

"But I thought they were dead." Ellie whispered. "Didn't the vampires kill them?"

"Yes, they killed the ones in the house with you, but they were there on the orders of another." The queen spoke slowly. "I wonder…"

"Carry on," James told Peter, "what else?"
Peter looked from the queen to Frances then settled his gaze on James.

"It was definitely the Gnomes that took Ellie, but Felix believes that some other group were involved." Here he glared at James with pure hatred.
James bristled and opened his mouth to reply, but Frances placed her hand on his arm in a calming motion, and he stayed silent.

"I think you are inferring here that we, the Elves, would wish harm to our daughter." Frances uttered through clenched teeth as she rose to her full height. A bluish haze appeared around her and seemed to make her hair and eyes crackle with electricity. She all at once seemed terrifying and powerful.

Ellie sat back further in her chair and squeezed her hands tightly together. She opened her mouth to say something but the words were not there.

"That is not for me to say!" Sniffed Peter with as much vitriol as his tiny furry frame would project. "I am merely repeating the findings of 'our' brother Felix"

"I don't understand any of this." Ellie cried. "What is happening? Are you saying that elves would hurt me? Why would they? They have no reason to."

"No reason at all." Said James softly as he looked at Ellie. He came and stood behind her chair and stroked her hair. "I swear that, by all that is holy, you're life is more precious than my own to me."

Oddly, Ellie believed him. "But why?"

"Not today." Whispered James in her ear.

"What else?" Yarrow interjected, seemingly in an effort to break the tension.

Peter sniffed loudly and made a show of smoothing his bristled whiskers before continuing, slowly.

"Felix followed the person following Ellie but lost them around the Mersea Road roundabout. They were on foot and quite swift. Felix ran down the steps to the underpass but could not see which way they went."

"Were there any other creatures there?" Asked the queen.

James hands tightened on Ellie's shoulders.

"He said that he could not be certain but he thought not. Normally the traffic is too heavy there to encourage wild life, so we believe that it would have been noticed. Any way, after running about trying to pick up the trail, he gave up and returned here. Felix had said that he would try to follow them again last night. When I woke and he was gone, I presumed that is what he had done."

"Why did you not accompany him?" James asked tersely.

Peter turned and looked long and hard at James.

"Because," he spoke deliberately, "my job is to guard Ellie, to keep her safe."

"And I thank you for such a fine job so far!" Spat James.

"Look!" Ellie shouted. "I don't know what the hell your problem is." She pointed at James. "But Peter, in fact everyone here, has gone out of their way to protect me. I don't know you. I don't know why you feel you can come into my home and act like a total jerk. Show respect to my friends or leave. Bloody elf or not! I will not tolerate any more crap than I have to."

Out of the corner of her eye, Ellie saw a small smile at the side of Frances' mouth.

"My deep, humble apologies." James dipped his head in contrition. "I will endeavour to leave my feud outside your door."

"Yes… well, thank you." Ellie sat forward in her chair and huffed. "So what now? We still know nothing and Felix is missing."

They all sat and mumbled ideas to each other, each as unsuitable as the next. The tension between Peter and James was still palpable, but they avoided each other sufficiently enough to be useful.

"Oh! Jeez! Bloody idiot!" Ellie jumped up so fast her chair tipped back and fell with a loud clatter.

"What is it?" Demanded James.

"I don't know why I didn't think of this before. How stupid can I be?"

"What?" Asked the queen.

The Fae

"My safe place. Don't you see? My safe place. If I can see myself from my safe place, surely we can see Felix from his? Can't we?"

"Well, oh, yes, I suppose. Hmm! Well, I should think we could." Frances thought out loud. "Has he been there do we know? I am not quite sure that I would know where his is. Does anybody know?" Frances looked around at everyone.

Peter looked blankly back at her, James and Yarrow looked as though they were searching their memories, the queen looked confused and Bunbury, who had been sunning himself at the window turned over and knocked the washing up liquid bottle over with a thud.

"Oh, I see." Said Frances. "Well, we must give it our best attention. See what we can come up with. It seems to be our best chance yet." She then sat back in her chair and Bunbury jumped up to perch on her shoulder. She absently rubbed her head against his as he purred loudly. "Oh, good boy." She mumbled.

After several hours of nothing happening and no further ideas being put forward, Ellie started fussing about with pots and pans, preparing a meal for all to share.

"One more thing though." She wondered aloud. "If we do find Felix' safe place, can we get there? I mean, can we go from one to another?"

"Yes." James answered. "We were in yours because at one time you invited us…"

"James!" Frances warned.

"Is that really relevant now?" He asked in exacerbation.

"Yes. It is. No more."

"Okay." Ellie continued. "Keep your secrets. So… and lets pretend someone else is asking this okay? Have any of you been invited to Felix' place before?"

"Good question." Frances replied. "I have not. James?"

"Nor I." He looked at the fairies but they just stared blankly back at him. "That's a negative then. We have to tell her." He turned to Frances.

"No. Let me think." Frances left the room, deep in thought with Bunbury still sleeping in her arms.

Several long, drawn out minutes passed with the group staring at each other vacantly around the table. Frances' footsteps could be heard walking back and forth in the living room. The occasional mumble and half snatched tune made its way to the kitchen, causing questioning looks all around.

"Here is what I am prepared to do." Frances re-entered the kitchen and pulled out a chair. "I will tell Ellie a little of what she needs to know…"

Everybody looked up quickly.

"Just enough mind you. The safety of our son exceeds that of all else at this moment. I pray that I am doing the right thing. But I cannot help wonder if this will cause more pain." She sat in the chair and looked at Ellie, kindly. "If everyone here could give us some time."

Everyone stood and left the room. At the door, James held back, a questioning look on his face. "Do you think I should…"

"No my son. Join the others. I will call you when we are through."

James smiled encouragement at Ellie, his face conveying strength and fortitude. Then he too left.

"My daughter." Began Frances, taking Ellie's hands in her own. "This is not my wish. My wish is for you to remember without intervention, but James is correct. The safety of Felix over-rides my wishes. What I am about to tell you will raise even

105

more questions in your mind. It may also jog your memory, but one thing is for sure. This will bring you pain. Are you sure you wish to continue?"

Ellie looked deep into Frances' eyes seeing compassion and pity struggle with love and fear. She took a deep breath.

"Felix risked his life for me. If I cannot do this, I dishonour him and myself. I am afraid. This seems to me to be something fearful, but I must. Do I want to? No. But I will. I have known Felix a few days and the whole of my life. I must do this."

"So be it." Frances sat back and sighed. She appeared to be reluctant to start. "Oh daughter. My beautiful daughter. When you were a small child, you used to visit your safe place as a refuge against the pain and suffering that awaited you in your life. Whilst there, you and Felix played together with Joachim and were mostly inseparable."

"That must be why our bond is so strong. It makes sense now, I could never understand why I felt such familiarity and love for him."

"Quite so. You spent many years locked away in your place, visiting your life only when you had to. Such was the despair that followed each visit, I wanted to forbid your returning there at all. But you cannot live completely in your place, you must revisit your life, else madness can overtake you in the world outside. Imagine a body with no consciousness. It would be terrible."

"Like a catatonic person?" Ellie asked, beginning to understand.

"Yes, some catatonic people are actually locked away in their safe place and wish not to return to their bodies. I could never allow that for you, so I permitted you to go back from time to time. I hated it but it was necessary."

"Okay, I can't say this jogs any memories and to be fair it all sounds crazy. But, I have seen so much lately that crazy is normal. Please, tell me more."

Frances sighed and struggled to continue.

"Felix and Joachim became your whole world. You were so young and refused to grow. I think you chose to be a child so that... Oh, that is for another time. What is important is that you were safe. You would play in each others places, flitting between the three like little butterflies. It was a joy to see you so happy. Of course, Felix and Joachim stayed children with you, but in the world, they grew. They began to know why you were there and the nature of their play changed. They became fiercely protective of you. Your every wish was theirs to fulfil. I might add that you became a little brat at times, but they did not care. They loved you deeply. Then one day, you did not return. The boys waited and waited, but you never went back. Joachim eventually stopped going to his own place altogether in case you returned and he missed you."

"This sounds so strange to me." Ellie began. "But even though I have no memory of this, it still seems true. Does that make sense?"

"Yes child." Frances stroked Ellies' face, looking into her eyes as though searching for the memory.

"I thought only fairies could chose when to stop ageing." Ellie commented. "I am not fairy, so how could I chose to stop?"

"Your body aged in the world but in your safe place you chose to be a child."

"So everybody, human and Other has a safe place?"

"Well, ehem! Actually..." Frances looked panicked.

"Well?" Ellie was now becoming suspicious. "All people regardless of race, have a safe place. Right?"

The Fae

"Oh daughter, I did not want you to find out like this."

"What? What did you not want me to find out?" Ellies' voice was deceptively calm, she was reigning in the turbulent emotions that were battling to explode. "What?"

"You are not human."

"What! Are you insane? Of course I am human. I remember all of my life, from a toddler to now. It stunk like hell, but it was mine. I was there. I remember it. I am human."

"I am sorry that you did not get to remember on your own. This must be such a shock for you." Frances was visibly upset but Ellie was furious.

"I have had my life turned upside down, been attacked and kidnapped, almost raped, my home invaded, no privacy, I think I've lost my job, I find I can visit make believe worlds, I have met fairies, elves, goblins and bloody Vampires and now you tell me I'm not human? Frances, you are a nice lady and all, but you have gone too far."

Ellie stomped into the garden where she found herself standing in the middle of the patio, staring at nothing, her head spinning and feeling sick. She flopped to the ground and sat with her knees pulled up under her chin. She had tears in her eyes and just wanted everything to go away. She sat for several hours before she noticed that the sun had been replaced by a harvesters moon. The stars were twinkling like they were the most important thing in the universe and she was cold. The air had turned much cooler. Bunbury had managed to squeeze between her knees and her chest without her noticing and was snoring away contentedly. She lowered her stiff, aching legs and painfully stood up. Clutching the cat she re-entered the kitchen to find Frances exactly where she had left her, sitting at the table. Ellie sat in the chair opposite and looked at Frances long and hard.

"I don't want to discuss the human not human thing at the moment. I am not ready for that. I don't really know if I believe it, but that is for another time. The important thing here is Felix. We have to find him. Now, I have no recollection of his safe place, I don't know where it is or if indeed I could get in if I could find it. Or even where his mirror is come to think of it. But I have to try. So what do we do now?"

Frances looked relieved and wiped her hands over her face in a scrubbing motion, as though washing herself clean of worry.

"Okay," she started, "I believe that it is quite simple. When I wish to visit your place I think of you and then I am there."

Ellie raised one eyebrow suspiciously. "And that's it?"

"Well yes. Sort of. I think of you and kind of say to myself that I wish to visit you in your safe place, and then I am there, with you."

"But don't you have to picture the place or something?"

"Yes, it helps. I always do but it is not a conscious thing. I am sure that if you just concentrated on Felix, that would be sufficient."

"What? Like how he looks sort of thing?"

"How he looks, feels, what he means to you. Just let the essence of Felix fill you."

"Uh huh!" Ellie was still very sceptical. "Well, I guess I may as well give it a try." She closed her eyes and let her thoughts of Felix fill and expand within her mind. She thought of his smile, his twinkling eyes, his snippy comments, the way he smelt, his sense of humour, his beautiful voice; and wished with all her heart that she were with him.

Chapter ten

Ellie opened her eyes to a warm, dark place. It felt like she was in a room with no light and obstacles hidden in the unseen spaces. She put her hands out to feel for any obstructions and to aid her balance, then started forward very slowly. Ellie slid her feet along the floor and tried to circumnavigate any unexpected objects. When she reached as far as she could go, she ran her hands over the high flat surface in front of her that she assumed was a wall. Reasoning that at some point she would find either a door or a window, she crab walked the surface, hands tentatively stroking, until she found what had to be a doorframe. Feeling the change in texture, she used her hands to search for the handle. Once found she twisted and turned the knob but to no avail. It would not open. Ellie was starting to feel closed in and slightly panicky. She began to tug and bang on the door, anxiety rising, terrified she would be trapped.

"Help, help, let me out! Please, let me out!" She sobbed to nobody. Ellie slid to the floor and started to cry. An overwhelming sense of futility washed over her. All the events from the last few days, all the anxiety at Frances revelation, the fear for Felix and worry about Fox threatened to drown her in a sea of self pity and hopelessness. She sobbed.

After a while, sniffing up the unattractive mucus and wiping at her swollen eyes, Ellie decided that she could not sit there forever and stood up. Her legs were frizzing with pins and needles but she welcomed the discomfort. At least that was real. *Come on you stupid sod*, she thought. *Think*! Ellie felt the door again, tried the handle again. "Stupid!" She said out loud. "Key?" Ellie returned to the handle and felt beneath it for a key. There it was! She turned the key and opened the door, wondering briefly why the empty room would be locked from the inside.

As she stepped through the doorway, she was greeted by the most welcoming smell of freshly brewed coffee. She followed her nose down a short corridor and into a wide, airy kitchen. The worktops were waist high, clear of clutter and made of a dully polished pale wood. The sink was an old fashioned Butler and she remembered seeing a similar one at a ridiculous price in a reclamation yard once. The cooker was a large, clean but well used Aga, with two pans bubbling contentedly on top. The left hand oven door was slightly ajar, allowing a buttery, nutty, apply smell to ooze out. Ellies' mouth watered. There was a long, scrubbed pine table with years of scratches and dents creating a restful and welcoming conversation area. The mismatched chairs sat tidily beneath and gleamed with the colours of a rainbow. Upon the table was a hand carved tray, china coffee pot, jug of milk and bowl of sugar lumps, a pair of silver tongs nestling inside.

"Hello." Called Ellie. "Is anyone here? Felix? Where are you?"
She received no reply so walked through the kitchen to the large French windows and pushed them open. The faintest of breezes caressed her still clammy skin and cooled her instantly. The roses that surrounded the door frame were in full bloom and greeted her with their rich, evocative scent. Ellie inhaled their sweetness and looked about. The garden was wild and exciting. Tall richly green trees along the borders created a verdant frame for the swaying hollyhocks and foxgloves. Full and fragrant rose bushes surrounded a pond that glinted through the foliage. Snatches of lilies could be seen nestling on the sparking water. Butterflies bounced gently in the air above clumps of lavender and brightly coloured wild parrots settled in the branches of

The Fae

plum and apple trees, calling to each other coarsely. The grass was short, neat and vivid; as though painted by a child, dots of yellow buttercups staking a claim with splashes of independence. A stone path meandered along one side of the lawn and drew her eye toward the back of the garden, where a crumbling wall supported an aged gate that stood slightly ajar.

Ellie followed the path to the gate and pushed it open. Beyond the garden were a series of fields, rough gorse bushes marking their boundaries. Large black birds swooped and dove in the hazy sun, rising to the clouds with fat worms and grubs in their beaks. The earth of the fields freshly turned and pungent with fertilizer. Looking about, Ellie could see no life other than the birds and a few horses in a distant paddock. She returned to the house.

Walking back through the kitchen, Ellie was faced with a hallway which held seven doors. Each door was closed bar the first, so she started there. The room contained a large utilitarian table and six chairs. A display case against the far wall stood empty save for a blue china bowl. The windows were large and framed with pale blue curtains that echoed the faint blue rosebuds on the faded wallpaper. Upon the table sat a folded cloth in the same blue as the curtains, Ellie assumed this to be the tablecloth. In the centre of the table were plain glass candelabra with fresh white candles reaching tall and straight. The floor was of bare boards. Pale rugs in blues, pinks and creams set the muted colours gently against the pine of the floor. Ellie retreated and tried the next door.

The next room was full of oversized furniture arranged around an inglenook fireplace. The large rounded armchairs were plumped high with cushions and throws, the sofa worn and comfortable looking, sported an assortment of books, one was open as though left for a moment by the reader. A jam jar upon the mantle held fresh daffodils and tulips. Ellie left, closing the door and tried the next. Door after door opened onto a room of domestic comfort. Each held a snapshot from time; with parlours and sitting rooms from across the ages. The last door however, was locked.

Abandoning the locked room for later, Ellie ascended the bare wooden staircase. Each stair sang as she placed her foot, a creak, a squeak, a groan, gently protesting her weight. A ghost of a memory teased at the back of her mind but she let it lay undisturbed. Hoping it would grow. The banister was smooth and warm, devoid of paint but patina'd from countless palms. At the top of the stairs, the hallway echoed the one below, with seven closed doors and one open. She started at the door closest to her and by time she reached the seventh closed door, all she had seen were empty, dusty neglected rooms. As she reached the open door furthest from the stairs, she heard a faint stirring from inside and the hackles on her neck stood up. She clenched her fists and drew in a great lungful of air. Her nerves resonating from memories of her kidnapping, she rushed into the room, fists raised in feminine aggression.

"Who's here? Let me see you! Come on out you bastard." She spun in the centre of the room but saw nobody. Feeling foolish, she lowered her arms but her fists remained clenched. The room held a high four poster bed, piled haphazardly with feather pillows and cushions. They were all covered in a pale sea green fabric that shimmered like taffeta. The bed was made and a change of men's clothes were folded neatly at one end, atop a clean looking white towel. One corner of the sheet was

The Fae

turned down and looked very inviting. Ellie felt tiredness wash over her as she stood there. Shaking it off, she continued to look about the room. There were ornate French inspired wardrobes and dresser, all neatly closed and polished. Upon the dresser sat a comb and mirror in a silver filigree covered ivory. Ellie stepped over to the mirror and picked it up. Looking in the mirror intently, she tried to see past her own reflection.

"Felix? Are you in there? Felix?" She called gently into the glass, feeling slightly silly. "Felix? Where are you? Can you hear me?" She called again.

She thought she heard a small sound coming from somewhere in the room and she stood perfectly still, listening. Ellie held her breath hoping to hear better and strained her ears to pick up the slightest noise. Nothing but the beating of her own heart. For a few more seconds, she stood, listening, then placed the mirror in her pocket and turned to leave the room.

As she was closing the door, she definitely heard a slight noise from under the bed. Ellie's heart thumped and her skin crawled, she felt very afraid. Closing her mind to any unpleasant possibilities, she quietly lowered herself to her knees and moved forward toward the bed. Holding her breath, and her nerve, she grasped the fabric of the valance and pulled it up quickly before she could change her mind. Nothing happened. Ellie leaned forward onto her other arm and peered under the bed. There, at the far side, was a pair of huge, brightly glistening blue eyes.

"Come on out!" Ellie called. "What are you doing? Who are you?" She scooted back a little keeping the valance high. "Come on. I won't hurt you."

Ever so slowly, the eyes inched closer until Ellie could see a nose and some blonde hair. The hair surrounded a beautiful face that then revealed a small, thin body. As the body grew arms and legs, Ellie saw that it was a small girl. She softened.

"Come on out sweetheart. I won't hurt you. Come on out."

The small girl slid out from under the bed and stood shaking in front of Ellie. She had long tangled blonde hair, a dirty and torn blue bibbed dress over a grimy looking yellow tee shirt. Her legs were thin and knobbly with grey socks pooled about her ankles. Her feet had on black plimsolls with rips and mud.

"What is your name?" Ellie asked gently.

The girl looked at her with huge wet eyes and said nothing. The only noise, the chattering of the girl's teeth and the beating of Ellie's heart as it fought to calm down.

"Come, let's sit on the bed." Ellie held out her hand to the girl whilst she sat on the edge of the bed. The girl meekly followed suit.

"My name is Ellie. Can you tell me yours?"

Still no reply.

"I am looking for Felix. He is my friend and I am not sure where he is. Have you seen him?"

The girl's hair stuck to the tears and snot on her face as she vigorously shook her head no. She stared up at Ellie with eyes the size of saucers and Ellie could see fear and apprehension struggle in their wetness.

Ellie took both her hands and held them gently.

"Is Felix your friend too?"

The girl hesitated a moment then nodded.

"Would you like to help me look for him?"

Again the girl nodded.

"Come on then." Ellie slid off the bed and the two left the room hand in hand.

The Fae

Having searched the house from attic to basement, they returned to the kitchen still not having found Felix. The girl had not spoken but Ellie kept a light and cheery dialogue to pass the time. She realised that by chattering she had kept herself from exploring the dark imaginings that crowded the corners of her mind. She was completely lost and had no idea how to find Felix. And who was this child? Why was she here? And so afraid? Where could he be?

"Phone!" Ellie yelled, patting her pockets.

The small girl yelped in fear and hid under the table. Ellie crawled under with her and gently prised her hands away from her ears.

"I am so sorry that I frightened you. That was very silly of me. I should not have yelled. It's just that I remembered that I have this phone. I might be able to call him and see where he is. Do you see?"

The girl was having none of it and started to wail in fear. The pitch grew in intensity and soon it seemed as though there were a speeding ambulance under the table with them, such was the resonance from those small lungs.

"Oh, ssh! Ssh! Quiet honey, I am sorry, I didn't mean to scare you. Come; let's see if we can call Felix. Here. Do you want to try?"

Ellie handed the small pink phone to the frightened girl and together they huddled under the kitchen table as Ellie explained how to use it.

The girl gave her a teary but withering look as if she were an imbecile and flicked open the phone.

Realisation flashed in the little girls face as she became aware that she would have to speak, so she handed the phone to Ellie who took it back with a smile and spoke into the handset.

"Felix please."

There followed a short ringing tone, then the connection was made.

"Hello?" Came Felix' voice. He sounded as though he were running and out of breath. "Poppy? Is that you?"

"No. It's me, Ellie."

"Ellie? What are you doing there? Is Poppy okay?" He sounded very worried, and breathless.

"If you mean this beautiful little girl that is sitting here with me, then yes. I believe that she is okay. A bit frightened maybe. Felix, where are you? We are all so worried and nobody knows where you are."

"Are you both at mine?"

"Yes, I came to look for you and found Poppy here under the bed."

Felix sounded puzzled and his voice was strained.

"Right. Look. I can not come there at the moment. I am uh... well, in a bit of a situation. But wait there please and I will get to you when I find a safe place."

"A safe place? Felix are you in trouble? Felix, what is it? Felix?"

But Felix had closed the connection.

"Well, little Poppy." Ellie said.

Poppy looked at her and appeared less guarded. Perhaps now she believed that no harm was meant.

"Well Poppy, Felix said he will be with us soon as he can. What say we go get a drink, and then you can show me around? Would that be okay?"

The Fae

Poppy nodded her assent and led Ellie back to the kitchen. Ellie poured herself a cup of the delicious smelling coffee and Poppy took some milk in a pink glass with flowers painted on it.
They sat at the table and Poppy watched every move Ellie made. She reminded Ellie of a newborn kitten that is alert to every possible threat. Ellie felt sad that she had caused this, but nothing she said seemed to take it back. They drank their drinks in silence. The only sounds were the birds outside and the gentle rustling of leaves in the breeze. Ellie tried to imagine who this child was, but it was beyond her. *Perhaps she is Felix's Joachim?* She concluded.

When they had washed their cup and glass, they entered into the garden to explore. Poppy took Ellies hand and pulled her around to the side of the house. Here, against the weathered red brick, climbed a full and fragrant wisteria, its gently swaying stalactites of mauve petals brushed their faces as they passed. Flowers of every kind covered the ground, trees reached to the skies and wildlife cheeped and chirped, burbled and barked its infinitesimal melody. Dragon flies buzzed on the breeze and bees hummed along, adding their voices to the choir. Poppy and Ellie explored every inch of the garden. The saw ants carrying a leaf, ladybirds basking in the sun, worms burrowing into richly scented soil and fledgling sparrows beg for food. They passed a pleasant hour walking amongst the lavender, disturbing the cluster of butterflies that had alighted amongst the stems. The lay between the rose bushes and watched the frogs hopping across the pond; a small and hungry stalk watching from the far bank in anticipation.

Ellie gave up trying to engage Poppy in conversation and they soon settled into a companionable silence. They lay on the grass near a bright patch of deliciously scented wall flowers and played with a pack of cards the Poppy had discovered in the kitchen. Poppy was currently beating Ellie hands down in their seventh game of gin rummy, and Ellie was in no way trying to lose on purpose.

The sun seemed to hang low and fat, skimming the tree tops; in no hurry to set. The air was warm and alive with the hushed sounds of nature. After being beaten eight times in a row, Poppy appeared to relent and they busied themselves by lying in the grass with their eyes closed, each apparently lost in their own thoughts. Hornets buzzed about their business and bees bumped about the flowers. The petals preened and turned themselves to the warming welcome of the suns final rays.

"Ellie? Poppy? Wake up, I can not stay long." Felix's voice came from a long way off and Ellie reluctantly swam back up to awake.
"Oh, where have you been?" asked Ellie. "We are all so worried. You look a fright, what's up?"
Felix sat on the grass beside the two girls and Poppy climbed into his lap. She looped her arms around his neck and snuggled against his chest. Her eyes were still watchful but she appeared to be more relaxed now that Felix was there.
"I am sorry that I frightened you. I got called away and there was no time to let you know." Felix looked over his shoulder as though expecting to see someone there. "It would be best if you return and tell the others that I will come when I am able. It should not be too long now."

The Fae

"This is all very mysterious my love but please can you tell me what's going on? I'm going to be grilled when I get back and have to be able to tell them something." Ellie tried to dazzle him into submission with her fluttering eyelashes.

"Do you have something in your eye? Here, let me look." Felix leant forward and raised Ellies' eyelid.

"No, it's okay thank you." Ellie said, slightly embarrassed. "It's gone now. Please Felix, what is happening?"

Felix looked away, out over the pond. It seemed as though he were conducting an inner dialogue. Ellie knew instinctively to stay quiet.

"Alright." He conceded. "I will tell you enough, but I cannot tell you all. It is a matter of security."

Ellie stiffened and opened her mouth to complain.

"I am not concerned about you. I believe that I could trust you with my life, which in effect I am doing. However, there are others that must not have too many details. There are things happening that need to be investigated. Yes, alright..." Felix had noticed Ellie's look of impatience. "Well, suffice it to say that I am helping the Vampires at present. You may remember that I swore to aid them? Well, they have called me on it. That is what I am doing at present. Only it has all ... Anyway, yes, I am helping them. Aurellio and I are currently looking into the black ball problem and are trying to gather as much information as we can. It is proving to be a bit sticky but we should have some answers at least by tonight. I promise to come to your house when I am done. Is Peter there still?"

"What? Oh, yes. Yes, he is." Ellie was thrown for a moment.

"Good. Yes, that is good. Please tell him that I have requested that he not leave your side. At all."

"Felix, you're scaring me."

"Well, that is good. You need to be scared. And alert, keep your eyes open at all times." Felix looked over his shoulder again. "I must go now. Remember, keep vigilant, I will be back as soon as I can."

And then he was gone. No puff of smoke, no glittery scene fade, just gone. Poppy dropped the few inches to the floor with a bump.

Ellie scooped her up and held her close.

"I have to go home. But what shall I do about you?" She asked. "Do I leave you here alone? No, I can't do that. I know that it is safe here, but I wouldn't feel right about it."

Poppy jumped up and twirled around, her hands above her head as she pirouetted, a big smile on her face.

"Are you telling me that it is okay to leave you here?" Ellie asked cautiously.

Poppy nodded and continued to twirl.

"I'm not really sure I should. But then, this is a safe place. Where else would be safer? Oh, if only I had thought to ask Felix." Ellie stood and took Poppy's hand. "Well, if you are sure."

Poppy gave Ellie a quick hug and ran off dancing.

Ellie opened her eyes.

Frances was holding her hand and looking at her hopefully.

"Did you find him?" She asked. "Did you find Felix? Is he alright?"

The Fae

"Yes I found him, yes he appears to be alright. He left in such a hurry that he didn't have time to let anyone know. He is helping the Vampires. He told me that they called him on his oath and he had to go. He said that they are investigating the black balls. He is with Aurellio." Ellie realised that she was exhausted. She slumped back in the chair.

"Frances? Who is Poppy?"

"Poppy? I do not know, why?"

"Oh, no reason." Ellie got up and went to the bathroom to splash water on her face. She not only felt very tired, but was feeling lethargic and morose. She was worried about Felix no matter what he had said, and she believed that he needed her help in whatever it was he was up to. And what was he up to? He had told her nothing that they didn't already know. She believed that he was with the vampires, but why couldn't he have told her something useful? Why was everything so sodding complicated all the time? Why was everyone so mysterious? What ever happened to straight forward? And how was she going to help him?

"Frances," Ellie started as she re-entered the kitchen. "How do I find the Vampires?"

"What?" Frances sputtered her mouthful of tea all over the table.

"The Vampires? How do I find them?"

"You do not!" came a voice from the garden.

Ellie looked up to see James closing the gate and stepping into the kitchen.

"Why not?" She asked petulantly.

"Need we spell it out? They are Vampires!" James replied in an exacerbated voice.

"I only want a quick word with them. I think there is something wrong, and I need to be able to get hold of Felix. They can tell me where he is." Ellie implored.

"Then eat you." Frances mumbled, wiping at the tea on the table. "Vampires aren't known for their generous spirit and sense of giving. Ellie, they are voracious appetites on legs. They will feed on you in a heart beat and then throw away your desiccated carcass. They were civil when you met them because it was in their interest to be so, but that is not their usual attitude. They are the most dangerous creatures on earth. Even if we knew where they could be found, which we do not, there is no way we would tell you. It would be suicide!"

"Uh, that's not strictly true." Interjected James.

"James! How could you!" Frances was dumbstruck. "I cannot believe this!"

"Look, I am sorry, truly I am, but this is Felix. Ellie, tell me how you feel." James sat down and indicated that Ellie should do likewise.

"Whaddya mean?" She asked.

"You said that you believe something is wrong. Tell me about that."

"It's just a feeling, that's all."

"We trust our feelings Ellie. We have them for a reason. They are sometimes like an early warning system. Come, tell me."

"Okay. Well, when I saw him in his safe place, he was very distracted. I suppose that could be normal, after all he is with Aurellio, but... Well, he kept looking over his shoulder as if there were danger coming up on him. He said he was okay, but he didn't look or sound it. He made me very nervous, oh and he left in such a rush that Poppy fell over, that was odd."

"Who is Poppy?" Asked James.

The Fae

"Oh, nobody." Ellie was confused, again! Why did nobody know who Poppy was. She must be important to be in Felix' safe place, but nobody had heard of her. *I guess Felix must be keeping her secret for some reason*, she thought to herself.

"Look." Ellie started, "I believe that Felix is in some kind of trouble. I don't know what or why, but I do know that I can help. I only need to ask the Vamps where he is, I will be in and out in seconds."

"No!" Frances declared.

"Okay." James said.

"James! No! You cannot let Ellie do this. It is madness." Frances was so upset, her face had paled and her throat was working hard to swallow.

"Mother." James took Frances hand and stared into her eyes, pleading silently. "This is Felix. I must. I will go with her. I promise to keep her safe."

"You cannot make that promise. I forbid you to do this. It is insanity." Large crystal tears rolled down her cheek and plopped onto the table. "James please."

"Mother I must. He is my son."

Ellie looked up sharply.

"Your son? Felix is your son? Yours and Fae's son?"

"Yes."

"But he doesn't know. Nobody knows. How do you know?"

James gave her a disgusted look.

"I'm sorry, I didn't mean that. I am just amazed. You and Fae? Wow! I never saw that coming."

"Did you not?" James smiled sadly at Ellie. "Did you not think I was him when we first met?"

"Of course, you look alike, I see that. But I guess I thought it was just the beautiful thing. Tell the truth, I had forgotten about it. Wow! You! Felix' dad. Who would have thought?"

"Yes well, if you are quite through?" Frances interrupted, wiping her eyes with a lace handkerchief that she had pulled from the sleeve of her dress. "Son or not, I forbid you to do this. That is my final word."

The rest of the day passed excruciatingly slowly. Ellie cleaned and tidied the house, fed Bunbury, made dinner, took a bath, all the usual things. But they all felt wrong. They felt as if she were outside watching herself perform the tasks. There was an otherness about the day that grew stronger as the sun grew lower. Frances reluctantly left after dinner. She had said little throughout the day, but kept casting glances at James as if she expected him to disappear in a puff of smoke. James, in turn, was remote and distracted. The pressure of knowing that his son was in trouble appeared to weigh heavily on his shoulders. He moped about the house, getting under Ellie's feet and on her nerves.

Moments after Frances had left, James' whole attitude changed. He became focussed and alert. He strode to the bathroom and threw open the cabinet. Grabbing plasters, disinfectant and medical tape, he stuffed them into his pockets.

"Get your coat, we are leaving now." He said to Ellie.

"Where? Where are we going? James?"

"Come on, the sun is going down soon, if we are lucky we should get there before it fills up. It could be dangerous if there are too many, however this early we should be okay."

"What are you talking about? Where are we going?" Ellie was growing excited as she pulled on her summer coat, she had an inkling but surely he wouldn't disobey his mother would he? Could he?

"Oh, I think you know. Come on." James held open the door and they hurried through. Ellie buttoning her bright pink coat as she went.

"This is serious Ellie. You have to listen and do as I ask. This will be the most dangerous thing you will ever do. We are going to the hive, of our own volition, and hope to heaven that we do not get killed. If we are lucky, we will get some answers. If we are not, well… it was a pleasure knowing you."

Ellie looked at James trying to decide if he was being serious or not. She decided he was and tried to damp down her rising fear.

The Fae

Chapter Eleven

Ellie and James arrived at a grand looking detached house set back from the road. The nearest neighbours were some distance away and the place was surrounded by trees; black in the night. Every window was lit from within and the house appeared cosy, warm and welcoming. Ellie shuddered involuntarily.

"Are you ready?" Asked James.

"As I will ever be. Come on, lets get this thing rolling." Ellie puffed up her chest and started toward the front door, James a half step behind her.

She reached out and took hold of the large brass knocker and lifted it high, ready to slam it down and announce their presence. She felt a moment of doubt and settled the knocker gently in its rest. Silently berating herself, she lifted the knocker again and rapped loudly on the door. They both took a step back so that they were not crowding the doorway and waited with held breath as a slight whisper of movement was heard from the other side.

Ellie took a deep breath and reached behind her to squeeze James' hand; for her own reassurance more than his. James squeezed back then let go as the door opened.

In the lighted hallway stood a small child of about seven or eight. He had black hair that shone in the artificial light, his eyes were large and wide, great pools of infinite blackness. Ellie looked closely but could detect no humanity there, nor her reflection. She sighed.

"How may I help you?" The child asked.

James stepped forward into the light cast by the interior. "Aloysius, is your father here?"

"Oh, good evening Uncle James. How kind of you to call, if you would be so good as to step inside, I will go and tell him that you are here." Aloysius stepped back and held the door open for them to enter. Ellie lifted her leg to step inside, but James touched her arm and stopped her.

"Oh, it is such a beautiful night, and we have been cooped up in the car so long. I think we will take the air whilst we wait if you do not mind." James said, perfectly reasonably.

Aloysius' eyes narrowed and he hissed under his breath in displeasure.

"As you wish." He remarked through clenched fangs, closing the door.

"Wow, that was intense!" Ellie whispered. "I really wanted to go in there."

"He was trying to glamour you."

"Glamour? What's that?"

"Its where a vampire can hypnotise you into doing as they want. Its how they feed mostly. Saves time fighting I guess. Makes people easier to overcome."

"Yuk!" Ellie shivered.

The door opened again and a tall, ginger haired man stood in the entrance. It was the man that Ellie had first seen at the meeting with the queen; the scary one.

"Oh, oh!" Ellie said under her breath.

"A pleasure to see you again Ellie. James." The Vampire said, inclining his head in greeting.

"Dougal." James half bowed. "Kind of you to receive us. I appreciate that you must be very busy. We only want to ask you a couple of questions, then we will be out of your way."

"As you wish." Dougal spoke down his nose, if you would follow me, we can at least be comfortable."

"Ah..."

"Really! How rude. Do you expect me to invite you into my home then eat you?" Dougal was annoyed. Maybe.

"Sorry if we seem a little reluctant, I was just remembering the last time we met." James sounded very enigmatic, but Dougal appeared to understand and his demeanour softened slightly.

"Of course. Upon my oath, you shall be safe here tonight, as will young Ellie here."

"Thank you." James entered the house, much relieved. Ellie followed very closely behind him, bumping into his back whenever he paused his steps.

They followed Dougal to the back of the house, where there was a large glass walled conservatory. There were thick blinds rolled up to reveal the stark moonscape outside. Ellie guessed that during the day, those heavy blinds would be tight shut. Or would they? Was that another myth? Did Vampires burst into flames and die in the daylight? Did they have reflections in mirrors or was that another Hollywoodism? Ellie realised that she was nervous as her mind was wandering off again.

Once inside the conservatory they saw a long banqueting table running the length of the room. There were piles of gift items on the table. A large pile of i-pads, another of perfume gift sets, yet another of jewellery boxes. Around the table were five people, three men and two women. The boy, Aloysius was under the table, opening a large cardboard box with a wickedly sharp looking knife. Ellie started to call out and warn him before she remembered who he was and where she was, so kept quiet. The men and women around the table glanced up and casually sniffed the air but showed little other interest in Ellie and James. That was reassuring. The people were sorting the contents of the large cardboard boxes into piles. They chatted softly amongst themselves but their hands were busy at all times.

"May I ask what they are doing?" Ellie asked.

"They are putting together care packages." Dougal answered.

"Oh. Was there another disaster then?" Ellie asked in all innocence.

James and Dougal looked at her for a long moment. James appeared horrified, Dougal had a small smile tugging at his mouth. Ellie opened her mouth to speak again but James squeezed her hand, hard.

"Perhaps we could get started?" He asked.

"What can I do to help you?" Asked Dougal as he settled himself into a large spherical chair that was suspended from the ceiling. With one foot on the floor, he spun the chair to face a rattan couch along the wall. "Take a seat." He instructed.

Ellie and James sat.

"We are worried about our brother Felix. We believe that he is helping Aurellio with some matter, but Ellie here and indeed myself, are worried that something is wrong. We believe that they are in some trouble and we need to find them."

"What sort of trouble?" Asked Dougal as he stroked his thigh with a fingertip and stared directly into Ellie's eyes.

"We are not sure, we just know that something is very wrong." Ellie supplied.

"Are you suggesting that Aurellio has in some way caused harm to Felix? That Aurelio would contravene the oath that was sworn?" Dougal appeared to grow in his chair. His back straightened even more and his fangs slipped past his pale, bloodless lips, his voice became sibilant and his eyes narrowed into slits.

The Fae

In her peripheral vision, Ellie saw the other Vampires stop working and tense. Ellie felt her hackles rising.

"No, not at all. I have no definite information, just a feeling. I believe that Felix and indeed Aurelio are both in trouble. Please, can you help? Do you know where they went?" Ellie pleaded.

"As it happens, I do." Dougal smiled benignly. "I spoke with Aurellio shortly before they left last night, they were going to the dwelling of a Gnome. It is believed that this Gnome has information about the death balls and they went to, ehem, ask them to share their knowledge." He licked his lips unconsciously and had a faraway look in his eyes.

"Oh, good. Do you know where this Gnome is?" Asked Ellie.

"I did hear Aurellio say that they were going to..."

At that moment, there was an almighty crash and glass flew everywhere. A fist sized gritty black ball landed next to Dougal and he jumped up, knocking the chair swinging. He scrabbled backwards away from the ball just as another came flying through the window and shattered on his brow. Fine dust and lumps of grit powdered around him and where it touched his skin, it seemed to sizzle.

"What have you done?" Dougal screamed at James as he began to twist in on himself and moan in pain.

"Nothing. I have done nothing. What is this? Who is doing this?" James shouted. His voice was lost amongst the smashing of glass and screaming of vampires. As Ellie looked around, she saw fine black dust covering every surface and every body in the room, her and James included.

"Oh god! We have to get out of here." Ellie screamed and pulled at James. "Now!"

James stood rooted to the spot, his mouth open, his eyes seeing too much. Ellie pulled at his arm, trying to budge him. James stumbled a step then realised that he was in trouble and started to look about wildly.

"What is this? Ellie? What is this? What is happening? Oh my, look." He pointed to Dougal. Where once his skin had been white as marble and smooth as stone, Dougal's face started to warm. The colour deepened by degrees, from icy white through pale blue, to blush of pink then to ruddy. His lips filled out and turned a kissable peach. His eyes, that moments before were black and soulless, were now a light hazel and very confused.

"Where am I?" He asked. "What is this... where am I?" Dougal looked about him in alarm and, frightened, dove under the table. He pulled his knees up to his chest and buried his face in his crossed arms atop them. He shook with fear and moaned a low keening that attracted the attention of Aloysius. The boy stood, bent over at the waist, his face forward, sniffing the air. His eyes were tears in his flesh, red and focussed. His hands were claws that swung at his sides, his knees bent and ready to spring. He sniffed the air in front of him and became still. His once black and shiny hair had become grey and dusty, great clumps falling to the ground. Aloysius took a step toward Dougal and breathed in deep through his mouth. Saliva pooled then fell from his lips, unnoticed. Dougal rocked back and forth, oblivious to the danger, keening and rocking. Rocking and keening. Aloysius stepped nearer, sniffing and growling from deep within his throat.

Ellie pulled at James.

"We have to go. Move. Come on. Now!" She whispered urgently.

James was transfixed, the scene before him played out in grisly repetition around the room. Some were dazed and bewildered, colour in their cheeks, confusion in their eyes. Others were feral, growling, snarling, hungry.
Ellie pulled at her friend. "James, please. You must come." She whispered between the tears. "Please."
James looked at her, incomprehension on his face.
"What? I don't... What?"
"James, please, come with me. We will die if we stay here. Please." She begged.
James took one faltering step, then another. Gradually they made their way to the door they had entered through. Ellie looked back behind her and saw Aloysius leap onto Dougal and sink his teeth deep into his cheek. She saw him shake his head like a dog and tear a chunk of flesh clean away, toss it into the air and then swallow it. Blood ran down his face as he bent to bite again. The room was filled with snarls and screams. Blood flew with pieces of vampire. The room was a charnel house.
Ellie and James ran for the exit.

Throwing open the front door, Ellie stumbled down the step, pulling James behind her. She recovered her balance and ran to the car they had left parked near the gate. James plipped the remote and unlocked the doors as they reached them. They slammed the doors closed behind them then sat, staring out of the front window, unable to move. Howls and screams could be heard faintly through the glass and they turned to look at each other.
"Oh my god! Oh my god! Oh my god!" Ellie repeated. She stared at James, his hair had come untied and was stuck to the sweat and grit on his face, his eyes were wild and darting. His mouth hung open and he was panting, each breath a shudder from his soul.
"What did we just see?" He asked in a small voice. "Ellie, what did we just see?"
Ellie took his face and wiped the hair from it. She stroked his arm from shoulder to fingertip, over and over, absently. And she told him.

When she had finished telling James all that she knew of the black balls, she sat back and closed her eyes. Visions of the carnage they had witnessed played on the inside of her eyelids like a horror movie. Over and over she saw Aloysius tear into Dougal and swallow his flesh. She shuddered and opened her eyes. Sitting upright she glanced at James.
"Swap seats, I'll drive. We need to get away from here. There is no telling what the feral Vamps will do when they are done in there."
James shook himself back to the present.
"I am okay. I can drive. Let's go."
He put the keys in the ignition and turned them. The car came to life and he flipped on the lights.
"Did you see that?" He asked. "Over there, did you see?"
Ellie strained against the black night sky.
"Probably one of the Vampires. We should go." She buckled her seatbelt and sat back in her seat.
James continued to look out of the window for a few moments more then drove the car through the gates.

As they turned right into the road, Ellie saw an old Volkswagen parked across the road. She peered through the window.

"Stop! Stop the car."

She had the door open and one foot out already before the car came to a halt. She ran over to the parked car and cupped both her hands on the window, she leant into them and struggled to see into the dark interior.

"I fucking knew it!" She fumed. "Bitch! I fucking knew it!"

Ellie stomped back to the car and threw herself into her seat.

"Mind telling me?" James asked politely.

"I want you to drive to Greenstead please. There we will wait for the owner of that car to return home and then you and I are going to kick seven shades of shit out of the bitch that owns it. That okay with you?" Ellie was apoplectic.

James started the car and with a quick worried look at Ellie, drove as directed.

They had been waiting for about ten minutes when James asked…

"So? Are you going to tell me what we are doing here?"

"That car, the one we are waiting for? It belongs to my boss's girlfriend. I recognised it, then when I saw her handbag I knew for sure. She must have been involved in the raid on the Vampires. The one where you and I could have been torn limb from limb and sucked dry. That has pissed me off a little."

"Okay, with you so far. Why though would your bosses girlfriend want to attack a Vampire hive, or for that matter, even know of a Vampire hive?"

"Because my sweet, stupid boss is dating a Gnome. She stinks, I don't see how he can stand it. She is such a creepy cow too. Should have seen how she kissed up to him when Felix and I found her at the…Stupid! Stupid! Stupid! Of course! Felix! She would know where he is. Okay, change of plan. When the bitch gets home, we find out where Felix is, then we kick nine shades of shit out of her." Ellie announced.

"I thought it was seven shades?" James teased.

"Longer we wait, the higher the interest." Ellie smiled back.

Just as they were beginning to think Scarlett would never return home, her headlights swept past them and turned into the driveway. Ellie and James bounded out of the car and pulled open the drivers door of the Volkswagen. Scarlett sat, mouth open in surprise, keys in hand.

"Hello dear." Ellie smiled. "Hope you don't mind, but we have popped round for a chat. Come on, out you get, let's get that kettle on."

"You? You? How did you..? How did you know where I live? Why are you here?" Scarlett stuttered in surprise.

"Lets just say a little birdie told me. Oh and the envelope on your dash with your name and address on it. Very careless that. You never know who might be looking. Come on old girl, out you get."

"I don't know what you want with me. It has nothing to do with me, you losing your job. I will call the police if you touch me." Scarlett tried for aggressive but fell short at scared.

"Oh, I'm going to touch you alright. A lot. And you are going to tell me everything I want to know. Starting with, why are you seeing my boss?"

They made their way into Scarlett's' house. The first door in the passage led to a comfortable looking living room, so Ellie pushed her in there. They took a seat with Ellie perched on the arm of the chair opposite Scarlett.

The Fae

"Now then." Ellie began. "How long have you been seeing Jack?"

"That's none of your…" Scarlett began but Ellie cut her off.

"You don't seem to understand how this works. Let me explain it to you. I know who you are. I know what you have just done and I don't much like you. Now," she held up a finger to halt interruptions, "you will tell me why you are seeing Jack, and then you will answer my other questions. Be assured, I will kick the shit out of you, however, the severity of the kicking depends entirely on the quality and expedience of your answers. Ready?"

Scarlett looked at her, then James. Her face a rictus of self righteous anger.

"You have no idea who you are messing with here human!" She snarled.

"On the contrary, Gnome, I know exactly who you are. And for the record? I am not human! Now, can we get on? Thank you." Ellie leant forward, her knee just touching Scarlett's.

"Why are you seeing Jack?" Ellie asked, pressing forward so that her knee moved Scarlett's apart slightly, subtly threatening her exposed vulnerability.

"Because I love him." Came the unexpected reply.

"What?" Ellie laughed. "Love him? Puhleese! You expect me to believe that?"

"I don't care what you believe, it's true." Scarlett pouted and tried to close her legs.

"We will come back to that." Ellie smirked. "Where is Felix?"

"Who?" Scarlett raised her eyebrow and feigned innocence.

Quick as a flash, Ellie's hand shot out and slapped Scarlett across the face. A large welt started to turn a vivid red before she had bought her hand back.

Utter shock registered on both James and Scarlett's face. Ellie herself was astounded, she had never done anything like that before in her life. It was as if her hand had a mind of its own. She decided to go with it.

"I will ask you again. Where is Felix?"

"I don't know who you are talking about!" Shouted Scarlett. "You have me confused with someone else."

Ellie slapped her again in the same spot. Scarlett reached and cupped her cheek gently, tears in her eyes.

"I don't know. I swear."

"Why were you at the Vampires tonight?"

"What? Vampires? Are you crazy?"

Ellie slapped her again, in the same spot.

"I saw you throw some of the black balls into the house." Ellie lied. "I saw you leave the building and scuttle back to your car. I ask you again. Where is Felix?"

"I don't know, I swear. I don't know!" Scarlett was shouting and snivelling.

"Please excuse me a moment." Ellie stood up and pulled the scarf from around Scarlett's neck. She then used the scarf to hog tie Scarlett on the couch. "I shall be back in a moment, don't go anywhere."

Ellie beckoned James to follow her.

They stood in the kitchen, cradling a cup of shop brand instant coffee each, talking in whispers and peering through the serving hatch occasionally to make sure that Scarlett was where they had left her.

"I don't know how to proceed." Ellie was saying to James. "I've never hit anyone before in my life and much as I enjoyed it, I don't believe it's getting us anywhere. I

The Fae

can't just keep slapping her. It will get old very quickly. What do you think?" She looked up at James.

"Uhm, well, I don't know. I've never had to torture someone before. I'm not really sure how you go about it."

"For crying out loud James! This is our only lead to Felix. Man up will you? Think!"

"We could threaten her." He offered unhelpfully.

"I thought we had been doing that." Ellie replied, taking a sip of her coffee.

"No, I mean, we could threaten to turn her over to someone really bad. Someone that would scare her." He said.

"That's good. Who?" Ellie asked thoughtfully.

"I'm not sure. Who would a Gnome be afraid of?"

"You're asking me? You are the bloody fantasy creature, I'm just a normal person. How would I know? Couple of weeks ago, you guys didn't even exist!"

"Okay, yes. Fair point." James mused. "Hmm. Who would a Gnome be afraid of?"

They stood sipping and thinking, occasionally looking through the hatch, but no new insights came.

"Well we cannot stay here all night can we?" Grumbled James. "We cannot very well untie her, say we are sorry and poodle off home now can we?"

"For crying out loud James, you are one useless prat, do you know that? It's your son we are trying to find, show some bloody initiative why don't you?"

"I can hear you in there you know!" Came the voice of their hog tied prisoner. "Why don't you just let me go? You don't have the balls for torture, this is pretty much a waste of all our time don't you think?"

"She's right you know." Whispered Ellie. "I can't do it. I don't think I could get information out of a speaking clock. But we can't just let her go can we."

"Can still hear you."

"Shut up!" James called through the hatch.

"Oh, what a numpty! Bloody phone. I have the phone. I can ask Fox." Ellie reached into her pocket and pulled out the small pink phone. She flipped it open and asked to speak to Fox. The phone rang. And rang. And rang.

"You have reached the fabulous Mr. Fox. Please leave a message and I will get back to you as soon as I am able. Cheerio."

"For crying out loud!" Hissed Ellie as she left a message for Fox. Something about useless, emergency and arsehole.

"I think he is still avoiding me." She mumbled.

"I cannot imagine why." James quipped. "You being such a charmer."

"Oh shut it. Let me think, who else? Do you think I should call Fae? After all, he is her son and she might know who to contact."

"No, I don't think that would be a good idea. Fae is very fragile, this may be difficult for her to handle. I think it best if we keep her out of it as long as possible."

"Okay. Who then? Oh! Yarrow and Milfoil. I met them briefly, they know about the balls and stuff, maybe they can help?" Ellie looked at James hopefully.

"Worth a try." He said encouragingly.

Yarrow and Milfoil both arrived after Ellie's confusing phone call. She apologised again for calling them, explaining yet again that they didn't know who else to call.

Telling them for the umpteenth time that she wasn't very good at torture but Scarlett was their best lead.

"Yes, yes, we understand." Milfoil said. Again. "Yarrow, a quick word outside? Do not want the prisoner listening in do we?"

"I've heard quite enough for a lifetime thank you very much." Came Scarlett's bored voice from the living room.

Yarrow and Milfoil stepped outside and left James and Ellie alone again.

"More tea?"

"Sure why not."

Ellie set the kettle to boil. Again.

"Could I have a drink please?" Came the voice in the living room. "Dying of thirst in here."

Yarrow and Milfoil stepped back into the kitchen. Their faces grave.

"We have spoken and decided that there is only one course of action open to us." Yarrow said. "It is regrettable, but we should hand the Gnome over to the Vampires." There came a high pitched squeak from the living room. Ignoring it, Yarrow continued. "As fairy, we are unable to inflict pain no matter how deserved. So the only avenue left is to hand her over to someone who has no such constraints."

"You can't. I mean it! You cannot give me to the Vampires. Do you have any idea what they will do to me?" Screamed Scarlett. "Ellie, please, don't let them do this."

"I have no choice." Ellie shouted back. "We need that information, this is the only way." She looked at the cup in her hands and saw the surface ripple.

"Ellie. Ellie. I will tell you everything. Honest. Everything. Just please don't feed me to the Vamps. You saw what I did? They will destroy me. Please!" She started to sob uncontrollably.

"I have to go." Ellie rushed out of the house crying. James followed behind her.

In the car, Ellie sat and sobbed.

"I don't know that person. I hit another human being. I wanted to hurt her, to smoosh her into the ground. Who am I?" She buried her face in her hands and cried. James pulled her to his chest and stroked her hair.

"Ssh! It's okay. You didn't do it."

"But I did James. I hit her. A lot. And I liked it! What does that make me?"

"It makes you someone who will do anything for family. It makes you a brave and formidable woman."

"Oh, if only you knew! The family I come from were…well lets just say that love, solidarity and honour were completely unknown concepts there. They would have let me rot in hell before lifting a finger. Sometimes I think they did. My life seems to have started the day I met Fae, everything before is growing pale. Thank god."

"You have no idea how special you are." James soothed. "Tonight, I do not know what happened. It has been one crazy night, but it has not affected who you are. The things we saw will have left a mark on us, especially you, but its only a mark. We can wash it off."

James sat and stroked her hair until she fell asleep, whispering to her of fairies and elves, of darkness and light, good and bad. She did not dream.

Ellie awoke stiff and painful in James' arms. He was carrying her toward her bed. She felt a brief moment of uncomfortable panic as he lay her down and kissed her head. But he pulled the duvet over her and left her to sleep. She turned to her side and drew her knees up. A soft thump landed by her head and Bunbury was pawing at the pillow making himself comfortable. He finally stopped fidgeting and curled up under her chin to sleep. Within moments, Ellie had joined him in slumber. Still she did not dream.

Chapter twelve

Yarrow proved to be an amusing companion and he made an excellent cup of tea. He had Ellie laughing for most of the day but he never lost sight of the gravity of Felix's disappearance. Peter and Bunbury had returned and slunk off to another room. They both had very guilty looking faces but Ellie left their secrets unexplored. Milfoil had called by to drop off a large casserole dish full of delicious smelling vegetables in a cheesy sauce that they all three dipped thickly buttered crusty bread into and ate whilst they talked. After thrashing the problem around for an hour, Milfoil excused herself, she had to get back to the hospital as her shift was due to start.

At about mid afternoon, Fox arrived. Ellie had sensed a shadow in the door frame, looked up and saw him standing there, scowling.
"Fox!" She exclaimed. "How long have you been here? Did you get my message? Felix is missing and we can't find him. I was hoping that you may know where he is." For some reason, Ellie felt very nervous and her words rushed over themselves; tumbling from her lips in a breathy torrent.
Fox stared at her for a moment then said, "I was here when he went missing Ellie. Remember? What has come over you?"
"Really? It all seems so long ago. I struggle to keep track of things sometimes. Okay. Well, have you heard any more? Has anyone seen him? Or even Aurellio? Surely the Vamps must be worried about him."
"The Vampires are not known for their caring or worrying natures. I am sure they probably think he got staked." Fox said curtly.

"Look here Fox." Ellie spat. "We need to sort this out once and for all. I have no idea what the hell is going on in that fairy brain of yours, but can you number one, speak to me with a little courtesy and number two, let me know why you seem to be so all fired pissed off at me?"
Fox looked at Yarrow who in turn made his excuses and left the room.
"I think you know what is bothering me." Fox told Ellie. "I have been ordered by the queen to stay away from you."
"And yet here you are." Ellie sneered. "Does that also mean being rude and offensive when you do have to see me?" she asked.
"I am not. I am merely trying to obey my queen. It is proving difficult to stay away when you appear to court such trouble." Fox huffed.
"When I..." Ellie was incensed. "When I court trouble? A few weeks ago I was just a normal person, now I am aufait with Fairies, Gnomes, Elves and sodding Vampires. Give me some bloody credit! I think that given the fact my life seems to be in constant jeopardy, plus the fact that I was tortured and almost raped, I think I am doing quite well. Don't you?" She stood and gripped the edge of the table to stop herself from jumping over it and throttling him. "So, basically, what you mean is that you are sorry you kissed me, sorry that you broke your precious fairy laws and no longer have any feelings for me? Right?"
Fox looked straight in her eyes "If you wish."
Ellie clenched her teeth to stop the pain pouring out.
"Then I shall make this easier for you. Do. Not. Come. To. My. Home. Again. Say what it is you came to say then get out."
"I came to see Yarrow actually." Fox spat back archly.

The Fae

Ellie hid away in the garden whilst Yarrow and Fox talked in the kitchen. She busied herself pulling weeds and dead heading flowers, occasionally wishing she could dead head a certain Foxglove. Ellie was so immersed in her anger that she did not see Yarrow enter the garden and sit watching her. She wiped at the tears that fell with the back of her dirty hands and smeared garden across her cheeks. She saw a ladybird alight upon a petal and had an overwhelming urge to squash it between her fingers. She reached out and the bug hopped onto her hand. As she lowered her pinched fingers toward it, she felt a hand around her wrist stopping her. She looked up to see Yarrows' face inches from her own, a look of pity in his eyes as he removed the ladybird from her and gently blew so that it could fly away. Yarrow kept a light hold on her wrist and led her to the garden chairs where they both sat.

"I do not know what words will soothe you." Yarrow said softly. "I am not familiar with relationships. Milfoil and I have been husband and wife for so many years that I have little memory of the anguish you feel. I know that Foxglove is in pain also but I am sure that does nothing to alleviate your suffering. The queen has forbidden him to see you. The question of your being human is too great an obstacle to overcome it would seem. It is unprecedented. We are such a small and shrinking race that we must do all in our power to preserve our lines. Marrying outside could cause irreparable harm. I see in your eyes that this is of little importance to you at present, perhaps ever, but it is all I can offer you by way of comfort."

Ellie looked at this strange, beautiful creature who knew nothing of her and who was clearly out of his depth but who wished to offer her something of himself.

"Thank you Yarrow. I know that you are trying to help. I'll be alright, I just need time to find a box in my head to lock this into." She sniffed and wiped at the last remaining tears on her face. "What did he say? Did he have any news on Felix?"

"Some." He replied slowly.

Ellie became immediately anxious.

"What has happened? Is he hurt?"

"No, no, nothing like that. At least as far as we know. The queen heard from Marcellus, who sent a messenger this morning. Aurellio and Felix were investigating the Gnomes as we now know. They followed them to a farm on the outskirts of town where it appears that they have some sort of base. At least it had a lot of them there so it was assumed it was a base of some kind. Well, apparently Felix and Aurellio were hiding at the back and listening in on the meeting inside when they were spotted and fled. They were chased for some time on foot and then captured."

"Oh my god! Are they okay? What can we do? How do we help them?"

"The queen and Marcellus will meet tonight to work out a plan of action, until then there is little that we can do." Yarrow shrugged his shoulders in defeat and stared morosely at the flower bed.

"Wait a minute. Hold on." Ellie jumped up. "How do we know this? Where did this information come from?"

"What do you mean?" Asked Yarrow looking up.

"Well, if Felix and Aurellio were captured, who told Marcellus?"

"Good question." Mused Yarrow. "I imagine they must have had somebody else with them." He guessed.

"No mention of anyone else before. I wonder who it was. And, why didn't they try and save them? Who will be at the meeting tonight?"

"As far as I know, it is just the queen and Marcellus."

"Isn't that dangerous?" Asked Ellie.

"I do not think the queen would agree to meet if she felt threatened in any way."

"But remember at that first meeting? Marcellus was openly disrespectful to the queen, if he felt confident doing that in front of all of us, why would he not feel confident enough to attack her if they were on their own. Or indeed if they will be alone. I really don't trust him. He gives me the creeps." Ellie shuddered and sat back in her chair. "I think we should follow and keep an eye on things."

"What?" Yarrow nearly choked. "What are you suggesting? That we spy on the queen? Are you serious?"

Oddly enough and much to her own surprise, she was.

"I am." She said. "Who else do you think could help?"

"I am not sure that this is such a good idea." Yarrow worried. "What if we are caught?"

"Well, what's the worst that can happen? The queen is angry and yells at us a bit. Surely that is nothing compared to what might happen if this is a trap of some kind?"

"Sure, if it is the queen that finds us, but what if it is not her but someone else? What then?"

"I imagine we would die." Ellie said quite calmly, even though her stomach was in knots and she wanted to be sick. "I know that Felix would move heaven and earth if it were any one of us. And could we really live with ourselves if something happened to the queen and we had done nothing?"

"Okay, you are right. I just do not feel very comfortable disobeying her like this."

"Did she actually say that nobody is allowed to follow her and keep a look out?"

"Well no, of course not."

"Then you will not be disobeying her will you?" Ellie smiled triumphantly.

Yarrow left shortly after to see if he could find anyone else that could come with them to keep an eye on the queen. Whilst he was gone Ellie had an idea.

"Begonia, Bluebell! Can you hear me?" She called out with her mind, concentrating as hard as she could. "Girls? Can you hear me? It's Ellie."

"Hello Ellie Bellie. How are you today? We missed you, you know, mommy said that we can come and visit soon, are you up for a visit? We know that you are very busy and that you have been a bit poorly lately, but could we? Visit we mean. Could we Ellie Bellie?" The girls were breathless in their excitement at being called telepathically by Ellie.

"Girls, you are welcome any time you like. I love having you come visit with me. Listen, I have a question for you. It's very important. Is that okay?"

"Of course." They chimed back. "Anything."

"Okay." Ellie dove straight in and asked, "can you hear other people or is it just me?"

"What do you mean?" Asked Bluebell.

"When we speak inside our heads, like now, you can hear me as if we were speaking out loud right?"

"Yes. Right" Begonia replied, interested.

"Well, let's say that it was a regular day and we were not together, can you hear inside other people's heads? Do you hear what they are thinking?" Ellie felt the girls pull away in alarm, suddenly unsure where the question was going and fearing that they were in trouble.

The Fae

"No, no my darlings. I am not cross and I promise that I will not tell you off, but this is very important. Felix needs our help and I may know of a way of us being able to help him. But I must know if you can hear other people."

"If we concentrate really hard we can." Bluebell said cautiously. "We have been practicing a little but it feels very wrong when we did it. Why do you need to know? How can that help Felix?"

Ellie felt awful for what she was about to say, but believed that she had no other choice.

"I believe that Felix is being held prisoner somewhere. The queen is meeting with a Vampire later tonight to talk about rescuing him but I think that the Vampire is dangerous and cannot be trusted. I believe that he may want to harm the queen."

The girls sucked in their breath and Ellie felt their thoughts go into a panicked free fall.

"It's okay." She soothed, "I could be wrong, I probably am wrong, but I want to follow the queen tonight and keep an eye on her. I thought that if you could hear others, you might be able to help."

The girls' curiosity had started to overcome their panic.

"How do you want us to help?" Asked Begonia.

"Ah!" Ellie hesitated. "That is the difficult bit. Firstly you see we would need your mother's permission. That means that she would need to know that you can speak to each other telepathically."

"Oh no! Oh no! We could not let mother know. Oh no! We could not."

It took a lot of coaxing and a lot of soothing, but eventually Ellie managed to secure the girls permission to share their secret with their mother.

"But you have to tell her." Insisted Bluebell.

It was agreed that the girls would ask their mother to call on Ellie as soon as possible and bring them along.

"Well, I must say that this is all very intriguing." Mertensia said as she arranged herself at Ellie's kitchen table. "The twins were very insistent and also very secretive. I have no idea what this is all about." She picked up a cherry biscuit from a plate that Ellie had baked whilst waiting for them to arrive. She had been so nervous that she found herself making cookies and cleaning. Her nerves had not yet abated and she found the prospect of telling Mertensia about the twins very unsettling.

"It is alright Ellie. We have though about this and we feel that mother should know. We hate keeping secrets from her." Begonia soothed silently inside Ellie's head.

"Okay." Ellie took a deep breath. "The thing is. Well, it's… you know that Felix has been captured right?"

Mertensia nodded, a half smile on her face as she listened and nibbled at the biscuit.

"Well, what it is… The queen has a meeting tonight. Alone. I mean alone with Marcellus and I really don't trust him. I believe that he intends to harm our queen and well, we have to do something don't we?"

Mertensia smiled, "But what do you suggest we do?" She asked politely.

"Erm, well. I need to borrow the girls." Ellie spat the words out quickly in case they stuck in her throat and choked her.

"I am sorry my dear. I do not understand. You want to borrow my girls? Whatever for?" Mertensias smile seemed a little stiff now, incomprehension clouding her eyes. "What could they possibly do? They are only small."

The Fae

"Yes. Yes I know. I promise that I wouldn't even dream of asking if I had any other way of ... well, it's for Felix you see? He may need us and I really think that there may be trouble tonight if nobody keeps an eye on the queen and Marcellus. I think he is up to something."

"Well, yes, I understand all that." Mertensia put down her biscuit and gathered her girls to her. One under each arm. "What do you think my babies can do exactly?"

"Mother, please may we help?" Begonia spoke inside her mothers head. "We know that we can be of use."

Mertensia looked at Begonia who had not moved an inch. Her lips were closed and no sound had come from them.

"Please mother." Joined Bluebell.

Mertensia whipped her head around and stared at her other daughter.

"I ugh! I... Well, I don't know what to...so you are telepathic? How long have you..?" She seemed completely at a loss for words. "Bluebell? Begonia? How long have you known?"

"About a year now." Answered Bluebell inside her mothers head.

"Out loud please, this will take a little getting used to." Mertensia looked somewhat perplexed. "Why on earth did you not come to me and say something? You must have been so scared." She hugged her daughters close to her and kissed the tops of their heads. "Ellie, how do you know?"

"Because we can speak to each other that way." Ellie shrugged. "the girls are much stronger than I am, they seem to boost each others signal if you know what I mean. I am very new to this, I think I can only hear these two. I don't even really know if I have the gift myself, or can just hear the twins." Ellie indicated the little girls who were clinging to their mother with a mixture of relief and trepidation.

"Are you cross with us mother?" Asked Begonia.

"Cross? Why on earth would I be cross? I am a little surprised that you did not tell me, but never cross." She stroked their hair as she spoke and the girls seemed to relax. The hardest part was over.

Ellie explained what she wanted the girls to do and Mertensia sat for a long time staring into space, apparently thinking. Eventually she came to a decision.

"Right well, here is what I will agree to." She started, looking Ellie square in the eyes. "Firstly, the girls can help..."

"Yay! Oh mother..." The twins broke in.

Mertensia held up her hand for silence and continued.

"The girls may help but there are conditions. First, I will go with them, we will sit in the car and they can listen from there. That way, we can get away if necessary. Second, any sign whatsoever of trouble and I take them away immediately and third, if I think that they are hearing anything that could harm them, I will take them away." She looked at Ellie. "I am sure you know what I mean."

"I do." Ellie said sombrely. "I am so grateful and of course, any sign whatsoever and I want them out of there too. Thank you Mertensia. I think we have a good chance of keeping the queen safe and maybe even getting a lead on Felix."

They sat and discussed details whilst waiting for Yarrow to return.

Some time later, Yarrow came back and with him were James and A tall heavy set man with blue black hair and bright green eyes. He had a full nose over curved lips and high, sharp cheekbones. He wore a pair of black jeans and a purple tee shirt. On his feet he wore a pair of battered plimsolls that had a small tear where his big toe was pushing against the fabric.

"Ellie, Mertensia, girls." Yarrow greeted them. "You all know James, this is Sean. He is an Elf and has agreed to help us out tonight."

Sean inclined his head and his green eyes twinkled brightly.

"Pleasure to be meeting you." Came a melodic Irish accent.

Ellie explained the role that Mertensia and the twins would be playing and Yarrow stared at the girls with undisguised curiosity.

"Well!" He finally said. "Well! I did not expect that. We have not had a telepath amongst us since old mother Forsythia died, and here we have two! Well!" He was clearly taken aback by the news.

James and Sean smiled at the girls and allowed them to climb up on their laps.

"Thank you so much for coming." Ellie said. "I suppose that we should talk about how this is going to work. Yarrow, did you manage to find out where and what time the meeting will be?"

"Yes. It will be at midnight in the band stand at Castle Park. Where we first met you I believe?"

"A hundred years ago and yesterday!" Ellie smiled. "Okay, that gives us time to go over what we need to do, and allows the girls to get some sleep. Mertensia, do you want to take them home? Or they can sleep in my bed until we are ready to leave?"

"Here! We want to stay here." The girls chipped in. "Please?"

"I think that will be alright. Let us get some food cooking, then you two can take a nap. Let me see what you have in here." Mertensia opened the fridge and started rummaging about.

As they all sat to eat at the table, Sean told them a little about himself.

"I am here sort of on my holidays you could say. I am from Dublin, born and made there, have lived there for hundreds of years, but I arrived here in Colchester about a month ago. I decided to visit after meeting Yarrow here on facebook. We got talking, realised we had a lot in common and he invited me over."

Ellie burst out laughing.

"Facebook? Are you serious?"

"Yes. Why not facebook? Do you not use it?"

"Well, sometimes, but you are an Elf! I just cant imagine Elves on facebook. Do you have your own groups?" She couldn't help but laugh.

Sean looked long and hard then decided to smile, he must have realised that she meant nothing by her outburst.

"I will have you know," he continued in a flat tone, "that I have over three hundred and sixty friends."

Ellie looked at him to see if he was serious and he winked. Great thick black lashes briefly brushing the ivory skin of his cheek bone. Then he laughed. His green eyes twinkling brightly.

"Sure it has been a great visit so far, and when your man Yarrow here asked if I fancied a little outing tonight, I thought and why not?"

"Well I'm very glad you could join us. We don't really know what to expect, hopefully nothing, but I just don't trust Marcellus. If we can find out anything to help Felix, that will be so much the better. Anyway, thank you. And you James, thank you for coming too."

James nodded but had a faraway look in his eyes.

"I really am grateful that you came," she told him.

The Fae

"Of course I came Ellie, I will always be here for you, but Felix is our priority tonight."
Ellie guessed that Felix' paternity was not open for discussion so she said nothing.

"Okay, yes. Well what we should do is…" Ellie, James and Milfoil sat in the car. Yarrow and Sean were outside, leaning against the car door and listening intently. Ellie continued.
"We should be completely out of sight here, and frankly I am impressed that we got a parking space! Anyway, Yarrow, Sean and James, climb over the fence and hide behind the café, Milfoil and the girls will stay here in the car. When you get there, call the twins in your head and we shall see if they can hear you. Then, as soon as the queen and Marcellus arrive, we start listening. If you see other Vamps, just call out silently and we will reassess the situation. If we hear anything untoward, we will let you know and then we can all charge in and save the queen. How does that sound?"
"Bloody awful, but it is the best we have." Sean smiled. "Right, I make it a quarter to, so we need to get going. Okay good luck."
James slipped silently out of the back door of the car and the three men disappeared over the gate of the park.

The two women sat silently in the front of the car whilst the twins yawned and curled up in the back.
"Don't fall asleep girls." Ellie whispered.
"We could not if we tried, we are too excited." Begonia said sleepily.
Milfoil and Ellie looked at each other and smiled.
"Ooh! That tickles!" Giggled Bluebell. "His voice is all fluffy and tickly."
"Who's voice?" Asked Ellie.
"Sean. They are there now, behind the café. The queen has arrived and is waiting outside the bandstand. Sean keeps saying it over and over like an old radio ham. But I do not think he can hear me. I have told him I can hear but he keeps on repeating himself."
"Okay, hopefully Marcellus will be here soon and we can get this over with." Milfoil said, beginning to get a little nervous.
Ellie reached over and took her hand.
"There is no way they can know we are here. The girls are perfectly safe."
Milfoil half smiled in hope.

They sat in silence for about twenty minutes. Nothing appeared to be happening.
"Ooh!" The twins jumped. "Tickly voice says that the stinking Vamp is walking toward the queen. He says he is a cocky bastard."
Ellie and Milfoil turned in horror to look at the innocent face of Bluebell.
"What is a cocky bastard?" She asked sweetly.
Milfoil cleared her throat.
"I will tell you when we get home. And I will tell that stupid great Irish oaf a thing or two, too!" She finished under her breath.
"Right. He is telling us to pay attention now, the queen and Marcellus are talking." Begonia hushed. "Funny though, I can not hear the vampire at all, only the queen."
"I thought that may happen." Ellie said to Milfoil. "Its alright, we should be able to work out what is being said by the things the queen says."
"Well, the queen is not very happy." Giggled Bluebell. "She is telling him that she has been waiting for some time and…Ooh! What a horrible man! He said something

132

The Fae

that made the queen very sad. She has tears inside her head, but she is making sure that the horrid man does not see them. Good for her."

"Yarrow is calling for you Ellie. He says that there are no Vampires around that they can see. He says that they are moving closer because the queen and the vampire have gone through into the bandstand." Begonia reported, sounding very professional.

Ellie realised that she could hear all of this for herself, but said nothing. It was too late to change plans now. Bluebell must have noticed the way in which her sister was behaving because she also became more serious.

"Sean is at the back of the bandstand and has nothing to report. The queen is asking Marcellus about the death balls and whether they have discovered anything else about them yet."

Begonia continued the dialogue.

"Yarrow says that James is making his way to the top of the wall so that he has a better view of the castle grounds, Yarrow is just out of sight by the ornamental garden and has a clear view of the entrance to the bandstand. He says that they are all set and ready if need be."

"You are doing a wonderful job girls." Milfoil told her daughters. "I am so proud of you."

The girls smiled at their mother then scrunched up their faces in concentration again.

"The queen is not at all happy." Bluebell said. "She told Marcellus that he had brought her there under false pretences. She is saying that she wishes only to know the whereabouts of Felix and Aurellio and that his internal politics have nothing to do with her. She seems a bit frightened but is putting on a stern face and a strong voice, hoping that he does not notice."

Begonia took over the narrative.

"She says that she demands he show some respect, she is a queen. Now she is really frightened. In her head she is trying to stay calm, she is thinking that she made a big mistake coming to meet him. She is trying to remember if she has anything on her that will fight off a Vampire."

"Oh ho! James is calling, sort of." Bluebell said. "He says that he can see movement at the bottom park near the pond. He says that it is too big for a swan and that it moves all wrong. He is asking if he should go and investigate."

Ellie started to worry. "They can't hear the girls, how do I communicate with them? I don't want James to go, he is better where he is in case he is needed in a hurry. Oh, how can I let him know?"

"Why not go and join them, the girls can talk to you and you can relay the information to the men." Milfoil suggested.

"But then you will be on your own." Ellie pointed out.

"You have already told us that nobody will know that we are here, so we shall be perfectly safe. In any case, if I even think we are in the slightest trouble, I am driving away." Milfoil smiled at Ellie to show that she was unafraid.

"Okay, if you are sure." She relented. "Girls? Is this okay with you?"

"Of course. We will be fine." They said.

Ellie climbed to the top of the gate and hung there panting. Her arms ached and her chest was sore where she had balanced her weight on it to pull herself up. *It all looks so easy in the movies.* She thought. *Don't see Angelina out of breath, sweaty and puffing do you?* She dropped down the other side and landed on her feet with a bump. *For crying out loud!* She berated herself. She shook out the crick in her ankle and made her way to the back of the bandstand.

"James!" She called in a stage whisper. "James! Where are you?"

"Ssh!" Came the reply. "Quiet! Vamps have exceptional hearing." He whispered back. "What are you doing here?"

"The girls said that you guys can't hear them so I had to come. You wanted to go investigate the shapes down the hill but I didn't want you to. There was no other way of letting you know."

James' teeth flashed white in the darkness as he smiled at her. "I was not going down there, I am needed here. It was just a thought I had. But I do appreciate you coming to rescue me. It means a lot!" He mocked her.

"Oh shove it bro!" Ellie replied.

James looked at her sharply then told her to get down.

"Look, they are moving this way. Go and warn Yarrow and Sean. Quietly. And for goodness sake, be careful!"

Ellie got on her hands and knees and began to crawl toward the front of the bandstand. She was positive that she heard James snicker behind her.

"Yarrow? Where are you?" Ellie whispered loudly into the dark.

"Here. Ssh!" Came the reply, and Ellie crawled toward the voice.

"There are bodies moving up the hill, James said to be careful." Ellie said as quietly as she could.

"Vamps?" Asked Yarrow.

"I would imagine so." She replied.

"So what is happening in there?" Yarrow indicated the bandstand with a nod of his head.

"Gimme a minute." Ellie told him, then silently asked the girls for an update.

"Okay." She said to Yarrow. "The queen is scared, she believes that this is a trap but is not sure how. She is trying to get information out of Marcellus, but he is toying with her. I imagine he is waiting for the guys on the hill to get here, Anyway, the queen is thinking that as soon as she gets what she came for she will scarper."

"Scarper?"

"Escape. Run. Get away."

"Oh, okay."

Just as they were talking, Sean slid down beside them.

"All clear behind us. Any news?"

Ellie gave him what little information they had and it was decided that Sean would be better positioned at the rear of the bandstand with James.

Just then there was a rustling in the undergrowth and a very damp and bedraggled looking cat appeared.

"Peter?" Ellie exclaimed in shock. "What on earth are you doing here?"

"I am supposed to be guarding you." He replied somewhat huffily. "And yet you slope off out without telling me a thing. How am I supposed to keep you safe if I don't even know where you are?"

"So how did you know where to find me?" Ellie asked in astonishment. "The only people who know are here now."

"You have your secrets, I have mine!" Peter retorted.

"Well. Okay then. But we are kinda busy right now." Ellie tried to explain.

"As I am here, I may as well be useful." Peter said. "What would you like me to do?"

Ellie snatched him up and gave him a big hug.

"You big softy." She told him. "I am so glad you are here. Do you think you could pretend you are a cat and wander into the bandstand? The queen will recognise you but Marcellus shouldn't. You being there may give her strength. Worse case, you could provide a distraction if it all goes wrong. It will give us time to come and rescue the queen."

Peter looked a little taken aback. "Uh, sure, no problem." He said unconvincingly. However, he gamely sauntered over to the bandstand and entered.

"Ellie, your cat Peter is in there now." Bluebell told her. "The queen was a bit surprised but very glad to see a familiar face, she is now thinking that maybe there is a chance of getting out alive. She has started asking Marcellus again where Felix is. He does not appear to be telling her because she is now getting angry. Oh my! I do not want to say those words. Do I have to Ellie? Mother will be very cross if I do."

"No my darling." Ellie told her. "you do not have to say anything that makes you uncomfortable."

"The queen is looking at Peter and trying to tell him something. I can not quite make out what. Oh, oh I see. The queen is trying to tell Peter to get help. Peter does not understand though. I think the queen knows that. She is becoming very sad. She is saying that she did not expect to be taken out by a Vampire, but that she has had a long and good life. Oh, wait! Peter has jumped up at the vampire. He is scratching and biting at him."

"Everybody, quick! Inside!" Ellie yelled at the top of her lungs.

Yarrow and Sean ran ahead of her, as she reached the entrance, James caught up and they entered together. They all pulled out a sharpened stake of wood from under their coats. Brandishing their weapons, they circled Marcellus, who was fighting to keep Peter from scratching out his eye.

"Get this bloody cat off me!" Marcellus screamed, trying to swat Peter away.

Peter hung on for dear life, his claws fully embedded in the face and neck of the Vampire.

Marcellus grabbed Peter around the middle and with a great scream, ripped him from his face. He threw Peter against the wall of the tent then kicked him hard when Peter ran at him again. Peter collapsed on the floor where he fell, his eyes rolled closed and his breathing appeared to stop.

"What is this?" Marcellus roared in anger. "A trap? You meant to trap me woman?"

The queen quickly positioned herself behind James and stood shaking.

"Trap? You accuse me? You who have led me here with a lie and false promise? I can smell your men climbing the hill toward us and you accuse me?" She shook with anger. "Tell me now where Felix is held and I will let you live."

"What do you think these fairies will do? They are incapable of harm. It is an empty threat Alcea."

Ellie stepped forward and placed the stake over Marcellus' heart area.

"I am not fairy." She said calmly. "I have no compunction in staking you. Tell me now, where are Felix and Aurellio?"

"You would not dare!" Growled the Vampire. "You could not even torture a Gnome!"

The Fae

"Do you wish to put that to the test?" Ellie asked reasonably.

"I also am no fairy." James declared as he stepped next to Ellie. "And I would love to drive my stake through what is left of your heart. So, the choice is yours. Answer the question or answer to your god."

Ellie looked over at James and smiled.

"Nice!" She said smiling a nod.

James shrugged his pleasure at the compliment.

"Aw shucks! Well Vampire? What is it to be?"

Sean tied the Vampires' hands behind his back with a silver chain that had been hanging about his neck.

"Me ma gave me that. Ah well, 'tis for a good cause."

Marcellus had relented and told them that Felix and Aurellio were being held at the Arena. Despite the obvious pain caused by the silver burning into his flesh, Marcellus had laughed when he said this, thinking it appropriate, what with Aurellio being an old Roman soldier.

"What is this Arena then?" Sean had asked.

"It's a sport centre that also has rooms that are rented out."

"Oh aye!"

"No, not like that. They are all health and beauty related, hairdressers, aerobics, that sort of thing. There are dozens of rooms there so I guess it could be possible. I would have thought it a bit public though." Ellie mused. "Oh crap! Peter!"

Ellie rushed over to where Peter lay crumpled on the floor. She gingerly stroked his fur, feeling for any broken bones. Her hand came away wet with blood and she wrapped him up carefully in her sweater.

"We have to get him home immediately." She said, making her way out of the bandstand, closely followed by the others.

"I will take him to the car, meet you guys back at mine as soon as you can." She called over her shoulder as she ran for the car.

Back at her house, Ellie lay Peter on a towel on the couch.

"Can you hear me? Peter? Can you here me? You are going to be okay. We are home now. You are safe. You were so brave. You're going to be okay." Ellie's tears fell onto Peters fur and glistened next to his spilt blood.

Ellie used a damp cloth to softly wipe his wounds. His jaw seemed to be broken and he was having trouble swallowing.

He tried to speak.

"Ellie?"

"Yes my dearest, I'm here, you're going to be okay."

"Need Fae." He managed to say.

Ellie felt a painful stab of jealousy but quickly brushed it aside. She took out her small pink phone and flipped it open.

"Fae please." She spoke into the handset then listened to it ring.

"Hello?" Came a sleepy, curious voice. "Ellie? Is that you? What has happened?"

"Oh Fae, please come, Peter has been hurt. Badly. Please come, I am afraid he might die." Ellie sobbed into the phone.

"Boil some water and I will be there immediately." Fae's voice had shaken itself free of sleep and was fully awake.

The Fae

Ellie put the kettle on to boil and waited for the others to arrive. Milfoil had taken the girls straight home thinking that they would be upset to see Peter injured.

"How is he?" Came the queen's voice before the gate was even opened. "How is he? Is it bad?" She rushed into the house closely followed by Sean, Yarrow and James.

The queen dropped to her knees beside Peter and gently stroked his damp fur.

"Come on old friend." She urged. "We have been through too many stories to end this now. There are many more books to be read as yet. Stay strong for me." She stood and looked at Ellie.

"What is being done for him?" She demanded.

Ellie stepped back as though slapped, but remembering that this was a queen, she bit back the sarcastic retort that was pushing at her teeth.

"Fae is on her way, she will be here any moment." Ellie said as politely as she could.

James took a deep breath and turned back into the kitchen.

The queen watched him leave and said, "Well, it was bound to happen. I could not keep them apart forever. Though heaven knows I have tried." She said under her breath. Turning to Ellie she said. "My apologies for being curt, I am frightened for Peter and it has been an eventful night. When Fae has seen to Peter, we will discuss your involvement in tonight's activities."

"Yes your majesty." Ellie said.

Joining James in the kitchen, Ellie poured the boiling water into a large red tea pot.

"Are you okay?" She asked him.

"Oh yes. I suppose so." James sighed. "I have not seen Fae for many years. She refused to allow me anywhere near her. I know that the queen ordered it, but I had hoped that our love was stronger than that. I rarely got to see Felix, usually only in passing or with the aid of a spell. I don't know that I should be here when she arrives."

"Do you want to see her?" Asked Ellie.

"More than anything." The pain in James voice touched something deep and hidden inside Ellie.

"This is my house and I am asking you to stay. The queen has no sovereignty here."

"Thank you." James said brokenly. "Thank you, but I shall leave. I would not wish to further harm Fae and my presence here would do that. It is best if I leave."

Wearily James stood and picked up his coat. He turned to the door just as it swung open and Fae stood there. Her face dropped and her mouth fell open. She seemed unable to draw a breath, but managed to utter, "You!"

"I am sorry, truly I am." James cried as he brushed past her and disappeared into the night.

Fae visibly pulled herself together and marched into the living room.

"Oh Peter!" She sobbed as she knelt by the sofa and took him in her arms. "What have you done to yourself?"

"Waited for you…" Peter's voice was becoming weaker. "Time to go now…" He managed.

"Oh no you do not!" Fae told him fiercely. "I am here now, I shall make you well. Come, let me see the damage."

"Let me go…" Peter breathed. "Time…"

Ellie and the queen looked at each other and back at the cat in horror.

The Fae

"Its only a broken jaw!" Ellie cried. "You can fix that surely?"

"Time…Good life…Love…" Peter's voice was becoming more and more faint as his body sagged in Fae's arms.

"No! Peter, no!" Fae screamed. "I can heal you. I can. Peter, you cannot die, I love you. We all love you. It is not your time!"

"Let…" Peter rolled back his eyes and became limp.

Fae laid him back on the couch and turned to look at everyone in the room. "He is gone." She whispered.

"No!" The queen cried.

"He can't be!" Sobbed Ellie.

Whilst the room stood in shock, Bunbury sauntered in unnoticed and stared at everyone in surprise. He followed their line of sight to the couch, where Peter lay supine. He jumped up and stood over Peters face, staring into his unseeing eyes. Bunbury leant forward and licked his friends ear. Over and over, Bunbury licked and prodded Peter, trying to get a reaction. None came. Peter was dead. Bunbury sat up on his back legs and looked at Ellie. Pain was visible in his golden eyes, but something else too, determination. He jumped down from the couch and stretched his front paws, arching his back as he did so. From his mouth came a fearful cry of utter pain and anguish. His claws extended and dug into the floor, his ears lay flat against his head and still the cry came, louder and louder. Bunbury's fur started to ripple along his body, each hair alive and electrified; from the tip of his bushy tail to the long curly white hairs that covered his belly and around to the thickly black and lustrous pelt that covered his back. His lips pulled back over his teeth in a rictus of despair and still the scream. Unending, feral and lost. Bunbury's body started to shake and a grey haze appeared, surrounding him. And still the scream, louder now; causing the window to crack.

The haze around Bunbury continued to grow, larger and more dense. From its centre; an atavistic cry of anguish. The haze grew to the size of a dog, shaking, snarling, screaming. The grey became red. The red became pain and blood and loss and fear, and still it grew. With a final yell of despair, the haze lifted, and there lay a man, curled and foetal. His body long and sinewy, his hair black and white, his face streaked with pain and tears. His fingers long and pointed, nails fearsome; both hands and feet. The man stood on two legs and carefully balanced for the first time. He woodenly reached down and lifted Peter into his arms. He held the lifeless cat tight to his chest and closed his eyes.

A warm light appeared around the cat, which grew in strength; becoming so bright that those present had to turn away. From the corner of her eye Ellie could see Bunbury cradle Peter within the light and mumble rhythmically at him. The sound had no words but it was a language. The language had cadence and pauses but no recognisable meaning. Bunbury lay Peter gently upon the sofa and leant down over him. The light stayed around Peter whilst Bunbury clumsily kissed his head and straightened up. When he had reached his full height, he toppled backward and landed on the floor with a thud, out cold.

The light around Peter began to fade. Ellie and the others looked at each other and then at Peter. Suddenly his chest rose and fell. Then it was still. Those in the room

The Fae

held their breath. Peters chest rose again, fell again, rose again. Peters eyes fluttered open and he looked around groggily.

Ellie and the queen clasped each other crying and Fae fell back to her knees beside the wakening cat. Yarrow and Sean laughed and punched each other in the arm, then cleared their throats self consciously and bent over the slowly awakening body of Peter.

"Fae?" Asked Peter weakly.

"Yes my precious, I am here. We all are here. We are so glad, so glad. Thank the gods!"

Ellie leant over so that Peter could see her too.

"Welcome back Peter. You has us very worried there." She told him.

"What happened?" Peter asked slowly. "I thought I died."

"You did. I don't understand any of this, but you did. You died. Bunbury saved you. Oh my god! Bunbury!" Ellie threw herself down next to the man that was her cat and stroked his hair "Oh my precious Bunbury. What have you done?" She asked the comatose creature.

The Fae

Chapter thirteen

Ellie rushed to her bedroom and snatched up the throw that lay on the chair. Returning to the living room, she gently covered Bunbury and wiped his hair back from his eyes, where it had landed as he fell. Bunbury was still out cold, but his breathing was strong and his chest rose and fell as it should. Ellie sat back on her heels and looked at the people gathered in her once familiar room. Sean and Yarrow were talking together quietly by the window, the queen was sitting in the chair, fanning herself with a magazine and Fae was sitting on the couch, stroking Peter and murmuring to him gently.

"Er, guys?" Ellie asked. "Did anyone else notice that my cat just turned into a man? A very large and very naked man?"
Yarrow looked over at Bunbury lying on the floor.
"Yes. That is to say that, well… It's not something that you need to worry about. He is perfectly harmless. He is still the cat that you know. He should change back in a few hours. Just keep him warm." Then he returned to his conversation.
"Okay, I see. Still a cat?" Ellie began to wonder if she were in an alternate universe. Again. This all seemed so normal to these people. Her cat had just turned into a man and she was to keep him warm and not worry? Didn't anyone get it? She was not used to cats that turned into men. Or fairy queens that needed rescuing from Vampires, come to that. This was all a bit much.
"Yeah, but guys?" Ellie tried again. "Guys? Why or even how did my cat turn into a man? Is this usual? Will he do it a lot? Do I need to make some sort of provision for this?" She was becoming a little irked to say the least.
Yarrow turned to her again and his face softened.
"I am sorry Ellie; I forget that you don't know any of this…" He waved a hand indicating the magical creatures. "Bunbury must be a shape shifter. They can be either people that turn into animals or animals that turn into people. I am guessing that when he saw that Peter had died, he felt strongly enough about it that he had to do something. He would not have been able to use his powers in cat form so had to change."
"Well that makes perfect sense." Ellie said sarcastically. "I fail to see why I even bother being surprised any more." She took another look at her man cat and got up from the floor.

Ellie made everyone a drink, checked that Peter and Bunbury were comfortable then reminded them all why they were there.
"Okay, so how are we going to rescue Felix?" She asked the room.
"Do you not think it would be better to leave that to the Vampires?" Asked the queen. "After all, they are much better suited to this sort of thing than we are."
Ellie and Fae gave the queen a very hard look and Fae placed her hand on Ellie's arm to stop her saying something she shouldn't.
"I think that as Felix is ours, we should be the ones to rescue him." Ellie said very calmly. "Besides, Marcellus knows where he is and has done nothing even though Aurellio is there as well."
"I have been thinking about that." Sean joined in. "You have to be wondering why the king of the Vampires is allowing one of his own to remain a prisoner. I know that they are not the most loving of creatures, but you would think he would be wanting him back if only for form's sake."

"Well yes, there is that." Yarrow said. "He certainly did not seem particularly bothered that one of his own, his second in command come to that, was being held prisoner. Unless he thinks that Aurellio has already been staked."

The queen glanced up.

"That is a rather vulgar term Yarrow; could you not use a different expression?"

"My apologies your majesty." Yarrow coloured.

Ellie looked over at the queen briefly, then continued.

"I for one intend to go to the Arena and rescue them. Who is coming with me?"

"Ellie, do you not think perhaps this is best left to the men?" Asked Fae.

"What?" Ellie spat in shock. "The men? Are you serious?"

"But it could be very dangerous." Fae insisted.

"Everything that I have been through since I met you guys has been pretty dangerous. I have no choice. I need to get him back, I know beyond any doubt that he would do the same for me." She looked everyone square in the eye, daring them to contradict her. "And you."

"Well, we can not let you go by yourself now can we?" Laughed Sean. "What did you have planned?"

Ellie shrugged her shoulders and smiled.

"I don't know. I'm new to this super hero stuff. Any ideas?" She asked the room.

They tossed back and forth a few ideas, each as useful as the other, none brilliant.

"We need James." Ellie declared. She noticed Fae's face drain of colour. "I am sorry Fae, but he is Elf so he's not bound by the pacifist thing that you guys are. No offence fella's but if it gets scrappy, you won't be much use will you?"

Yarrow and Sean just shrugged their shoulders and appeared not to be offended in the least.

"I would rather not be here when he comes." Fae said in a small voice. "I shall take Peter home and look after him. Oh, that is if you do not mind." She asked Ellie.

"I don't mind, I think you will be more use to him than me. Thank you."

Ellie didn't really notice when Fae bundled Peter in her coat and took him home. She was busy trying to think of a way of getting past the Gnomes and rescuing Felix.

"Okay, so how do we get James here?" She asked nobody in particular.

"I will call him, I have his cell number." Yarrow answered.

Ellie was oddly surprised to know that James and Yarrow had mobile phones. It seemed incongruous somehow.

They were on their third cup of tea when James arrived. He had bought Frances with him. She rushed over to Bunbury and started to stroke his hair whilst murmuring to him in a sing song voice.

"Thank you for coming back." Ellie smiled at James. "Frances, thank you for coming too. Has Yarrow told you about Bunbury?"

"Oh yes, we know all about Bunbury don't we my darling?" Frances cooed, attention on the man cat beside her.

Odd, thought Ellie. *Oh well*!

"Right." Started James. "So basically, we need a few weapons…"

Frances' head snapped up.

"…a lot of nerve and, actually, do you think that you would be able to…? No, no, not you. The twins. Do you think that they could listen for Felix and well, sort of pin point him in the sports centre?"

The Fae

"Oh, great idea!" Ellie clapped her hands. "I don't think we will be able to borrow them until the early morning, before school. They must be tired out and asleep just now."

"Pity." Yarrow commented. "Understandable though." He finished quickly.

"I don't think that there is any other way of locating them quickly without alerting the Gnomes that we are there." James supplied.

"No, I think it's a great idea." Ellie repeated. "So, who is coming?"

It was decided that Yarrow, Sean, James and Ellie would go. Frances would return in the morning to stay with Bunbury and the queen would stay at home. They agreed to meet at the Mersea Road roundabout car park at dawn and everybody left for whatever sleep was left to them.

Ellie was too worked up to sleep. Images of Bunbury screaming and turning into a man played over and over in her head, making sleep impossible. She got back out of bed and went to sit with Bunbury. The men had lifted him onto the couch before they left and Ellie had tucked a spare duvet around him. It felt absolutely surreal looking at the sleeping form of a grown man, knowing that he was actually her cat. Her cat that slept snuggled under her chin at night and watched her in the bathroom. She stroked his head over and over, talking softly to him, telling him that things would be alright, they would get better, that he would soon be a cat again. *Can you hear yourself?* She muttered under her breath.

Ellie eventually dozed sitting on the couch, bolt upright and head tilted back. She awoke with a gripping pain in her neck, drool on her chin and a bundle of black and white fur on her lap. The fur was fast asleep and purring.

"Oh my darling, you beautiful boy. I am so glad that you are back." She hugged Bunbury tight to her chest and covered his head in kisses.

Bunbury lazily opened one eye, looked at her then closed it again and returned to his dreaming. Ellie spent several minutes hugging and stroking the cat, overjoyed that he was back to normal, with no apparent ill effects.

Eventually she got up and saw to her breakfast. The house felt empty without Peter singing and chatting. She kept expecting to see him jump up onto the sill or sit at the table for his food. In a short space of time he had become a large part of her life and she missed him. Ellie scolded herself for feeling jealous that Fae had taken him home. *After all, he is her cat.* She thought sadly. *At least Bunbury is okay.*

Ellie dressed and tidied the kitchen whilst she waited for the hands on the clock to crawl round. Finally it was time to leave, just as she was picking up her jacket, Frances arrived.

"Oh, he's all better now." Ellie gushed. "I mean he is back to being a cat, you don't have to baby sit him. Well, unless you want to that is."

Frances told her that she would still like to sit with Bunbury to keep an eye on him.

"That way I will be here when you get back." She reasoned.

"Good idea. Well, I should go. Wish us luck." Ellie grabbed her keys and set off.

It was only a ten minute walk up the hill to the car park and as she got there, Ellie could see that the others had arrived before her. They stood in a huddle,. Breath misting in front of their faces as they spoke together.

"Hi guys. Ready?" Ellie asked.

The Fae

The group walked up the slight incline, past the abbey walls and skirted the small green. The infant school stood ancient and proud, garlanded with scaffolding whilst awaiting its make over. Blossoms hung heavy on bows as they made their way past gardens ablaze with colour. The scent of wall flowers preceded them and fat flies floated lazily in the still summer air. When they arrived at the sport centre, they split up into pairs and approached nonchalantly. Yarrow and Sean went around to the back of the building, whilst Ellie and James walked calmly toward the front door.

"We see you loud and clear Ellie." Came the voice of Bluebell inside Ellie's mind. "We are in the car park, you walked straight past us." She giggled as though this were a great adventure.
"Yes, mummy borrowed a different car. She is so clever." Begonia added.
"Hello my darlings. Thank you for coming. I don't know what I would do without you." Ellie told them in her head.
The girls giggled.
"Can you hear Felix?" Ellie asked them.
"Hang on a minute…Yes. We hear him. He sounds really poorly. I think he is asleep." Bluebell said. "His mind is all dark and yucky. Do we have to go in there?" She asked in a small worried voice.
"Oh no my precious, just try and tell me where he is. Do you think you can do that?"
"Well yes. Sort of. We have never done that before." Begonia said. "It cannot be that hard though can it?"
Bluebell agreed and Ellie had to smile as she felt the girls scrunch up their minds to concentrate.
"Okay." Begonia started. "He is in a dark room. There are pictures on the window, stopping the light from getting in. The pictures are on backwards."

Ellie looked up at the building and saw that to the right of the entrance were a long line of windows on the ground floor that were blocked out with posters of the services available within the centre. To the left of the entrance, on the first floor right in the corner, two windows were similarly blocked with posters, these bearing the sport centre name and logo.
"Girls," Ellie called silently, "do you know if he is upstairs or downstairs?"
"No!" They chorused.
"Okay. Can you tell me if there are any other noises near them? Or smells? Can you tell smells?"
"Not sure, hold on a bit."
Ellie and James went over to the nearby bench and stretched out, to all intents and purposes they looked as if they were waiting for someone. For appearances sake they spoke quietly together.
"Ellie!" Called Bluebell inside Ellie's mind. "Ellie, we can hear lots of banging and music, it sounds like when we dance on the floor in our house. Felix is feeling squashed, we think he is in a small room. Does that help at all?"
"Very good girls." Ellie relayed the information to James. "Okay, if possible, can you send him a message? If he can hear you, tell him that we are coming."
Ellie perked up a little as she and James walked into the centre.

James and Ellie waited until the reception was busy, and the girl behind the counter was flustered and distracted.

"My wife here is thinking of joining a dance class and was wondering if she could get some information and maybe have a look around?" James asked the harassed looking receptionist, who held a phone under her chin and a pen in her hand. The woman absently swept her hair back where it had flopped and left a scar of blue ink in it's place.

Ellie was standing meekly beside him, trying to look interested whilst endeavouring not to breathe, as the smell emanating from the Gnome they were addressing was making her gag.

The receptionist was apologetic and told them that she could not leave the desk, but they were welcome to look at the room by themselves, if that was okay?

"Oh, well, I suppose so." James huffed. "Come on dear."

As they walked away, arm in arm, James winked at Ellie who let out the breath she had been holding.

"You know that you were turning a little blue there?" James smiled.

"If we had been any longer, I may have passed out!" Ellie exclaimed. "I really don't know how you guys can stand the smell."

"All species smell Ellie, it's just a question of degrees. Unfortunately you appear to have a very sensitive nose."

"Yes well!"

They climbed the stairs and made their way down the long corridor; listening for the sounds of music. About half of the rooms were occupied and a variety of noises escaped the aged doors as they passed. When they reached the end of the corridor, they opened the door and went in. The room was a mess. It appeared to be used as a store room, there were old desks, filing cabinets and huge net bags with balls of every kind inside. The room smelt musty and dust motes spun lazily on the beams of light that had escaped through rips in the posters covering the windows. From the room next door, they could hear the thump, thump, thump of dancers going through their routine. The music sounded tinny and disjointed through the wall, but was recognisable as a popular R and B song from the charts.

"Yes, you are in the right room!" Ellie heard Bluebell say. "Can you see him? Is he alright? Ellie?"

"No darling, I can't see him yet, there is a lot of junk in here. Did he hear you at all?"

"We do not think so, we tried but think that he just cannot hear us, or he is asleep!"

Ellie and James explored the room, moving piles of old curtains and towels, opening cupboards and kicking aside black bin bags full of god knew what, all the while trying to be inconspicuous. The detritus filled the room, in places it was stacked as high as the ceiling. It made small passages between the piles, like an alien landscape.

They heard a small bump and nearly jumped out of their skin, both sets of eyes swivelling to the door in panic. Nothing. The bump again, Ellie and James looked at each other and started to search faster. They heard a muffled grunt and stood very still, trying to identify the source and direction.

"Felix?" Whispered Ellie loudly. "Felix, let us know where you are."

Again there came the muffled bang followed by a low moan.

"Over there!" James jumped over a pile of stuffed bin bags and tore open the door to a cleaning cupboard that they had previously overlooked.

The Fae

Felix tumbled out and landed on his side, mouth gagged and hands tied behind his back to his bound feet. Another quiet moan and Aurellio fell on top of him similarly tied up.
Felix stared up at Ellie with a mixture of surprise, pain and exhaustion on his face.
"You get them untied, I will watch the door." Ellie told James. "Hurry though, we have to get them out of here."

Aurellio started to twist and moan within the confines of his bindings. A slight wisp of smoke curled from his face and he closed his eyes against the pain of it.
"Oh my god!" Ellie cried. "The sun! I forgot about the sun! We will have to find something to cover him with. Quick, grab a couple of those curtains. Hurry James!"
James grabbed a handful of the dusty curtains and threw half to Ellie. They both covered Aurellio from head to toe hoping it would be enough to block out the harmful rays from the sun. Ellie went to the door and opened it an inch so that she could watch. The beats and bangs continued from next door and the ordinariness of the setting sat, incongruous, in her mind.

"Ellie, help me, I can't carry them both, you need to help me get them moving." James called as quietly as he could.
Ellie made her way back to the bedraggled trio and took Aurellio's arm to help him stand.
"No, you take Felix!" James demanded. "I will help the Vampire."
They swapped places and Ellie helped Felix to his feet. They shuffled toward the door, injuries and exhaustion making the progress very slow.
Felix leant heavily against her as she half pulled and half dragged him through the door. Ellie strained to hear if anything outside the room had changed.
"We can do that." The girls said.
"What do you mean?" Ellie asked them, slightly confused.
"We can let you know if anyone is coming towards you."
"Really? That would be great, thanks."
Ellie hoisted Felix a little higher and the foursome made their way to the stairs.
They had descended a couple of steps when Bluebell called out.
"Quick, someone is coming, they are about to start up the stairs."
Ellie and James pulled their rescuee's back up and looked around desperately for somewhere to hide. The stairs had a dogleg halfway up so they were unable to see who was coming. But equally, they could not yet be seen either.
"Oh God, it's a Gnome, I can smell her." Ellie hissed. "Quick, we have to hide!"
They searched for a door that had no sounds coming out, found one, threw open the door and pushed Aurellio and Felix inside. The two injured men landed with a soft 'whump' but did not cry out.

Several minutes passed. Long agonising minutes where Ellie expected the door to be opened at any time. They found themselves in another dance studio. This one had the ubiquitous floor to ceiling mirror and bar. The floor was polished wood and shone dully in the early morning sun. The room smelt faintly of old socks and sweat. Ellie caught sight of them all in the mirror. James was up against the door, ear pressed to the wood, listening. She looked like a stranger, her hair was loose and wild, her eyes wide with adrenalin. But Aurellio was not reflected. There was his cover, the curtains all dusty and old, but there was nobody in them. Ellie looked round and saw Aurellio staring at her. He winked. She looked back at the mirror, but he was

The Fae

defiantly not there. The curtain made a sausage shape on the floor, but she could see all the way through it. *Wow! I always thought that bit was a myth*! She thought to herself. She looked back at the vampire and shrugged her shoulders with a smile.

"You can come out now." Ellie heard Bluebell say. "That awful Gnome has gone. There is nobody else up there."
"Thank you guys." Ellie told them. "James, we need to go." She said out loud. "Up you come handsome." She smiled at Felix as she hoiked him back up.
James and Aurellio between them managed to get the curtains back in place, covering every inch of skin. As they left the room, James pointed to the other end of the corridor, where a fire exit door was situated.
"Thank god for that." Ellie mumbled as they made their way over.
Reaching the door, Ellie pushed Felix against it to lower the bar and they stepped out onto the top of a rickety staircase. Aurellio let a groan escape as he left the building and they all tried to descend a little faster.

Yarrow and Sean were positioned one at the bottom of the stairs and one at the corner of the building. They both appeared alert and tense. Yarrow reached out and helped James with the Vampire.
"It will be quicker if we carry him." James puffed, so they picked him up like a large bag of laundry and hurried toward the car park.
"What if we are seen?" Asked James.
"What are they going to do?" Ellie wondered. "Its not like they can call the police is it? 'Excuse me officer but my kidnap victims have been stolen. Would you mind awfully helping to get them back?'" Ellie replied.
"Quickly." Sean shouted, no pretence at stealth. "There are some coming. Hurry!"
Ellie and the men picked up their pace and hurried to where Sean was standing.
"There, look. I think they have clubs! Ah! I do not know how to fight. What should we do?"
"Okay, Sean, you and Yarrow get these two to the car, James and I will keep them busy."
James raised his eyebrows in alarm but said nothing.
Sean and Yarrow grabbed hold of the two injured men and rushed as fast as they could toward the car park and safety.
"I'm not exactly an expert fighter." James whispered.
"Me either, but if you had the same childhood I did, a couple of goons with bats is nothing, I can tell you!"
James looked at Ellie with pain in is eyes.
"Oh my darling girl, I am so very sorry."
"Oh shish! It's not as if you could have done anything about it. Come on."
James took a deep breath then turned to the matter at hand.

Ellie peered around the corner and saw two large muscle bound men walking slowly toward them swinging equally scary looking baseball bats. Ellie felt her insides turn to water. She had always thought that was a stupid saying, but now, faced with the prospect of imminent pain, she knew it to be true.
"Look for a weapon." She hissed at James.
"I can see two." He replied. "Baseball bats."
"Jokes? Now we have jokes?" Ellie laughed.

"It may be the last chance I get." James replied. "We could get seriously messed up in a minute."

"I know. And you know what?" Ellie asked.

"What?"

"I'm glad I'm here with you being a hero and rescuing those two. But more importantly?"

"What?" Asked James, clearly interested.

Ellie grabbed up an old branch that was laying near them.

"It could be kinda fun!" She yelled as she took off running and screaming toward the Gnomes, brandishing her branch.

"Oh what the hell!" James yelled as he ran toward the Gnomes with equal vigour and comparable yelling.

The gnomes stopped dead in their tracks, looked at each other, looked back at Ellie and James running at them screaming like banshee's then they turned and fled the way they had come.

Ellie and James came to a stop and bent over, gulping lungfulls of air and panting with the fear and exertion.

"Did they really just run away?" James was incredulous. Between pants.

"See, that is where it helps to have a human by your side. I understand meat heads. They are too concerned with appearance, hence the huge muscles and silly track pants. If we were meek, they would beat the hell out of us, but as we looked like we could take care of ourselves, they were having none of it. Funny really. Got the blood pumping that's for sure."

"Could have let me in on it!" James laughed. "I nearly messed myself there I was so scared."

"Me too. It was only something I read in a girls mag once. Didn't know if it would work or not! Bloody glad it did!"

"I think we should get going quickly just incase they decide they are tough after all." James suggested.

"Good idea." Ellie agreed as they ran back toward the car park.

Finding Sean alone had Ellie worried for a minute.

"Not to worry love." He told her. "Yarrow went with Frances and the girls, they are taking the vampire and your friend to your house to get them fixed up."

"Oh, that's okay then." Ellie puffed in breathless release.

The three of them started to walk back to Ellie's house, laughing in relief at a job well done. They got a lot of mileage out of the muscle men running away, and a glint of respect shone in Sean's eyes as he heard how Ellie had run at them screaming.

"Like Queen Boudicca of old she was." James said in admiration. "You would have liked her, you are very similar in many ways."

Ellie looked at him in astonishment.

"You knew Boudicca? Seriously?"

"Why are you so surprised? Did you think that royalty would not want to associate with the likes of me?" James was hurt. "Or maybe because I don't know how to fight, a warrior would not speak with me?"

"No! Don't be so bloody precious!" Ellie punched him in the arm. "I just cannot imagine what your life must have been like. To actually know Queen Boudicca! Wow! I mean that's incredible. She was amazing!"

"Yes, she had a fun side." James commented mysteriously.

The Fae

They reached Ellie's house in high spirits. Entering they saw Frances and Fae at the table in the kitchen, Yarrow was in the living room, tending to Felix' wounds.

"Where is Aurellio?" Asked Ellie.

"Ah! Well, that was a bit tricky." Yarrow replied looking sheepish.

"What do you mean?" James asked sharply.

"Oh nothing bad, just…Well, perhaps you had better look for yourself." Yarrow led them through to Ellie's bedroom. He lifted the valance sheet that skirted her bed and there, underneath the bed, lay a swaddled, body shaped lump.

"I see!" Ellie tried not to laugh.

"It was the darkest place in the house." Yarrow explained. "With the curtains being so thick and heavy, there is very little chance of him getting crispy."

"Ssh! You can't say that, he will hear you." Giggled Ellie as they were leaving the room and closing the door behind them.

"No, they sleep the sleep of the dead during the day." James told her.

"Literally!" Yarrow interjected with a smirk.

"But he was awake when we rescued them." Said Ellie.

"Well, yes. In emergencies they can stay awake but it takes a lot out of them."

"Careful, you'll have me worrying about him soon!" Ellie retorted.

"Ellie!" Yarrow was shocked. "What was that for?"

"Well, if it wasn't for him in there, Felix would be okay." She pointed out.

On the couch, Felix lay covered with a sheet. Someone had removed his clothes and every inch that Ellie could see of him was covered in bruises, burns, bites and cuts. He was very pale, his hair tangled and lack lustre. His closed eyelids were almost transparent, a reddish tinge battled with the vivid blue of the veins that stood out in sharp relief. There were large dark circles around them. His cheeks were hollowed and his lips dry and cracked. Ellie could see where his cuts had been wiped clean and some were dressed with plasters and bandages. Felix looked all of his many hundreds of years and Ellie's heart felt as though it would crack. She sat on the floor by the couch and took his hand in hers.

"You're safe now. We are all here. You're safe." A tear rolled down her cheek and disappeared into her hair that swung over the unconscious body of her friend.

Fae entered the room and stood looking at her son's broken body. Her face was hard. She took a long, searching look then left the room. James followed her out and into the garden. Through the window Ellie watched as they stood toe to toe, angry faces mouthing harsh words that could not be heard. She saw Fae turn to walk away and James reach out and grab her hand, turning her back. Not letting go. She saw her body language stiffen, hands fist, head held high and tight. She saw James lean toward Fae and whisper into her hair. She saw Fae soften. Ellie watched as the pair walked out of sight, hand in hand.

Frances had been watching too. Ellie saw concern writ large upon her face. Saw her take a step as if to follow, then not follow through. Indecision chased worry through her features then settled into acceptance. Ellie went to her and took her hand. They stood for several moments, hand in hand, watching through the window.

The Fae

Chapter fourteen

Fae and James came back to the house after about an hour, they looked slightly flushed and sheepish, but nobody commented on it. Perhaps nobody but Ellie really noticed. Frances looked long and hard at her son and seemed to want to say something to him, but she appeared to shake herself and the moment passed. Yarrow had left to go to the hospital and start his shift. Sean was spread across the armchair in the living room watching Felix and reading a book. The twins had gone straight to school from the sport centre but Ellie herself felt peculiar.

Ellie was in her own home, with people she cared about, having rescued her friend but she felt really out of sorts. A black cloud seemed to have settled over her, turning all her thoughts dark. She was listless and tired. Everything was too much effort. Talking seemed to drain her. Thinking was out of the question. She wanted to be on her own but she didn't want anybody to leave. The tea she was drinking tasted like soap in her mouth so she put the cup down. Then she lifted it and took another long sip. Realising that it still tasted bad, she put the cup back down again. She did not know what was wrong. She should be happy. Things were great. Okay so she kidnapped and tortured her bosses' girlfriend and may no longer have a job to go back to, but she had new friends and a family of sorts. She had always wanted that. To have people in and out of her home, as if it were their own, comfortable around her. What was wrong with her? She went to the bathroom, locked the door, sat on the closed toilet seat, put her head in her hands and quietly sobbed.

She must have been in there for a while because there came a knock on the door and Frances voice asking her,
"Are you alright my daughter?"
"Yes, thank you, I won't be a minute." Ellie sniffed and replied, grabbing a handful of toilet tissue and blowing her nose.
She stood to leave and burst into tears again. She sat on the side of the bath and hugged herself. What was happening? This was stupid. Everything in her life was great, why the tears? She cried harder.
Looking up, Frances stood before her. Ellie didn't question how she got in, just looked at her with bright shining eyes that were brimming with sorrow.
Frances knelt in front of Ellie and wrapped her arms around her. She did not say a word, just rocked and held tight until the tears stopped.
As she stopped crying, Frances held Ellie at arms length and said,
"You have done nothing to be embarrassed about. After all you have been through; I am surprised that it took this long to have a cry. I don't think you realise how much you have had to assimilate in the last few days." Frances wiped Ellie's tears from her cheek. "I want you to know that now I have found you, I will always be here for you. I will never lose you again. I swear it."
Ellie sniffed and rubbed at her nose.
"Thank you. That means more to me than you know."

After her face was washed, cooled and back to normal, Ellie went back to the living room. James and Fae were sitting on the floor, hand in hand, watching Felix so intently that they appeared to be burning his image onto their retinas. They both looked up when Ellie walked in and smiled gently at her.
"I do not think that we have thanked you for saving our son." Fae said.

"It wasn't just me." Ellie blushed.

"No, but you were the driving force. If not for you, we fairies would still be talking about it and James would never have known. You are the lynch pin that holds the two species together. We have never worked in such proximity before. I believe that your coming to us was a blessing."

"Aw! Fae! Cut it out." Ellie was embarrassed.

"No, she is right." Frances agreed. "We have had a long history of distrust and enmity." Here she blushed and looked at Fae. "But you seem to have bought us together. I think that this is the beginning of a new age for the Fairy and Elf."

"Way to be dramatic." Ellie joked, trying to lighten the mood. This was a bit deep. Fae looked at James and smiled.

"Here is to hope that it may be so." He agreed.

"Ahem!" Sean cleared his throat. "If you kind people have finished with the mutual appreciation club, you may be interested to hear that your man here is waking."

All attention turned to Felix who lay with his eyelids fluttering, trying to open. They looked like wounded butterflies flapping desperately, trying to take off. They eventually opened. The whites of Felix eyes were a deep crimson that made Ellie suck in her breath with alarm.

Felix achingly slowly turned to her and croaked,

"Hey you." Then collapsed back into the cushion.

"My dearest boy." Fae said gently. "I am so happy to see you awake. We were so worried."

Felix's blood red orbs sought his mother and his parchment lips tore in a smile.

"Mother." He whispered, then closed his eyes and returned to his sleep.

James squeezed Fae's shoulder and stood up.

"May we put him in your bed Ellie? I think he would be better rested there."

"Oh of course, why didn't I think of that?"

James and Sean lifted Felix between them and carried him reverently to the bedroom, where they lay him down and covered him over.

Ellie took a quick peek under the bed to make sure that the vampire had not moved or woken.

Frances and Ellie sat on the couch whilst James and Fae stayed with their son in the bedroom. Sean resumed his position across the armchair. The radio played softly in the background. Saxophone and piano chased each other lazily through the still summer air whilst the trio lay back and listened. No words were needed nor welcome. Through the open back door, the sun could be seen to reluctantly set. The orange and red of its defiance sat heavily on the horizon. The birds called their farewells and blossoms curled in for the night. Bunbury appeared and jumped onto Ellie's lap. He arched his back against her fingers then settled in a ball to sleep. Within moments his purr accompanied the jazz that soothed their souls.

Ellie must have dozed for she jolted awake as she felt someone sit on the sofa. Opening her eyes, she saw that she had fallen asleep against Frances, who was stroking her hair absently. Sitting upright, she stiffened when she saw that Aurellio had come into the room and sat alongside her.

"I'm sorry if I disturbed you." Aurellio still held onto a hint of his Roman accent, making his words sound exotic and romantic.

"Oh, no it's okay." Ellie soothed. "I didn't realise that I had fallen asleep. How are you feeling?"

As she looked at him she saw that he bore little resemblance to the wretched creature that they had bundled into dusty curtains and hidden under her bed.

"Well, thank you." Aurellio gave a bow of his head. "I thank you very much for your timely rescue. I do not believe that either of us could have lasted much longer. I can see that Felix is still not come round even though his mother is tending to him."

"We are hoping that he will be awake soon, but he looks awful. I cannot imagine what you guys went through. I think it would be better, if you don't mind, to wait for the queen tomorrow night before we de-brief. If that's okay with you?" Ellie asked. "That way you only have to tell it once and it will give Felix time to recover a bit more."

"I agree." Aurellio said. "I do have another favour to ask you, although I realise that you are not compelled to help me." He looked somewhat unsure.

"I will do what I can." Ellie sighed. "What do you need?"

"Um! Well, I do not think that returning to my home would be a terribly good move at the moment. There are things in play that need careful exploration and I do not know who I can trust. I was wondering, hoping if there was somewhere I could stay during the day, and well the night I guess. I am mostly healed, but I could do with the rest and there are a lot of things that Felix and I need to discuss when he is able."

"Oh, sure, as long as you don't mind sleeping under the bed, it's the darkest place I have. I can block out the windows in there even more too, that will be no problem." Ellie assured him.

Frances gave her a quick look of alarm.

"I see that your mother is concerned for your safety." Aurellio soothed.

"Oh, this is Frances, she's unfortunately not my mother. And that is Sean." Ellie indicated the lounging Irishman on the chair.

Sean tipped his head in greeting.

"Pleasure." He smiled.

"You have every right to be nervous around me, I am a dangerous man. But I swear that no harm will come to you whilst I am here. In fact I owe you my life, so it shall be my honour to be your protector from now on."

"Well, thanks but it wasn't just me you know."

"I know, and I do not renege on my debts." Aurellio said proudly.

It was agreed that Aurellio stay with Ellie until the situation changed. Whatever that meant.

"There is one rather embarrassing yet urgent problem though." Aurellio looked Ellie in the eye. "I haven't eaten since the day before we were captured and it is staring to make me rather ill."

"Oh god! I am so sorry. Here let me make you something." Ellie jumped up and started toward the kitchen.

Frances grabbed her hand and shook her head.

"No child. He has not fed. There is nothing in your kitchen that he can use."

"I don't under... Oh!" Ellie's face paled. "Oh!"

"I have a supply in my fridge at home, but I think it would be too dangerous for me to go there."

"We can..." Ellie interrupted.

The Fae

"Thank you but no." Aurellio answered. "I am sure that now my escape is known, my house will be watched. It would not be safe to go there. If I can make a phone call, I know someone that can bring me a couple of packs…"
Sean sat up.
"Sure, it will be fine. I know a man; I think it best if you stay away from all your known associates for now. Do you not think? Give me a couple of minutes and I shall be right back." He stood and left, whistling a jaunty tune as he reached the back gate.

"My apologies again. How thoughtless of me." Aurellio said. "Of course, you do not want any more Vampires at your door. Please forgive me. I can only say that I am unused to not knowing who to trust. It has been many years since my life had any colour in it; I had quite forgotten the possible implications. Do you forgive me?"
He looked as if he genuinely wanted to be forgiven, Ellie was not sure why. She was sure that she was glad there would be no more Vampires coming to her home. One was certainly enough.

They sat awkwardly for some time. Ellie had offered Aurellio a drink and he had explained that vampires don't drink. Ellie felt revulsion sweep over her as she realised exactly why they didn't. It was one thing to read about sexy vampires sucking your blood during hot and heavy sex. That was quite titillating. But to have a real live vampire in your sitting room, propped on your couch? One who had recently been tortured and starved? Ellie realised that this was perhaps not an ideal situation. Maybe allowing him to stay was not such a bright idea. After all, she didn't know him from Adam. Now that she thought about it, he did appear to have a wild, almost desperate look in his eyes. He did not seem able to sit still, jumping at the slightest of sounds.

"Tell me a bit about yourself." Ellie realised she had spoken out loud when Aurellio looked at her in surprise.
"Really?" He asked. "You want to know about me? Why?"
"Well, if you think I'm being nosey…"
"Oh no, not at all. It is just that I cannot remember the last time anybody was actually interested in me."
"Oh Puhleese! Seriously?" Ellie smiled. "I have been told that you came over with the Roman invasion. You have been around since Jesus! Christ! You have to be incredibly interesting! I don't even know where to begin asking you questions."
"Oh! How kind. Well, yes, as you know I came over with the Romans. We did not see it as an invasion at all. We had been invited here."
"No way!" Ellie interrupted incredulously.
"Yes way!" Aurellio smiled.

"Have you heard of the Trinovantes?" Aurellio asked. "They were the first tribe based in Britain to establish trade links with the Romans. Well, Camulodunum which as you probably know is what Colchester used to be called, was the capital city of the Trinovantes and they became ruled by King Cunobelin in around 10 BC. King Cunobelin was the only King to have the title Rex Britannorum, which means King of Britain. Try though he might though, he could never unite all the tribes of Britain into a single fighting force, so when we Romans came we were able to conquer most of

Britain. Had he been able to unite the tribes? Well, we cannot know for sure, but I believe that we would not have been as successful.

"Ok, so before the tribe splits, you have Verlamion up in Hertfordshire and Camulodunum here in Colchester. These are the most important cities in Britain, which are ruled first by the Trinovantes then the Catuvellauni with King Cunobelin. With me so far?"

Frances and Ellie were sat with their mouths open and eyes wide. They nodded.

"Right now came Mandubracius, an exiled Trinovantian prince. King at the time was then Cassivellanus who had been elected leader of the British resistance. Mandubracius then fled to Caesar begging for aid. Caesar forced the Britons to surrender and forced Cassivellanus to sign a treaty forbidding him to attack the Trinovantes along with their rightful King Mandubracius."

"So..." Began Ellie, interested. "Colchester was an important place then? Cool!"

"Colchester, or Camulodunum as it was then, was the capital of Britain. It was the most powerful place in the land. Verlamion was the second capital. Between the two, most of the south of England was covered. The Trinovantes trade and government reached far beyond her borders to influence many other tribes."

"But you said that the Romans were invited. I can't see where, only the treaty to set that Mandy bloke back on the throne." Ellie said.

Aurellio took a deep breath whilst he appeared to be gathering his thoughts.

"Right. Yes, I forgot that bit. Okay I am not too sure when he became King but we do know that the first coins minted for King Cunobelin were around 5 BC, forty something years later in 39 AD one of his sons Adminius fled to Rome to ask Emperor Gaius Caligula for military support, he wanted some of the power his two other brothers had. Basically he was saying to Caligula that the Britons were wealthy but unorganised and ripe for conquering.

"So now Claudius succeeds Caligula and Cunobelin dies. In 43 AD four of the Roman legions arrive at the Thames Valley where they wait for Claudius. He arrives with his Praetorian Guard, elephants and even several Roman senators. They advance on Camulodunum and accept the surrender of the British Kings. Claudius is led on a victory parade through the city to gloat over his new subjects. Claudius then sets up a legionnaire fortress for the XXth legion and the First Thracian Cavalry. Camulodunum was given highest rank of the Roman Cities and its people became citizens of the Empire. This was in part for, and here I quote.." Aurellio made quote marks with his fingers in the air. "For initiating the allies in the requisitions of the laws of Rome." Basically for inviting them in and making their stay such a pleasant one." Aurellio showed no emotion in his face as he recounted a history that he had lived through, but that Ellie had not even heard of before.

"I remember the invasion." Frances said quietly. "I do not remember it quite as you do. I remember the slaughter, the hunger, the raping of our women and of our land to build fortresses. The Castle in the park? That was built atop a wooden fortress. And the beautiful Boudicca, Queen of the Iceni. The Romans killed her in sixty one. She and the Celts razed the city to the ground before they caught her. You can still see evidence of her destruction in town. They call it the Boudican destruction layer. She slaughtered our citizens in their hundreds."

"We bought more than destruction." Aurellio said hotly. "We built you temples, the Temple of Claudius housed three thousand people, and it was the largest and finest in the country. We bought you underground heating, sanitation. We built the first city wall…"

"Only because Boudicca destroyed your defences and you had to replace them, don't try to tell me that was for our benefit!" Frances was becoming annoyed and it showed in her voice.

Ellie was too fascinated to interrupt.

"We bought you culture and learning…"

"You bought the royal family and the wealthy culture and learning. How more separate from their people could they possibly be when the royals were speaking in Latin? Sycophantic, pretentious, preposterous…"

"Okay, okay!" Aurellio held up his hands. "Please let us not re-fight the battle of over two thousand years ago."

Frances smiled. "You are right, my apologies. Tell me, if you don't mind that is. Were you a Vampire when you came over or were you turned in Camulodunum?"

"Oh no, I was an idealistic young man with a beloved back in Rome. I came from a noble family. We were not as wealthy as the senators but we were accustomed to fine things. My beloved was also from a good family and we were pledged to marry upon my return. I came to Britain, marching long and hard. Straight across Europe as it is now known. We were so fit in those days. There was plenty to eat and the villages we passed by would give us what they could willingly, for the most part. The journey across the water to Britain was my first time at sea. I hated it. It was most undignified, my head over the side for the whole journey. My comrades were merciless in their torment." Aurellio smiled at the memory. "When we landed, I actually threw myself to the ground and kissed the earth, so glad was I that we were arrived safely. It had been a long and perilous voyage. Storms had followed us here and tried many times to rip apart our vessel.

"I was with the First Thracian Cavalry. I was so proud. Eager too! Any opportunity to get myself noticed by my commander and I jumped at the chance. I came to his attention that is for sure!" Aurellio said darkly. "One evening, I was called to his tent to serve him and his guest at dinner. I had never seen this man before. He was short and squat, he wore a black cloak over his winter toga and seemed to prefer to sit away from the firelight. I waited upon them, staying in the shadows, ready to jump when called. As the meal wore on, I overheard small snips of information. I wasn't listening in you realise. It is just that I had no choice but to hear what was said. It turns out that the man was called Marcellus. He requested that I escort him back to his accommodation outside the camp. He told my commander that he was afraid of possible roaming bandits in the area. My commander agreed. He seemed overly obliging, obsequious even. So after the meal, Marcellus and I set out. He spoke very little and it was not my place to question him, only to speak when directed to do so. We arrived at his accommodation and he asked me to step inside a moment. He told me that I was to take a package to my commander. I had no reason to believe otherwise, so I went inside.

"Before I knew what was happening, I had been lifted from the ground and thrown against the wall where I landed with a crunch. My head was bleeding and my wits were scrambled. Marcellus was upon me in a flash. He held me with one hand as if I

The Fae

were a child. He stretched my head back and bit into my throat. I could feel the flesh tear. I had never known anything like it. I could not believe that this man was attacking me. And in such a way! I can honestly say that I was terrified. I had never known such fear. My throat felt as though it were being pulled away from my neck! I realise now that he was sucking, drinking my blood. But then? I could not conceive of it. When he had had his fill, he thrust me aside like a used goblet and I passed out. When I came too I was compressed. There was no air, no light, and no space. Every inch of me was tight. I had been buried. We did not use boxes, we wrapped our dead in a sheet and buried them. I had been buried alive! I tried to scream but there was nowhere for the sound to go. I tried to claw and kick but I was bound and squashed into dirt. I thought I should go insane. I could see no way in which I could free myself. I wondered what had happened. Why did they think I was dead? Perhaps they saw my throat and believed me beyond help."

"Oh my god!" Whispered Ellie in awe. "How did you escape?"
"I didn't. That is to say that I did not escape, I was dug up."
"Eow!"
"Yes, quite! Marcellus had come back and dug me up. He took me back to his accommodation and cleaned me up. Luckily they did not waste good embalming on mere soldiers in those days!" Aurellio joked. "He kept me a prisoner at his place. I tried to escape several times but in the beginning I was weak and he was fast. I began to notice that I no longer thirsted or felt hunger. I began to feel strong, stronger than I had ever felt in my life. My skin had become what you see now, pale and dull, my teeth felt strong and sharp, my fingernails never seemed to break, which was odd as I had always had a habit of biting them before. Then I became ill. I had such a need, but I knew not what for. It was overpowering, visceral. Every fibre in my body screamed out for…something. I could not sit, stand, lay. I paced back and forth like a tiger in a cage. I would roar and howl in frustration. I wanted to tear down the fabric of life itself to satisfy this need. It was all consuming. Then Marcellus told me how to stop it."

"How? What was it?" Ellie asked in all innocence.
"I had to feed." Aurellio shrugged. "I had to feed or I would die. For good this time. I would not, I could not do to another what Marcellus had done to me. He told me that it was the only way. I refused."
"But what happened?" Ellie was entranced.
"I held out for two and a half weeks. I thought I had lost my mind. The pain and need were all there was. Then, when I was too weak to fight any more, Marcellus bought me what I needed."

Sean walked into the room, swinging a supermarket carrier bag. He stopped and glanced around at the Ellie and Frances sitting and looking at Aurellio. Their mouths were open, eyes were huge and staring. A look of fear and incredulity upon their faces.
"Hey guys, what did I miss?"
The spell was broken and they all turned to look at Sean. Huge sighs of relief and a release of tension cleared the air.
"Well Mister, I have your dinner here. Would you like me to nuke it in the microwave or heat it in a saucepan?" Sean continued to look at everyone trying to guess the reason for the strange atmosphere.

The Fae

"Thank you. Uh, if you good people will excuse me, I will just see to this then." Aurellio stood and accepted the bag from Sean. He went through into the kitchen, rustling and pings could be heard through the open door.

Ellie and Frances looked at each other then up at Sean.

"Wow!" Said Frances.

"Wow indeed!" Echoed Ellie.

"Wow what?" Asked Sean.

The evening drew darker and eventually the stars were permitted to dazzle. The night creatures chirruped and hooted in the undergrowth and trees. A stillness settled upon the house that felt wholesome and welcome to Ellie. The company had chatted of things light and distracting. Dancing around the reason for their presence, they spoke of Holidays taken and holidays dreamt, of cars they desired and clunkers they had owned. Ellie forgot to see the different races around her as they gradually became ordinary people with ordinary histories and ordinary jokes. Fae and James had joined them in the living room and although they participated in the conversation, they were on constant alert to any sound from their son. As the night drew on Ellie started to yawn. She had not realised how tired she was. It was agreed that Fae and James would stay the night, Sean would go home, Aurellio would amuse himself with twenty four hour television and Ellie would sleep on the couch as her bed had been taken by Felix.

Laying wrapped in a duvet and wearing her longest most old fashioned night dress, Ellie was convinced that she could never fall asleep. Aurellio had the TV turned down low and was watching an episode of Being Human. James and Fae were in the bedroom with Felix. She closed her eyes and heard the soft murmurings of the TV and the occasional grunt of incredulity from Aurellio.

"You have my word that I will do nothing to harm you." Came Aurellio's voice faintly. "Nor indeed will I allow anyone else to harm you. Please be at peace and try to sleep."

"I know, thank you." Ellie sighed. "I don't really know what is wrong with me. I am not worried having you here although I suppose I should be. I am even used to having mythical creatures in and out of my home and thoughts. I have been involved in things that are straight out of a fairy story. I suppose that I am still trying to adjust to it all. It tends to make sleep a little difficult when new and incredible things are around every corner for me."

"Yes, I see what you mean." Aurellio was thoughtful for a moment. "Would it help to talk about it do you think?" He asked in all sincerity.

Ellie laughed and turned over to face him.

"So I finally meet a man that wants to talk about my feelings and he's already dead! Typical!" She laughed.

"Yes, I see what you mean." Aurelio smiled in return.

"Do you have a boyfriend? Girlfriend?" Asked Aurellio.

"No. Yes. Actually, I'm not really sure. I don't think so. Not now anyway."

"This sounds interesting." Aurellio sat back and stretched his legs out comfortably.

"Not so much interesting, more frustrating."

"I'm a good listener."

Ellie found herself telling Aurellio all about her confusing feelings toward Fox and about his changed attitude toward her.

"I feel really guilty for starting something I shouldn't have and I feel really angry that he is just accepting what he is told to do. I don't know, I guess I want him to fight for me, to tear down anything that stands in our way. I'm beginning to wonder if I should have just left well alone. I'm not completely sure that I want it to happen any way." Ellie looked at Aurellio from under her lashes. "I know that I seem like an awful person. I guess I must be. I am pretty sure that I am not ready for a relationship anyway." She shrugged and snuggled further into her duvet. "All this must sound so vanilla to you. So one dimensional."

Aurellio smiled kindly.

"Not at all. We no longer have the longings and desires of mortals. We are so used to taking what we want that the nuances are lost to us now. I can hardly remember the last time I yearned for anything, let alone felt confusion about a possible mate. I don't think I can remember the last time I had a mate!" He seemed genuinely amazed. "Do you know that I actually can't remember? How weird is that?"

Ellie laughed.

"You know what? Me either! It seems so hard to remember much of my life at the best of times, but recently I have felt that my time before was the fantasy and now is the reality. I know that I have dated, nothing very serious though. I always felt that whoever I was seeing was too flat, too insipid. I never seemed to find someone that made me feel alive. Made me feel whole. Maybe that's why I went for Fox? Maybe it's because he isn't human; the fairy prince thing? Yeah, that's probably it."

"Probably." Aurellio agreed.

Chapter Fifteen

Ellie had awoken with Bunbury under her chin and a welcome waft of freshly brewed coffee on a table beside the couch where she lay. She stretched out her legs and scrunched her toes, then stretched her arms past her head and yawned loudly.

"Good morning my darling." Came Fae's voice from the kitchen. "I have some porridge on, do you like yours salt or sweet?"

"Um, neither thanks, just straight up with a handful of the chopped fruit in the fridge."

"Oh that sounds good, I shall make that for all of us." Fae called back.

"How is Felix?" Asked Ellie.

"Not much change I'm afraid. He woke a few times in the night but not for long. Sleep is the best thing right now."

"I agree." Ellie said sitting up. "There is nothing to beat sleep when you need to heal. Did Aurellio get under the bed in time?" She giggled at the image.

"Oh yes. You know he is rather charming for a blood thirsty creature. We chatted for a while after you fell asleep. He is very interesting." Fae replied as she came toward Ellie with a tray, upon which sat a steaming bowl of porridge.

"You know," began Ellie. "A girl could seriously get used to being woken with breakfast in bed." She half joked. "I don't know that I will ever get used to being alone again after the amount of company I have had these last few days."

Fae just smiled in acknowledgement and returned to the kitchen.

"He is awake Fae." Announced James as he strode into the room looking very tired.

"Oh, coming!" Fae replied rushing past whilst drying her hands on a tea towel.

James sat heavily on the chair opposite Ellie.

"Good morning." He acknowledged.

"It is for me, but you need to sleep." Ellie scolded him. "Here." She scooted up to sit on the sofa. "Lay here for a bit and rest."

"I can't. They may need me."

"They may well need you but you will be no use to them dead on your feet. Now shift!"

James smiled and changed seats.

"Okay, I will just close my eyes for…" He fell asleep as soon as his head hit the back of the sofa.

Ellie smiled and covered him with her duvet then got up and sat in the freshly vacated chair. James slid down until he was laying on his side. With a half snort, half snore, he appeared to be out for the count and Ellie resumed her breakfast.

Ellie was in the kitchen washing dishes when Fae came back in.

"He is looking much better." She answered Ellie's enquiring look. "He spoke for a while but it tired him out."

"Fae?" Ellie asked. "I hope you don't think I'm being rude, but.."

"Yes dear?"

"Well, why don't you heal him? You know, how you healed me when you found me?"

"That is not rude dear, that is just complicated."

"How?" Ellie wanted to know.

"I know that you have been told that I am to face disciplinary action for what I did for you. Well, I have been forbidden to use my powers until after my trial."

"That's just bloody stupid!" Exclaimed Ellie heatedly. "For crying out loud! He is your son!"

"Yes, I am aware of that." Fae sounded a little offended at the implication. "You cannot possibly understand. I don't mean to be rude in the least, but please can we drop this? It pains me greatly to be unable to help him. I am contented only with the knowledge that he will recover fully naturally. His injuries are superficial. Mostly he is suffering from dehydration and exhaustion."

"Yes but..."

"Please Ellie? This is hard for me."

"Okay, I shan't talk about it but please know that I feel awful knowing that it is my fault you can't help him."

"It most certainly is not your fault! Never let me hear you say that!" Fae was incensed. "Had I not helped, you would have died. I will never regret doing what I did. Felix will recover, have no fear. He will probably be up by time the queen arrives tonight."

"Ah crap! I had forgotten that she was coming." Ellie huffed. "How many do you think it will be this time? Shall I prepare food?"

"How many? I am not sure. As to preparing food? No. Mertensia will bring something with her. She may even treat us all to her famous lavender cake." Fae smiled and the mood in the kitchen lightened considerably.

The day was spent cleaning the house and shopping for groceries. Fae accompanied Ellie to the supermarket and together they wandered the aisles examining produce and choosing delicacies to replenish her dwindling supply at home. They chattered like two starlings as they walked arm in arm around the store. Ellie felt that she must have known Fae in a previous life as they got along so well. They seemed to know a great deal about each other and they were very relaxed in each others company.

Must be the blood I suppose, thought Ellie at one point when they both said the exact same sentence at the same time.

When they reached the checkout, Ellie lifted her bag and reached inside for her purse.

"Oh no, let me." Fae smiled.

"I couldn't possibly. There must be almost a hundred pounds here." Ellie was shocked.

"A small secret?" Whispered Fae leaning toward Ellie conspiratorially.

Ellie leant in also. "Ye-es."

"We fairy have a, let us say," here Fae made speech marks in the air with her crooked fingers. "*Special* kind of credit card." She said drawing out a pale blue credit card sized piece of plastic. It had a small pimpernel in the left hand corner but no other markings.

Fae swiped the card and entered a PIN number. The sale went through.

"Well its certainly very pretty," remarked Ellie, "but what makes it special?"

"It is unlimited." Cried Fae in girlish delight.

"Well, many credit cards are." Ellie replied. "Of course, it doesn't matter what the limit, I don't earn enough to have one and keep up the repayments."

"Ah!" Winked Fae. "These ones? We do not repay. They are unlimited!"

"Are you telling me that you guys have a credit card that you can spend on anything you like, as often as you like and yet don't have to pay back?" Ellie was sceptically impressed.

"That is exactly what I am telling you." Fae laughed.

The Fae

"Man! What I wouldn't give for one of those!" Ellie tried hard not to show the jealousy she felt rising up inside her.

"You do not have to give anything." Fae laughed harder. "This one is yours!"

And with that she handed the card to Ellie, who stood dumbly with her mouth open, staring at the tiny piece of blue plastic in awe.

Ellie and Fae went crazy! They went to every shop in town. Ellie bought every single pair of shoes that took her fancy, she bought dresses, skirts, tops, jackets, pretty underwear...

"I have never had pretty underwear before..."

...Sunglasses, hats, a diamante collar for Bunbury, clothes for Aurellio and Felix. She bought a beautiful waistcoat for James that reflected the colour of his eyes. She bought Bluebell and Begonia frilly dresses and matching lacy socks, she bought Fae a long cardigan of such fine and irregular lace that it looked as though spiders had woven it especially. Ellie and Fae went to the ancient George Hotel in town for lunch and ordered a bottle of champagne. They laughed and shopped until they could think of nothing else to buy and nobody else to buy it for.

The pair arrived back at Ellie's house exhausted and smiling. Ellie had never dreamt that a day like that was possible. Nothing was denied her. She felt amazing.

As they unloaded all their purchases onto the kitchen table, Felix gingerly walked into the room.

"Oh my darling." Sighed Fae, "You should not be up. How are you feeling?"

"Better." Felix managed as he slid onto a chair. "Much better."

Ellie squeezed his shoulder. "Good to see you in one piece." She smiled at him.

"Good to be in one piece." He smiled back. "Thank you. For everything."

"De nada! You would have done the same." Ellie shrugged.

"No, Ellie. I am serious, what you did was amazing. I shall never forget it."

"Way to get emotional!" Quipped Ellie back. "Just get better soon eh?"

"Er, mom?" Felix started.

"Yes my love."

"Why is James here?"

"Ah! Yes! About James..."

"I think I need to go check on Aurellio." Ellie got up and started backing out of the kitchen. "Just gotta check he is... um! Gotta check it's..." Ellie made a hasty exit.

Ellie was on the couch reading a book when Felix stumbled over and sat next to her. His eyes were glassy with exhaustion but his jaw was set and hard.

"Are you unhappy?" Ellie asked him.

"You knew? You knew that James was my father?" He asked.

"Only because of.. well, only because you were missing and I tried to find you. When I went to my safe place there you were. Only it wasn't you, it was James. He was upset at your disappearance and I could never have found you without him..."

"I am not unhappy Ellie. I am a little shocked. It certainly explains Peter's dislike of him. Wow! James? I never saw that coming."

"Really?" Asked Ellie. "You really never saw it? He looks just like you. I thought he was you."

"Well of course, now that I know, it all makes perfect sense. And yes, I can see the likeness now, but...wow!"

Ellie took his hand in hers.

The Fae

"I must go and speak with him." Felix stood uncertainly and went to talk with James, who was still in the bedroom.

Ellie returned to the kitchen and found Fae sitting at the table, staring out of the window; a faraway look in her eye.

"That seemed to go well..." Ellie interrupted.

"Oh yes, not so bad. He is such a strong boy. I know that they will work it out."

"May I ask why he never knew?" Ellie asked tentatively.

"Why he never knew?" Fae repeated distractedly. "Well, he was taken from me as a small child, I do not know if you have been told this?"

"Yes, I have been told a little. You don't have to tell me if it is too painful." Ellie said.

"Painful? Yes, I suppose it could be called painful." Fae still seemed to be distracted. "I had two...James and I had two beautiful babies, one boy and one girl. Although we had to keep our relationship a secret, we were very happy. James and I were so in love, we were perfect for each other. What did we care that we were different? To us that just made it more romantic. We were young then, naive. Felix was our first born. We had him with us for almost two months before he was stolen away. One morning we awoke, went to his crib and he was gone!

"We had to tell the queen and the council. We needed their help to find him. We were out of our minds with fear. The council ruled our relationship unlawful and forbad us to see each other again. We were incensed! That was not what we were there for. We needed help in finding our son, not a ruling on our love! The council offered us minimal aid. I truly believe that they did not wish him to be found." Fae covered her mouth in alarm. "Oh forgive me! I did not mean to say that. Of course they wanted Felix found. Please forget I said that." Fae was deeply upset.

"What happened then? I have been told that he was held for years. How on earth did you manage?" Ellie gently asked.

"Years, yes. James and I fought a lot after Felix was taken, we both secretly blamed the other for allowing it to happen you see. We split up. We had agreed that it was because we were breaking the law, but that is not true. We could not bear to see our son in the other's eyes. We searched constantly for our son but every thread we followed fizzled out into nothing. James and I would still meet and talk, we searched together and shared leads. We still loved each other. That had never changed. Years and years passed. We had made a daughter together after a while, but she too was taken. We could not believe that it was happening again. I am ashamed to say that my mind snapped. I became a recluse, I rarely left my home. I refused visitors. I grew my vegetables and herbs and flowers. I did not need to mix with anyone. James stopped coming. I believe it broke his heart to see me the way I was. He continued to search for our children. The only information we had was that the Gnomes had taken them. We never knew why. What possible reason?

"And then one day, out of the blue, there he was. My son. An adult but I would know him anywhere. His father is strong in him. He was broken completely. He had no memory of his life to that point. He was so damaged that it took years for the physical wounds to heal. As to the psychological? Who knows? We have no blue print to check against. We love him and care for him and try to protect him. As to why he did not know that James was his father? It was selfishness on my part. I wanted him to be strong. The council knew that he was half Elf and chose to accept him anyway. To give them their due, they have never treated him any differently to other fairy. I just did not want him to suffer as I had. Being forbidden to love whom I chose was a torment that scarred me. I did not want that scar to touch my son." Fae blushed slightly. "Also I suppose that I did not want to share him. I had missed so much…"

"I understand." Ellie soothed. "But how did James react?"

"I am ashamed to say that I did not care. I loved him still, that had never changed, but I was fiercely protective of Felix. I did not want anyone else to share his love. I had so many years of it denied me… I was so wrong! The suffering that I caused to the kindest man. I can never forgive myself…"

"I have already forgiven you." Came James' voice as he entered the kitchen and sat beside Fae. He took her hand in his and tilted her chin so that he could look directly into her eyes. "The past is gone. We are here, today. We have our son, he is alive and will soon be well. We will find our daughter, I swear it. We have each other and nothing will ever part us again." He leant toward Fae and kissed her lightly on the lips. A tear fell from his eye to join the one slowly rolling down Fae's cheek.

After a while, Ellie heard Bluebell and Begonia chattering away inside her head, they were on their way and drawing closer.

Ellie stood and put the kettle on to boil, she leant against the sink and stared out of the window at the setting sun. One by one the street lights beyond her garden blinked to life.

"Ellie, Ellie, Ellie." Sang the twins. "Can you hear us Ellie Belly?"

"Yes my darlings, I can hear you. I have a present for you."

"Ooh! We love presents." They squealed in delight. "What is it? Tell us. Oh please tell us?"

"Nope! You will have to wait and see."

"Well, we have sort of a present for you." They sang back at her.

"Will I like it?" Asked Ellie suspiciously.

"Oh yes. We think you will loooove it!" They giggled manically.

"Really?" Asked Ellie with a sinking feeling. "Can you tell me what it is?"

"Nope!" They echoed. "You will have to wait and see."

Oh crap! Thought Ellie.

Just as she had dreaded, Fox arrived with Mertensia and the girls. He managed a quick word alone with her before he was bustled into helping unload the car.

"This was not my idea. I was ordered to come by my queen."

"Well, orders must be obeyed!" Ellie retorted acidly.

And then he was out the door and helping Mertensia with the food she had prepared. Ellie took a deep breath and plastered a wide smile on her face.

"Where are my favourite twins?" She called. "Come out, come out wherever you are."

"Boo!" The girls shouted, jumping out from behind the gate. "Can we have our present now please?" They asked in mock seriousness after flinging their arms around Ellie's neck for a kiss.

"Girls, please mind yourselves." Mertensia semi scolded as she tripped over Begonia, nearly dropping a large plastic cake platter piled high with pale lavender coloured buns.

The Fae

"Sorry mother." The girls chorused as they stepped out of the way. "Ellie, Ellie, Ellie, may we? Please?"

"May you what?" Asked Mertensia sharply.

"Oh, I hope you don't mind but I bought the girls a present. I just couldn't resist. Please say it's okay?" Ellie grinned at a harassed looking Mertensia, taking the platter from her and setting it down on the table.

"Well, I must say that was very kind of you." Mertensia smiled. "I can not see any harm in it. What do you say girls?"

"Can we have it now?" Asked Bluebell.

"That is not what we say, and well you know it you saucy minx! What do we say to Ellie for thinking of you?"

"Thank you Ellie Belly." The girls giggled impatiently.

"Oh well, as you don't seem that interested, I shall just take these back to the..."

"No!" Screamed the girls. "We are interested, very. And happy." Shouted Bluebell.

"And we are very thankful, are we not Bluebell?" Chimed Begonia.

Ellie laughed and handed the girls a present each and watched with joy as they tore open the tissue paper and pulled out the dresses. The twins' eyes were huge with excitement.

"They are beautiful. Oh thank you Ellie. May we put them on mother?"

"Go and change in the bathroom then." Mertensia relented in mock seriousness.

"Hurry up though, the queen is right behind us."

The girls ran shrieking with delight to put on their new dresses.

"That was very kind of you." Mertensia said.

"I couldn't help myself." Ellie replied. "I saw the dresses and knew that the girls had to have them."

"It is so rare that they have shop bought clothes." Mertensia said wistfully.

"Ah, I kinda saw this too. I hope you don't mind." Ellie said nervously, holding out another prettily wrapped package to Mertensia.

Mertensia took the gift and looked at Ellie with huge wet eyes.

"You did not have to...I do not know what to... I can not remember the last.. Oh! What is it? May I open it?" Mertensia was as excited as the children.

Ellie nodded, embarrassed, and watched as Mertensia carefully untied the ribbon and unwrapped the package. Tears ran down her face as she lifted out a russet coloured dress made from almost sheer silk. She held it against herself and the fabric swished down toward her feet.

"Oh it is beautiful." Mertensia whispered reverently.

"It reminded me of your hair, just a shade or two darker. I hope you like it." Ellie said.

"Like it? You have no idea. I am going to put it on now!" And with that she ran lightly to the bathroom to join the girls.

Fox managed to stay out of Ellie's way until the queen arrived. Alcea came into the house followed by Yarrow, Milfoil, Sean and a woman that Ellie had not yet met.

"Good evening Ellie. Thank you for allowing us to use your home again." The queen smiled disarmingly at Ellie.

"You are very welcome." Ellie replied. "Is anyone else coming?"

"No my dear, this is it. May I introduce you to Datura"

"Pleased to meet you." The woman said, sounding anything but.

"Likewise." Replied Ellie in the same tone.

The hell is that about? She wondered.

The woman made no pretence of looking around. She was shorter than had appeared usual with the fairies, her hair a dullish brown with coppery highlights. Her cheekbones were not as high as the others and her lips not as full. Her nose had a tiny kink at the tip making her face seem off centre.

That accounts for the attitude, thought Ellie, *short arse syndrome*! She smothered the smile that crept up.

Datura Looked up sharply as though she had heard.

Crap! Ellie said inside her head. *I hope she can't read minds. Shut up then! I can't. She's looking at me. If she can read minds, she will think I am a lunatic. Well if she can read minds, the snotty cow, read this*! Ellie tried to see whether the woman's face had registered anything at all. The woman had looked away just as Ellie glanced at her, so she could not tell.

You do know that you are losing your mind don't you? Ellie told herself sternly.

The woman turned back and Ellie could have sworn she saw her smirk.

As everyone was taking a seat around the table Ellie had an odd thought. *Why are there always enough chairs? I only have four, yet everyone always has a seat. Where do they come from? Where do they go? Hmm! Strange.*

Whilst Ellie was musing, Felix entered, leaning heavily upon his father's arm.

"Your majesty." He nodded.

"Felix. I am glad to see that you are recovered." The queen said.

"Hardly recovered!" James interjected pointedly.

"James, I see that you are here also. Do you believe that it is necessary?" The queen asked imperiously.

"I am here because my son is here." James replied calmly. "Nothing will keep me from my family again." He looked straight at the queen then helped Felix to sit down.

"Quite!" She sniffed. "And the Vampire? Where is it?"

"If you are referring to me..." Aurellio strode into the kitchen, "I am here." He sat and winked at Ellie.

"Is that all then?" The queen enquired politely.

"I believe so." Fae answered slightly nervously, but with defiance in her voice.

The meeting started with Aurellio telling the group how he had heard that there was a lead on the black death balls. He told how he had asked Felix to join him and that he had agreed.

"And why did you ask our Felix? Why not one of your own?" Asked the queen sweetly.

"If you don't mind your majesty, may I come to that later?"

The queen visibly struggled to hide her annoyance at being denied so early in the proceedings.

"Continue then." She waved at Aurellio to carry on.

"Thank you your majesty. As I said, Felix joined me and we followed the suspect over several hours. They appeared to be delivering a message, or news. They went to many houses and flats, knocked, spoke briefly at the door then left."

"Wait a moment." Fox interrupted. "I thought that Marcellus was dealing with that now? We gave you people all our information. That should have been the end of it."

"And yet it is not." Replied Aurellio. "We were watching this Gnome from across the road, when we were knocked out from behind. We woke to find ourselves in a tight dark place, bound hand and foot. As it turned out, this was a blessing for Felix." He nodded to Felix who smirked in recognition of the fact. "The captors took us away in turns and tortured us. I will not go into details here, it is unnecessary. Suffice it to say that I wish never to go through anything like that again. I have the power to regenerate, so in that respect it was easier for me. Felix however does not and as you can see, he has come away from it worse than I."

"What did they want?" Asked Yarrow. "Surely if they designed the balls…"

"It was not really about the balls." Aurellio said. "They were more interested in how much we knew and whether we knew the identity of the players."

"And do you?" Asked the queen.

Aurellio flinched as he replied. "Your majesty, please. I am so sorry to be rude but that information is not something that I am willing to share. I survived torture without giving it up, surely you cannot expect me to tell you just because you ask me nicely?" He tried to smile as he said this but it never reached his eyes.

The queen's face drained of colour and her mouth dropped open. "Sir, I was under the impression that we are all on the same side here." She was furious.

"Madam." Began Aurellio. "With respect. We are not. There are more than two sides to this. I am on my own side in a party of one. Until I know all the facts, I shall stay this way. I am indebted to Felix for his aid, but that does not automatically place us in bed together."

Felix snorted a laugh, then tried to make it a cough as the queen shot him a look.

Ellie watched the scene before her as if it were a movie.

"So why exactly are we summoned here then?" The queen demanded.

Fae spoke up. "We believe that an attack on one of our own deserves investigation at the very least. Is that not still so?" She asked pointedly.

"Well, yes of course. We will look into this, of course we will." Spoke the woman Datura. "I believe that the queen wishes to know why this Vampire is here at all? Why is he telling us what he has told us?" She smirked with self satisfaction as though she had said something deep and insightful.

Aurellio ignored the woman. "Your majesty. I believe that what Felix and I are investigating will have far reaching effects for all the Others, not just the Vampire. The information that I can share with you, should be enough to help you to prepare yourselves."

"And what sir, are we to prepare for?" Sneered Datura, looking around the table.

Aurellio looked at Felix who nodded his permission. He took a deep breath, looked at everybody seated then said, "War. You will need to prepare for a war."

Chapter sixteen

Sharp intakes of breath could be heard following Aurellio's declaration. The queen tightened her lips and furrowed her brow, Fox stared insolently at the vampire and Fae clutched at her breast as if to calm her pounding heart. Ellie sat stock still, eyes trained on Aurellio watching for any sign that he was in jest. None came. Aurellio sat back in his chair and swept his gaze across those seated in the kitchen. His pale skin reflecting a subtle sheen from the moon, creating a landscape of peaks and troughs in his stern face. His bloodless lips were a small, thin line beneath his aristocratic nose. His serious, black eyes a void in the ashen marble of his countenance. Aurellio's hands rested atop each other on his lap and his ankles were crossed beneath the table. His demeanour, calm and stoic against the insanity of his words.

"War?" Asked the queen. "Between whom?" The shock that had shown in her face moments before was now replaced with a haughty indifference.

"The vampire and the Gnomes most certainly." Aurellio told her. "But there may be some fallout that affects the Fairy and Elves."

"Do not be ridiculous!" Snorted Datura. "What possible reason could you have for involving us? We have nothing whatsoever to do with you or the Gnomes."

"Be that as it may." Aurellio answered. "War is no respecter of boundaries but it *is* a great leveller. War does not respect your desire to be pacifist, nor does it respect your belief that you are above such things. War is coming and will roll right over you if you are not prepared."

"What can we do?" Asked Ellie.

"I do not believe you!" Datura spat at the same time. "We would never scrap like animals, you are mistaken."

"It is no mistake, there is war coming. I am trying to find a way to prevent it. Felix here is helping me, as you are aware, but I fear that we will not be successful. Things have moved too far and too fast. Those death balls that you found seem to be the final piece. Whoever developed them knew what they were about. They are the deadliest thing we have ever encountered. James, I believe that you and Ellie witnessed first hand their power and destructiveness?"

James looked harrowed at the memory. His face paled as he replied. "Yes, it was instantaneous. I would never have believed that something could affect the vampires like that. What we saw? It was pure carnage. But I don't understand, how does it involve us? And the Fairies?"

"I simply cannot believe that anyone, even vampires, would involve us in their petty squabbles." Datura sniffed, looking around the table for support. "Everyone knows that Fairies stay out of the affairs of Others. If you people wish to destroy each other, go ahead it is no concern of ours!"

"There are some of the Others who feel that you have sat aside too long." Aurellio answered. "There are also ones who believe that you had a hand in the development of the death balls."

"Preposterous!" Shouted Fox jumping to his feet. "How dare you suggest…"

"Foxglove! Be seated." The queen commanded.

Fox sat. He glared at Aurellio whilst clenching his fists and grinding his teeth with impotence.

"This feels wrong." James said quietly. "I don't doubt what you say, but this feels wrong. Why now? Why would the Others turn against us? There is something else at work here."

"Yes well thank you for your input!" Datura mocked. "I do not believe any one else here could have added anything less relevant."

Aurellio glanced at Datura dismissively. "I agree, something here is wrong. Felix and I are trying to put it together but so far have hit a brick wall. It is highly unusual, the lack of information in itself is telling."

"Telling what exactly? That the dead have lost what is left of their minds?"

"Datura! Enough!" The queen snapped. "This is not helping matters. Aurellio, what have you so far?"

"So far, we have the attacks on Ellie, the development of the death balls, the taking of Ellie, then myself and Felix…"

"Yes, yes, but what leads you to suppose that this is building up to a war? Why do you not believe that this is localised?" James asked.

Aurellio took a moment to reply. "There are things happening that I simply cannot share with you at present. But please be assured that the attacks on us so far have been unprecedented. We have not had a problem with the Gnomes for centuries, not since long before they came from Europe in the eighteen hundreds. They are unlikely to have had the skill to develop a weapon such as the balls. They must have had help. The question is from whom? I believe that the taking of Felix and his sister as babies is a part of this also, the combined powers of Elf and Fairy in one person? Or two? We cannot know what was learnt, what use that knowledge would have been put to."

"Yes," interrupted James, "but why war? Why is this not simply Gnome against Vampire?"

"I believe the attacks on Ellie prove that it is bigger than just the two of us. Because Ellie is human, it must mean that the attacks are meant to be more widespread. The intelligence that we have so far discovered bears this out."

"But I am not human." Ellie blurted out.

All eyes swung to look at her. Datura snorted in disbelief, the queen raised one eyebrow questioningly and James smiled and took her hand for support.

"What do you mean you are not human? Of course you are. What else could you be?" Asked Yarrow. "I know the queen asked us to accept you as family, but, and I am truly sorry, that bit of blood you have from Fae does not really make you Fairy. I wish it did for I love you like family, but you are still human Ellie."

Ellie smiled crookedly, wishing with all her heart that she had kept her mouth shut. "Frances told me a few days ago, when Felix went missing. She told me that she had wanted me to remember on my own, but that we hadn't enough time. She only told me the barest details. But she was adamant that I am not human."

"Well, what are you then?" The queen asked, stunned.

" Ah! That I don't know. Sorry. You will have to ask Frances."

"Did you not ask her?" Sean was incredulous.

"I kinda had other things on my mind at the time." Ellie said, smiling at Felix.

"Oh really! Who actually believes this rot?" Datura was furious. "This is pathetic. Here we have an insignificant, damaged Mundane wishing it were more than it is. Please tell me you are not taking this nonsense seriously!"

"Datura, that is enough!" Warned Fox, standing and leaning over her in a most non-pacifist manner.

"Oh please. Just because you wish…"

"I am warning you Datura. One more word from you…"

"And what Foxglove? You will do what exactly? Marry me again?"

The room fell silent. Nobody dared breathe. Fox sat down slowly and stared at Datura with pure hatred. All eyes were on Datura as she sat there smugly. Her face wearing a triumphant smile whilst malice shone from her eyes.

Ellie looked at Fox. She was stunned. Of all the reasons for his behaviour, she would never have dreamt that he was *married*!

"You… You… Are you telling me that you…And her?" Ellie stood on shaking legs and pointed to Fox. "This is the second and last time that I will tell you to leave my house. Get out. Now! And take your wife with you." Shaking, she stood and waited for Fox to stand and leave.

Datura remained seated. Her face was a mass of confusion and triumph.

"Woman." Ellie told her. "Get your snide, sarcastic, lopsided arse out of that chair, walk toward the door and get the fuck out of my house. NOW!" She shouted the last word so loudly that the spell around the table was broken and everyone started to speak at once.

Datura looked at the queen then to Ellie. Her face drained of colour and she scuttled out of the house without uttering another word.

"Now. Are there any more surprises? Hmm? Any more revelations? No? Shall we get back to the matter in hand then? Yes?" Ellie sat down and willed her stomach to stay out of her throat.

As she sat, Ellie felt Bunbury jump up onto her lap under the table. He padded in a circle then settled to sleep, purring gently. Ellie stroked the cat and with each pass of her hand she felt her heartbeat slow.

Sean looked at Ellie and smiled the saddest smile that she could recall ever seeing. She smiled back and took a deep, shuddering breath.

"Right then." Ellie said, staring at everyone in turn. "Where were we?"

James smiled a dazzling smile of pride, and with the smile shining through his voice said "We were discussing whether or not you knew what species you were."

The whole table seemed to be intent on discussing Ellie's parentage. She had tried to explain that she not only did not know, but actually was not quite ready to believe it either. But nothing could detract them all from speculating. James was the only one who kept out of it. He busied himself making drinks and tidying up, but he made no contribution to the debate.

Eventually, they returned to the matter in hand.

"I don't see that it makes any difference." Aurellio insisted. "If we didn't know, then the Gnomes certainly would not have known. They must think Ellie is human. It is the only thing that makes sense."

"I agree." The queen said. "The question of Ellie's origins, whilst intriguing, cannot have a bearing upon this threat. Also I believe that it is for Ellie to discover, not us to guess."

"Thank you." Ellie smiled. "I am not ready to open that door yet, so please can we pretend I never mentioned it?"

The Fae

It was decided that they would not learn anything further that night, so all but James, Sean and Aurellio made their farewells. Felix went home to be looked after by Fae. As she was leaving, the queen took Ellie aside.

"I hope it turns out that you are fairy." She whispered with girlish excitement. "I should love it to be so." Then she disappeared into the night behind the others.

Ellie set about clearing the last of the dishes and wiping down the table. She was emptying a plate into the bin when James spoke.

"Do you truly have no memory?" He asked her sadly.

"No. I really don't." Ellie replied. "It's odd though. The more I think about it, the more true it seems. But I have such clear memories of my life. Believe me when I tell you that I would much prefer not to, but I do. I remember every stinking moment of it. I remember praying that I was adopted, that my real parents would come and find me, rescue me. Clearly that never happened! How can I be something else entirely if I remember my life so clearly?" She looked at James with so much pain.

"I wish I could help you. But Frances is right, you must remember on your own."

"Why can't I remember? Would my life have been so bad that I blocked it? Surely it can't have been as bad as the one I do remember."

James put his arms around her and let her cry.

"I think that your life before was wonderful. I think that the reason you do not remember is that you are afraid. You only have pain in your memories, so the thought of something good would be terrifying to you. Enough to make you block it out. I promise you that when you do remember…"

"You are so kind to me James. Thank you." Ellie wiped her face with the tea towel in her hand and stepped away from James in embarrassment. "Sorry about the tears, I don't know what comes over me sometimes."

"While you are already upset…"

"Uh oh! This sounds like I wont like it."

"Maybe not, but I think it might be important. Do you remember when Fae found you in the woods?"

"Sort of, I have a hazy recollection. I'm not sure if it is a genuine memory or what I have been told though."

"What do you remember?"

"I remember the dark mostly. Everything was dark. The sky, the woods, my clothes." Ellie looked at James, vulnerability naked in her eyes. "My mind."

James held out his arms for her to settle into again. "What else?" He pushed.

"I remember the sun was warm although I couldn't see it. My wrists were cold and heavy. I was choking on the pills, trying to get them all down. The vodka was making me feel sick but I thought that if I just kept drinking it, I wouldn't taste it after a while. My whole body felt like concrete, sinking into the ground. I felt so lonely James. I wanted to die so badly. I couldn't stand to be alone any more. I just wanted it over, to stop being me. I hated my life. I hated every breath that sustained my life. I hated the reflection in the mirror, I hated the tiny pulse in my wrist. I hated everything about myself. I just wanted it to end. I thought that if it all stopped I would be okay. Do you know what its like to hate the very skin that wraps you? Every freckle on my arms was a torment to me. Every hair on my head was an insult. Being me was worse than dying James. Can you understand that?"

"No my love I can't." James held her tight until the tears had stopped, Ellies and his own.

The Fae

"Why were you filled with such self hatred?" James asked her gently.

"Oh, I don't know." Ellie sighed. "It all seems so pathetic when you put it into words, but when it rolls around and around in your head, for the majority of your life…Well, it eats away at you. It poisons every aspect of you."

"Can you tell me?"

"It's embarrassing really. I have never been loved. I know that sounds melodramatic, but it's true. My mother hated me. I never knew why. I was so obviously a great disappointment to her. I was too fat, too ugly, too stupid. Everyone else had a better child than her. My hair was too straight, my teeth too crooked, my attitude too slow. She kicked me once when I was about six or seven. I was playing on the carpet sweeper, pretending it was a car or something. She was mad at me as usual and kicked me from behind. She always wore court shoes with pointed toes, this time the toe of her shoe went straight into my groin and I thought I would die from the pain. Another time, she bit me, here…" Ellie rolled up her sleeve and showed James the faint outline of a human bite mark on her upper arm. "I was six. The scar has nearly gone now. She would hit me for breathing it seemed like. She always spoke to me through gritted teeth and never had time. Whatever I asked, she was too busy. I sat at the table for dinner? Because I scraped the cutlery against my teeth, she stabbed my arm with her fork. I have never known what I did to cause her to hate me so much."

"What of your father? Where was he in all this?"

"He was the lucky one, he worked overseas. He married her when she had children already, so he worked like a mule to support her. I became invisible. I would hide under the stairs or in the attic. Anything so as not to draw attention to myself. I would go out after breakfast and stay gone until it started to get dark. It was different then, you could do that. It was safer, less cars you know? I used to try and get hit by a car though. I used to jump out into the road, but it was a small village and nobody seemed to drive fast in those days. I thought that if I were…well, I don't know what I thought really."

"Do you have any good memories from then?" James asked her.

"Not really. I actually managed to block it all out for a long time, but when I had my first nervous breakdown it all came back to me. That and the abuse. It was a hard time for me then."

"How do you get through each day?" He asked in amazement.

"Knowing that the one person who should love you unconditionally hates the very essence of you? Well, let me just say that denial aint just a river in Egypt you know!" Ellie tried to joke, but it fell flat. "It is what it is." She shrugged. "I can't change the past. I also can't keep carrying it with me. Since I met you guys, I have been so thankful that I am alive, I cannot believe that I tried to end it all. I am incredibly glad that Fae found me. I feel as if I have been given a second chance to live. And believe me, I will not blow it again!"

"You did not blow it the first time. You are amazing Ellie, I am so proud of you."

"Uh, yeah well. Let's talk about something else now hey?"

They went to sit in the living room with Sean and Aurellio who were playing a game of scrabble and arguing light heartedly about the spelling of a word that Ellie had never even heard of.

The Fae

"What exactly are you guys doing? That is not a real word; you're cheating Sean." She laughed.

"We are playing in Old English." Aurellio said. "It gets boring after a few millennia and we old guys have to try to keep it interesting." He joked. "We wrote the missing symbols on the blank tiles. I hope you do not mind, it will wash off."

"No, no. Knock yourselves out. It's nice to do something ordinary for a change."

The rest of the night was spent playing board games, telling jokes and horsing around. Ellie managed to put the turbulent feelings from earlier to the back of her mind. She refused point blank to talk about or even think about Fox. *The lying married bastard*! She enjoyed watching the boys play about. She even forgot that they were magical beings for a while and just settled back to relax in their company. After her revelation to James, she realised that despite the constant danger she seemed to always be in, she was actually, oddly, very happy.

The Fae

Chapter Seventeen

Ellie ate breakfast alone the next morning. Sean and James had left late the night before and Aurellio was dead to the world under the bed. Ellie had felt peculiar waking up to a relatively empty house but determined to make the most of it and took a leisurely breakfast in the garden. She had walked up the hill to the shop earlier and bought a newspaper to read. She had also bought a can of tuna fish to give Bunbury a treat. Ellie sat at the small wrought iron table in the garden with her best china tea cup and plates. She had a bowl of porridge and two slices of toast and honey. She had made a pot of Earl Grey tea and was enjoying the fragrant brew whist skimming the paper looking for the cartoon section. Bunbury sat by her feet noisily devouring his equally fragrant fishy treat.

Ellie looked up as she heard her garden gate open; briefly wondering who it would be this time. She was pleasantly surprised to see a very nervous looking Ciara standing there.
"Hi, come on in. Would you like a cuppa?"
"Oh, hi Ellie. I am sorry to disturb you. I hope you don't mind me coming round. I asked at your shop for your address and that woman gave it to me. I do hope that was okay? To ask I mean."
"Of course. Come, sit down. What can I do for you? I must say, this is a lovely surprise." Ellie was genuinely happy to see Ciara. She had hoped to run into her again at some point.
"Oh thank you. Yes, thank you I would love a cup of tea, oh! Earl Grey, my favourite. Thank you." Ciara sat down and fiddled with the hem of her scarf nervously.
"Um, I hope you don't mind me coming round like this. I mean uninvited and all. Its just that, well… Do you remember me telling you about that old woman? When I was walking Flopsy in the woods that time? Its just that, well, she sort of showed up again. She was a bit scary to tell the truth. She told me I was to pass a message to you. I told her to do it herself but she laughed at me and said it was my job. I don't know what she meant. I must say, I think she is an awful woman. She really frightened Flopsy."
"Why don't you tell me what happened?" Ellie suggested as Bunbury chased after a butterfly that had passed by his nose.

Ciara sat at the table and took a dainty sip of the tea Ellie had poured for her. Placing the cup back into its saucer she looked around nervously before speaking.
"Well, Flopsy and I were in the woods for a walk. Friday woods? Up Berechurch Hall Road? So, we are wandering about, I pretty much let Flopsy take the lead when we go there. I have to admit I was miles away, I do let my mind wander when I walk her, I find it such a peaceful place. Well, parts without the dog walkers anyway." She smiled. "So, there we were minding our own business when that old crone just appeared in front of us. I swear I never even saw her approach, she was just…there. She looked at me and said 'Its you again, you need to give that to Ellie.' And she thrust this in my hand." Ciara passed over a dirty cream coloured envelope made from thick, expensive looking paper. "Like I said, I told her no, to do it herself, but she just sort of cackled and said it was my job. I asked her what she meant by that, that I hardly even knew you, but she was gone. I was turning the envelope over in my hand, looked up and poof! She wasn't there. I'm not a fanciful person, despite

appearances." Ciara smiled self deprecatingly. "But if I didn't know better, I would think she were a witch. There one minute, gone the next! And oh boy she stank! I know I shouldn't be rude, or say mean things about the elderly, after all she probably cant help it, but she really stank!" Ciara looked at Ellie slightly embarrassed and shrugged her shoulders as if to say, 'what can you do?'

"Well, that is certainly very odd." Ellie commented distractedly whilst turning the envelope over in her own hands. "I wonder who she is. It was the same one that you saw before?" She asked.
"Oh yes. I'm certain of it. She definitely recognised me anyway. I hope I did the right thing. Bringing the envelope to you that is."
"Oh… Yes, thank you. It is very odd isn't it?"
Ciara continued to sip at her tea whilst Ellie stared distractedly at the envelope. Bunbury sauntered over and sat looking from Ellie to Ciara and back again. Seemingly making up his mind, he jumped onto Ciara's lap and proceeded to make himself very comfortable. Ciara made a fuss of him, stroking his long fur and telling him he was beautiful. Bunbury purred his assent.

The gate swung open again and a tumble of curls, lace and squealing giggles exploded through and made its way to Ellie. Tiny mocha coloured arms threw themselves around her neck and cupid's bow lips pressed themselves all over her face.
"Hello my darlings, I didn't hear you coming." Ellie smiled in delight.
"We are practicing being quiet." Bluebell told her proudly. "Did we do well?"
"Very. I had no idea at all you were here." Ellie told them. "You are very clever girls."
The twins beamed proudly and turned to Ciara.
"You are very pretty." Begonia told a blushing Ciara. "What is your name? Can we be friends? Are you an Elf? I love your dress, do you like ours?"
Ciara sat with an amused expression on her face. "Nope, not an elf. I used to think I was a fairy princess but not any more unfortunately." She smiled at the girls.
"Oh no." Bluebell said seriously, studying Ciara's face. "Not a fairy, you could be an elf though, they are just as beautiful as us, are they not mother?"
Mertensia came over and sat in a chair, she was followed by a tall slim man with similar features to the girls, but a deeper shade of skin.
"Girls! The young lady could be an elf or even a fairy queen. She may be whatever she likes, may she not?"
"Oh, oops! Yes. You are correct mother, sorry." Begonia said with a smile. "We forget that not everyone is magical do we not?"

"What beautiful girls." Ciara told a flustered looking Mertensia. "And such wonderful imaginations. I remember when I was their age, I was the most beautiful fairy princess in the world." She told them fondly.
Mertensia looked a little relieved and turned to introduce the man beside her.
"Ellie, this is Clematis my husband. Clem, this is Ellie and…?"
"Oh sorry, how rude of me. This is Ciara. Very pleased to meet you Clematis." Ellie continued the introductions and the adults sat chatting whilst the twins chased Bunbury round the garden trying to dress him with the clothes from their now naked dolls on the ground. The letter lay temporarily forgotten on the table.

The Fae

Ciara had stood to leave when the gate opened a third time and Felix walked into the garden. Spotting the group seated at the table, he walked over scooping up the twins on his way. The girls were caught one under each arm, kicking and screeching with delight as Felix spun around and pretended to drop them.

"Uncle Felix, stop, stop!" The screamed.

Felix bent to put them down.

"No. Again, again!" They cried, so Felix spun them some more until his face started to look a little green.

Ciara had stopped dead in her tracks and was staring at Felix with wide eyes and her jaw almost resting on her chest.

"May I introduce…" And so the introductions began again.

Felix took Ciara's hand in greeting and as he looked at her to speak, it seemed as if the words were stuck in his throat. He appeared unable to say a single word. Felix held onto Ciara's hand and Ellie thought that he would never let go.

"Ciara was just leaving, perhaps you might persuade her to stay a little longer." Ellie suggested with a twinkle in her eye.

"Okay." Ciara said as she blindly sat back to where her chair should have been.

Clematis, noticing that she was about to miss and land on the floor, twitched his finger and the chair slid silently behind Ciara so that she landed safely. She did not notice a thing, she only had eyes for Felix.

Ellie smiled her thanks and tried hard to keep the grin from her face as she watched Felix at a complete loss for words, still holding Ciara's hand.

Ellie, Mertensia and Clematis chattered away like pigeons whilst Felix and Ciara stared at each other. After a while they were not even noticed any more. They had faded into the background. The girls continued to run around and torment Bunbury. Mertensia had produced from her bag a tin that contained American style biscuits. Large golden fluffy creations that tasted like buttermilk heaven. They were still warm and when spread with butter, simply melted in the mouth. After the biscuits were devoured, the adults sat back, bellies groaning, and watched the girls play.

"Oh! I forgot. Mertensia? Ciara bought this to me today. She told me that an old crone gave it to her in the woods, I think I mentioned her before?"

"What is it?" Asked Mertensia.

"Well, I haven't looked yet." Ellie admitted. "I don't really want to. Ciara said that the woman stank, so I was thinking that…"

"Ah yes. I see what you mean." Mertensia said thoughtfully. "Well, the only way to find out would be to open it."

"But what if it is dangerous?"

"I am quite sure that whatever it is, it will not be nice. Still, the quickest way to deal with it is to open it. Do you have any kitchen gloves? Oh and a sandwich bag?"

"Whatever for?" Asked Ellie.

"Just something I saw on CSI once." Mertensia laughed.

"Not a bad idea though." Interjected Clematis. "You cannot be too careful. After all, we know nothing about this crone do we?"

"Good point." Ellie agreed, jumping up to get the items from the kitchen.

Ellie came back with rubber gloves, a roll of clear sandwich bags and a sugar tong. She placed the envelope inside one of the bags, put on the gloves and reached the tongs inside to try to open the letter.

The Fae

"Well, that's not as simple as it looks." She said. Ellie put the tongs down and tore off two more bags. Opening the bags, she slipped one over each gloved hand and manoeuvred the envelope open. Inside was a sheet of paper, folded once with writing on one side. Ellie drew the page from the bag and unfolded it so that she could read what it said.

"Well, that's odd." She said distractedly. "Take a look at this." She handed the sheet of paper to Mertensia, who took it with the sugar tongs and held it up to read. Mertensia squinted her eyes and Clematis snatched the paper away from her with a laugh.

"Give it here you blind old bat!" And he proceeded to read the letter.

"Well what does it say?" Mertensia asked, excitement evident in her tone.

"It says 'Bring the Vampire to the woods, Friday at midnight. I have information that can stop this war.' What on earth…"

Ellie took the letter back and turned it over. There was nothing on the back. No matter how many times Ellie read the letter, the words did not change.

"Bring the Vampire to the woods. I have information that can stop this war? I wonder what she has?" Ellie asked nobody in particular.

Clematis looked alarmed. "You cannot be seriously thinking of going Ellie? It could be a trap."

"I am sure that it is, but what other lead do we have? We must have more information."

"But Ellie…"

"I will be with Aurellio, how much safer can a girl get?" She joked, trying to ease their worry.

Just then, Felix appeared to return to his senses and cleared his throat in embarrassment. Talk of the meeting ceased as they remembered that Ciara was not one of them.

"Oh boy!" Felix said, blushing.

"You can say that again!" Clematis laughed. "Nice of you to join us."

"Oh boy! Wow, I feel like I have been hit by a train." Felix shook his head.

Ciara looked around sheepishly, her face a bright red. "Uh, I think I should be getting home." She said, gathering her things together.

"Stay for lunch." Ellie laughed. "I'm sure Felix would like that." She teased.

"Oh no, I really should be…" Ciara stood and hurried backwards toward the gate. She almost tripped over Begonia. "Sorry. So sorry. Thank you for… I will see you soon…Thank…Bye. Bye." Then she was gone.

Felix stared after her. "She has left her scarf. Wait, Ciara wait." He called. Receiving no answer, he snatched up the scarf and ran after her.

Ellie, Clematis and Mertensia fell about laughing.

"What is funny?" Asked Bluebell.

"Oh nothing." Sniffed Ellie, wiping at the tears on her cheeks. "I think Uncle Felix has fallen in love."

"Well of course he has." Begonia told her seriously. "It is alright though, Ciara is Elf."

"Now girls, please remember we must not discuss these things when we are around mortals, that could have been very awkward earlier." Mertensia lightly scolded the girls.

"It is okay mother. We know." Bluebell told her. "But Ciara is Elf. She just does not know it yet."

"What makes you say that?" Asked Clematis. "Many people are beautiful, it does not mean they are magical."

"We know!" The girls giggled as they ran off to play with Bunbury.

After lunch, the group decided to take a trip to the beach, so they all piled into Mertensias car and set out for Mersea Island. As they reached the bridge, they had to wait twenty minutes for the tide to go out and the road to clear of sea water so that they could pass. They drove over as the water lowered to about an inch deep and the girls squealed in delight as the spray from the wheels made huge swans wings either side of the car.

"One way of giving this old heap a wash!" Clematis giggled, much to Mertensias feigned chagrin.

Arriving at the car park by the beach, they saw that many other people had a similar idea. There were dozens of cars and Mertensia had to wait for someone to leave before she could park her car in the vacated spot.

Finally parked, they threw open the car doors and raced each other to the sand. From nowhere, Clematis had conjured up buckets and spades, so the twins set about creating the biggest sand castle on the beach. Ellie sat back on a large stripy towel that had appeared and watched the girls industriously turning the pebbly sand into a cockeyed masterpiece. They had dug a moat around their castle and were running back and forth to the waters edge, filling their buckets with the brackish sea water then emptying them into the thirsty sand. After several trips and still no sign of a filled moat, Clematis clicked his fingers and the water stayed put, allowing the girls to complete their castles defences.

Mertensia rolled up her long purple skirt to reveal surprisingly shapely legs and lay back against her husband as she soaked up the sun. Clematis had undone the top button on his shirt and removed his shoes and socks. The twins were running about in knickers, having discarded their clothes as soon as they were allowed. Ellie wore a light summer dress and a floppy, wide brimmed hat. Although she loved the sun, she did not want to expose her skin to it, so her dress had long floaty sleeves whilst the skirt reached to her toes. It was made of a light filmy fabric that helped protect her delicate skin from the sun's harmful rays.

"If you are Other like us, you will not burn in the sun." Mertensia told her with closed eyes, as she raised her skirt a little higher.

"Really? Wow, how cool. I like my colour though." Ellie said. "I don't really want to tan. I can't abide all those tan lines. I would rather be the one colour all over than a patchwork quilt."

"Fair enough." Clematis agreed. "I prefer not to tan also."

Ellie looked at him from under her hat to see him smiling at her. "Ha, ha!"

Whilst she lay on the beach, watching the world at play, Ellie felt herself dozing off. She opened her eyes to find that she had gone to her safe place. Joachim stood anxiously by the fountain as though he were expecting her.

"Hi. This is a lovely surprise." Ellie told her friend as she hugged him to her.

"Is it? I called you." Joachim replied. "Did you not hear me?"

"No. When was this?"

The Fae

"I have been calling for about a day now. Never mind, you are here now."

"Sorry, I never heard you. What was it you needed to see me about?"

"I wanted to warn you."

"Warn me? About what?"

"There is a woman that is trying to reach you."

"Oh, yes, she gave a friend of mine a letter to give me. How much of what happens in the world do you know?" Ellie asked him. "How did you know that this woman wanted me?"

"I am the same as you. In the world, I know everything I am exposed to, same as you. Here I am cut off somewhat, same as you. I knew about the woman because I was told. I thought you should be warned, after all she may be a Gnome."

"Thank you, its okay though, she just gave me a letter. She wants to meet up. Both me and Aurellio. She wrote that she has information that could stop the war. Why would a Gnome want to stop the war? I thought it was they that started it?"

"Yes, I suppose they did. But they must have had help, they do not have the training to launch an all out attack by themselves. Someone must be helping them."

"That is what Aurellio said. He thinks he might know who but is keeping that very close to his chest. They tortured him and Felix but he still didn't give in." She said proudly.

"So I heard." Joachim said. "Will you meet the Gnome?"

"I have to. We need more information. So far we have precious little. If our going could help to stop this war from happening I have to."

"You do know that it will be a trap? They have been trying to kill you. You have no idea who this woman is or why she wants to meet you. You must not go. It is too dangerous."

Ellie laughed, not unkindly. "Joachim, ever since I was rescued I have been in danger of one sort or another. It is becoming normal for me. I will be safe, I shall have Aurellio with me."

"A Vampire? You cannot trust a Vampire! They are the most savage race that we know of. Ellie, please reconsider."

"Don't you see? This is an opportunity to stop a war! I have to go."

"Then at least take your brother with you."

"Pardon me?"

"At least take brother James, he could be useful. The fairy family are pacifist, at least as an Elf, James might be able to do something useful if need be."

"Yes, I was thinking of asking him along. Do you think he would come?"

"Do you think you could stop him?"

Ellie opened her eyes to see the sun beating down on the sand castle that the twins had decorated with sea shells and stones. Mertensia had loaned them one of the flowers from her hair to decorate the flagpole they had created from a discarded lolly stick. Ellie looked around to see Bluebell asleep on her fathers lap and Begonia playing quietly with her mother.

"Welcome back." Whispered Clematis.

"Pardon me?"

"You fell asleep there." He answered. "We should be heading back soon, the girls will want feeding. Are you coming back to ours?"

"Thank you but no, I need to get hold of James. I think it would be a good idea if he came with me. When we go to meet the Gnome that is."

The Fae

"Good idea." Clematis agreed. "So, midnight tomorrow eh? I wonder what she has to say for herself?"

"I wonder what sort of trap it will be." Ellie half joked.

Back at home, the sun had just set in a spectacular red and gold explosion on the horizon, when Ellie heard Aurellio moving about in her bedroom.

"Mind if I jump in the shower?" He called.

"Sure. When you are ready, I have some new information."

"What is it?" Asked Aurellio walking into the kitchen, clutching a towel and bottle of men's body wash.

"Where did you find that?" Ellie asked.

"Oh, Felix popped it round last night after you were asleep. What is the information?"

Ellie told him about the letter and about her visit to her safe place. Aurellio was very interested in the safe place. Apparently Vampires don't have them.

"Okay, let me think this over whilst I am in the shower." He said thoughtfully, walking back to the bathroom.

"Felix? Hi it's Ellie. How are you after your little surprise this morning?" Ellie spoke into her tiny pink phone. "No, I am not calling to tease, that is just an added pleasure." She laughed. "Okay, I promise to tell you all about her, firstly though, do you know how I can get hold of James? Why? None of your business nosey! No, joking! It's about that letter I got today. Well if you had not been mooning over my friend you would have known...Okay, that's fine. See you both here in a bit. Bye!"

As Ellie was returning the phone to her pocket, Aurellio came out of the bathroom. He was wrapped in a large white towel, his wet curls even darker against his pale skin. A few black curls hung on bravely to his chest as he continued to rub at them absently with the towel.

Ellie felt herself staring and dragged her eyes away. *Get a grip, for crying out loud*! She scolded herself. Aurellio continued to the sofa and sat, rubbing at his calves as he thought.

"Okay." He said. "Well we know that it will be a trap. I am concerned that she knows I am here with you..." He thought some more.

"She may not." Ellie said. "The letter told me to 'bring the vampire'. That does not mean she knows where you are. But I agree that it is a possibility."

"Right, so... What could be gained from leading us into a trap? We have both been held by the Gnomes before..."

"Maybe they miss our sparkling conversation?" Ellie commented.

Aurellio looked up at her. "Possibly. What else?"

"If I knew that... I have been trying to figure that out since all this started! That poor woman, Jane something was killed because they thought she was me."

"You don't know that for sure."

"Did you see a picture of her? Apart from the nose ring, it could be me. It was the same white van that knocked me down too."

"Okay, okay. Well, we have to go, there is no question about that."

"Yes, I agree. I have asked James to join us here, I will ask him to come with us. The Fairies are great and all but not a lot of use in a fight, he being Elf should mean that he can fight back if we are attacked."

The Fae

"Yes, good. I can ask some of my guys to come too, they can be almost invisible. The woman would never know they are there. You are sure that she is Gnome?"

"Pretty sure. Ciara told me that she stank, so far it's only the Gnomes that smell bad…in my vast experience!"

"What do you mean?" Asked Aurellio.

"Well, this is a bit weird, but I can smell different species. Gnomes smell like rotting nappies. It's really gross, but there you are. I can't control it."

"Can you smell me?" He asked genuinely interested.

"Ye-es."

"And what? Do I smell bad too?"

"Not bad so much."

"So much as…?"

"Well musty, you smell musty. When I saw Marcellus, he smelt musty too, but stronger, so I guess that must be the vampire smell. When James and I were in that house, where the attack took place? It was overpoweringly musty in there."

"Musty?" Aurellio mused, a half smile on his bloodless lips. "Well, it could be worse. Better than the Gnomes at any rate. What do Fairies smell like?" He asked.

"Fairies are like flowers. But I suppose that makes sense. Elves smell like cookies." Ellie laughed. "There was this doctor, when I was in hospital, he smelt like blood. I hated that, it was all cloying and coated the back of my throat. I didn't like him at all. He sort of slithered rather than walked. I have no idea what he was. But then I am new to all this supernatural stuff."

They chatted about different species and what they might smell like for a few minutes. Aurellio joked that teachers might smell like chalk, that wood sprites might smell like pine and doctors may smell like ointment. They were laughing as the door opened and James walked in followed by Felix.

"What the hell is going on here?" Demanded James.

"What?" Ellie was stunned.

"I walk in and you are cavorting with a naked vampire! What is going on?"

"Cavorting?" Ellie asked then burst into laughter. "Cavorting? Don't be so bloody stupid! Cavorting indeed!" She laughed so hard that tears were streaming down her face.

"Easy there." Aurellio sounded put out. "Its not that funny!"

"Cavorting with a naked vampire!" Ellie was rolling on the floor, clutching her sides.

"Do I have to choke you again?" Felix asked as he helped her up onto the chair.

"What? Choke? What the hell is going on here?" James was incensed.
Ellie laughed harder whilst Felix explained about Ellie's laughing fits, and his having to choke her to get them to stop.

"And as to 'cavorting with a naked vampire'." Aurellio interjected, hurt. "We were talking. I do not 'cavort' with humans. I haven't 'cavorted' for several decades. In fact, I don't particularly wish to 'cavort'…"

"Okay, okay, I am sorry." James sat down heavily. "Its just that I walked in and I saw… And you two were… And I just thought that… Look, I am sorry. Please, can we start again?"

Aurellio looked down and seemed to notice for the first time that he was not dressed.

"Oh my god! No wonder! I am sorry! Please, let me just go and get dressed. Ellie I apologise. I am truly sorry to have put you in this position."

Ellie looked at Aurellio, who was apparently mortified and started laughing again, Felix gave her a stern look. Ellie laughed harder.

Aurellio left the room and returned moments later tucking a tee shirt into his jeans. He ran his fingers through his hair combing back his curls.

"Is it true that when you cut your hair, it goes straight back to the length it was when you died?" Ellie asked Aurellio.

"You do ask some peculiar questions Ellie. What made you ask that?" James questioned.

"Just a thought. Is it? True I mean?"

"Yes. That is one of the stories about us that is true." Aurellio smiled.

"So, does that mean that you stay the same size? If I were say a size ten, got turned etcetera, would I stay a size ten for all eternity?"

"Yes I suppose you would."

"So I could eat anything I wanted, and stay slim?"

"No. You would never eat anything again." Aurellio said looking a little uncomfortable.

"Oh." Said Ellie, disappointed. "Oh! Yeah, sorry forgot the sucking your blood thing. My apologies." She was embarrassed.

"No need. It is true. We do need blood to survive, but we can live relatively well on synthetic blood. Of course the real thing is much better but acquiring it can be…let's say 'problematic', if you see what I mean."

"Not like the old days eh?" Joked Ellie. "Bloody CSI!"

"Ellie!" Felix was shocked. "Seriously?"

Chapter Eighteen

With Aurellio suitably attired and James somewhat calmer, they all sat in the living room whilst Ellie filled James and Felix in on the letter she had received. James blustered a little and Felix looked exhausted.

"Well, I guess we have to go and see her then." Felix sighed, deeply tired.

"Well we do, us three. But you my darling are no use to us in your condition."

Felix tried to argue. "But by tomorrow night I should be back to normal, I cannot let you go without me. It is just is not right."

Ellie looked at him long and hard. "I love you Felix. Truly I do, but you won't be an awful lot of use, you are exhausted. If only Fae could do something." She looked around sheepishly. "I know its not fair, but she is your mother, you think she might break the rules…"

"I forbad her to do so." Felix interrupted. "I am not so unwell that I will not heal naturally, but I take your point. I will be of no use in a fight. Perhaps there is some other role I can play so that I do not feel completely useless?" He half joked.

Ellie smiled at him. "I know that there will be plenty that you can do. Can I ask you a personal question?"

"You have never felt you could not do so before. What is it?"

"Well I have these, let's say, *abilities*. Right? I can talk to Bluebell and Begonia in my head and can smell other species. Which is not so great let me tell you… Anyway, I was wondering…What do you do?"

"Cheeky mare!" Felix laughed. "I am only slightly hurt, I am not totally useless you know!"

"Oh god!" Ellie clasped her hand over her mouth. "I didn't mean it like that at all. I meant do you have any powers? Everyone seems to have them to some degree or other, I just wondered what with you being half and half as it were…Well, I wondered what your powers were. Sorry, I really didn't mean to imply anything. I should have kept my big mouth shut. I am sorry Felix, please, forget I asked."

Felix laughed at her. "Gottcha!" He smiled broadly. "Only getting you back for teasing me earlier. As to powers? I do not really know. I have not noticed anything out of the ordinary. I guess I must not have any. That is probably the Elf counteracting the Fairy, eliminating any possible powers. That must be why the Gnomes eventually let me go." He looked thoughtful, as though the idea of Gnomes had triggered a memory for him.

James looked at his son with concern and Ellie stroked his hand briefly.

"Well, powers or not, I will be there tomorrow. Humans manage all the time and they do not have any powers either." He pulled himself out of his reverie and smiled.

"Yep, you're right." Ellie told him. "Won't be much use to us in a fight though will you?" She laughed.

"I am only half Fairy you know, the Elf half can kick Burt with the best of them." Felix clenched his fist and attempted to make a muscle on his slender arm.

"Well," giggled Ellie, "let's hope Burt is there for us to see it!"

It was decided that Ellie and Aurellio would go together in one car. James and Felix in another and would arrive earlier to hide in the wood where they would be able to keep an eye on proceedings. Aurellio would have the aid of two Vampires in the woods also, just in case.

The Fae

"Do you have anyone in mind?" Asked Felix, giving Aurellio a long look.

"There are still one or two that are loyal to me, that I can trust." Aurellio replied. "It is still dicey but we have no alternative. The Fairies are no use to us, no offence. I don't know any Elves that I could ask. It's all we have."

"We should be alright." Ellie chipped in. "After all, too many and we would be spotted. This way you should be able to hide and keep watch. If anything looks dodgy, please don't hesitate to ride in and rescue me. I did not vote for women's lib and am quite happy to be a weak woman in need of manly assistance!"

"Weak woman you most certainly are not." James smiled. "But we take your point."

Aurellio had decided that he would not invite the other Vampires to Ellie's house but that they would meet somewhere else. So Ellie dressed in a warm pair of jeans, a light jumper and a jacket to fend off the chill night air and they walked into town. They chattered together as they made their way up Queen Street and headed for Castle Park. The angel stood proudly, gleaming in the moonlight and a wreath of poppies lay discarded at her feet. Instead of entering into the Castle grounds, they went next door to the closed pub and sat on the bench tables that were still outside. Ellie had prepared a flask of coffee and she set about pouring a cup for herself, James and Felix.

"So how many have you managed to ask?" James addressed the Vampire, who was staring into the grounds of the castle through the iron fence work.

"Oh, I managed to get two. It is tricky because I am not sure who can be trusted. These two I would trust with my life." Aurellio said grimly. "Which is what we are doing." He added ominously.

The group fell silent, seemingly remembering why they were there.

"I was just remembering when we used to be stationed here, defending the fort against the neighbouring tribes. It seems so long ago now…" Aurellio said wistfully. "So many things have changed since then. I hardly recognise this town sometimes. Ah! Here they come."

Ellie looked through the fence and saw two dark shapes approaching. They were indistinct, a mere ghost of a presence, ephemeral. As they drew closer, they began to gain substance. From voids in the night they became two brooding, darkly dressed figures. The closer they came, the more fearful Ellie felt. James took her hand.

"They will not harm you whilst you are under my protection." Aurellio assured her. "They have served me for centuries. You are safe."

Ellie did not feel safe. Darkness rolled off the two men approaching. Ellie felt as though her soul were being probed; like carrion crow examining a carcass. She felt exposed and vulnerable; she shivered.

As the two Vampire approached, they became clearer. Each stood at about six feet tall, heavily built and dark featured. Their faces were all angles and planes. Deep shadows lay across their eyes and Ellie had to strain to see them. They both wore long coats that hung open to reveal on one, a pair of skinny jeans and a deep v tee shirt, whilst the other had on a pair of dark trousers and a dark coloured shirt, open at the throat. At the thought of throat, Ellie tightened her own jacket and pulled up the collar, feeling uncomfortably exposed. The two Vampires had dark, thick hair that hung to their collars and the same bloodless lips that seemed to be the norm. As they

The Fae

approached they ignored everyone present except Aurellio. They spoke to him as though he were alone.

"Well, here we are. What do you need?"

Aurellio outlined the situation, explaining that they would be needed as lookouts.

"Any chance of a snack whilst we are there?" Asked one, looking at Felix and raising an eyebrow, as though assessing a steak.

"No, it is an information situation. We need to make sure that she is not followed, that there is no trap, that no harm comes to these people." He indicated Ellie, James and Felix. "And that if anything were to happen, we need you to 'handle' it."

"Tomorrow then." The vampires turned and walked away.

"Oh boy!" Ellie shook. "I cant believe how scary they were."

"Do you think so?" Asked Aurellio, raising an eyebrow in a parody of the Vampire earlier. "Interesting."

"I so do not want to be on their shit list." She continued. "I almost peed myself!"

Aurellio laughed a short bark of a laugh. "You won't want to come to any Vamp parties then?" He asked her. "Any impromptu Vamp get togethers? Hmm?"

Felix and James were speaking quietly by themselves, sitting on the step of the monument. Ellie decided to speak with Aurellio while they were occupied.

"Who don't you trust Aurellio? Is it Marcellus?"

"What makes you ask that?" He looked at her inquisitively.

"The things that you don't say. The things that you hint at. If you trusted him, you would have gone to him for help surely?"

"Not necessarily. Marcellus is in Rome for a while. He has been called back to attend a council meeting. He is not here for me to ask."

"So who is it that you don't trust?" Ellie pushed. "You seem to have cut yourself off from everyone that could help you."

"Gnomes mostly. In our world, the world of the Others, word gets around so fast that you would not believe it. I know that they must have had help to start this war, or whatever you want to call it, but I don't know who from. I just don't want things to be any harder than they already are. We have not had anything like this for a very long time. Mostly people, Others, are so caught up in their own existence that they are unaware of any danger, and that is as it should be. We need to get this sorted and ended without a full scale eruption."

"But surely Vampires would welcome war? I thought that you guys were bloodthirsty."

"But it is us that face extinction from these death balls."

"Yes, sorry, I had forgotten them." Ellie thought for a moment. "Maybe we are going about this all wrong."

"What do you mean?"

"James, Felix! Come here a moment please." Ellie called out. "What if we have been looking at this all wrong?"

"What do you mean?" Asked Felix.

"Okay, bear with me, this is an unformed idea..." Ellie started. "Right. We have been on the back foot from day one with this yes?"

The others nodded their assent.

"Okay, we react to every situation that is thrown at us. Right? Well, let us think for a minute. You all say that the Gnomes do not have the wherewithal to create the death balls by themselves."

"Yes, definitely! Gnomes are a bit of a sub-species. Think chav." Felix chipped in trying to be helpful.

"Okay, so we have these 'chav's' who all of a sudden have the technology to eradicate the Vampires from the face of the earth. Who would benefit from that?"

"Okay, I see where you are going." Aurellio said, thinking. "Well, up until recently I would have said humans, but since we developed the synthetic blood, we don't really bother them too much now. We do have the die hard traditionalists, but not so many as before."

"Good, who else? Think guys."

"Well, we had that war a couple of centuries ago with the Goblins, but I don't think it would be them, we pretty much decimated their numbers."

"Okay, that's a motive right there. Are they smart?" Ellie asked.

"Yes, pretty smart. It could be them though I doubt it. Still it is worth keeping them in mind. Right, who else..." Aurellio screwed up his face in concentration.

"Are you sure that the humans would not be involved?" Ellie asked nervously. "They, well some of them are certainly smart enough. Also it was a human that was developing the balls when Milfoil found them."

"I cannot say that it isn't a possibility, but they don't know of our existence. Except as stories and movies." Aurellio said.

"Well, that isn't quite true is it? The guy was a human."

"Okay yes, point taken."

They threw back and forth ideas, trying to come up with a species that would have cause to destroy the Vampires and also have the technology to do so.

"Don't forget that the Gnomes killed that woman thinking she was me. They tried to kill me too and when I was taken, the Gnome said that he was under orders. So we should think about that as well. We need to know why they want me dead. After all, I have been just a human for all these years, what possible threat am I to a species that I didn't even know existed?" Ellie looked around at the men seated with her. "Why on earth am I important?"

Nobody had an answer.

"James, whilst we are discussing this, erm..." Ellie began nervously. "Joachim referred to you as my brother, so... Are you? My brother I mean?"

James looked amazed and it took him a few moments to speak. "I would love nothing better than to claim you as my sister. The goddess knows I love you like one, but... and I am truly sorry, I am not your brother. We are all one family so are referred to as brother and sister, both Elves and Fairies. We are closely related to each other you see? But no. I am sorry, I am not your brother."

Ellie was surprisingly saddened to hear that, so forced a grin on her face and joked,

"Anyone here that wishes to claim kinship with me? My heritage must play a role in the Gnome's desire to kill me, I can't think of any other reason."

There was a shuffling of feet and an embarrassed chorus of 'No, sorry's'.

"Worth a try." Ellie shrugged and they started back home.

Ellie went to bed leaving Felix and James chatting with Aurellio in the living room. She felt sad that James was not her brother, she had been secretly wishing that he were and would have been overjoyed to have Frances as her mother. Thinking of

The Fae

mothers bought the past that she did remember into her mind with the subtlety of an armed intruder. She fell asleep with tears in her hair and knees to her chest.

Ellie called at the shop to see Jack the next morning. She was unsure to the status of her job, so decided to talk to Jack in person. As she pushed open the door, Ellie was overwhelmed by a sense of displacement. She had the all encompassing feeling of not belonging, as if the shop itself had ejected her from it's existence. Everything was where she remembered but it all felt different, wrong somehow; alien. There were no customers and the counter was empty. Ellie forced a cheery smile on her face as she tried to breathe through her nose, to counter the smell, and closed the door. Seconds after the jangling of the bell, Scarlett appeared at the till.

"What do you want?" Scarlett asked unkindly.

"Is Jack here? I need a word."

"What you need is of no concern to me."

"Please, I am not here to fight. I just want a word with Jack." Ellie started to walk to the door at the back of the shop that led to Jacks office.

"You have no business back there." Scarlett stood and blocked her way. "I will tell him that you came by."

"So you work here now do you?"

"And that is your business because?"

"Because, to the best of my knowledge, that is my job you are attempting to do."

"Well your knowledge, like so much else about you, is sorely lacking." Scarlett sneered. "You got fired! Or were you too busy cosying up to the fairies to notice?"

"Okay, if I don't work here anymore, I guess it doesn't matter if I do this then does it?" Ellie asked sweetly, stepping toward Scarlett.

"What?"

Ellie drew back her head then snapped it forward to land heavily on Scarlett's nose. She felt a satisfying crunch and smelt the coppery tang of freshly shed blood. Smiling despite the agony, Ellie left the shop.

As she turned the corner, Ellie leant heavily against a wall and took several steadying breaths. Her head was pounding and she was now definitely out of a job but if pressed, she could honestly say that she had never felt better in her life.

Ellie spent the afternoon alone in her garden with a book and a headache. She had always found that reading helped to quiet the chaos of her mind when she was anxious. She did not want to think. She wanted to lose herself in someone else's fairy tale and be a witness for a change; instead of a participant. The sun beat down and warmed her skin as she buried herself within the pages. Bunbury lay stretched out at her feet, his paws above his head, toasting the curly white fur on his belly. His whiskers twitched as a fly flew too close and his chest rose and fell steadily with each languid breath.

Ellie's grumbling stomach notified her that it was time to put the book down and think about food. She went into the kitchen and rummaged about in the cupboard. There was so much to chose from, thanks to her recent shopping trip, that she stood staring blankly for several moments.

"I recommend action." Came Felix' voice behind her. "Inaction tends to leave one's stomach in turmoil. How about I cook?"

"Good idea." Ellie closed the cupboard door and sat at the table. She watched her friend deftly set about preparing a meal.

"Worried about tonight?" Felix asked.

"Yes. I have to admit that yes, I am worried. I have no idea what to expect and that makes me nervous. But also..." Ellie fidgeted in her seat. "Well, its this thing about my background. It is really starting to bother me. I couldn't believe how upset I was that James is not my brother, it would have been so cool."

"That would have made you my aunt. That would be weird."

"I suppose so." Ellie sighed. "I just think that this whole thing has to be a mistake. I have no memory whatsoever of my life before, but a whole lifetime of memories of my life as a human. Surely Frances must be wrong? It is possible for her to be wrong isn't it?"

"Sure, I have never known her to be wrong, but of course, this could be the first time. But if she is say, how do you account for the abilities you have?"

"Easy! Fae's blood. I never had any before she saved me. Oh! Maybe that's what Frances can 'read'? She probably can sense Fae's blood in me and thinks it is more. That has to be the answer. It's not possible to wipe out a whole lifetime! I have memories from being a baby for goodness sake! That has to be the answer. Thank god for that! I thought I would go crazy!"

Felix smiled distractedly as he appeared to think that through.

After a light meal of omelette and salad, Felix sat back in his chair and stretched his arms above his head working the kinks out of his neck. Bunbury sat on the counter watching Ellie wash the dishes.

"He looks sad." Ellie commented to Felix. "I think he misses Peter. Have you seen him? Is he better?"

"Yes. I saw him this morning, he was asking after you too. He is much better, getting under mothers feet again, being rude and sarcastic. I think he is bored, but mother is keeping a tight reign on him. She was so worried when he got injured, I don't know what she would do if he died again for real."

"Do you think she would mind if Peter came for a visit? I really miss him and I think Bunbury is confused. His best pal was dead, then gone."

"I will ask, I do not see how she would mind." Felix passed her the last of the dirty cups. "So, only a couple of hours to go. I do not mind telling you, I am a bit nervous myself. I hate that I have to sit in the car. I wish I could be more useful."

"Honey, if you could fight, it would be different, but being Fairy...Well."

"I know. It is somewhat emasculating though! Having to sit in the car while you are in danger."

"I will have Aurellio and James." Ellie told him. "Oh, I meant to ask, how are you two getting along now that you know...that he is your father I mean?"

"Really well. I thought it would be difficult but it is not. I have known James on and off for a long while; bumping into him around town, gatherings etcetera. He used to visit mom occasionally too so I already knew I liked him. Knowing that he is my father just seems to add to that. Our relationship has not particularly changed the way we are with each other I mean. We Fairy and Elf are quite close knit anyway. We share more traits than we have differences. It is like a piece of my puzzle has been slotted into place, which makes the big picture easier to see. I am not sure if that makes sense? It is the best way I can describe it."

"Sounds pretty good to me." Ellie smiled. "Aurellio should be up soon, the sun is setting."

"How is that working out for you? Having a Vampire under your bed?"

Ellie laughed. "If he were under it when I were in it I think I would be very uncomfortable, but as he is there when I am awake, its okay. I cannot believe how much my life has changed. Hanging out with Fairies and Elves and a Vampire under my bed! Who would have thought? It's pretty surreal. I feel quite safe though. I am not afraid of him in the least and I don't worry about being attacked. Who would be stupid enough to take on a Vampire?" She laughed again.

"Well he is only any use at night."

"Yes, but I am hardly ever alone anymore am I? My little house is becoming *the* place to be. Speaking of which…"

They both laughed as the gate swung open and James walked in.

"What?" He asked, puzzled. "What?"

Ellie and Felix just laughed harder.

The Fae

Chapter Nineteen

Felix pulled up in the car park and switched off the engine. As the darkness closed around them, Ellie tried to see if she could spot the Vampires. The woods looked forbidding and impenetrable. Dark twisted shapes reaching further than the ambient light could penetrate. Ellie felt her stomach clench in nervous anticipation.
James leant forward and touched her shoulder, making her jump.
"You ready?" He asked.
Ellie was nowhere near ready but she took a breath and replied that she was.
"Come on then, let's go." She reached for the door handle. "Felix, you have the walkie talkie?"
Felix held it up in response and switched it to receive.
"Everything you say, I will hear." He told her. "Any sign of trouble and I will come running."
"Good." Ellie sucked in a breath and blew it out through her teeth. "James? Aurellio? Set?"

Aurellio led the way along a dirt path between the trees. His predatory eyesight an advantage in the inky blackness. Ellie could feel her heart tapping against her chest and she felt dizzy with dread. Further into the woods they went. Night birds chirruped and howled whilst unseen creatures scuttled amongst the foliage. The air was heavy with the scent of rotting vegetation and loamy earth. Against the black of their surroundings, shadows and voids could be glimpsed from the corner of Ellie's eye, adding to her tension. She stumbled and nearly fell. Throwing out her hands to steady herself, her fingertips brushed against a thick cobweb and made her skin crawl. Aurellio powered on and Ellie stumbled blindly behind him, with James bringing up the rear. Something fluttered past Ellie's face, causing her to yelp with surprise. The sound amplified against the thick night air.

Reaching the clearing, they approached slowly, with great caution. Sitting on the ground, her legs folded beneath her, sat the crone. She appeared to be by herself. Her long coat was wrapped close despite the warm night. Her head was bare, allowing her long hair to lift in the slight breeze. Twigs and leaves wove about the filthy strands. She appeared in monochrome, the night leeching all colour from her features. Ashy grey skin wrapped around her bony face. The crone watched closely as the trio arrived. She did not move but greeted them politely.
"Thank you for coming." She said. Her voice was cultured; diction crisp.
"Why did you want to see me?" Ellie asked, stepping closer.
"All in good time."
"I would prefer you told me now. I have come as you asked, but please do not be under the misapprehension that I am here to do your bidding. Now, why have you asked me here?" Ellie spoke gently but there was steel in her words.
"I need your help." The crone told her.
"What?" This was the last thing Ellie had expected. "What could you possibly need from me?"
"I need protection, and in exchange I will give you information that could if not stop, then seriously shorten the war that is about to break out."
"What information?" Ellie asked sceptically.
"No. I need your guarantee that I will be safe, then I will tell you."
"Not interested." Ellie turned and took a step away.

"I am not bluffing, and I will not play. My life is in danger because of the knowledge I have. If you will not help me, I will take the information to your enemies. Believe me when I tell you that you would not want that to happen."

Ellie turned back to the crone and studied her for a moment. "Who is threatening you?"

"Ah! I see you are not so stupid!" The woman said smiling. "If I tell you that, you will know who your enemy is. Very clever."

"Thank you. I try."

"I cannot tell you until I have your promise. But... I accept that you have no reason to trust me, so I will tell you a little about myself. Please, sit, be comfortable."

Ellie sat in front of the woman, but James and Aurellio stayed standing and alert.

"I have lived in these woods for centuries. I tend to my own business and do not involve myself with the trivialities of other races. I am self sufficient and do not need to interact with humans or Others. The woods have provided me with a home, far from wandering eyes but that privacy is a double edged sword. I am invisible here yet that invisibility works both ways. I am not noticed by others either. I blend into the trees and am one with the earth. People come to my woods for many reasons. To walk their dogs and let them foul my footpaths, to play with their children, to ride their bicycles, all manner of reasons. But lately I have discovered that it is also a meeting place. Not just for trysts of the romantic nature, but for subterfuge and intrigues. I happened across such a meeting some weeks ago and could not help but listen. What I heard filled me with panic. Then again a few days ago, these same individuals met and I heard more. Now I was sure that something awful was to happen. Their third meeting, they discussed war. They spoke of the plans that were in place, those that were yet to be and they also spoke of you Ellie."

"Me?"

"Yes, they were very keen on finding you. They knew that you had a Vampire protecting you along with the Fairies and Elves and they were plotting how to take you."

"Calling me to a meeting in the middle of the woods in the middle of the night might be a good way." Ellie said sarcastically.

"I take your point." The woman conceded. "And yet you came anyway."

"We are aware that war is coming. We have not been idle." Ellie said proudly. "I am also aware that the Gnomes want me dead or captured. I have escaped them once already. What do you have for us that we do not already know?"

"Arrogance will be your undoing child!" The woman hissed. "So you know that the Gnomes are involved, but do you know who is pulling the strings? Do you know why you are so important? No? Well I do, and that is the information that I have to trade for my safety."

Ellie looked at the woman for a long while then stood and went to Aurellio.

"What do you think?" She asked him. "Do we trust her? She is not Gnome. I don't know what she is, she certainly smells but it's not like the stink of a Gnome."

"We need that information."

"Yeah, but it could be lies, or a trap, or just complete bullshit from a crazy lady that lives in the woods."

"Yes, but it could be what we need. I say we agree."

"And where exactly do we put her? There is no room at my house, and besides, she smells bad."

Ellie went back to the woman and sat on the ground in front of her again.

"You said to bring the Vampire. I have, he is there." Ellie pointed at Aurellio. "What do you want with him?"

"Bring him closer." The woman said.

Aurellio took a few steps closer and the woman seemed to sniff the air.

"Aurellio. You need to help me. I have never hurt or betrayed the Vampire so you have no reason not to trust me. What I have to tell concerns you greatly. Do you agree to aid me?"

"Woman I do not know you. Tell me what you must and I will protect you." Aurellio spoke gently to the crone.

"Come closer I cannot see you."

Aurellio stepped closer but Ellie could see his body thrum, alert to any danger.

"Closer fool, I am near blind!" She hissed.

"I am close enough, now tell me and we will take you to a safe place."

The woman leant forward sniffing the air. "Yes, it is you. We must be quick, I sense the Gnomes are approaching."

"So this is a trap?" Ellie yelled into the walkie talkie. "Felix, look out, Gnomes in the area."

"I set no trap, they are following you." The woman pointed to Ellie and beckoned Aurellio closer. "I know who instigated this. I heard them speaking together, he and the Gnomes. I was shocked, but when I thought it over, it made sense."

"Speak woman, tell me what you know." Aurellio demanded while he was looking around.

"They spoke of a design, of death balls that can destroy the Vampire. They were developing them to wipe you all out. They believed that with the Vampire out of the way, the Others would be easier to conquer. That they could defeat everyone and control all."

The woman inched closer on her bottom.

"They said that the balls would turn the Vampire human and therefore they would be easier to defeat. Quick, listen close. The Gnomes are almost upon us!" The woman started to shake and gabble her words.

Ellie and James looked about wildly, straining their ears to hear the Gnomes approach. Aurellio swooped down and lifted the woman into his arms.

"Come, back to the car." Aurellio called out and they all started to run back the way they had came.

"Why can't secret meetings be held at the edge of the woods? Why do they have to be way deep in the middle so it's hard to run away?" Grumbled Ellie as they ran, trees and undergrowth grabbing at them as they passed.

Aurellio had stopped suddenly and Ellie ran into him in the dark. He was standing still as stone, sniffing the air and growling deep in his throat.

"James." He said thrusting the crone into his arms. "Take her to the car. Now!"

James ran with the woman in his arms back toward the car. Ellie and Aurellio stood, back to back scanning the area around them, alert for any sign of movement.

"Ssh! There." Whispered Ellie pointing to her left.

"And there." Aurellio whispered back indicating the trees in front of him.

"Crap! What now?" Ellie was terrified.

"Wait and see I guess." Came the helpful answer.

The Fae

From between the trees, hooded shapes emerged. Ellie felt as though she would throw up, the smell was overpowering making her gag.

"Gnomes!" She yelled and they started to run.

She could see Felix, sitting at the wheel of the car, yelling silently and thumping the dash in frustration. The engine could be heard faintly over the pounding in her ears. All at once there were Gnomes in front of them, waiting. Aurellio and Ellie stopped, nearly toppling over, their momentum interrupted. Ellie looked wildly about, they were surrounded. The Gnomes carried weapons, bats, knives and something that looked like a bolas.

"Oh god!" Ellie yelped.

She froze in panic. Her body did not know what to do, how to move. The woman wailed, a piteous sound that caused the hackles on Ellie's skin to raise. Looking around she saw the Gnomes approach, and James gently lower the woman to the ground, mere feet from the car. James looked terrified, but he ran back to Ellie and stood his ground. He reached for the club that he had secured across his back.

Aurellio hissed. A low, menacing sound. Ellie could see his eyes roll upwards and his jaw open wide. Two wickedly sharp fangs appeared and glistened in the moonlight. Aurellio crouched slightly at the knee and his body shivered. He was one moment the man she knew, the next a feral animal with death in his eyes.

Aurellio leapt forward and landed on the nearest Gnome. His teeth found and closed upon the neck. With a brief shake of his head he tore the flesh apart. The Gnome screamed and fell, clutching at the ragged hole and Aurellio flew at the next. The spell was broken and hell visited Friday Woods that warm summer's night.

Ellie snapped out of her trance and reached for her own club. She relaxed her knees and waited for the attack. A large dark Gnome lunged at her from the left. She pivoted on one foot, raising the club as she did so, and swung with every ounce of strength she had at the Gnome's head. Her arm vibrated dully as wood struck bone and contact was made. The Gnome dropped to the ground and Ellie almost dropped her club as her fingers numbed from the impact. She swore loudly, readjusted her grip and raised the club to swing again. The club was grabbed from behind and she lost her balance, falling to one knee. Keeping a tight hold on the club, she rolled forward and yanked it free. Jumping up she spun around and swung the club at her new attacker. She hit the female Gnome across the chest and drove the air from her body. As the Gnome doubled over, Ellie swung the club upwards and caught the Gnome under the chin, forcing her backwards into unconsciousness.

Ellie smiled widely, her blood on fire, and spun to see who was next. She saw James rolling on the ground, his club some feet away from him. He was wrestling with a female Gnome and looking embarrassed. Ellie ran over and smashed the Gnome across the head then kicked her comatose body away.

"Don't be such a gentleman! Kill the fuckers!" Ellie told him handing him back his club. Holding out her hand, she helped hoist James to his feet then turned back to the fight.

Aurellio was on top of a fallen Gnome, wiping his bloody face on his arm. His eyes were wild with blood lust and his awful mouth, bloody and sharp, was drawn back in a mockery of a grin.

When all the Gnomes were dead or unconscious. Ellie ran to James to see if he was alright. He had blood on his face and his arm hung limply by his side. His sleeve was torn and bloody. James had trouble standing so Ellie propped him up with her shoulder and eased him to the car. Dumping him in Felix' arms, she ran back to Aurellio and the woman. Aurellio was cleaning his face from a packet of baby wipes that he had pulled from his pocket. Ellie looked on in surprise.

"Live and learn!" Aurellio smiled offering her the pack.

Ellie bent down to check the crone. She was huddled up on her side. Her knees to her chest and violently shaking all over. Her hands were covering her face and Ellie could hear her mumble, "No, no, no!" Over and over.

Ellie gently prised the woman's hands from her face and wiped her filthy hair from her eyes.

"It's okay, you are safe now."

The woman's eyes grew round and stared at a point just over Ellie's shoulder, she struggled to claw herself away. Her mouth a perfect round of fear. She wailed in terror and Ellie started to turn to see.

Ellie felt herself pulled back sharply by her throat. A coarse, hairy arm was around her neck, pulling her upwards. The smell was almost unbearable.

"Well, well. Now what do we have here?" A voice whispered in her ear. "If it's not the prettiest prize of em all."

Ellie stopped struggling and allowed herself to be manhandled to a standing position. From the direction of the voice, Ellie judged her captor to be roughly the same height as her. She let her body sag slightly and the Gnome was thrown a little off balance whilst still trying to maintain his hold on her. Ellie lifted her leg and ran it as hard as she could down the inside of the Gnome's calf, stomping on his foot with her Doc Marten's. The Gnome howled in pain but instead of letting her go, he pulled her tighter to him and ran a knife under her chin.

"That wasn't so clever was it little girl? Try it again and I shall stick this in you." He pressed against the knife for emphasis and Ellie felt the hot prick, tight against her throat. She tried to swallow but her mouth had gone dry.

The Gnome swung her around so that he could see Aurellio.

"Get here where I can see you." He ordered in a strong, confident voice. "You, Fairies, get here too. Stand with your hands up, all of you."

"Please. Do as he says." Ellie called calmly. "I have a prick at my throat!"

Aurellio, stepped forward; nonchalant, relaxed. Felix helped James over and they stood together with their hands up.

"Now what smart arse?" Ellie asked. "You are on your own, your pals are dead or fucked up. You cut me again and that Vamp will tear your throat out."

The Gnome looked toward Aurellio, who smiled as he daintily wiped a drop of blood from the corner of his mouth.

"Happily." Grinned the blood covered Vampire.

The Gnome looked about distractedly at his fallen brethren. He tugged Ellie around as he looked behind him. The knife sliced deeper into Ellie's throat and she felt her blood leak out beneath the blade. Suddenly Ellie did not feel quite so cocky and wondered if she would get out of this alive.

Aurellio growled deep in his throat and his eyes started to roll back. The Gnome began to tremble and Ellie felt her leg dampen as he soiled himself. Ellie struggled in his grip and the Gnome started to panic.

"I mean it! Don't start anything. I have nothing to lose. I am dead anyway. I may as well take her with me!" He pressed the knife deep into Ellie's flesh and she felt the scratch of it, hot and cold at once. Ellie began to feel light headed and she swayed in the Gnome's embrace.

Felix was as white as a sheet, his whole body was shaking with rage. Ellie's last sight as she blacked out was Felix screaming at the top of his voice in fury.

"Let her go. NOW!" He screamed so loud that the air around them vibrated with the force of it, their ears rang and ceased to hear, the skin rolled against their frames as though in a wind tunnel. The Gnome dropped his arm from Ellie's throat and clutched at his head. As Ellie started the timeless fall to the ground, she saw the Gnomes' head explode spraying out bits of blood, bone and brain. Then she saw nothing.

Chapter Twenty

Glimpses of faces hovered over Ellie. All encompassing pain and an overriding dizziness accompanied her as she jounced in the car. She felt hands and heard disconnected words as she became aware of a cool breeze on her burning skin. The surface beneath her changed to cool and smelt like laundry. Ellie slept.

Ellie awoke to a dim room and a tight pain across her throat. Slowly her heavy eyelids rolled up and she could see Felix sitting beside her on the bed, his back toward her and talking to Aurellio who was in the chair opposite. She stayed quiet and listened.

"But where the hell were your guys? Ellie could have died!" Felix whispered angrily. "We all could have died. Where were they?"

"I do not know. They agreed to be there, promised to be there. I just do not know. I cannot believe that they would have betrayed me."

"Well it certainly looks as though they have. What will you do? When is Marcellus back?"

"Do you think Marcellus would do a better job than me? Do you think it is because of me that this happened?" Aurellio was becoming angry and his voice took on a slight growl as he spoke.

"No." Felix insisted. "No, I do not think that. I just can not help but wonder what is happening. There are forces at work within the Vampire ranks that are puzzling. You speak yourself of trust, of betrayal, but will not tell me more. Have I not earned the right to be included in your thoughts? I have risked my family for you."

"For your vow."

"Yes for my vow, but also because we are friends."

Aurellio looked shocked. "Friends? You consider us to be friends?"

"Yes Aurellio, I consider us to be friends. Please let me help you."

"I need to find them and question them."

"Then let me come with you. I can help."

"You are Fairy, you cannot help me."

"Did you not see that thing with the exploding Gnome? That was me. I made his head explode!" Felix raised his voice in awe and determination.

Ellie shifted on the bed in remembrance of the Gnome that had held her, and a small gasp escaped her lips.

"Oh I am sorry, I did not mean to wake you." Felix turned to her. "How are you feeling?"

Ellie opened her mouth to speak, but the pain was too great and her eyes watered with the effort.

"Oh, no! I am sorry, how stupid of me. Do not try to speak. Here, try this." Felix held a tall glass with a long straw toward her and placed the tip of the straw in Ellie's mouth. She sipped the soothing cool water gingerly then lay back on her pillow.

"We were talking about last night." Felix informed her. "We are trying to decipher the meaning behind the lack of back up." He looked at Aurellio then back to Ellie. "We were lucky to get away at all."

Ellie lifted her hand to her throat and felt the rough bandage that encompassed it.

"We patched you up." Aurellio said proudly. "It was a first for me. I think I did a good job." He did indeed look pleased with himself.

"Nk yew…" Ellie mumbled painfully. "Rone…?"

"The crone?" Asked Felix and Ellie nodded slightly. "Ah, she is here. Would you like me to send her in?"

"Ot et." Ellie struggled to sit up. Aurellio leapt off his chair just as Felix reached out to help her.

"Stay in bed, what do you need? Lay back down." Felix fussed.

"Oy led." Ellie managed with a half smile. She eased herself to the edge of the bed and stopped, looking bewildered. "Ep ee?"

Aurellio and Felix looked at each other in a slight panic. Aurellio back pedalled to his chair and sat back down with a bump.

"Hazel" Called Felix. "Can you help Ellie to the toilet please?"

Ellie looked at them questioningly.

"Hazel is the ahem, woman we met in the woods."

Ellie's eyes widened in discomfort.

"Ah, well…it is okay Ellie, look." Felix turned toward the door as they heard the woman approach.

Into the doorway stepped a tall, very thin woman with thick, old fashioned glasses. She had long auburn hair and green eyes. Her hair glowed and her face was high cheeked with a straight nose and thin lips. Her eyebrows were arched and the same vibrant red of her hair. Her skin looked a little dry and pale but she was beautiful. She stood uncertainly in the doorway and looked from Felix to Ellie with a nervous twitch of her head.

"Oo yoo?" Ellie asked. "Ey lowse?"

"I am Hazel we met last night in the woods, you probably do not remember." The woman said shyly. "As to your clothes, the boys here seemed to think you would not mind. Just for a bit that is."

"Ont ell!" Ellie said then held her arm out to be helped up.

"I am sorry, what did you say?" Hazel asked.

"She said that you do not smell." Aurellio supplied. "Ellie has a peculiar talent."

"Ell ars igh."

"Well yes, I had been in the woods for some… Let us just say that I availed myself of your shower too."

"And about three bottles of your body wash!" added Aurellio.

The woman scowled at Aurellio and helped Ellie to the bathroom then left her seated whilst she waited outside. When Ellie had finished she helped her back to bed and handed her Aurellio's pack of baby wipes to clean her hands.

Ellie grimaced with the distasteful memory the baby wipes invoked but used them anyway.

"Appen? Urt?" Ellie asked, nervous of the answer.

"James has damaged his arm and cannot use it at present but we are all okay. Apart from you that is." Aurellio told her. "You had your throat cut. It was deep but not deep enough to kill you. Clearly. So it should mend soon. You can have some of my blood if you wish. I have regenerative powers that could sort that out in no time." He offered helpfully.

"O an oo." Ellie tried not to look as grossed out as she felt. "Ey aw iyt."

Ellie sat back against her pillows and waved Hazel to sit on the bed.

"Ell ee owt oo." She said.

"Well, like I told you last night." Hazel Began. "I have lived in the woods for many, many years, keeping myself to myself. I do not like to be around people very

The Fae

much and feel... Whatever! Anyway, I come from a long line of woods dwellers, we have an affinity with the trees, I guess you could say that we are their guardians. My race is called the Dryads. We are very few in number now. We used to belong to just one tree each but now we have whole woods to protect."

Ellie looked fascinated. "Ood o ba?" She asked.

"Well we like to think ourselves good." Hazel Laughed. "But if you hurt our trees we can get quite riled up. Currently I am keeping a close eye on the developers across from me. They have torn up the army estate and built a whole new village there." She said emotionally. "They had not better think of coming near my..." She looked up and saw that all three were staring at her. "Sorry, not used to polite society, I am used to speaking to myself." She shrugged.

"O ay. Ss o ay." Ellie replied.

"We need to talk about what you saw and heard." Aurellio spoke up. "It didn't exactly go as planned last night, so anything else you can tell me...?"

"Pretty much what I said. I know who started this war."

"Well damn it! Who?" Aurellio was becoming angry. "Just spit it out! We kept our side of the bargain, we kept you safe, got you out of there."

"Not quite, I cannot stay here indefinitely, I need a safe place to go until this is over. But... I cannot leave my trees." Hazel seemed upset and genuinely fearful.

"We can find somewhere more appropriate." Felix joined in. "As to the trees? This should be over very soon, depending of course on your information, so you should be back with them in no time. Not much can happen to them."

Hazel raised her eyebrow and looked at Felix. "You know nothing of trees." She sniffed. "Many of them I have nursed for hundreds of years, all it takes is one careless... No! I cannot bear to think of it! You must end this so I can go home. You must!"

"We need to call the queen and have her listen." Felix mused aloud.

"Queen? Alcea?" Hazel asked in surprise. "Never! I will never share a room with that creature! Never!" She pulled her spine straight and clasped her hands together primly in her lap. Hazel set her face in a defiant scowl and her eyes dared anyone to argue with her.

"Yes our queen, Alcea. Why? What is the problem?" Felix looked shocked.

"We have unfinished business and I will not see her." Hazel spoke with finality and looked away as if to put an end to the matter.

"Ih o ay." Ellie soothed with her broken voice. "Ell er ayt er."

"Alright." Felix agreed stiffly. "We can fill her in later. Now, can we get on?"

Aurellio leaned forward, flint in his eye, his mouth a bloodless slash as he prepared himself to listen. Felix sat further back at the foot of the bed and Hazel drew a deep breath.

"As you know, I am a Dryad." Hazel began. "One of my race has lived in the woods here since Roman times, when they were begun. I myself have been here a relatively short while. We are unseen by humans and keep to ourselves, tending our trees. We are so used to anonymity that we live independent of outside influences. We almost never speak with people, whether human or Other. I tell you this as explanation for my delay in bringing this to your attention." Here she looked at Ellie and her face conveyed both sorrow and a pleading for forgiveness. "As I said before, I overheard conversation, as I overhear many conversations, and I paid little heed to its content. Only when they returned some nights later and took up their talk again did I place any value on their words. Then, you must understand, I still believed that it did not concern me or my trees, so I did nothing. The third time I overheard them I knew that I had to do something, that I had to find help. They mentioned you Ellie so I thought that if they were so very afraid of you, you must be the person I should go to. I spoke to your friend. The one who walks her rabbit in the woods."

Felix blushed and Ellie felt a smile tug at her mouth.

"She thought me infirm." Hazel smiled. "That or she dismissed me as unhinged. I questioned her about you. At least I attempted to. You chose your allies well Ellie, she gave me no information. In the end I wrote to you, hoping that you would meet me."

"Yes, yes, we know this already." Felix was frustrated at the meandering pace of Hazel's tale. "Tell us what we need. Tell us who was meeting. What did they say?"

"Another impatient soul!" Hazel snapped. "Allow me the luxury of telling my tale in my own fashion. It has been many years since I used my voice and I enjoy the sound of it!" She settled herself more comfortably on the bed and smiled at Ellie. "As I was saying." She began again in her previous tone. "I do not care so much if the Gnomes, Elves, Fairies and Vampires wipe each other out, but whenever there is war, my woods are damaged; destroyed irrevocably. I cannot allow that you see. So something had to be said. Something must be done to prevent this war."

Ellie moved against her pillow as she struggled to get words past her damaged throat.

"Aw ih oo? Oo ith ih?"

"Ah yes." Hazel said. "Well Patrick, I gather he is the Gnome leader, he was there along with his brother Philip I believe his name was and the person they were meeting..." She looked at Aurellio with pity in her eyes. "The person they were meeting was a Vampire."

"No! This is a lie!" Aurellio jumped up, teeth fully extended and a growl in his throat. "You lie, crone!"

"I am sorry but it is true. The person behind this, the one who wishes to start this war is Vampire." Hazel said sadly as she watched Aurellio pace up and down angrily before finally flinging himself back into the chair.

"But why would a Vampire wish to wipe out his own kind?" Felix asked, stunned and confused.

"That I can only guess at." Hazel spoke softly, as though to undo the damage of her words with the softness of her tone. "I have known Vampires, indeed all Others to commit heinous acts against each other for the most asinine of reasons. It never makes sense, except to the perpetrator. I am truly sorry to tell you this Aurellio. I have never wished to be involved in the machinations of people and it grieves me to have to do so now." She looked at Ellie gently and continued. "You my child play such a role in this. Your mere presence was enough to start this war. Had you stayed hidden, I do not suppose this would be happening at all. But... It cannot be undone. They know of you now and you have to end it before it is too late."

"Own unna san."

"I know my child. You do not have the memories yet that would make this puzzle clear. I cannot help you with that, though I actually wish that I could. Your memory cannot be forced. It was protected by magic. Only you can undo the spell and remember. You can only do this when you are ready."

"E-ee ow!" Ellie insisted.

The Fae

"No, I am afraid you are not ready now, though it would be most opportune." Hazel smiled kindly. "I am, afraid things do not work like that."

"Ay I in or ant? Oo an ay?"

"I cannot say." Hazel stood and walked to the door. "I think that you have a lot to discuss, so I shall make myself busy elsewhere and leave you to it."

"Well! That would certainly explain why your buddies did not show up in the woods." Felix said to Aurellio.

"I do not believe this." Aurellio said, but he looked as though he were seriously considering the possibility.

"Who could it be? Are there any rogue Vamps in the area? I thought that your hive was pretty settled now. There has not been any dissention there for decades. Not since…Well, I cannot remember when." Felix looked at his friend. "Aurellio, what are you thinking?"

"I am thinking that if this is true, then it is Vampire business and not yours!" Aurellio stood and strode to the door. With his hand gripping the handle, he stopped. His whole body ceased to move, as if he were frozen in place.

Felix stood and went to him. He placed his hand on Aurellio's shoulder and spoke gently. "You cannot do this alone. We do not know who is involved. We must stick together and sort this out. Together we are stronger than alone. Come, Aurellio, sit. Let us discuss this."

Aurellio returned to his seat like an automaton. He sat and let his head fall momentarily into his hands. Aurellio rubbed at his face as if he was washing it, then sat upright. A tiny spark flamed in his eye and a grim determination took residence on his face.

"Eed iynd oo." Ellie croaked painfully.

"Yes, you are correct, we need to find who. Do you have any ideas who could be behind this Aurellio? Failing that, who do you know that would benefit from the Vampires being destroyed? I cannot see what benefit there would be to a Vampire, to wipe out his own kind."

"There is someone." Aurellio began thoughtfully. "Someone who may know well… More than we do."

"Okay, who? And when do we leave?" Felix slid off the bed and started to button his jacket.

"Not we. Me. This is not a man that you would survive. He is an ancient and lives hidden away. Very few know of him and he is, let us say… Unfriendly. There is no guarantee that he will help or even speak with me, but I shall go now and see what I can do. If I am not back before day break, then I am not coming back at all."

"Eewiussy?" Ellie said in surprise. "Ee at ad?"

"Yes, he is that bad. Well, wish me luck." And with that Aurellio left the room.

Felix turned and looked at Ellie. He sat by her on the bed and took her hands in his.

"Ellie, will you allow me to help you?"

"oth ourthe." She smiled uncertainly.

"I have spoken to James and Aurellio, they have both sworn to say nothing. But then Fairy laws do not apply to them so it is not such a big ask."

The Fae

Ellie looked even more puzzled as Felix pushed his sleeves up then flexed and stretched his fingers, slightly popping his knuckles as he did so. Ellie watched as his hands came closer to her neck and gently lifted the bandage from her throat.

"O Elis, oo usn." She sighed sadly.

"Ssh!" He whispered as he lowered his fingers to gently rest across her wound. Felix closed his eyes and his face assumed a beatific expression as all about him the air shimmered and turned a deep and luminous green. There were golden sparks chasing white pin point flashes and the room filled with the scent of growing things.

Ellie felt a soothing warmth about her throat and her limbs appeared to be as light as gossamer, floating just above the sheet. Her body was wrapped in a cocoon of clouds as she felt both weightless and connected to the earth at the same time. A gentle frisson of sensation swept around her injury, feeling as though each cell was knitting itself to the next. Ellie felt the fog of pain lift, to be replaced with a feeling of wholeness. She lifted her hand and stroked her throat feeling nothing but the smooth, unbroken surface that was so familiar to her fingers. Tears pooled on her lashes as she lifted her eyes to Felix in thanks.

Chapter Twenty One

Aurellio returned to find Ellie sitting up on the couch, absently listening to James and Felix bickering. He took a bag of blood from the stock Ellie kept for him in the fridge and dinged it in the microwave. Porting his meal to a tall dark glass, he sat with the others and sipped slowly.

"Well?" Asked Ellie with only a hint of an injury in her voice.

Aurellio turned to Felix and nodded curtly. "Yes, I found him."

"And...?" Ellie leant forward, eager to hear. James gently pushed her back against the cushions with one hand.

"And yes, he had information. Forgive me, I am not being deliberately obtuse. This has come as a... Well to say surprise would be understating in the extreme, but I cannot think of a suitable word to convey the utter, complete, absolute betrayal I feel right now."

"So it is Marcellus?" Ellie asked softly.

Aurellio looked at her, a peculiar movement deep in his eyes made Ellie uncomfortable for the first time ever in his company. She shifted slightly in her seat and looked down.

"Yes." He sighed, deep from within his soul. "It is Marcellus. My friend. My leader. My companion for centuries and my maker. It is he that has betrayed all Vampire and he that commissioned the design for the black death balls. Marcellus."

"Oh I am so sorry Aurellio. So very sorry. I wish that it had been someone else, truly. But we need to deal with this. Now. When is he due back?" Ellie asked.

"Back?" Aurellio was still stunned.

"Yes, back. You told us he was away, Rome I think, anyway that is irrelevant. When is he back? How long do we have to put a plan together?" Felix was brusque, even cold in his questioning.

"There is a council meeting for all hive leaders in the middle of next week, so he will probably be back Tuesday."

"So, then that would be a perfect time to wipe out all the leaders at once. That must be what he has planned. I wonder what he hopes to gain from this? It makes no sense." Ellie was confused.

"It matters not at this moment what his reasons are, I believe that you are right and that the council is his target. That gives us just under a week to put together a counter attack. Aurellio, are there any Vamps that you can trust? Any at all?" James was oddly excited. Ellie wondered at that.

"No." Aurellio shrugged disconsolately, "None. Who can I trust? My maker and friend is not who I believed. Who could I trust?"

"Snap out of it for gods sake!" Ellie spat. "Get over it. So your best pal is an arse that wants to commit vampicide? So what? Get a grip! Start thinking with your head, you have no heart so it can't be broken!"

Aurellio looked at her and his eyes narrowed in anger, his teeth slid out over his thin lips and a growl started in the back of his throat.

"You dare to speak to me thus?" He hissed.

The skin along Ellie's arms started to prickle and she could feel every tiny hair stand erect in fear. Her nostrils flared and her throat dried uncomfortably. Ellie felt the bubble of her bowel threaten to void but did not back down.

"Yes. I dare. Who else is there? I am here, I am your friend, I am in a world I know nothing of but I understand pain and betrayal. Crying about it changes nothing.

The Fae

I am sorry that you have to face this but you have faced worse I am sure. Marcellus is planning to wipe out your whole council of leaders. Does that mean anything to you? If it does not then fine, we all go about our business with a few less Vamps to worry about. I lived this long not caring, I can manage longer. If it is something you wish to prevent, then here we are. We, the three of us in this room will fight with you. Not because we care about a bunch of blood sucking strangers but because we care about you. What matters to you, matters to us. Now. Have you pulled your head out of your arse? Are you ready to make some decisions? Hmm?"

The three men in the room stared at Ellie with mouths open and shock writ large upon their faces. Aurellio fidgeted in his seat, opening and closing his mouth several times to speak, seemingly trying to find words that were audible to the others.

"Vampicide?" He asked, stunned. "Vampicide?" Then he collapsed in a heap, laughing uncontrollably. "Vampicide!" He roared.

The others in the room stared at the incongruity of the sight. A terrifying, atavistic creature who held a glass of human blood in his hand was laughing like a child. They were each unsure how to respond.

"You would make such a fine Vampire." Aurellio sniffed as he brought his mirth under control. "You go straight for the throat!"

"Yes. Well!" Ellie harrumphed.

Aurellio looked at Ellie with something new in his eyes that made her feel uncomfortable for a whole new set of reasons.

"You can forget about that, thank you very much!" She told him primly.

"Right. Well..." James broke the tension with an uncertain little cough. "Back to matters at hand yes?"

"Indeed." Aurellio laughed. With a last strange look at Ellie he said, "Yes, back to more immediate concerns. What to do? Do I care about the council? As my friend here suggested, I have no heart so to care would be impossible. Is it important that they remain as they are? Note that to keep in with Ellie's line of thinking, I omitted the word 'alive'." He giggled a little. "Yes, I believe it is important to keep the council, let us say 'alive'. If they were to be killed, there would be chaos. The Vampire are an unruly bunch and the current leaders have held the peace for decades. Were they to be removed? Yes, definitely chaos. Many human deaths would ensue as it is the current crop of leaders that keep the peace there. I know of many that would rejoice at being able to hunt again. Yes, I believe that it would be better to try and prevent Marcellus from carrying out this attack."

"Right. Good. That's one problem done." Ellie tried to recover from the uncomfortable feeling that Aurellio had evoked. "How and what I suppose is the next thing."

"James, do you have any people that might help?" Felix asked.

"I have been wondering about that." James said. "It is not as if the Vampires have ever helped the Elf, so I think we may struggle there."

"Yes, and Fairies do not fight, so my guys are no use." Felix added.

"I am pretty sure that you don't want humans knowing about Vamps and others." Ellie said. "Not that I know of any that would be of use here. Wow, what a crap army we three make."

"Four." Aurellio said.

The Fae

"Yes four, I know that. It just didn't rhyme." Ellie looked quite serious. "Plus also, the three musketeers were four but referred to as three."

"So we three musketeers will take on the evil Count Marcellus at the Kings court and undo the plot to overthrow the kingdom?" Laughed James, joining in the game.

"Yes. Why not?" Felix laughed.

"Indeed." Agreed Aurellio. "The three musketeers! We need no others. All for one…"

"And one for all!" The others replied, laughing and jumping up to high five each other.

The rest of the night was spent conjuring ever fantastical plots to save the council. The three musketeers invented dragons that swooped in and ate Marcellus, whilst incinerating his army. They created witches that cast shrinking spells and spent hours imagining a miniature Marcellus nipping at the heels of the council, trying to drain them as they sat, and being swatted aside like insects. The three friends imagined potions that made them invincible and others that made them invisible.

"Are there witches? Do they exist?" Ellie asked.

"Yes." James told her. "But they are very few and live away from people. They prefer solitude, living mainly in places of natural beauty. Most of their magic comes from nature, so they like to be surrounded by it. It would be very rare indeed to find one in a town or city. Unless they were visiting, or on holiday."

"And Werewolves? Are they real too?"

"Oh yes." Aurellio said coldly. "Very real. There is no friendship between them and Vampires. We have been fighting for centuries."

"Are there any in Colchester? Would I know them?"

"Yes, there is a pack in Colchester. You probably have seen them about. They prefer to be builders, workmen, anything that requires muscle and brawn. They tend not to go for the, let us say, more refined career choices. I suppose it is because of all the Others, they are the closest to animal, they possibly find the higher brain waves harder to command." Aurellio said smugly.

"I do not think that is quite, well, yes they tend to do more manual work." James defended them. "But as to being doctors or scientists… Well I think that it is just that being dogs, they have more of a cunning than intelligence. Oh I am not really …Well, they tend to be like Aurellio says, builders, labourers. But they also join the police. They like order, belonging. It is the pack mentality. They are usually quite strong, tenacious. Never underestimate them though, they are certainly smart. Just, well, they are not so much book learned. If you understand." He finished lamely.

"So… Unlikely to help us fight Marcellus then?"

"Not necessarily…" Aurellio surprised them by saying. "Their pack leader, Chris, he and Marcellus have a long standing feud. It goes back years. Any opportunity and they will attack each other. It might be worth asking them."

"Would that not be, well, problematic?" Asked Felix. "If they do not like the Vampire, would they not take it as an opportunity to attack themselves? If they know that there is a possibility of dissention or weakness? Do you know what I mean?"

"It is a possibility." Aurellio agreed. "But, it could be put to them that it would be in their interest. Or, a strong possibility is that Chris would just like an opportunity to have a go at Marcellus. He does not need much of a reason."

"Can you contact them? See whether they want to join in?" Ellie asked excitedly.

The Fae

"No. Not me." Aurellio looked slightly embarrassed. "We don't exactly have the best of histories ourselves. Last time we met, I er... Well I may have kind of... Well, let's just say that I may have killed his mate."

"Oh my god! You killed his wife?" Ellie was sickened.

"Well, yes. It is not as bad as it sounds though!"

"How can it not be so bad? You killed his wife? He must hate you with a passion."

"Not really. She was trying to kill him at the time, I sort of stopped her and she kind of got dead in the process. He is not unhappy that his mate is dead, he did not much like her anyway. It is more that, well it is more that I did it and not him."

"That is disgusting!" Ellie looked away in contempt.

"Seriously, Ellie. It is not so bad. He did not like her. It was an arranged marriage and she was a bitch!"

"Harrumph!" Ellie was not appeased.

"James and I could go. We could ask them." Felix offered. "Our species have never had any kind of dealings with them. We should be okay."

"Me too. I would love to meet a true life Werewolf." Ellie piped up excitedly.

"No. It is not a game Ellie." James told her.

"Really? Wow! And there was me thinking that this was all for chuckles!"

"I am sorry, I did not mean it like that, it is just that this could be dangerous."

"You condescending prick! What do you think I have been doing since I met you all?" She was incensed.

"Yes, but also, look at the injuries you have sustained since you met us. Surely you cannot be angry that we want you healed? What use will you be to us next week if you are still damaged?"

"Oh. Well okay. I see your point." Ellie allowed.

"Right, if we are going to go, it may as well be now. Aurellio, where will we find this Chris? And how will we know him?"

"He works at the Bull, in Crouch Street."

"But that closed ages ago." Ellie said looking at the clock on the wall.

"Yes, but he has lock-ins most nights. Go round the back entrance and ask for him. He should be there tonight."

"How will we know him?"

"Not a problem, you should be able to spot him." Aurellio smiled.

James and Felix grabbed their coats and waved goodbye. As they disappeared out of the gate, Felix could be heard challenging James to see who could run to town the fastest. Ellie smiled to herself and settled back against the cushions. With her lids half closed she asked Aurellio to tell her more about himself.

Well." He began. "As I told you, I was turned during the invasion. It was a strange time. The town was full of different languages, Latin from the Romans, Old English from the Trinovantes, some French and German., much Celt. It was a very unsettled time. People coming and going, settling, dying. Disease was rife, hygiene poor. The town was interesting. On the one hand you had the small round houses of the locals and on the other you had the grand brick and stone of the Romans. There were temples being built, markets trading, churches being erected. Noise everywhere, and dust! Dust in your hair, clothes, nose. Trade came in along the Hythe river, just down from here. That was a busy area, many people would gather when a vessel was due and then the noise! When the vessels docked, people shouting, bartering, all for a good deal, better price. And the poor merchant trying to unload and get his wares to market. Horses and cows were everywhere, and with them came their stench. It permeated our clothes and skin. When I first arrived here I found the filth and smell intolerable. The longer I stayed, the less I noticed it. Some days you could feed a family of seven with a slice of that air!" He laughed with the recollection. "There was order for the most part. The Romans bought their laws. The locals had their ways and mostly we all rubbed along quite well. History paints it as a violent time, and it is true that there were times when things were very bad, but it helps to remember that history can never paint the nuances. It can only record one persons interpretations, not a whole cities."

"I have always been fascinated with that period of Colchester's history." Ellie told him. "I walk through town staring up more than down. The buildings fascinate me. I often imagine the countless lives that have been lived inside them. I love the old photographs showing snapshots of a time long past. I look to see if any of it is familiar, I look at the faces of the people and wonder at their descendants."
"There are a couple that I have seen where the people in them are still alive." Aurellio told her. "Queen Alcea is in quite a few. She has always loved her own image. I think there is even one with James in somewhere. I must dig about at home and see if I can find them for you."
"That would be fantastic. Thank you. So, did you ever marry? Have children?"
"No, I was too young when I was alive. I had my beloved back in Rome, but I never saw her again. As to children? No. I had never even lain with a woman when I was turned. In the army, there were many that took comfort with other men, but I never did. Marcellus tried to seduce me in the beginning, but I just never felt that particular desire. After a while, he stopped trying and found himself a new toy to play with. I have loved many times since then, but as I tend to live much longer than they, I stopped about a century ago. Despite having no heart, it still hurt too much to watch those that I loved age and die before me."
"Oh that is so sad!" Ellie whispered. "There has been nobody?"
"There have been none that I love but several that satisfy my desires." He winked.
"Oh Aurellio!"

Ellie and Aurellio spent a pleasant couple of hours chatting and gossiping. It turned out that Aurellio was an amusing font of local knowledge. He regaled her with tales of Others that had crossed his path. He spoke of a particularly funny episode where he had been invited to King James' coronation but had to decline as it was in daylight. He told how he had tried to attend later in the evening but arrived at the wrong door and spent a rowdy night with several buxom servants. He spoke of the changes to Colchester that he had witnessed and his sadness as the beautiful buildings were replaced with ugly boxes with no soul. Ellie was surprised to hear him speak this way. She had supposed Vampires to be like the ones on TV, all sex and killing. It amazed her to find out that Aurellio wrote poetry and had even had some published in books that were still available in the library.

As the night was nearing its darkest point, the peace was shattered by rowdy, drunken singing growing louder and louder. The gate swung open with a crash as it bounced off the wall, and in stumbled a large mass of moving limbs and off key noise. As it entered the back door, the mass broke apart into three distinct shapes. James and Felix were ruddy with drink and a third, hulking creature leant and threw up outside the door. Felix and James looked at each other in alarm then burst into laughter as they clutched at each other to stay upright.

"Sorry 'bout that!" Hiccupped the newcomer. "I shall clear it up presently madam." He swayed toward the closest kitchen chair and collapsed into it. He lay his shaven head on the table and proceeded to snore loudly.

Felix, who had spun to watch his progress, did a small pirouette and fell daintily in a heap on the floor. James laughed so hard that snot flew out of his nose. He swung his hand up to cover it but missed and punched himself in the face. James looked so amazed that Ellie started to laugh.

Ellie set about making the revellers some coffee and when she was done, she nudged the sleeping stranger with her foot.

"Wake up sleeping beauty." She prodded. "Come on sunshine, coffee here for you."

Felix held his cup with both hands and sipped gingerly whilst James looked morosely into the tan depths of the mug.

"I don't know what happened." He told Ellie. "I think we were poisoned."

"I think I am going to die." Moaned Felix. "I am defiantly going to die."

Ellie looked at them long and hard. She could smell the beer on their breath from where she stood at the sink.

"Yes, I believe you are. Is there anything you would like me to do for you, you know... when you are gone?" She asked sweetly. "Have you considered what type of funeral? Who you would like to attend? Let me get a pen and paper so I can make notes." And she rushed out of the room before collapsing with giggles next to Aurellio on the couch.

"Have they never had beer before?" She asked, tears streaming.

"No. Fairies and Elves do not drink. I can see why now."

When Ellie looked back into the kitchen, she saw that all three were asleep. James had his arm around Felix' shoulder and was nestled into the crook of his neck. Felix was sitting bolt upright, head back, mouth open and snoring like a steam train.

In the morning Ellie entered the kitchen to find it gleaming and smelling faintly of bleach. There was a pot of tea and breakfast laid out on the table along with three sheepish, hung-over men staring up at her from their seats. Ellie's lips twitched as she tried to suppress her smile. She glowered at them as if they were miscreant children.

"Uh, we are very sorry." Felix mumbled, looking down.

"Pardon? I can't quite hear you." Ellie said loudly.

"Sorry, I said we were sorry. Please do not shout. The poison is still eating our brains. We are near death Ellie, I swear." Felix looked up at her like a small kicked puppy.

Ellie could not help but laugh. "You prat! You were drunk that's all. It's no big deal. You will have a headache for a while but I promise you won't die of it." She sat at the table and poured herself a cup of tea. She looked toward the guest and asked, "is anyone going to introduce us?"

"Oh my apologies. My name is Chris. Pleased to meet you." The dark man said, standing up and holding out his hand in greeting.

Ellie shook his hand and noted that his grip was firm and dry. Chris was tall and heavily built. He had black hair shaved close to his skull. His body appeared to be quite fully covered with the same thick hair. His shaved hair the tide mark indicating the beginning of his chest hair. His eyes were brown and seemed to be bottomless. Ellie thought that you could drown in those eyes if you were not careful. He had an ordinary face, one of many that you passed every day, but there was a stillness to him that set him apart. His body almost hummed with energy and he made Ellie feel as if he could bound into action at any moment. She felt calm and safe near him and noted that he smelt faintly of dog, but not unpleasantly so.

"So the boys found you then?" Ellie asked him, releasing her hand from his grip. "Did they explain what we need?"

"Yes, they asked if I might help you to fight Marcellus. This is a bit sticky. I cannot ask my pack to help you. I am sorry…" He said quickly when he saw Ellie's disheartened face. "It is just that we have no cause. No reason of our own to fight. We have had a fragile truce now for about six months and need this time to recoup our strength. We suffered heavily in our last encounter and need time to heal. I however, am very happy to lend my support on an individual basis. From what these two tell me, I believe that the fewer we are the better."

"Really? Why is that? Surely we would need an army?"

"No. The fewer we are the stealthier we can be. We do not need an all out war, just… let me say *careful pruning*."

"Oh, well, I suppose you would know better than me. I am still quite new to all this. There is one potential problem though. How do you feel about working alongside Aurellio? He told me of the part he played with the death of your mate. Could you work together?"

"I don't see why not. She was a bitch. If he hadn't of killed her, I would."

The three men and Ellie ate their breakfast and chatted about commonalities they had discovered between them. Chris remembered Ellie singing in a karaoke bar some time ago, much to her embarrassment. Felix remembered seeing Chris play American Football several seasons back and they even shared a few friends.

"I do not know why we are so surprised." Ellie commented. "This is a small town. And you guys have been around for centuries. I am surprised that you don't all know each other better!"

"We don't live as long as these guys." Chris told her. "We have the same life span as humans. Also, we tend to hang out whereas the Fairies and Elves keep to themselves. We have always considered them aloof; untouchable. It's fun to find out how normal you are." He smiled widely. "And to know that you have such wild sides." He added ambiguously.

"Why?" Ellie asked, perking up. "What did they get up to last night?"

"Ah, that would be unfair. I cannot possibly tell you."

"Why not?" Ellie wanted to know.

"Because then I couldn't torment them!" Chris laughed.

Ellie got the feeling that a whole new type of Other had entered her life now.

It turned out that Chris was a bit of a ladies man. He made it clear on several occasions that should Ellie fancy 'a bit of rough,' he would gladly oblige her. During one of his propositions, James happened to walk into the room and overhear. He became very agitated and started shouting at Chris to show more respect. Ellie had felt compelled to intervene and explain that it was just Chris' way of being friendly and that he meant no harm. She went on to tell James that if she had said yes, Chris would likely have run for the hills. James appeared to be placated but kept a close watch on their new friend all the same.

After lunch, Chris told the three that he had to leave but would return at dusk when Aurellio awoke, so that they could plan. The house appeared much quieter and somehow bigger after he had left.

There was much discussion between them as to whether Felix should heal James' damaged arm. Felix wanted to do it but James was concerned that it would land him in trouble with the queen. Ellie reminded them that only their small group even knew of his injury. They argued about it for some time when Ellie, becoming impatient with the lack of progress, declared…
"Well. If you're arm does not work, you will not be able to join us in the fight, so you may as well start rolling bandages and boiling water ready for our return."
James blustered some more but it was clear that his heart was not in it, so eventually he allowed himself to be persuaded.
"I think," said Felix. "That we should go into Ellie's room, that way any residual energy should seep into Aurellio. I am not totally sure, but it can not hurt."
"Yes, good idea. Come on then before I change my mind." James left the room muttering to himself about parents looking out for children, not the other way around.

Ellie put the kettle on to make tea. Whilst she was standing, staring into space and enjoying a moments solitude, there came a scratching at the door. Walking over and opening the door, Ellie let out a screech of delight when she saw Peter sitting on the step.
"Oh my god! Peter! I have missed you so much. How are you? How is Fae? Are you well?"
"Well let me in and I shall answer all your questions." Peter quipped as he strode past her and jumped up onto the table. "Where is Bunbury? I haven't seen him for a while."
"Oh he should be back soon, it's time for his dinner. Tell me, how are you?"
"Oh me, I am good. Totally healed. I wanted to see you of course, but I really need to thank Bunbury for, well for everything really. Who would have thought that he was a shifter? I did not see that coming. How has he been since?"
"Oddly, its as if nothing happened. He is the same as ever, still affectionate, still well a cat. I was a bit weird with him for a couple of hours but he is still Bunbury no matter what shape he takes. I don't let him in the bathroom with me any more though, that is a bit too weird."
Ellie and Peter chatted and filled the other in on what they had been up to since they last saw each other. If Peter noticed the strong earthy smell and occasional green flashes from the direction of the bedroom, he did not comment.

Ellie told Peter about meeting the Dryad and how she was staying with her for a while.
"Although I rarely see her." Ellie told him. "She is in the garden more than I am. I think she really misses being outside with her trees."
She told Peter about the battle in Friday Woods and about how Felix had taken a fancy to her friend Ciara. She did not tell him about Marcellus and the plan they were hoping to put together. She felt that it was not her place to do so. She trusted Peter implicitly but did not want the information to go any further than the three musketeers

and the wolf. She felt a twinge of guilt for keeping a secret, but figured she could live with it.

As the church bells started to chime from the bell tower across the road, Bunbury strolled into the kitchen and wove himself around Ellie's ankles. When he noticed Peter, he stopped and looked at him with his head on one side, unblinking. Bunbury stayed like that for several minutes, and when Ellie turned to look at Peter, she saw that he was mirroring the action. After a few moments, they broke eye contact and Bunbury went to his food bowl and started to eat.

"He tells me that it is like Piccadilly Circus here. People coming and going, drunken Werewolves, all sorts. What has been going on Ellie?"

"What a tattle tail." Ellie laughed, ruffling Bunbury's fur along his head as he ate. "Am I to have no secrets, puss?"

Peter gave Ellie one of his old fashioned looks that seemed to say that he was completely aware that she was avoiding answering him. "Well, he does say that he is well and that he has almost no memory of being human-ish. It is most unusual. Most shape shifters are human in form who then turn to other creatures, I think Bunbury is the only one I know of that is the other way around."

"Well, he is my special little man." Ellie said, scooping up her cat and nuzzling him with her chin. "What else did he say?"

"He did say that he finds being called a special little man somewhat demeaning." Peter told her.

"Tough." She kissed the top of the cats head and put him on the floor where he cocked his leg and started to lick his nether regions.

"Told you!" Said Peter with a smile in his voice.

Chapter Twenty Two

James was swinging his arm round and round in circles as he, Ellie, Felix and Peter sat in the garden. Bunbury was curled up on Ellie's lap, snoring gently; his tail and paws twitching in sleep. Peter and Felix were talking quietly and Ellie lay back against the chair with her eyes closed, completely relaxed, soaking up the dying rays of the sun.

"Boo!" Came the stereo shout of tiny voices by Ellie's ear. "Ha, ha, gotcha!"
Ellie almost jumped out of her skin as she bolted upright, turning toward the twins who were giggling furiously by her side. Clutching her hand to her racing heart, Ellie smiled.
"You certainly did." She told them when she was sure her heart would not leap out of her mouth. "Boy you two are getting good at being stealthy. I didn't hear you coming at all. You must have been practicing."
"That they have!" Mertensia told her seriously. "I miss the days when this was a secret. They sneak up and scare me to death on a regular basis. I am ageing at a rate of knots and I am sure my hair is more grey every day." She ruffled Bluebell's hair affectionately.
"It is so good to see you," Ellie told them, "it has been way too long. How are you? How is Clematis?"
"We are in excellent health thank you." Begonia said in a playfully regal voice. "Papa is away with work again. We do miss him ever so much."
"Well my darlings, if he did not work, you would not have so many pretty dresses. The ones you have on today are gorgeous." Ellie smiled.
"Oh do you think so?" Mertensia blushed. "I made these. It is my first time. I was not too sure, I thought they may look a little amateurish."
"Not at all, they are incredible. You could sell these. I know lots of little girls who would love to have one."
"Do you think so? That I could sell them I mean? I did so enjoy making them."
"Absolutely. They are fantastic."
Ellie and Mertensia discussed dressmaking whilst Bluebell and Begonia ran about the garden chasing Peter. Bunbury raised one sleepy eyelid then shut it again quickly when he saw what could be in store for him.

The sun was sinking lower and the bees droned mournfully in the background. Starlings chittered to each other as they prepared for nightfall and the friends went inside out of the chill air for a warming mug of chocolate. From somewhere within her enormous carpet bag, Mertensia produced a can of squirty cream and a bag of mini marshmallows to complete the treat.
"Your bag." Ellie said in wonder. "It is almost as if, well, if I think of something, you are able to pull it out of your bag. Is it magic?"
"No." Mertensia laughed. "I have just been shopping and the girls wanted hot chocolate when we get home, so I bought these. It is merely coincidence I promise." She smiled and then winked, leaving Ellie unsure as to the truth.
They all sat cradling a warm mug of chocolaty sweetness, each lost to their own thoughts.

Aurellio entered into the kitchen stretching and yawning. He absently scratched at his crotch before he noticed that there were people watching him. He paused a moment before going to the fridge, removing a pack of blood and placing it in the microwave.

"Good sleep?" Asked Ellie.

"Oh, what? Yes. Thanks. Uh hello everyone." He said grumpily.

"Get out of the wrong side of the coffin?" Asked James.

Aurellio growled quietly and went back to the bedroom, having retrieved the warmed blood and a glass.

"Hnf! Dunno what his problem is." Mused Ellie lazily. She stretched out then collected up the dirty mugs, placing them in the sink to wash later.

Mertensia gathered the twins and announced that she ought to be going as she had only popped by for a hello.

Ellie kissed Mertensia and the twins goodbye then went to the sink to wash up.

"Here," James moved her out of the way. "You sit down, I will do them. Need to get the blood flowing in this arm again." He said as he swung his arm around some more.

Aurellio came back into the kitchen and sat at the table with a sigh.

"Did I scare your friends away?" He asked, not sounding particularly interested in the answer.

"Yes you did. How come you are so out of sorts? Did you have a bad dream or something?"

"Ellie, we do not dream, when we are asleep we are dead. We are not aware of anything. We have no thoughts, dreams or feelings. Just dead."

"That is disgusting!" Ellie declared. "How do you know you are dead?"

"I don't know. We just are. Why do you question everything?"

"Because if I didn't, I wouldn't know anything. Duh!"

Aurellio looked at her for a moment as if he were thinking over what she had said, then he dropped his head into his hands and rubbed at his temples.

"I do not know what is the matter with me. I feel wrong."

"What do you mean?" Asked Felix in alarm. "Wrong how?"

"I'm not sure. I feel all fuzzy and weird. I have not felt ill for centuries, maybe it is that. Although..." Aurellio mused aloud. "I should never feel ill again. I am dead, I cannot exactly catch anything. Very odd."

James and Felix exchanged a worried look.

"Erm..." Felix began. "Erm, it may be me. I healed James in the bedroom earlier, I thought that any residual energy may soak into you and make you sort of...better. It must be that which is making you feel wrong. I am truly sorry. I meant no harm."

"Will it wear off?"

"Oh yes...sure, of course. Any time now." Felix blustered.

Not long after, Chris arrived looking much better than he had earlier. He was wearing clean fresh clothes and had showered. He even wore some form of cologne. He smelt faintly of vanilla and wood smoke. It was an odd but pleasant smell. As he entered, he grabbed Ellie's hand and kissed her palm.

"My apologies again for my unceremonious entry last night." He told her. "Ah, Aurellio. Are you well?"

Aurellio had the decency to look a little sheepish as he returned the greeting. But it was gone in a blink and he was back to normal in a heart beat.

"The mate thing." He got straight to the point. "Is it going to be a problem?"

The Fae

"No, but next time I want a divorce, let me do the tearing okay?" Chris laughed. "You may want to stay away from the pack though. They seem to think I should be more upset. Give them time to calm down."

"Whatever." Aurellio replied eruditely.

"Okay, the gang's all here." Ellie said. "Let's make a plan. Right…firstly, Aurellio please explain to us how the council works, how they arrive, sit, stand, mingle. How long does it last? Where is it? You know, any details that may help us to build up a picture of what we are facing."

"The council consists of five hive leaders from England, two from Scotland, two from Wales and one from Northern Ireland."

"What about South Ireland?" Ellie asked.

"They are not a part of the British Isles." Aurellio told her as if that were obvious.

"Seriously? You guys recognise borders? Wow!"

"Yes, well it helps to keep things simple. If I may continue?" He certainly was in a bad mood. "Right. This council meeting is to be held in Colchester this year. They take it in turns, visiting each hive so as not to show favouritism. I do not yet know where in Colchester, but that should be easy enough to find out. It is normally a formal event. Each leader brings their entourage both for safety and to show the others how well they are doing. It might help to know that Vampires are, well they can be a little vain…"

"Really?" Ellie asked sweetly.

"Oh yes. Anyway, they bring their retinues and that means that they need a large, auspicious meeting place. Somewhere like the Masonic Lodge or the Town Hall. They have a sit down conference that can last for several nights. It depends on what issues are discussed and whether there are any enmities that need tiptoeing around. All sorts. Generally, you can expect there to be upwards of a hundred people."

"That many? I had no idea." Felix interrupted.

"They generally arrive at midnight as is tradition and the meeting goes on until just before dawn. The host has to provide suitable accommodation for everyone attending and as you can imagine, it needs to be close by. If the business is not completed, the meeting reconvenes the next night and so on until nothing is left to discuss. There is quite an honour attached to being a part of the council meeting, even if you are only there as decoration."

"Okay, this is good." Ellie rubbed her hands together and looked at the men around her. "As soon as we know where it will be, we can refine the plan, but until then we have a lot to sort out. Firstly, the plan. I say we ambush any attack, wipe them out and scuttle off home before anyone is the wiser."

"Good plan except for one tiny detail." Aurellio said. "Marcellus will be host, so he will be inside the building before anyone else. He will have his entourage of minders with him as well."

"Well yes, okay. But… He will have to leave at some point else he will be slaughtered by the death balls himself. We can get him then."

"I think that is certainly an idea, but we should explore other possibilities just in case there are problems, or it does not happen the way we expect." James said gently.

"Yes, good idea. There are only five of us though." Ellie conceded. "We really should have more people."

"I don't agree." Chris said. "The fewer the better. Aurellio, does the event have, and excuse me here, catering?"

"Yes, the host lays on snacks for the guests."

"Maybe I could be a waitress and alert you to his movements or something." Ellie offered helpfully.

Chris laughed loudly. "I don't think so little lady," he said not unkindly, "the snacks are generally in the shape of familiars."

"What is a familiar?" Asked Ellie.

"A familiar is a human that is enamoured of Vampires and will do anything to be allowed the distinction of remaining in their presence." Aurellio supplied.

"Oh." Ellie said, thinking it over. "Oh! That's gross! They allow you guys to suck them? Willingly?"

"They consider it a great honour to be able to serve their masters in this way." Aurellio told her with a hint of pride in his voice. "Would you prefer we hunted?"

"No, no. Sorry. I am just… it is just that this is all still new to me. Things like this have only ever been on TV before. It takes a bit of getting used to." Ellie apologised.

"The idea of an infiltrator is not to be dismissed so lightly." James said. "Obviously it cannot be Ellie, but if we could find someone that Marcellus does not know, it would be a good idea to have someone on the inside."

"I could never allow anyone I know to offer themselves to get chewed on!" Ellie was incensed. "Surely the Vamps know who their familiars are?"

"Not always. They will never turn down a willing snack and sometimes these familiars bring along a friend." Aurellio looked as though he were thinking hard.

"Do you know any familiars? Anyone who might be going? Would they help us?" Felix asked hopefully.

"I know many familiars." Aurellio answered. "But as to whether they would help. No. That they would not. They see Marcellus as a god."

Ellie shivered with disgust. Aurellio ignored her.

"They would never betray their god. But I may be able to get someone in as a friend of one of the familiars. They would willingly do that for me. They do not have to know why. They will just obey."

"But we don't know anyone that could do it. He knows all of us here." Ellie repeated.

Felix shifted uncomfortably in his seat. "We could ask Ciara." He offered, reluctantly.

"We most certainly could not!" Ellie shouted. "How dare you offer one of my friends as bait? She has nothing to do with this. She would never agree anyway."

"Erm, actually…" Felix started. "I rather think that she would. Marcellus killed her parents when she was a child and she has told me that she would do anything to hurt him."

"But she is an innocent." Ellie pointed out. "You cannot seriously ask her to do this? It would be far too dangerous."

"Do you not think it would be polite to ask her herself if she would like to do this?" Felix said sounding stronger, more assured. "I can get her and bring her here now."

Ellie was not happy about involving Ciara, but agreed that it should be her own choice. She was hoping fervently that Ciara told them where to stick the idea.

Felix almost flew out of the door, so great appeared his eagerness to see Ciara again. He returned an hour later, more sedately, with her.

"Hi." She said nervously, staring at Aurellio and Chris with a hint of concern on her beautiful face. "Felix has explained what you want me to do, and on the whole I shall. Do it I mean. I just have, well, a couple of conditions."

"Conditions?" Asked Aurellio raising one eyebrow imperiously.

"Ah, yes..." She took a step backwards, toward Felix and felt behind her for his hand. "I want to help. That is beyond doubt, my condition is that..." Another look at Aurellio before taking a deep breath and continuing. "Should anything happen." She swallowed. "Happen to me that is..." She looked behind to Felix who squeezed her hand and nodded encouragement. "Well, what it is... If anything should happen to me, please Ellie will you take care of Flopsy? She would be so frightened."

With a sigh, not realising that she had been holding her breath, Ellie told her, "of course I will. But if there is any sign of anything happening, we would get you out straight away."

"Damned right we would!" Felix added fervently.

"You said a couple of conditions." Aurellio prodded.

"Ah, the second is a little more... Well the thing is... You see what I mean is..."

"For pity's sake spit it out woman!" Aurellio snapped.

Ellie shot him a look of contempt. "Hold your tongue and mind your manners. Number one, you are a guest in my home and number two, we are asking my friend to do something insane. Be polite."

Aurellio looked at her for a moment then nodded. "My apologies." He said stiffly to Ciara. "Please..." A look at Ellie, then back to Ciara. "What is your other condition.?"

Ciara shifted about onto one foot then the other as her face took on a pained expression.

"Uh, well, the condition is that I go in disguise and nobody, and I mean nobody can reveal that it is me. Felix may have told you that Marcellus killed my parents?"

Everyone nodded.

"Well, I am the double of my mother and have been mistaken for her before. Marcellus must never know that I am alive. I am concerned that should he see me, he will kill me. He does not know that I survived the attack you see." She looked at Aurellio with utter terror written on her face.

"I shall never reveal your secret." Aurellio told her gravely.

Ciara did not look convinced, but she did look resigned. It were as though now that she had told her secret, the rest was out of her hands.

"I am honoured that you would share that with us." Ellie told her. "Everyone in this room will take that knowledge to the grave. I swear it." She stood and held out her arm, palm down.

Felix stepped around Ciara and placed his palm over Ellie's.

"I swear it." He said.

"I swear it." Chris stood and placed his palm above Felix's.

James and Aurellio stood and placed their own hands in the circle and swore to keep the secret also. Ciara seemed to relax slightly at this show of solidarity and took a seat, thanking them.

"I guess that means that you have made up your mind?" Ellie asked Ciara sadly.

"I must. I may never get another opportunity to avenge my parents. Alone I am not strong enough. If I do not help, Aurellio will kill him and I will lose my chance forever. I have no choice."

"I understand, truly I do." Ellie begged. "But please reconsider. It is madness. You will be inside a room full of Vampires. I can imagine nothing more dangerous than that."

"Please accept my decision Ellie. Please do not make it harder for me. I am terrified, believe me that I am. But I must do this. I trust Felix to keep me as safe as possible."

"But Felix is Fairy, he cannot fight, please Ciara."

"I am only half Fairy." Felix interrupted. "My Elf half has been practicing and taking lessons." He smiled at his father in acknowledgement.

"Oh I give up!" Ellie pouted. "The world has gone crazy! I don't even believe any of this is real. I am still locked into a crazy dream and will wake up soon!" She stood and flounced out of the room to her bedroom. She slammed the door closed behind her in a childish fit of pique.

Feeling a sense of Deja-Vu, Ellie realised that this was her house and she would have to leave the bedroom and face the people in her kitchen. Reluctantly she stood and walked to the bathroom. She flushed the toilet hoping they might believe that was where she had been, instead of skulking in her room. She entered the kitchen and filled the kettle. Ellie reached for clean cups and set about making yet more tea.

The people around the table were talking amongst themselves and Ellie's entrance went un-remarked. They were discussing variations on the theme of Ciara entering the meeting and reporting back to the others. It was generally agreed that there was very little Ciara could do except keep the team apprised of the movements inside the meeting, then to run like hell when told to do so. Everyone except Ellie seemed satisfied with this. Ellie's objections were voiced repeatedly until she was told to shut up by Ciara who was becoming more and more distressed the more Ellie stressed the danger. The actions to be taken by the rest of the team was not so easy to figure out. They imagined many different scenarios but without hard facts, each one was as useless as the next.

"We need to find out where it is going to be." Felix said. "Until then, all this speculation is just that. Speculation."

"Agreed." James added. "Aurellio, can you find out tonight where it is?"

"I can go and see Umberto. He should know. I will go now." He stood and picked up his jacket from the back of his chair, then left the house.

Overcome with curiosity and not a small amount of perversity, Ellie slipped out behind him. Aurellio walked briskly to the end of the road and Ellie followed, keeping as quiet as she could, thanking her luck that the traffic sounds hid any noise she may have made. Reaching the junction at the top of her road, Aurellio crossed over then turned right. Ellie waited for a break in the traffic then hurried after him. She walked in the shadow of the high crumbling wall that ran down the hill toward the Hythe. At the entrance to the church, Aurellio turned and entered. Ellie stopped in shock, thinking of all the stories she had heard where Vampires could not enter churches.

The church lay in complete darkness. It was no longer used for any form of worship and Ellie remembered seeing a notice asking visitors to call at the house opposite if they wished to have a look around. The graveyard was a collage of blacks and greys, absences of light and strong earthy smells. Despite the road being mere feet away, there seemed to be no sound at all in the churchyard. Ellie felt as though she were in a vacuum, all sound and sensation sucked away. She felt a little light headed and reached out to steady herself on a jagged headstone. Instead of the rough stone that she expected, Ellie felt a cold, unyielding softness. Her fingers inadvertently closed around dead fingers and she screamed deep inside her throat, allowing only a whimper to escape her lips.

"I imagine this child is with you?" Came a bloodless, harrowing, scratch of a voice. It sounded as though it had squeezed itself up through centuries of tightly packed earth. The fingers turned in her hand and grasped her wrist, firmly. "I was under the impression that I need not reiterate the rules to one such as you." The voice continued past Ellie's ear.

"Apologies Umberto. I did not think she would follow me…"

"Think?" The voice screamed. A putrescence filled Ellie's nose and images of decaying flesh, animated by crawling maggots and other disgusting creatures filled her mind, pushing at the edges of her reason. Ellie felt her knees weaken and her stomach turn. She desperately tried to stay upright. In a flash of understanding she knew that if she fell, she would never rise again. Not as herself.

"Let me take her." Aurellio's voice came from far away as Ellie felt her temples press inwards, crushing her sanity. "I am her master, she is too keen. Too eager. I will punish her…" His voice faded to nothing as Ellie felt her mind slip under and the crawling things begin to eat away at her.

The Fae

Chapter Twenty Three

Ellie felt herself lifted up. It seemed as though her feet were suspended in midair whilst her head burrowed deeper and deeper into the dank soil. She felt small burrowing insects prod and poke all over her scalp, searching for a way in. Her nose felt clogged with putrid earth and her mouth, open in a silent scream, spewed bile and insect shells. She swayed as she was carried and the crawling things dug deeper, clinging on. Ellie felt cold, rough stone beneath her as she was placed gently down. Her skin roiled against her frame and Dante danced behind her lids. Snatches of sound whispered past the insanity screaming inside her head, a car, a bird, a word. Ellie had no control over her limbs as she felt them thrash. Fear turned her bowels to water and she felt them give. A howling screamed around her mind and she felt the last vestiges of her sanity snap. She floated in a disconnected bubble of blacks and reds. Sound became pattern and vision became oil upon water. Sliding, slipping, falling.

"Wake up. Ellie, wake up." A voice whispered to her from far away. "Ellie, wake up my dear. Come on."

Ellie felt cool fingers prise her lids apart and a harsh light burned away some of the decay inside her mind.

"Come on old thing, that's right. Open your eyes. Come on back to us." The whispering continued.

Her other eyelid was pushed up and a scalpel of light sliced into the darkness.

"Ellie, come on, you can do it. Concentrate my dear. That's my girl. Now the other one."

"I'm blind. I can't see." Wailed Ellie.

Her eyes were opened roughly and cool drops sizzled onto her burning retinas.

"Blink, Ellie, blink." The whisper ordered.

Ellie blinked and the oil on water shifted to reveal new psychedelic patterns of pinks and blues.

"Blind..." She cried. "I'm blind."

"No you are not. Pull yourself together and open your bloody eyes." Aurellio's voice pierced her ears with its harshness. "You have absolutely no... You could have been... You bloody stupid woman!" He was furious.

Ellie summoned all her resolve and forced her eye lids open. As the rainbows receded she saw the hazy outline of Aurellio, leaning over her. His fangs were extended and he was incandescent with rage. Beside him stood Hazel, wringing her hands and looking as if she would rather be anywhere else but there. Aurellio had his shirt sleeves rolled up and his top three buttons undone. His hair was askew and his trousers were spattered with what she hoped was mud.

"What happened?" Ellie asked quietly. "I thought I was dead. I thought I was..."

"Why did you follow me? What did you possibly hope to see? To hear? My god Ellie, you could be dead. If he had held you a moment longer, we would never have been able to bring you back. Why? Why did you do it?"

"Don't know." Ellie said in a small voice. "What happened? It was beyond horrible; I can't believe that such horror... Hell would be a picnic after that. What happened to me?"

Aurellio looked at her long and hard then turned on his heel and left the room. He slammed the door closed behind him.

Hazel sat on the bed and stroked Ellie's hair away from her hot forehead.

"What happened?" Whispered Ellie as she watched the shadows dance in Hazel's eye. "'s his problem…" she sighed as she fell asleep.

When she awoke it was fully day. The sun scorched her retinas as she strained to raise her eyelids. Her bones felt like lead and movement was a monumental endeavour. She slid her legs over the side of the bed and tried but failed to grab the headboard to pull herself upright. As she struggled erect, her knees gave way and she fell to the floor. The lead in her bones made ambulation impossible so she decided to crawl to the bathroom. Unable to rise to her knees, Ellie turned her head ready to pull herself along. Out of the corner of her eye she saw a glint from under the bed. Straining to see through the dust and darkness, Aurellio's face shone at her with porcelain delicacy. His attenuated lips pursed lightly beneath his unbreathing nose. Ellie stared in fascination at the glassy coolness of his eyes, open and staring into the depths of the bed base. She saw a mote of dust swirl and settle on his unseeing orb, causing not a flicker of movement, nor an acknowledging flutter. Ellie strained to make out his chest and waited, breath held, for the rise and fall that did not come. Shuddering slightly, she pulled herself away and snaked her course to the bathroom.

Ellie lay panting on the floor for some time. She made pacts with both God and the Devil if only they would let her get onto the toilet. Neither was listening that day and she gave up begging when she felt the hot wetness expand about her. Ellie did not cry. She was furious. Here she was in her own home, lying in a puddle of her own piss with a dead guy under the bed and a fairy floating about God knew where. She was fed up to the teeth of being on the back foot all the time. She was fed up with never knowing what would happen to her next and she was certainly fed up with that lying scummy bastard Fox!

Whoa! Where did that come from? She asked herself. She had not given that married bastard a moments thought since she threw him out of her house. *How long ago had that been?* Time seemed to have lost all meaning lately. Ellie was pretty sure that she did not even know what day it was. She lay back in the cooling puddle and tried to think through the last few days, trying to understand what had happened to her and how much she had changed. If Fae was to be believed, she had tried to kill herself what? A week? Two weeks ago? Three? She had become a part of a community of people that she had hitherto believed only existed in movies and books. She had been beaten and had beaten in return. She had fought Gnomes and parlayed with Vampires. She had visited an imaginary world that apparently she had spent her youth inside, *oh and let's not forget… I'm not even human*! Ellie sulked inside her own mind. On a deeper level, Ellie was aware that this would have sent her insane only a few weeks ago, but now it just made her angry.

"What on..? Ellie? What on earth is…? Come, get up out of that mess." Hazel leant down and offered her hand for Ellie to pull herself up.

"Can't." Ellie said laughingly. "Bloody body is on strike." She reached painfully slowly for Hazel's hand.

Hazel clasped tight around Ellie's forearm and hauled her upright. Feeling a little stronger, Ellie leant against the Dryad and allowed herself to be half dragged, half pushed into the shower. Hazel leant Ellie against the shower wall and turned on the water. Unable to stop it, Ellie laughed as the hot water found its way into her eyes and nose. Hazel worked her sodden clothes over her head and used the shower nozzle to douse her off. Ellie managed to stay upright, pressed against the wall by one of Hazels' hands, as her embarrassment was sloughed away and disappeared down the drain. She smiled brightly at Hazel and thanked her for helping. Hazel looked at her with a mixture of confusion and worry.

"What happened?" Hazel asked, her voice tender with concern.

"Dunno. Woke up and the old body refused to obey. Needed a pee but couldn't get up on the loo. Nothing for it but to let it go. Sorry you had to find me like this, but I figured it would wear off soon and I could clean up before anyone noticed."

"I am glad I was here. You should have called me, I would have come and helped you sooner."

"Bit fed up with needing help all the time to tell the truth." Ellie's tone shrugged as her body couldn't. "Did Aurellio tell you what happened last night?"

Hazel pulled Ellie out of the shower, wrapping a large, rough white towel around her. She managed to drag Ellie back into the bedroom where she let her fall onto the bed. Hazel rubbed at Ellie as if she were a child being dried off by her mother and Ellie felt the whisper of a memory evaporate at the back of her mind.

"No. He was furious though. I do not know what you did but he was speechless with rage. What do you remember?" Hazel rubbed roughly at Ellie's skin with the towel.

Ellie thought for a moment. "I remember following him when he left here. I have no idea why, maybe I just wanted to see what an ancient looked like."

"Aurellio and Marcellus *are* ancients, you know what they look like."

"Yes. I suppose that's true. I don't know… I just felt an overwhelming need to follow him. He went to the church down the road, st Leonards. Funny but I walk past there on a regular basis and never paid it any attention before. Well, anyway, I was hiding behind one of the tombs and, here it gets a bit iffy. I felt as though someone were holding my hand. It was awful. Cold, dry and it sort of made me feel afraid. I suppose I have not really thought of Aurellio as a Vampire before, he's just Aurellio. But I was really scared there in that cemetery. Terrified. Next thing I know…" Ellie shivered with the memory. "Next thing I know, here I am." She finished simply. She did not want to talk about or even remember the feeling of being eaten alive. That was one memory she would happily suppress.

Hazel seemed to know that Ellie had left bits out of her story but said nothing.

"So…" Hazel stood staring thoughtfully at Ellie's naked body. "I suppose I should get you dressed." She went and looked through Ellie's wardrobe. Moving hangars aside she finally decided upon a simple dress that she could pull over Ellie's head. Levering Ellie to a sitting position with one arm, she eventually managed to get the dress over her head and covered her nudity.

"That's better." Hazel smiled.

"Thanks." Ellie replied distractedly.

"Is something the matter? Do you want me to get you anything?"

"Oh a cup of tea please. I'm gasping."

Hazel left the room with Ellie lying where she had dropped. Ellie painfully inched her way up to the head of the bed and managed to position herself across the pillows so that she was not flat on her back. She flexed her hands and arms, pleased to see that some movement was returning.

"Here you go." Hazel had returned and placed a mug of tea on the table beside the bed. "How are you doing?"

"Better thanks, got a bit more movement. Come, sit with me."

Hazel popped out and returned with her own mug which she placed next to Ellie's.

"You must be missing your trees." Ellie said softly.

"Oh yes. Very much, but hopefully I will be able to go home soon."

"What's it like? Living in the woods I mean."

"It's mostly all I know." Hazel said thoughtfully. "I grew up in those woods. I have lived there all my life."

"Don't you ever want to see what it's like somewhere else?"

"No! Why on earth would I?" Hazel was shocked.

"I don't know, I suppose because nowadays people move about all the time."

"Not me. I love my home."

"Do you have a house or something? I don't recall seeing anything in the woods."

"You would not see my house. It is protected by magic and only visible if I wish it to be so. You may come and visit when I return home, if you would like." She offered.

"That would be fabulous. Thank you."

Ellie tried to lift her mug but it was too heavy for her. Hazel took the mug and put it to Ellie's lips, allowing her to sip the scalding brew.

Felix arrived mid afternoon and was also furious with Ellie. He ran his hands over her body and she felt the weight lift. Ellie wriggled her fingers and toes, letting out a satisfied sigh as she did so. She flexed her arms and knees as she gently turned her neck; testing her newly returned mobility.

"Sometimes I wonder if I know you at all!" Felix finally exploded at Ellie with an exacerbated huff. "What on earth do you think you were doing? Why did you follow him?"

"Dunno." Sulked Ellie, scootching down further into the pillows. "Why is everyone so pissed?" She asked in a little girl voice.

"You have no idea do you?" Felix was amazed. "You really do not know who he is? What he would have done? My god Ellie!"

"What makes him different then? Why is he so super scary?" Ellie made her eyes big and batted her lashes innocently.

Hazel turned but Ellie caught the beginnings of a smile as she did so.

"Oh Ellie!" Felix sighed, sitting by her side on the bed and taking her hand in his. "I do not wish to frighten you further but Umberto is the worst of the Vampire. Even Marcellus is afraid of him. He keeps away from people for a reason. He is rumoured to be unable to curtail his desires and has even been known to…Well, I shall not frighten you further. You have been through enough."

"Thank you Felix." Ellie sighed. "I truly am sorry for causing such a nuisance."

From the doorway, Ellie heard Hazel sniff back a laugh in a most un-lady like manner. She shot her a quick look whilst Felix was occupied stroking her hair.

"Fe-elix?" She asked him slowly.

"Yes?" He answered distractedly, seemingly absorbed with the task of soothing her.

"Do you think Aurellio will be cross with me for long? He is so frightening when he is cross." She whimpered.

Hazel snorted loudly and crushed her hand to her mouth as she fled the room.

"I will make sure that he understands and is more careful with you." Felix reassured her.

As Ellie was confined to bed for the rest of the day to recover her strength, she spent the time thinking over the plan they had put together. She was not happy with what they had come up with but could think of nothing better given the limited information they had. She was deeply troubled by Ciara's involvement, she was going to be in the most precarious position. So much rested on her, was it fair to let her do this? Ciara had made her desire to help very clear but she couldn't possibly know what she was letting herself in for. Ellie decided that she would talk to her again and try to dissuade her. *But what if she does change her mind?* Ellie wondered for the umpteenth time. *We need someone on the inside. If not her then who?* As Ellie lay on top of the bed she became more restless and agitated. She felt as though things were happening and being decided without her. The more she thought this, the more sure she became. Ellie finally could take it no longer. Believing that the others were making plans that she knew nothing of, she eased herself off the bed and made her way to the kitchen, where the faint sound of voices convinced her she was right.

As Ellie pulled out a chair and wearily sank into it, Felix, Hazel and Peter stopped talking abruptly and looked at her.
"Are you sure you should be up dear?" Asked Hazel kindly.
Peter sniffed loudly as he stood and turned to face the window, he cocked his leg high and straight then proceeded to clean himself.
Ellie wondered at his behaviour for a moment.
"I feel fine, nearly as good as new." She smiled reassuringly.
"Well, if you are sure…"
Felix and Hazel exchanged guilty looks then busied themselves sweeping invisible crumbs from the table and straightening the cloth.
"So what have you been talking about?" Ellie enquired.
Peter dropped his leg and spun to face her.
"Stinks being left out of the loop does it not?" He hissed superciliously.
Ellie recoiled as though slapped.
"What? What are you..? I don't know…"
Peter harrumphed and jumped from the table. He straightened his tail and slowly walked through the open back door.
"What was that about?" Ellie asked, perplexed.
"Ah, he is a little put out that he was not told about our plans. He is now of the opinion that you do not trust him." Hazel told her. "We were not aware that you had not done so, or we would have…well, perhaps things may have gone better."
"Oh hell!" Elli sat back with a thump on the chair. "I didn't deliberately not tell him. It just never seemed the right time, then the longer I left it, the more absurd it seemed. Oh crap!"

When Ellie felt her breath was back to normal, she went into the garden and called for Peter. She sat in the sun warmed garden chair and sipped at the lemonade she had carried outside. Peter seemed to have disappeared but she stayed put, hoping that he would come back and she could talk with him. Ellie sat back against the warmth of the chair and stared up into the sky. Wisps of white wandered across her vision, providing cushions for the starlings to bounce below. The sun shone smugly through the lacy veil of cloud and glinted upon the roofs of her neighbours. Turning slightly,

The Fae

Ellie could just about see the spire of st Leonards Church. She strained to peer through the curtain of leaves that were mostly blocking her view. The topmost point was visible through the foliage and beneath the spire she noticed for the first time, the gargoyles that guarded the church. To the left an eagle stared out over the town and to the right an angel. The clouds appeared to skirt the church and the sun did not reflect upon its slated roof. Ellie looked harder and noticed that no birds nestled within the churches eaves. *Odd*! She thought. As she stared at the building, Ellie felt an overwhelming desire to go there. She realised that she had half risen from the chair already. Deciding to give in to the urge, Ellie left her garden and walked the short distance to the church.

The nearer Ellie came to the church, the greater her desire to be there. She felt as if a rope were around her stomach, pulling her closer. She relaxed and allowed herself to be tugged along. Reaching the gate, she felt a small thrill of fear but entered anyway. The gate had long since rotted away and the surround crumbled grittily at her touch. Immediately there was a steep rise leading to the church entrance. The vestibule stood cold and uninviting, the door to the church closed. Ellie looked at the cracked cream walls and saw dirt and detritus blown into the corners, a spiders web hung heavily from the curved ceiling and an old notice board informed visitors how to gain access. Ellie tried the handle and was not surprised to find that the door swung open, noisily. She pushed the ancient wood and stepped into the cool interior. Before she could enter fully, the door swung hard, pushing her back outside where she landed on her backside with a thump. The door groaned in its frame as the catch fell closed. Ellie sat amongst the crisp packets and empty beer cans staring at the door in surprise. She stood and pulled at the handle again. Try as she might, it would not budge. It felt locked and immoveable. Ellie turned and looked outside. There were gravestones either side of the entrance but access seemed impossible as there was a barrier preventing egress. A steep wall of earth holding back the raised ground that housed the resting place of so many departed appeared to block her way completely. She looked about for a way in but could see none. *So how did I get in last night?* She asked herself. Ellie noticed how quiet it was. The road was five or six feet away but standing there in the entrance to the church, it was silent; like a vacuum. She could hear her own breath.

To Ellie's left stood a raised stone grave upon the hill-like rise that sat either side of the entrance. It was so old that the inscription had long since worn away. The top of the tomb was askew and Ellie shivered with imagination. *Maybe this is where Umberto sleeps*, she thought. *No, surely he would close the door to keep the sun out*! She giggled to herself. Ellie stood on tiptoe and leaned out over the wall as far as she could, trying to see inside the crypt. It was no use, the grave sat too far away. She noticed that the corner of the lid had been broken away and wondered who would have done such a thing. And why. Ellie went to the other side and searched for a way in but could find none. *Well that's stupid*! She thought. *How is anyone supposed to get to the graves?* Deciding that she would see nothing, Ellie left the church and stepped back onto the pavement. Immediately, sounds of traffic filled her ears. A car passed by with the windows open and Rhianna playing at full volume. The birds could be heard in the roof of the house opposite. The noise seemed over loud after the quiet of the graveyard. Ellie started to walk away, but felt herself being urged back. She leant into the hill and walked as though through snow. Every step an effort. In her mind she heard a voice calling her softly.

"Come. Come back. Join me." It whispered seductively in her mind.

"Not bloody likely!" Ellie doubled her effort and soon found that the pulling sensation eased as she neared the Royal Nelson Pub just along the road.

Rounding the corner to her house, Ellie saw Peter sitting on top of the wall beside her gate. Relief flooded her as she saw him and she knew that he was watching her walk closer.

"Peter, I am so sorry. I didn't mean to keep you in the dark. I have no explanation other than it never seemed like the right time. I mean, how do you say 'oh by the way we are about to take on the whole of the Vampire hierarchy and will probably all get killed!' ? Please don't be angry with me, I can't bear it."

She reached up and Peter allowed himself to be scooped into her arms. Ellie rubbed her cheek against his fur and breathed him in.

"You are such an important part of my life Peter. I cannot even remember how it was before you came along. Maybe a part of me just wants to keep you safe. I couldn't bear it if anything happened to you again and if you had known of our plans, you would have wanted to come along."

"Well, it would be churlish to hold that against you." Peter nuzzled her back. "Okay, I forgive you."

Ellie smiled gratefully into his fur and said nothing.

Chapter Twenty Four

Nobody appeared to have noticed that Ellie had left the house, much less that she had returned. Hazel, Felix and James sat at the kitchen table, the men arguing loudly. Ellie put Peter on the floor and set about making cups of tea. When finished, she placed a steaming cup before the combatants and sat down with them.

"Oh, thank you. What do you mean I will have to sit in the car? I will not be left behind like some recalcitrant child whilst everybody else is in danger." Felix was furious.

"Listen." James replied. "It is not that we do not want your help…"

"Well it surely sounds like that to…"

"Please, listen. You are Fairy, what use will…"

"Oh so now I am useless?"

"For crying out loud, will you please…?"

"Oh no. No, that is fine. Now I know that you guys do not trust me enough to be a part of this suicide mission. I shall just stay here and make snacks for your funerals shall I?"

"Now you are being ridiculous…"

"Ridiculous is it now…?"

Ellie stood up and rested her weight on her hands that were gripping the table.

"That is enough! James, shush! Felix, wind your neck in and shut up being so childish!"

"How dare…" Felix half rose from his seat in anger. "What makes you…?"

Ellie looked him square in the eye then turned and did the same to James.

"Felix is a vital part of this team." She held her palm up to stop James from interrupting. "And as such, even though he is Fairy, he has a role to play tonight. As do we all. This is going to be hard enough without us fighting each other. And I certainly do not wish to hear any more about suicide and funerals. Don't you think I am scared enough already? Seriously guys, rein it in please." She sat and glared at both men until they nodded their acquiescence.

Hazel sat fidgeting and looking uncomfortable.

"Was there something you wanted to add?" Ellie asked her, her tone tired.

"Uh, well…yes. The thing is, I know that I cannot fight; I would not know where to start. Well, the thing is… I think I can still be useful."

"Of course you can." Ellie tried to smile. "What did you have in mind?"

"Okay, well. As you all know, I am a Dryad. That means that I take care of the trees, yes? Well, also I have some, I call it, gift with plants."

"Yes…" Ellie could not see where this was going.

"Well, the thing is… The thing is that I could probably make up some… Well, we could call them wards."

"Wards?" Ellie asked.

"Yes, they can well, ward off danger, hurt, injury, that sort of thing. Do you think that might be useful?"

"Absolutely!" Ellie grinned. "I think they would be extremely useful. What can I do to help?"

"Nothing really, but if James would not mind accompanying me home, I can collect my bits and pieces. I do not really want to go by myself. I am not sure if the Gnomes are still in the woods."

"Of course I do not mind." James smiled at her kindly. "If you are ready, we can leave now."

Whilst James and Hazel were out, Ellie sat and talked with Felix.
"I don't get it." She said to him. "Why are you and James fighting?"
"Oh I do not know!" Felix sighed. "I think we both wish to protect the other and both feel that we are ill prepared for what we have to do tonight."
"You and me both!" Ellie quipped. "I don't think anyone could be prepared. We just have to hope that luck is on our side, do our best and try not to die."
"Simple then." Felix smiled.
"Simple."

Aurellio sauntered into the kitchen and sat at the table. He nodded a greeting to Felix and smiled hello to Ellie.
"What's the plan then?" He asked
"We are still working on it." Ellie told him. "Hazel has some kind of wards that we can use and has gone to get them. James is with her so we can go through it when they get back."
"Sounds good. I'm getting a snack, anybody else want one?"
"Yeuk!" Ellie answered. "No thanks."
"Try it, you may like it." Aurellio smiled wickedly. He went over to the fridge and removed a blood bag. Placing the bag in the microwave he leant against the counter while waiting for it to warm up.

The three sat at the table idly wondering at the myriad outcomes that could occur that night. Very few ended favourably. No matter how they looked at it, Ciara was not coming out of it in one piece. Ellie complained so often that she did not want her friend involved that the boys got fed up and left the house for a walk. Peter sat on the kitchen window sill, eyeing her thoughtfully.

"Why do you suppose Ciara wishes to do this?" He asked her.
"Because Marcellus killed her parents and she believes that this is her only way of striking back at him." Ellie told him.
"So she is no stranger to violence? To loss?"
"Well, yes I suppose so."
"Does she strike you as an imbecile? Someone not in control of their faculties?" Peter wondered.
"Of course not. She has always seemed really smart, together."
"So do you not think that she has thought this through?"
"Well…"
"Do you suppose that Felix made it sound less dangerous in order to secure her participation?"
"Oh no! Felix would never…"
"So then, perhaps she is aware of the danger, aware of the risks, yet wishes to do this anyway? Perhaps her need to strike back at the murderer of her parents is greater than her need for caution?"
"Well yes…"
"Forgive me for this Ellie, but…Perhaps you fear her participation because you fear you may lose her? She is your friend and maybe you worry about the loss to your life if something were to happen?"

The Fae

"Well, I wouldn't…"

"Perhaps it would be less selfish to allow her this chance to avenge her parents. Perhaps she needs to do this and maybe you need to let her. You would be a poor friend to put your own needs before hers would you not?"

"I hate you sometimes Peter."

Felix and Aurellio returned a couple of hours later then the gate swung noisily open again. Several sighs could be heard as James and Hazel walked into the room. James stood and looked about, confusion on his face.

"What? What happened?" He asked worriedly.

Ellie, Felix and Aurellio looked at each other and must have realised how nervous they all appeared. Smiles broke out tentatively and the tension eased a little in the room. As the day wore on, the friends became more nervous. This manifested itself with monosyllabic grunts in answer to half hearted questions. Nobody appeared able to sit still for any length of time so there was much door opening and kettle boiling. Mertensia arrived with the twins and set about preparing a meal for everyone. She appeared to know that something was happening and even the girls were unusually reticent. Begonia and Bluebell sat at the kitchen table, studiously completing their homework, looking up only when addressed directly.

Quietly, Mertensia plated up the food and set it around the table. Again, there appeared to be enough chairs, though Ellie knew not how. Knives and forks scraped lethargically against the prettily painted china and the sound of chewing broke the oppressive silence.

"Man, seriously!" Ellie sighed. "Here we are about to do something insane and we are all acting like we won't be coming back!"

"We may not be." James supplied softly.

"Okay then. Let's say that this all turns to custard and we all get wiped out. Do we really want our last hours on earth to be dull and dismal?" Ellie urged. "Wouldn't we rather go out kicking and screaming? This should be fun!"

Everyone turned and looked at her with varying degrees of incredulity.

"Okay, maybe 'fun' is the wrong word." Ellie blushed. "But…well, shouldn't we make it unforgettable at least?"

"I suppose so." Felix said, unconvinced. "What did you have in mind?"

"Dunno. I haven't thought that far yet." Ellie shrugged. "But…well, shouldn't we make it memorable? I just don't want what could be my last hours on earth to be miserable. I've had enough misery. I want to go out fighting."

"I do not want you to go out at all." Mertensia told her softly.

"Me either. But lets face it, this is a pretty stupid thing we are about to do." Ellie smiled. "Oh, and guys? Promise me one thing?"

Everyone looked up at her expectantly.

"If I get turned, stake me. No disrespect to Aurellio and all that, but I do not want to be a Vampire. I'm a vegetarian, I would starve!" She laughed.

The others around the table smiled and the tension eased a little.

"There is always that synthetic blood. You could take that." Begonia offered helpfully. "I think that's Vegetarian Society approved."

Laughter erupted around the room and the twins looked at each other in confusion. "I was only saying." Begonia pouted.

"Thank you." Giggled Ellie. "But I would not want to live forever as a night creature. Never to see the sun? I would miss too many things to ever be happy again.

The Fae

I cannot imagine how hard it must be for them to live as though cursed; for all eternity? No. I would not want that. Promise me?" Ellie looked at the team.

"We promise." Came the unenthusiastic mumbles.

From Mertensias' extensive carpet bag, she withdrew two large plastic tubs. One was filled with small, prettily decorated, lavender coloured cakes and the other held equally attractive rose pink ones.

"Shall we go and sit in the garden?" Mertensia asked, taking a jug of lemonade from the fridge and heading to the door. The twins gathered glasses and plates whilst Ellie scooped up the boxes of cakes and followed Mertensia outside. The sun hung fat and full, inches from the horizon and st. Leonards chimed in the background. Sitting in the warmth and familiarity of her garden, Ellie felt some of the days tension ease. Looking at her friends who had joined her in the garden, she saw that they too were relaxing somewhat in the muggy evening air.

Bunbury came padding over from behind the wisteria bush and, having stretched nonchalantly, jumped onto Ellie's lap. He placed his paws on her shoulder and nuzzled against her neck. Ellie inhaled the earthy scent of him and kissed his sun baked head. Bunbury's whiskers tickled her cheek in response and he flopped down onto her lap. Laying on his back, front and back legs stretched out fully with his belly fur curling between Ellie's fingers, Bunbury fell asleep. Ellie ran her hand absently through the warm white curls on his stomach and felt a wave of sadness wash over her.

"Do not worry." Mertensia said softly. "If anything does happen, Bunbury will come home with me. Peter will probably go back to Fae's."

Feeling oddly relieved, Ellie thanked her. She felt such an overwhelming love for the fluffy ball of mischief, she hadn't realised how much a part of her heart he had become. She pulled him up over her shoulder and hugged him tightly. Sleep disturbed, Bunbury allowed the sentiment for a moment then oozed down and curled up under Ellies chair in the shade. She smiled fondly at the peek of his tail twitching in a patch of fading sunlight.

"You need a man." Sniffed James.

"What?" Ellie looked up sharply.

"Well, let's face it, you are a romantic novel and a box of chocolates away from being a cliché." He told her.

Ellie threw a cake at him and laughed. "Thanks! Cheeky sod!"

But her thoughts turned to Fox and her mood darkened a little.

"He was never going to be good enough for you." Felix said softly, noticing her face.

"But married?" Ellie sniffed. "Married! How come you never told me?"

"I never knew." Felix told her. "I never really trusted his intention toward you…"

"You made that clear." Ellie interrupted.

"But…" Felix continued. "I never knew he was married. And to her of all people? Wow! Who would have thought? I did not know that they even knew each other."

"Who is she?" Ellie asked. "She seems so different to the rest of you."

"That is a polite way of putting it." Sniffed Mertensia. "Stuck up bitch!"

"Mamma!" The twins recoiled at their mothers outburst.

"Sorry girls." Mertensia sighed. "But really? She so is."

"I could not agree more." Added James.

"As to why she is... Let us just say 'different'?" Felix continued. "Well, imagine growing up and looking so different to everyone you know? Would that not make you a little bitter?"

"Cruelty makes you ugly." Bluebell piped up. "Cruelty and malice."

"Yes, there is that." Mertensia agreed thoughtfully. "As to why? Who knows. Maybe she does not know herself."

"She must have some good points, else Fox would not have married her." Ellie surprised herself by defending the vile woman.

"I imagine she hides them very well in company then." Felix snorted. "She clearly felt no compunction to be nice when she came here."

"Yes, well." Ellie tried to close that particular avenue of conversation. Her hurt at Fox had lessened a little but she was not yet comfortable talking about him.

"Well James." Ellie smiled at him mischievously. "I will have you know that I have a perfect boyfriend. In fact, I see him almost every night. So there!"
Everyone turned again and stared at Ellie, curiosity burning in their eyes.

"Well? Who is he?" James demanded.

"My dream man." Ellie laughed. "He comes to me in my dreams."

"That does not count!" Felix smiled at her. "You need a flesh and blood man."

"Do I?" Ellie asked. "Why?"

"Did I hear someone say blood?" Came Aurellio's voice as he stepped out of the kitchen and joined them in the garden. He looked up at the darkening sky and appeared satisfied that the sun was not about to pop back out.

"Not really." Bluebell smiled up at him. "Aunty Ellie was just telling us about her new boyfriend."

"Boyfriend?" Aurellio asked darkly. "I know nothing of this. Who is he?" He demanded.

"Keep your fangs in." Ellie laughed. "He's not real. Just some guy in my dreams."

"I do not like the sound of this." Aurellio said, looking at her intently. "How long has it been going on?"

"Aurellio, it's just dreams. It's not real." Ellie protested, half laughing and half nervous.

"Be that as it may," Aurellio sniffed. "You have to be careful Ellie."

"You're not...jealous are you?" She asked shocked.

"Do not be absurd!" Aurellio shot back. "I am just telling you to be careful. Mind what you talk about for instance."

"Get a grip Aurellio. It's just dreams. He's not real!"

"I shall say no more." Aurellio turned abruptly back to the kitchen and moments later she heard the ding of the microwave.

Aurellio came back into the garden with a tall, opaque glass and a black straw. It appeared to be an attempt to disguise his meal. For that Ellie was grateful.

"So, what is the plan then?" Aurellio asked again, bringing everyone in the garden back to their reason for being there. Sighs and moans could be heard as the group appeared to consider the night ahead.

"What time do you collect Ciara?" Ellie asked Felix.

"It is okay, Chris is getting her on his way here." Felix told her.

"Oh. Okay." Ellie was surprised.

"Nothing to worry about. If he makes a pass at her she will either accept or reject it. I am not going to drive myself crazy worrying about it."

"He would not do that? Would he?" Asked James.

"He is a wolf, a dog, of course he will. It is his nature to mate as much as possible with as many as possible. I doubt she would be interested though." Felix didn't sound as sure as his words implied.

"Let's hope so." Ellie smiled at her friend.

Mostly the group sat back and chatted softly amongst themselves. The reason for their being there was carefully avoided as the dusk deepened into night.

Ciara and Chris arrived looking solemn and nervous. Ciara was dressed in a short blonde wig, glasses, shapeless trousers and a shirt and tie. She had done something to her make up that made it difficult to ascertain her gender. The effect completely altered how she looked and Ellie found herself staring, trying to put her finger on how. Ciara went straight to Felix and kissed him hard, darting a look to Chris as she did so. *That answers that question then.* Ellie thought to herself. She noticed the small smile of triumph on Felix' face as they broke apart. He scooped Ciara onto his lap and she appeared content to stay there. Chris seemed oblivious to the mini drama he had inadvertently starred in.

"Can I ask you a personal question?" Ellie asked Chris.

"Sure. What is it?"

"Do you need a full moon to turn into a Werewolf? I mean…of course, if you do. Turn that is. Or is that another Hollywoodism?"

Chris laughed, loudly. "I am always a Werewolf. So, do I need a full moon to change into a wolf? I suppose the correct answer would be 'no'. When we are in our teens and start, well…okay look. When the process starts in our teens, it makes it easier I suppose, but as we age, we learn control it and can change back and forth at will."

"Does it hurt?" Ellie was fascinated.

"Well, yeah. It does. Kind of a good hurt though. Bitches say it is a bit like giving birth."

"Bitches?" Ellie asked sharply. Eyebrow raised.

"Yeah, female dogs, bitches." Chris smiled knowingly.

"I hate when women are referred to as bitches." Ellie declared.

"But ours are." Chris laughed. "However, I do take your point. Our *ladies* say that it is akin to giving birth. So yeah, it hurts like a … son of a bitch!" He winked. "But it is also the best feeling in the world."

"Do you have any memory of what you do and think when you are a wolf?" Ellie pressed further.

"Not as a youngster. But the more control you learn, the clearer the experience, the memory."

"Are you limited to how many times you can change?"

"Never been asked that before." Chris looked at her. "Do you work for the C.I.A?" He laughed.

"Sorry. If its too personal…"

"No. Not at all. No we have no limits but we do need time to recover between changes. It can take a lot out of you, especially if you are active."

"So, do you like, roam the countryside, hunting and killing?"

"I'm sure you said a question." Chris laughed evasively.

"Yeah. But do you?" Ellie really wanted to know.

"Yes, but there is more to it than that." Chris looked thoughtful. "When we have time, I will take you to meet my pack and you can learn all about us. If you want to that is?"

"Oh cool! That would be great." Ellie smiled and stopped the cross examination.

It seemed as though everyone present ran out of distractions at the same time. All the conversations petered out and the group sat looking around at each other; uncomfortable and expectant.

Chapter Twenty Five

"This feels so weird." Ellie said to nobody in particular.

"How so?" Asked Aurellio.

"Well, here we are, walking up the street like we don't have a care in the world, and about to probably do battle with the most terrifying creatures on the planet. It just feels, well I mean now, right at this moment…It just feels so…ordinary."

"You were expecting the Ride of the Valkeries perhaps?"

Aurellio, Ellie, James, Felix, Chris and Ciara were walking up Magdalen Street. They passed the petrol station, car showrooms, the Aldi supermarket and then waited at the road-works where the crossing used to be.

"God that is one ugly building!" Ellie muttered, looking over at the partially built court house. Floor upon floor of concrete and scaffolding loomed up beside the train station opposite them, blocking out the moon as traffic crawled past, unwilling to cede a second of their hectic lives to let them pass.

"When is it due to be finished?" Asked James, staring up at the building, his nose wrinkled in distaste.

"Dunno. Preferred it as waste land. Bloody horrible thing. Why are all new builds so ugly and soulless? What is up with architects these days?" Ellie answered.

"You look fine honey." Felix said to Ciara. "Really you do. You can still back out if you want. It is not too late."

Ellie didn't hear Ciara's reply but guessed that it was a refusal by the loud sigh she heard from Felix.

"Okay my love. I promise. Not one more word. I am so proud of you." She heard him say.

Finally a kind Kia driver let them pass. Ellie noticed a wide smile on Aurellio's face as the woman behind the wheel blushed and dipped her head.

Outside the pub newly named the Judge and Jury, there was a large huddle of people puffing furiously on cigarettes. A choking blue cloud enveloped everybody as Ellie tried to hold her breath through the fug.

"I smoke more now than when I had the habit!" Ellie muttered. "Let them stink up their own homes. I can't walk anywhere without getting a lungful from some rude, selfish, inconsiderate…"

"Ellie! Chill!" James put a hand on her shoulder. "Come, we will all be fine."

"Fucked up, indifferent, neurotic and emotional?" She asked, annoyed.

"If you like." James laughed. "Let us just get through this, then you can run for office and change the law back again. Okay?"

Ellie harrumphed but kept walking.

They crossed onto Osborne Street and walked the short distance to the Brewers Arms.

"Why here? It is gross!" Ciara asked screwing up her face.

"Uh, let's just say that it has a reputation of being blind and deaf." Ellie said mysteriously. "We wont be disturbed or overheard in here." She pushed open the door and the others trundled in nervously behind her.

A long wooden bar stretched along the back wall, broken by a low arch above a step; leading into a separate room that held a pool table. Cotton Eye Joe was playing loudly in the background whilst about half a dozen men and women stood about talking and holding drinks. The barman was wiping down the counter with a dirty looking grey cloth whilst listening half heartedly to an older woman wearing a skirt that skimmed her buttocks. Her bare legs led to swollen feet that were squeezed painfully into a pair of stripper shoes with a two inch platform made from the same clear plastic as the seven inch heel which had her tottering forward against the bar. Her heavy, unsupported breasts swung into the spilled drinks and the filmy fabric of her nearly transparent top soaked it up greedily. The tattoos down her arms wobbled dangerously as she gesticulated her wishes to the myopic barman.

"A bloody pint, ya daft wee shite! Where's ya bleedin' specs? Oh fe feck sake! There!" She leant further over the bar, pointing and Ellie was witness to the scariest looking lady garden she could ever have imagined. Coarse grey hair poked out either side of a discoloured, tired looking thong and veins ran blue and bold from her crack.

Swallowing audibly, Ellie ushered her friends into the round snug set into the bay window.

"So." She smiled at the shocked and puritanical faces. "What would you guys like to drink?"

"Hi there Ellie." The woman at the bar called as she turned, beer in hand, and spotted the group.

"Hi mom."

Ellie smiled to herself as she heard the whisper, soft as a breeze, blow round the table and back again.

"Get you and yer pals a wee drink hen?"

"No thanks. We're here for a quiet one." Ellie smiled. It was a smile full of unconditional love.

"I'll make sure yer no bothered then hen." The woman waddled off, teetering on the edge of a fall, all the way to the door, where she exited through it.

"Your mom?" Asked James. "But I thought that, well, I did not think that your mom was…"

"Scottish?" Asked Ellie, smiling benignly.

"Yes. Scottish." Finished James lamely.

"Well, Jeanie here isn't really my mom. She kind of took me under her wing when I was a kid. She gave me a place to run to, fed me, bought my clothes and whatnot. Saved me really."

"Oh." Came a relieved chorus.

Ellie raised her eyebrow and her face dared anyone to comment further.

"Right. So the familiar will meet us in here in a few minutes." Aurellio began. "Let us run over this again."

A few unconvincing groans escaped around the table.

"I go with the familiar," Ciara recited unenthusiastically. "Watch for Marcellus, whisper a commentary into my tie pin whenever possible. The minute I see any of you run in or the Vamps get feisty, I get out." She pulled at her wig and adjusted the glasses. "Are you sure he will not recognise me?" She asked for what seemed like the hundredth time.

"Honey, if I had not helped you with that get up, I would not recognise you." Said Felix sincerely. "You can still…"

"Enough!" Ciara cut him off. "We are doing this! What's next?"

"Me." Ellie piped up. "I wait in Mc Donald's out of sight until either Marcellus comes out or we go in. I listen to Ciara through the earpiece here." She moved her

The Fae

hair to show them that she had remembered to insert the earpiece that was linked to Ciara's microphone.

"Good!" Aurellio waited a beat then added. "I'm going in too."

There was a chorus of protestations but he was adamant.

"I have the best chance of stopping the slaughter."

"But what if you are hit by a ball? You are an ancient," Felix was upset.

"My friend." Aurellio put his hand on Felix' shoulder. "My only friend. It has to be this way."

A battle raged across Felix' face but resignation won out.

"I know." He sighed.

A large, brutish looking man filled the doorway. He peered about nervously and, when he spotted Aurellio, made his way over.

"Master." The man bowed quickly, his eyes never leaving Aurellio.

"Food. Sit." Aurellio commanded and the lump sat down, immediately, on the floor at Aurellio's feet.

Ellies mouth made a small moue of distaste.

"At the table Food!" Aurellio admonished quietly.

The big mans face broke into a toothy grin as he leapt up and sat at the end of the bench. His knees were pressed together tightly and he held his hands clasped in his lap. A look of adoration on his face. Ellie could swear she heard him panting with pleasure. The man gazed worshipfully at the object of his idolatry.

"You understand my command?" Aurellio asked regally.

Ellie turned away so that nobody could see the smirk on her face.

"Oh, yes master." The man lisped in ecstasy.

"Take my snack and I will have her at the feasting. Guard her well."

"Oh, yes master." The man nearly orgasmed in his pants as he stood and waited for Ciara to join him.

With a quick look back at Felix, Ciara stood and joined the familiar. There were no words of support, her role had begun. She straightened her spine, pulled her shoulders back and lifted her chin, then followed the brute out of the pub. *The long walk to the gallows.* Thought Ellie, then she shook herself free from the unwanted image. She resisted the overwhelming urge to run after Ciara and drag her back.

"So explain to me..." Ellie turned to Aurellio. "If you are going in, why is Ciara putting her neck on the block by being in there too?"

Felix looked over sharply.

"We need her there." Aurellio explained. "Between the two of us, we will see more."

"But you have super Vamp endowments." Argued Ellie.

"Yet even I cannot be everywhere at once." Aurellio answered reasonably.

"I suppose..." Ellie conceded as she got up and made her way to the ladies room. Closing the door behind her, she wiped then sat on the closed denim effect toilet seat and shallowly breathed in the strong scent of bleach that must have recently been used in there.

Trying to quieten her mind, she reached her thoughts out past the pub and toward the Town Hall. She sensed the staticky noise of peoples minds as she searched for Ciara. Snatches of mundanity flew past her as she made her way up Scheregate Steps, past the Purple Dog and along Trinity Street. There were fewer people here as The Bell was long gone and the night revellers had no cause to congregate in the sleepy street.

At the edge of her consciousness, Ellie felt a surge of pride and a Pavlovian obedience as she came across the man that Aurellio called Food. She stopped and looked out of his eyes briefly, seeing as he saw. She felt his excitement at the forthcoming event manifest itself sexually. The more he anticipated, the harder he got. Disgusted, Ellie started to leave when she felt his thoughts turn to Ciara. She stayed a little longer.

If I please him maybe he will let me have her. The man thought. *Dare I ask for her? But if I don't ask, someone else will take her. I want her. I deserve her.* Feeling disgust but no danger, Ellie moved over to Ciara.

"Oh I am glad you are here." She surprised Ellie by saying. "Can you stay?"

"Er, not really." Ellie said, taken aback. "I'm just checking that you are okay."

"Yeah, I am fine, but meathead here keeps touching himself. He thinks I can't tell." Ciara said in disgust.

"Men!" They chorused, then laughed.

"Oops!" Ciara said. "He heard me. Wonders what I'm thinking I'll bet."

"I wouldn't be too sure." Ellie said. "I don't think his big brain is driving the train, I think his little brain makes the decisions." They both smirked again and Ellie told Ciara to 'stay in touch'.

"Let me know quietly when you get there. I don't want the others to know we can talk."

"Why not?"

"I'm not sure exactly. I just think that for now it's best they don't know."

"Whatever you say."

"Stay alert Ciara, please. If at any time you feel threatened, leave!"

"I will. I shall call you when I get inside."

"Good luck."

"Bye."

Back in the bar, Ellie found that Felix was checking his watch every couple of seconds. His face a perfect picture of anxiety.

"She is okay." Ellie whispered to him. "I just peeked in her mind. She is almost there, nothing to report yet."

Felix looked at her, his need to believe that Ciara was alright written plain all over.

"Okay, yes I know. Okay." His mouth muttered distractedly.

"We should all get into position." Aurellio interrupted. "It is almost time for my grand entrance." His thin, bloodless lips twitched into what Ellie assumed was a smile.

"Okey dokey." She said getting up, faking cheerful. "Let's get this thing started."

"Ellie. We are here." Ellie heard Ciara's voice trembling inside her mind.

"Ciara and Food must have reached the Town Hall by now." Ellie told the others. "Let's go."

The group made their way to the High Street. Ellie watched Aurellio enter the side of the Town Hall as she sat at a window table in McDonalds. James, Felix and Chris split up and found doorways to lurk in. Of them all, only Chris looked natural, lighting a cigarette and leaning back like an old pro. Ellie briefly wondered how useful he would be when she noticed that he appeared more interested in trying to catch the eye of a group of young girls sitting at the bus stop giggling. Ellie cupped her latte and let her mind reach out to Ciara.

"Can I sit in your head for a bit?" She asked. "I just want to watch."

"Sure. Help yourself." Giggled Ciara nervously. "Truth be told? I am terrified."

Ellie opened her eyes and looked out through Ciara's. Her first sensation was disorientation; of being closer to the ground. Ciara was shorter than she and the perspective was unsettling to say the least. Ellie looked around the beautifully appointed room at the Vampires gathered there, accompanied by their minders and assorted snacks. The dress code was formal, exquisite tailoring alongside glittering jewels. The room was infused with an amalgam of scents that whispered wealth and status. Every Vampire head was high, back straight, movement subdued, gestures hinted. Ellie had the strange sensation that the Vampires were moving in slow motion. She felt Ciara's distress as a palpable thing, her blood was humming through her veins and Ellie could sense the paralyzing fear that threatened to overwhelm her friend.

The room was set out for a meeting, row upon row of chairs faced a small stage at the front of the room below the beautiful picture window. The moon shone through, bringing the coloured glass to life. Several Vampire sat talking quietly whilst others appeared to float across the floor, seemingly buoyed up by their individual entourages. There appeared to be no universal look to the Vampires present. Unlike the popular movies, they ranged in ages, heights, ethnicities and appearance. Some were indeed beautiful whilst others bore scars and deformities as evidence of their existence before turning. Yet all exuded a confidence and assurance that even the very rich aspire to. Ellie spotted Marcellus standing near the stage. He was in the process of kissing a short black woman on the cheek as she smiled regally at something he had said. Marcellus' minders stood either side and slightly behind him. Both were well over six foot and heavily built. They stood feet slightly apart and hands clasped lightly in front, eyes alert and scanning.

Marcellus' head snapped up and he appeared to be sniffing the air. His eyes thinned to slits as he spun around to face the door. Ciara and Ellie turned to look also and saw Aurellio standing in the doorway. He appeared relaxed, was smiling confidently and stood with one hand in his trouser pocket; the other idly checking the time on a ruby encrusted pocket watch that hung from a glittering chain at his waistcoat. He looked up and slowly scanned the room. After a lazy sweep of the attendees he eventually acknowledged Marcellus and his face broke into a wide and welcoming grin. Aurellio made his way over to his leader who, in turn, was struggling to regain his composure. Aurellio placed his palm on Marcellus' shoulder and held out his hand to be shaken. Mechanically, Marcellus complied, his bloodless face frozen blankly. Ellie could not hear the words exchanged but she saw Aurellio warmly greet the people Marcellus had been speaking with, then move on to another group. Marcellus' eyes followed him until eventually he recovered his wits and continued his conversation; darting glances at Aurellio as he moved artlessly about the room.

Eventually Aurellio strode over to Ciara and told her in an imperious tone, presumably for the benefit of those listening, to follow him and stay close. He then leant in and licked her exposed neck, smiling cruelly as he did so. Ellie felt the revulsion and fear course through Ciara's system and tried to keep herself separate from its welcoming insanity.

"Stay with me. Please?" Begged Ciara of Ellie. "Oh god, what am I doing here?"

Ellie tried to offer words of support as Ciara followed Aurellio to a seat on the edge of the stage. Three other seats were taken and their occupiers each had a minder behind them. Aurellio told Ciara to sit at his feet. She did so.

Looking at the other snacks scattered around the room, Ellie told Ciara to behave more like the thug Food.

"You can't let them see your fear." She told her. "Act obsequiously, copy Food."

Ciara tried her hardest to act as though this were the greatest honour she could receive. Ellie felt how very hard it was for her.

Gradually the Vampires started to take their seats; their snacks at their feet, fawning and preening. Marcellus walked to the stage and turned to face the crowd. The Vampires that remained standing took to their seats and eventually gave him their full attention.

"Fellow leaders. I welcome you to this, our two thousand and eleventh annual meeting." He smiled at those assembled. "It is good to see so many familiar faces and I would especially like to welcome Tomas, our new hive leader from Minsk. Welcome."

The seated Vampires all turned their heads toward a large, muscle bound copy of the actor Dolph Lundgren and applauded daintily. Tomas in return nodded his head in acknowledgement then turned his face back to Marcellus.

"We have much to discuss and many issues to get through, so if you are all ready I would like to invite the leader of the East Kilbride Hive, Jordan Kirk, to take the stage."

As he stepped aside, he looked at Aurellio who was sitting most comfortably on the stage, and hissed. "What the fuck do you think you are doing? You are supposed to be dead. Get off this fucking stage now!"

"I think not my leader." Aurellio whispered back. "It is a good place from which to keep an eye out for, let us say, surprises? We would not want anything to surprise our illustrious visitors would we?"

"I will deal with you later." Marcellus growled.

"As you wish." Aurellio looked away, dismissing his leader.

Angrily, Marcellus left the stage and took his seat facing Aurellio. He paid little attention to the Scottish Hive leader who was speaking of a suspected uprising in his borough just south of Glasgow. Marcellus' gaze was riveted on Aurellio. His dark eyes flashing dangerously and his fangs biting into his lower lip.

Ellie felt Ciara trembling.

Leader after leader took to the stage and spoke. Some for a few moments and others, apparently relishing the spotlight, droned on for quite some time. Each laid out the most pressing issues facing their hives and requested that the information be recorded in The Great Book. Ellie began to realise that this part of the meeting was not to seek aid as she had first thought, but to simply record any grievances. Becoming bored, Ellie decided to see if she could find any information about the impending attack. Although she knew that she was unable to enter a Vampire mind, she still tried a few at random. As she thought, it was impossible so she tried a few of the minders. Many were Vampire also but occasionally she came across a human mind that she could enter. Slipping into the mind of one of Marcellus' minders, Ellie tried to be as unobtrusive as possible. She felt that the minder noticed a slight tickle in his head but he assumed it was the beginning of a headache as he too was bored senseless.

The Fae

Ellie looked out through the minders eyes and saw the back of Marcellus head. His dense black curls were gelled into place and Ellie could smell his cologne. Marcellus sat rigid with fury, his beautiful suit vibrating slightly with his suppressed anger. Ellie felt the minder turn his attention to his leader.

Why doesn't he just stake the bastard and have done with it? He thought to himself. *Where the fuck has he been hiding? That's what I want to know. I searched everywhere for that slippery bastard. Nobody knew a thing? Right! When I find out who was hiding him, I'll introduce him to my old pal the sun. Got a lovely post in my back garden I can chain em to. God! How much longer does this whiney crap last for? When do we get down to the fun stuff?*

Ellie felt a flicker of excitement, *he must mean the attack*, she thought to herself. But the minder had started thinking about something else. Ellie slipped out of his head and went searching for more information.

After a good two hours searching through the minds open to her in the room, Ellie found that the closest she had come to learning about the attack was with Marcellus' human minder, so she returned to him. She sat in his head and listened to endless drivel regarding his obsession with weight training. He ran through drills in his mind and examined his workout from every angle, trying to find ways of improving it. Ellie had never been interested in exercise so found the subject extremely tedious. He did not seem too concerned with the upcoming attack as he did not think of it again whilst she was there.

This is no good! Ellie thought. *How can I find out more? There must be some way.* She popped back to Ciara and told her that she would be outside for a while but would come back to her as soon as she could. Ciara seemed to have overcome her fear to a large degree and replaced it with abject boredom.

Outside, Ellies mind searched the area around the Town Hall, looking for anyone that shouldn't be there. She passed James who was cold and bored then she passed Felix who was worrying himself insane about Ciara. Ellie stopped with him a moment and tried to put his mind at rest.

"I have just scanned in there. Ciara is sitting with Aurellio, bored out of her skull. She isn't as scared as she was, just bored. She will be fine. Try not to worry. Have you seen anything out here?"

"Not really. I saw a few guys go down towards that night club round the back there. The old Valentino's?" Felix pointed down the road. "But apart from that, nothing."

"Okay, chin up and eyes open." Ellie left him and continued her search.

Hang on a minute! She thought. *"That club is closed for repairs. Its not due to be opened for at least a month*! Ellie turned her mind to the way Felix had pointed and went in search of the men he had seen.

Ellie concentrated really hard but could only pick up the minds inside the houses of the Dutch Quarter. Each going about its nightly routine, watching television, washing dishes, sleeping. There was no sign of the men Felix had seen. Ellie felt a tiny movement in the churchyard and sprang inside its mind. She found that she was very close to the ground when she opened her eyes. She felt tiny, twitching, nervous movement followed by scratchy scuttling. Fear and food the only thoughts within this primitive mind. She smiled to herself as she realised that she must be inside some sort of animal. *I wonder what?* She thought as she decided to stay for a few minutes.

The Fae

The creature Ellie inhabited darted out from under the iron fence toward the shelter of a broken headstone. Once inside the dark cave like shelter, she felt the creature's relief and sense of safety. As the creature bought it's tiny paws up to its face and begin to nibble at a discarded crust of bread, Ellie heard voices speaking quietly nearby. *It's either tramps or my guys*. She thought. *I wish this little fella would eat quietly so that I can hear better*. The squirrel must have sensed something, for it stopped eating and stood on its back legs, ears twitching like satellite dishes tuning into the speakers. *Wow! Cool!* Ellie strained to hear through the animals tiny ears. *If only we were a little closer*, she sighed, never satisfied. The squirrel darted out from the grave and ran up the trunk of the ancient oak that stood in the centre of the grave yard. Ellie felt the animals pleasure as it ran, defying gravity and as it stopped, sitting placidly on a branch above three men sitting on a tomb, speaking together quietly.

"We're to wait here for the signal." Said one dark silhouette to the others.

"No problem." Replied another. "You got the stuff?"

"Yeah, here."

"Keep em away from me you bloody idiot. Don't you know what them things can do to us?"

Ellie was sure she had found the men she was looking for. She figured that the best thing to do would be to stay with them until they made a move, then alert the others.

"Did e tell you when this thing is supposed to start?"

"Nah, just watch for is signal is all e said. We can see the windows from ere, so it should be a good enough place to wait. I'm bleedin 'ungry though. Aven't eaten all day. Mebbe some lucky sod will walk past or pop in ere for a crafty fag or some fink."

Luckily, Ellie's squirrel seemed content to sit on the branch above the men and nibble on its crust of bread.

Chapter Twenty Six

Ellie noticed that the squirrel was becoming restless, she thought perhaps that it had never sat still for this long before so she let it run loose and scamper about the tree. She felt such a visceral elation from the tiny animal. The simplicity of it's desires was so refreshing to her complex mind. The squirrel appeared to love nothing better than to eat and run up tree trunks as fast as possible. She felt the little creature's jubilation as it clung, suspended from a branch, hanging only by it's claws, tiny eyes darting at every shadow or sound.

The men below Ellie, who were sitting on a large tomb, appeared to be settled in for some time. One had his feet resting against the faded stone of the grave and was whittling away at a fallen branch he had picked up from the base of the tree. The other two were talking quietly to each other, trying to discover any mutual acquaintances. Ellie supposed it made sense that these men did not appear to be local. After all, it could be dangerous for Marcellus to involve his own hive in any attack. There would be little point staging a coup if your own men were wiped out in the battle. No, better to risk outsiders and keep your own people safe.

Ellie decided that she dared risk a quick visit to check on Ciara and see how things were progressing in the hall. She located her friend exactly where she had left her. So deep into a daydream was she; that Ellie's arrival jolted her awake with a yelp. They both saw Aurellio look down at her, his face questioning.
"Oh I am so sorry. I must have nodded off for a moment." Ciara apologised sweetly.
Aurellio scowled slightly then turned his attention back to the room.
"How's it going here?" Ellie asked.
"God I could not possibly be any more bored!" Ciara replied. "And there was me scared out of my wits before."
"Still." Ellie warned. "Don't be complacent, there are guys outside waiting for their cue. Keep alert and get ready to run out the second you see anything. Promise me!"
Ciara promised and Ellie thought that she would take a quick peek into Marcellus' minders head.
For crying out loud, she heard him complain to himself. *How much longer until we get started? I'm going to fall asleep here soon.*

Ellie darted back to the squirrel in the churchyard. When she opened her eyes, all was black and the squirrel's heart was tripping like a jack hammer with fear. Ellie was scared and confused. She felt a damp warmth enveloping the squirrel, like hot breath; then the sudden shock of pierced flesh. Ellie felt the squirrel scream in agony then fall silent and dark. She felt the final thump of the tiny heart and the last thought was one of confusion as the mind she was inside stopped. With a sob, Ellie wrenched herself back into her own body. She sat shaking in the hard plastic seat in the window of McDonalds, tears falling down her cheek unabashed.

"Ellie, Ellie, come quick!" Ciara called inside Ellie's mind.
Ellie sniffed loudly then reached into Ciara's thoughts.
"I'm here."

"Something is happening. I do not know what exactly, but a few of these guys are sort of moving weirdly."

"What do you mean?"

"They are moving toward the doorways and have peculiar looks in their faces. I thought it best to let you know."

Ellie told her to get ready to leave quickly then she popped to Felix outside.

"Get ready, I think it's time." She whispered inside his head.

Feeling Felix come to attention and start to move silently toward the Town Hall, Ellie went and warned James and Chris.

Returning to the room, Ellie sought out the mind of the human minder. She found him sitting behind Marcellus, who was listening attentively to the current speaker on the stage. Ellie gently entered into his mind and tried to sort through his thoughts.

"Come on, come on! What is taking so long?" He repeated over and over to himself. *"Get on with it can't you? Things to do, people to stake."* He laughed to himself expectantly. Ellie felt his attention slip to Aurellio and found that she could not easily discern his thoughts. They appeared to be a mixture of hate, awe and fear. The sense of expectation was almost overwhelming and Ellie believed that whatever was about to happen would be soon.

After a brief check on Felix, James and Chris, Ellie went back to Ciara.

"I'm going to be out for a few moments possibly." She warned her friend. "I have to make my way over here and don't know if I can stay in your head and navigate my body at the same time. Keep talking to me just incase. But either way, I will be back in a couple of minutes, I'm only over the road."

Ciara was not particularly happy so urged her to hurry. Her pulse was increasing and she was starting to become a little breathless with panic.

"Promise I won't be long. Keep talking to me." Ellie urged as she opened her eyes back at the table. A cold latte sat in front of her and as she looked around, she saw that a couple opposite were staring at her and whispering together furtively.

"Up yer arse!" Ellie mumbled to herself as she got up and passed them on her way to the door.

Ellie rushed across the road to join with Chris who was just walking away from a trio of giggly girls who were somewhat the worse for drink.

"Really?" Ellie admonished him. "You couldn't focus just this once?"

"'Hey!" Chris smiled broadly. "What can I say? I'm a dirty dog!"

Ellie groaned loudly, but a small smile tugged at her mouth. Together they ran the few steps to the Town Hall and met with James.

"Where is Felix?" Chris asked.

"Round the other side, seeing if he can get a look through a window or something." James told them. "What do you want us to do Ellie?"

"Oh man! I have no idea! This is Aurellio's show. Let me see if I can find out. I don't know why he had to be in there, we need him out here."

Ellie closed her eyes and opened them inside Ciara.

"What has happened?" She asked.

"The doors are all covered, Marcellus is just sitting there. He must be a good actor, he looks like he does not have a care in the world. Aurellio told me to sit here and is walking the room, looking for anything suspicious."

The Fae

"Okay then, so far so good." Ellie said. "We need him outside with us. We don't really know what we are to do. Tell you what, can you walk over to him and we can have a word? He will have to know we can speak I suppose, though I would rather that remained between us."

"I have the microphone and ear piece, remember?" Ciara told her. "We can say that we are communicating that way."

"Of course!" Ellie mentally slapped her head. "Come on then."

Ciara stood and started to make her way over to Aurellio. Marcellus looked up at her and frowned as she passed him. He then turned back to his minder and said something that caused him too to look over with narrowed eyes. Ellie noticed that as they walked around the large crowded room, trying their best to avoid drawing attention to themselves, several Vampires raised their faces and sniffed the air as Ciara passed. It was not a comfortable observation. At each doorway, there stood two Vampires, each solidly planted, feet apart, eyes scanning the room. Ciara hurried around to where Aurellio leant against the far wall. He turned at her approach and scowled.

"I thought I told you to stay put?" He said, none too pleasantly.

"Yes, yes you did." Ciara said in a small voice. "But Ellie is on the earpiece, she said they are all outside and need to know what to do. Could you go out and well, let her know?"

Aurellio stared at her for a moment then appeared to reach a decision. He took Ciara's elbow and led her to an empty chair at the back of the room.

"Sit here, I will be back in a minute. Do not move."

He strode toward the door, where the pair of Vampires stepped aside and let him pass.

Ellie watched Aurellio step outside and turn toward her. His eyes were moving constantly up and down the road, strafing like machine guns. Felix arrived back with the group at the same time, looking expectantly toward Ellie. He shook his head indicating that the back of the building was clear, for the moment.

"Okay, nothing is happening yet." Aurellio told the team. "Go back to your positions, Ciara will call Ellie on the mike when I tell her to. Then I would like you all to come. I will ensure that the doors are open, or at least unlocked. Come in and if possible restrain Marcellus and his minders, I will try and clear the room and secure the balls. Okay guys?" He smiled. It was not reassuring.

"Uh, yeah. Sure." Ellie said hesitantly. "What is happening in there at the moment?"

"It's the part where the Hive leaders all record the disturbances and trespasses. It is pretty boring but necessary. All good so far. No sign that Marcellus is about to attack. His minders are all looking pretty relaxed, so it may be some while." Aurellio ran his hand through his hair. "Okay then, back into position." With that he turned and re-entered the building.

The three men turned and started to go back to their positions.

"No. Wait." Ellie called softly.

They all turned back to her.

"This is not right. Aurellio is mistaken. Something is happening, they are getting ready. I know it."

"But Ellie." James said. "Surely Aurellio knows these people better than us? He will tell us when we are to charge in."

"I don't know James." Ellie thought aloud. "There are three Vamps down the road with some of the balls…If we attack them now, whilst we wait for Aurellio, we will save time and possibly eliminate the threat. What do you think?"

"Sounds good. Are there any more do you think?" Felix asked. "Vampires outside I mean."

"I am not sure. We can definitely deal with those three though. Yes?"

It was agreed, so they walked down the road until they came upon an opening for a small residential car park. The four ducked inside and Chris turned to the others, saying,

"Okay, you say they are sitting on a tomb at the back of the church?"

Ellie nodded.

"Right. You guys stay here, I will deal with them. You will probably want to stay back a bit." He grinned.

Chris mimed a strip show whilst humming the infamous tune and removing his clothing. He carefully folded them into a pile that he handed to James as he stood, buck naked, in front of them all.

Ellie blushed and looked away, turning back in curiosity as she heard a barely perceptible hum emanating from him.

Chris had gone down to the ground on all fours, his neck stretched out and his teeth bared in a grimace. His body vibrated, gently at first then violently. His fingers lengthened and large sharp claws grew from his neat nails. His back legs bucked and elongated into an animalistic shape, thick black fur sprouted out all over his body and just before his face pulled into a wolf's head, he turned and winked at Ellie. The rest of his body changed in an instant. One moment he was a man, the next; a snarling wolf that loped away toward the church.

Cursed with curiosity, Ellie tried to enter Chris' mind. All she saw were swirls of red; desire, need and savagery. His mind was a boiling pit of blood and sex, each as compelling as the other. Ellie slipped out, shocked and faintly aroused. Blushing, she turned to the others and they stood silently; straining to hear the sounds of savagery from the church yard mere meters away.

What felt like moments later, the group heard a hair raising howl coming from the graveyard. It seemed to echo across the walls of the tightly packed houses that surrounded them. Ellie was sure that in seconds, windows would open and sirens would screech. They all ran toward the noise and entered the graveyard to see Chris, as a wolf, licking at blood that had splashed against his paw. He looked like a naughty puppy until he turned and they saw more blood smeared and dripping from his muzzle. Three broken and torn bodies lay about, their life's blood soaking into the rain starved ground.

"We can't just leave them out like this." Ellie said, ever practical. "Help me shift this lid. We can hide them in here." She went over to a large tomb and started to heave on the heavy concrete lid. Centuries old moss making her grip unsteady.

James and Felix moved her out of the way and tugged the lid open. They then lifted the bodies and dropped them into the musty darkness. Chris growled, low in his throat, watching intently as the last body was dropped unceremoniously into the tomb and the boys pushed the lid back into place.

"Do you understand me?" Ellie asked the wolf. "Do you?"

Chris stood on all four legs, blood congealing on his muzzle and stared at her, his head canted to one side as though listening.

"Chris! Do you understand me?" Ellie asked him again.

The wolf yipped.

"Is that a yes?" Ellie asked.

Chris pawed at the ground, staring straight at her. His wide maw open and drooling, a mix of saliva and black blood.

"Hang on a minute!" Ellie nearly shouted. "They were Vamps, why the blood? Open the coffin again please."

Felix and James looked at each other, shrugged, then set about sliding the heavy stone lid aside again.

As the lid opened, a hand reached up and grabbed the side of the tomb from the inside. It gripped tightly as a ravaged head appeared, its one undamaged eye searching.

"James! Quick, stake them!" Ellie yelled.

James swiftly withdrew a small stake from his pocket and leant over the coffin. He raised his arm and stabbed down twice with all his might. A fine dust blew up and glinted in the moonlight as he stepped back.

"The other is human, hence the blood." James told Ellie. He is pretty dead, the Vamps are dust though."

"Okay, don't close it yet. We can hide the balls in there until later."

"Good idea" called Felix as he loped off to pick up the bags that were laying beneath the huge oak tree. Dropping them in the coffin, the boys set about sliding the lid back into place.

"Now what?" Asked Felix.

"I'm going to check on Ciara." Ellie said as she closed her eyes and sought her friend.

Ellie opened her eyes and looked out through Ciara's. They both scanned the room searching for Aurellio and spotted him standing by a window, staring out with a preoccupied look upon his face whilst he absently twiddled with his pocket watch. Almost as though he could sense he was being watched, Aurellio spun round and his eyes found Ciara. She took a sharp intake of breath and forced herself to smile at him, desperately trying to calm her nerves. Aurellio looked a moment longer then pushed himself away from the wall and walked off in the opposite direction.

"I will be back in a minute." Ellie said as she spotted Marcellus' minder watching Aurellio. She slid into his mind and looked out through his eyes. His gaze was riveted on Aurellio. He followed every movement hungrily. As Aurellio bent to kiss a tall red headed woman on the cheek, Ellie felt the minder stiffen and his thoughts turn ugly.

"Goddam bitch, how dare she?" She heard him think. *"Get your stinking paws off him before I stake you."*

Ellie sat dumb struck. *Whoa! Whoa! What?* She thought, her mind blank. *Wait just a minute. What the…*

She saw Aurellio turn toward the minder and raise an eyebrow. The minder relaxed a little and Ellie, stunned, jumped out of his mind back into Ciara's.

"Ciara, quickly! Go to Marcellus. Now!" She screamed inside her friends mind. "We have been so very wrong! Go! Now!"

The Fae

Ciara jumped up and ran along the aisle of seats toward the front where Marcellus was sitting.

"What? What is it? What is wrong? Ellie?" Ciara shouted back at her. Unfortunately, Ciara shouted using her voice not her mind and every head in the room turned toward her, including Aurellio and Marcellus.

"Faster Ciara. Quickly."

Marcellus minders stood and surrounded him as they must have realised Ciara's destination. The other Vampires in the room stopped talking and growled, some slipping their fangs out and rising from their seats. Aurellio ran toward Ciara, his hand up as though to stop her.

"Call him." Ellie urged.

"Who? Marcellus? Why?"

"Do it. Tell him he is about to be attacked. It's Aurellio. We were wrong. He played us. Tell him!"

Marcellus stood and stepped toward Ciara.

"What do you want Food?" He hissed at her.

As Ciara ran she tripped on a large handbag that sat in the aisle. She reached out to grab a chair and stop herself from falling. As she did so her wig slipped over her eye. Unthinking, she swiped it off.

"You?" Marcellus spat. "You are dead."

"Marcellus, there is an attack... It's Aurellio he..." She was cut off as a large heavy body landed on her and crushed her to the ground. Breathless, she tried again. "Got to get out. Balls... Danger." Then she passed out.

Ellie flew back to her own mind and screamed for the boys to follow her as she ran into the room. The unexpectedness of the doors being pushed open from the outside must have caught the guards unawares as the doors met little resistance. Entering the room she shouted loudly. Every head turned to her and she saw Aurellio stop in his tracks and look over. One of Marcellus' minders that had pinned Ciara to the floor, rolled off her and looked up also.

"Everybody out. There is an attack. Marcellus, Aurellio has the balls." She shouted.

James and Felix stared at her as though she had gone mad. Marcellus swung his gaze to Aurellio who in turn dove over the chair that stood in front of him and, reaching into his pocket, took out a fist sized gritty black ball and threw it at Marcellus. He kept running, delving into his pocket as he fled.

Ellie felt herself pushed violently from behind, as the door she had just entered through swung open. Four masked Vampires entered, looked around and reached into long strapped, leather bags that hung across their shoulders. They each took out a rough black ball and threw it into the crowd that had finally realised there was something amiss. Within seconds the room filled with gasps, screams and a fine, gritty dust. The ball thrown by Aurellio had smashed against Marcellus and he was shrieking wildly as his body roared back to life. His porcelain smooth skin shrank against his skull, becoming dry and powdery, as his lips pulled back in a snarl. Marcellus sniffed the air and leapt upon a minder standing to his right, sinking his teeth into the now human flesh and tearing at it. He spat the bloody chunk of skin aside and pushed his face hungrily into the gaping hole.

At the same time, there were screams of terror from the beautifully dressed Vampires who had suddenly developed a pulse and a heartbeat. Some stood, frozen to the spot, uncomprehending and alive. Others had turned into a whirling mass of teeth and blood, growls and desire, intent upon feeding. Atavistic in their need. Bones could be heard breaking and blood sprayed where teeth ripped.

Felix ran to Ciara and half lifted, half dragged her toward the door. James took out his stake and strode into the melee. Ellie ran after Aurellio, betrayal lending clarity to her turbulent mind. As she ran, a feral Vampire leapt on her from over a chair and pinned her to the floor. His hot breath, fetid and damp, played across her skin as his teeth neared her flesh. Ellie struggled against the weight that held her, kicking and twisting. The Vampire, slick with blood, could not get a tight hold of Ellie's wrists so she managed to twist out of his grip. With her free hand, she reached for her stake and forced it up and into the chest of the snarling creature above her. Ellie watched with grim pleasure as the Vampire turned to dust then blinked furiously as the dust settled into her staring eyes. She rolled over and jumped up, spitting dust from her mouth and trying not to retch. She rubbed furiously trying to dislodge the grit from her eyes. Suddenly she was face down on the floor again; another Vampire had crushed the breath from her body as he landed on her. He pulled a fistful of her hair, forcing her head back and leant down to tear into her throat. Ellie closed her eyes against the pain in her scalp and tried to draw breath back into her crushed and aching lungs. She squirmed and bucked beneath the Vampire but he held on tight. She felt one of his teeth scrape her shoulder then the weight was gone and Felix was standing over her, hand out indicating that she should get up, dust was all about him.

As Ellie gratefully pulled herself up with James' aid, she saw Chris, as the wolf, leap over the head of a falling Vampire and launch himself onto the minder that had pinned Ciara to the floor. Chris' great head sank below Ellie's line of sight then re-emerged with a hank of bloody hair and meat in his mouth. He tipped his head back and swallowed the flesh, growling as he did so, then sprang up and sought out other game. Ellie saw Ciara from the corner of her eye, trying to pull herself over to the door. She appeared to be hurt and out of breath. Her eyes wide and staring as she groped her way to safety along the wall. As Ellie started to turn, she saw Marcellus; shrivelled, ancient and terrifying, leap toward her friend. Ellie screamed out for Ciara to move and as she did, Felix turned to see the woman he loved pounced upon by a creature intent only upon devastation. Ellie saw him rush over calling Ciara's name louder and louder until he reached a piercing pitch that caused Marcellus to stop dead. Marcellus' hands came up and his withered claws held fast against his ears, trying to block out Felix' death cry as it assaulted his frame. Ellie saw Marcellus' eyes register pain and incomprehension as his head suddenly imploded; thick black blood and brain matter spraying as he crumpled to the floor. Centuries of life extinguished. Felix reached Ciara and swept her up into his arms, he rushed through the door and returned moments later without her.

Ellie spun around, searching for Aurellio. All about her the creatures tore at flesh, bones crunched and screams echoed. The once eggshell blue walls were awash in gore and blood. The chandeliers sported new decorations that had never been in the designers thoughts. Nothing was still. Movement, swift and deadly, surrounded her. Ellie searched the insanity before her for a glimpse of Aurellio. She spotted him, near the picture window, reaching into his pocket and pulling out a ball. He threw the ball as he leapt at the window. Glass shattered and gave way as the force of his body propelled him through to the outside. Ellie mindlessly followed and, climbing upon a

The Fae

nearby table, threw herself headfirst through the broken window, feeling her skin tear as her arm caught on the knife sharp glass. Landing in a painful heap on the pavement outside, Ellie ran a quick check to see if she had broken any bones. Finding only cuts and bruises, she climbed painfully to her feet and looked around for Aurellio.

Stanwell Street was quiet, there was nobody within sight. Disconnected voices floated down from the High Street and the occasional swoosh of a passing car reached Ellie's ears over the surreal back beat of carnage behind her in the Town Hall. She tried to think which way would Aurellio have gone. She strained to see down toward the Stanwell Arms, a twelfth century pub on the corner that was being renovated; its scaffolding throwing eerie shadows across the deserted road. There was no sign of Aurellio so she turned and ran a few feet to the junction with the High Street, stopping at the corner and looking about desperately for a glimpse of the man that had betrayed her, causing her to become involved in a war that was none of her concern. She saw nothing through the haze of tears that she realised were falling steadily from her eyes.

"Where is he?" Panted James as he reached her side. "Aurellio? Where did he go?" James bent over supporting both hands on his knees and drew in deep, ragged breaths.

"Gone." Ellie replied. Her voice flat and emotionless. "I missed him. What of the others? Are they alright? Come." She turned, grabbed his arm and ran back toward the melee, dragging a wheezing James behind her.

Climbing back through the window, Ellie stopped a moment to survey the scene. All about the room was carnage. Broken bodies lay twisted where they had fallen. Blood and gore smeared the walls and two frightened people, clothes torn and bloody, huddled shivering in a corner of the room. Their eyes impossibly wide with terror. Gritty black dust lay about on every surface and a fine grey powder gathered in body shaped piles where the feral Vampires had been staked. Chris was prowling the room, flipping furniture aside with his great snout, sniffing and searching for fresh sport. Felix was pulling a stake from the body of a Vampire and watching coldly as it disintegrated. He then turned and walked from the room. James jumped down from the window and walked over to the newly-humans in the corner and squatted in front of them. Ellie climbed down and joined him.

"What are your names?" James asked in a tired voice. "Your names?"
The two women stared up at him in mute terror. Their eyes unfocussed and mouths slack.
"Leave them; we can deal with them later." Ellie said, standing up. "God what a mess. What do we do now?"
James got to his feet and surveyed the butchery about him.
"I do not know. Where is Felix?" He suddenly became agitated; looking about wildly.
"I saw him go through that door. Over there." Ellie pointed.
James sprinted in the direction she pointed and wrenched the door open, disappearing through it. Ellie followed slowly, in no rush for more.
In the darkened hallway, Ellie could see James kneeling and trying to gather Felix in his arms. Felix appeared to be struggling against his father and Ellie became aware of a low keening, growing in strength and volume. She walked closer and squatted down to see what was happening.

"Nooo…" Wailed Felix with such primal anguish, it caused Ellie's blood to run cold.

Ellie closed her eyes. Her mind battled against the desire to know what had caused so much pain. She heard James mumble words of love and comfort as Felix wept. Edging closer on her knees, Ellie saw Felix bowed over something large, dark and limp in his arms. James was holding tightly to his son, gently trying to draw him away. Moving closer, as though against her will, Ellie saw a pale hand flop lifelessly to the floor. She gasped a sharp intake of breath then dared not breathe as she followed the arm with her eyes, past the ripped and bloodied shirt on to the caved-in face of her once beautiful friend. Felix' bloodless lips inches from Ciara's; gently kissing and whispering.

Fin

Epilogue

Rain fell from the heavens in an unrelenting deluge, whilst the wind moaned and cried out, working itself into cracks and gully's. People stood around, heads bowed, tears soaking into sombre funereal clothes. Umbrellas jockeyed for position at the yawning chasm awaiting the simple pine box that held the body of Ciara Jane Owen, aged twenty seven years, four months and eight days.

Felix groped for Ellie's hand as he stared into the puddle that had gathered in the depths of the dark, terrifying hole. His eyes wide and unblinking as rain fell against his impossibly long lashes. His hair, tied back with a black band, lay sodden and heavy across the sopping wet of his suit jacket. His cheeks gaunt with bereavement and remorse. Wasted opportunities and love unfulfilled squeezed into the painful, thin lines that were his lips.

Ellie squeezed Felix' hand and tried to convey a library full of words in that small, inadequate gesture. Her stomach was cramping with unleashed screams and her throat was raw from crying at the unfairness of the world. James and Mertensia stood together across the hole, tears rolling freely down their cheeks as the winch began its creaky song. The coffin lifted jerkily from the ground and began its slow descent into the fragrant earth. Eventually coming to rest in the mud at the bottom with a small splash and a sickening slurp that had Ellie thinning her eyes, lost for a moment in memory.

Felix slipped his hand free from his friend and stepped toward the gaping hole. He stood silent for a moment then dropped a single stem of sweet-scented freesia onto the coffin. He stepped back, turned and continued walking straight ahead and out of the graveyard. Ellie watched him go, her heart breaking. James stepped to the grave and mouthed a silent prayer. He then dropped his own bloom atop the other and slipped away. Friend after friend said goodbye and walked away until only Ellie was left. Alone. She dragged her steps to the edge of the hole and stared bleakly into the cavernous depths.

"I am so sorry Ciara. Please forgive me." She cried as she too dropped a flower into the final resting place of her friend.

The scent of crushed freesias rose from the scattered blooms that adorned the coffin and Ellie breathed them deeply, tasting the damp earth in the back of her throat. She looked up as a bird flew past, struggling against the foul weather. Returning her gaze to the grave, Ellie sighed from deep within her soul.

"I am so sorry Ciara. So very sorry."

"I know." Came the voice of her friend; weak and ephemeral. "Come, let's go home."

Words: 136 699

Made in the USA
Charleston, SC
12 February 2014